Praise for
The Wood's Edge

"Meticulously researched. Alive and engaging [...] through the footsteps of America's formative years, with characters so wonderfully complex and a story of redemption so deep, only Lori Benton could tell it. I was transfixed from the first absorbing page to the last."

—KRISTY CAMBRON, author of *The Butterfly and the Violin*
and *A Sparrow in Terezin*

"From the opening scene to the last line of the book, I was captivated by *The Wood's Edge*. Rich in history, with characters to weep for and to cheer for, this is a novel that will linger in my heart for a long time to come."

—ROBIN LEE HATCHER, best-selling author of *Love Without End* and *Whenever You Come Around*

"Open *The Wood's Edge* and see the secret. Then, hold it—page after page—breathless. Rich in history and lush in story, Lori Benton's novel brings to life a cast of characters in a tale that spans two generations, two cultures, two worlds. In an era underrepresented in Christian historical fiction, Benton takes on the challenge of presenting the message of faith in its purest form. Love, grace, rebirth."

—ALLISON PITTMAN, author of *On Shifting Sand*

Praise for
Lori Benton

"Seldom has a tale swept me away so powerfully I'm left both breathless and bereft at its end, reluctant to let go. Lori Benton's *The Pursuit of Tamsen Littlejohn* is such a book, a gentle masterpiece destined to be treasured and acclaimed."

—JULIE LESSMAN, award-winning author of the Daughters
of Boston and Winds of Change series

"Founded on a fascinating little-known moment in early American history, *The Pursuit of Tamsen Littlejohn* is one of the most beautiful love stories I've ever read. In this tightly paced flight into fear, hope, and mystery, author Lori Benton emerges as the quintessential artist, able to pull her readers into the story through her well-drawn, multidimensional characters, their emotions, motivations, and dreams."

—SUE HARRISON, international best-selling author
of the Ivory Carver trilogy

"An authentic rendering of frontier life, full of heart and hope. *Burning Sky* takes the reader on a vivid journey into New York's wilderness at a time when cultures collided and lives were forever changed. A memorable debut!"

—LAURA FRANTZ, author of *The Colonel's Lady*
and *Love's Reckoning*

"Lori Benton gives us seasons in her debut novel *Burning Sky*. Seasons of planting corn, beans, and pumpkins as backdrops to the ripening and challenges of lives working through chaos after a war and a terrible personal tragedy. The author gives us seasons of the journey through loss, risk, family, and love. The author's voice is mesmerizing with evocative phrases like 'The air inside the cabin swirled with stale memories, echoes of once-familiar voices trapped within, awaiting her coming to free them.' Set on a frontier homestead in New York in 1784, we meet distinctive characters I came quickly to care about. And the promises of the opening poetic question of Burning Sky / Willa, 'Will the land remember?' is answered with passion and grace and the satisfaction of a good harvest. Enjoy this wonderful novel."

—JANE KIRKPATRICK, award-winning author of *One Glorious
Ambition*

"By turns exciting and heart-wrenching, *Burning Sky* is a deeply engaging story with a tender, thoughtful heart."

—DIANA GABALDON, author of the Outlander series

The
WOOD'S
EDGE

BOOKS BY LORI BENTON

Burning Sky

The Pursuit of Tamsen Littlejohn

The WOOD'S EDGE

A NOVEL

THE PATH FINDERS
BOOK ONE

LORI BENTON

AUTHOR OF BURNING SKY &
THE PURSUIT OF TAMSEN LITTLEJOHN

WATERBROOK
PRESS

THE WOOD'S EDGE
PUBLISHED BY WATERBROOK PRESS
12265 Oracle Boulevard, Suite 200
Colorado Springs, Colorado 80921

All Scripture quotations and paraphrases are taken from the King James Version.

This book is a work of historical fiction based on many recognizable persons, events, and locales. Content that cannot be historically verified is purely a product of the author's imagination.

Trade Paperback ISBN 978-1-60142-732-8
eBook ISBN 978-1-60142-733-5

Cover design by Kristopher K. Orr; cover image by Trevillion Images, Victoria Davies

Published in the United States by WaterBrook Multnomah, an imprint of the Crown Publishing Group, a division of Penguin Random House LLC, New York.

WATERBROOK and its deer colophon are registered trademarks of Penguin Random House LLC.

Library of Congress Cataloging-in-Publication Data
Benton, Lori.
   The wood's edge : a novel / Lori Benton. — First edition.
      pages ; cm
   ISBN 978-1-60142-732-8 (softcover) — ISBN 978-1-60142-733-5 (ebook)
   I. Title.
   PS3602.E6974W66 2015
   813'.6—dc23

                                                      2014040030

Printed in the United States of America
2015—First Edition

10 9 8 7 6 5 4 3 2 1

This book turned out to have much to do with fathers.
It is dedicated to mine, who is loved and missed.

Larry George Johnson
August 24, 1943–December 22, 2013

Thus saith the LORD, Stand ye in the ways, and see, and ask for the old paths, where is the good way, and walk therein, and ye shall find rest for your souls.

— JEREMIAH 6:16

Thou wilt shew me the path of life . . .

— PSALM 16:11

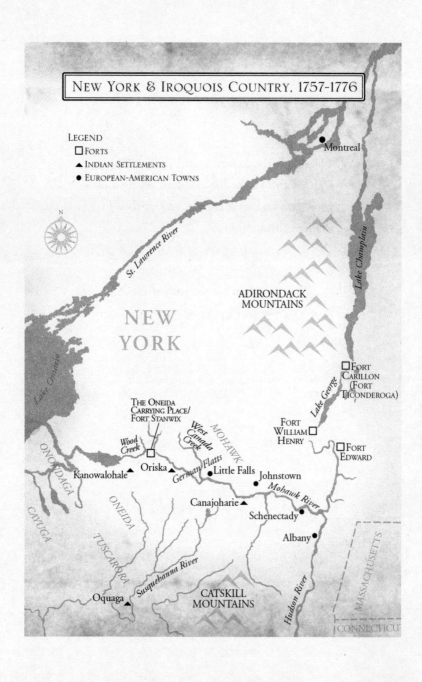

NEW YORK & IROQUOIS COUNTRY, 1757-1776

LEGEND
□ FORTS
▲ INDIAN SETTLEMENTS
● EUROPEAN-AMERICAN TOWNS

N

St. Lawrence River

Montreal

Lake Champlain

ADIRONDACK
MOUNTAINS

NEW
YORK

Lake Ontario

Lake George

□ FORT
CARILLON
(FORT
TICONDEROGA)

THE ONEIDA
CARRYING PLACE/
FORT STANWIX

West
Canada
Creek

MOHAWK

FORT
WILLIAM □
HENRY

□ FORT
EDWARD

Wood
Creek

Oriska ▲

German Flatts

Little Falls

Johnstown ●

Mohawk River

ONONDAGA

Kanowalohale ▲

Canajoharie ● ▲

Schenectady ●

ONEIDA

CAYUGA

TUSCARORA

Albany ●

Hudson River

MASSACHUSETTS

Susquehanna River

Oquaga ▲

CATSKILL
MOUNTAINS

CONNECTICUT

1757
FORT WILLIAM HENRY — LAKE GEORGE, NEW YORK

1

August 9, 1757

A white flag flew over Fort William Henry. The guns were silent now, yet the echo of cannon-fire thumped and roared in the ears of Reginald Aubrey, officer of His Majesty's Royal Americans.

Emerging from the hospital casemate with a bundle in his arms, Reginald squinted at the splintered bastion where the white flag hung, wilted and still in the humid air. Lieutenant Colonel Monro, the fort's commanding officer, had ordered it raised at dawn — to the mingled relief and dread of the dazed British regulars and colonials trapped within the fort.

Though he'd come through six days of siege bearing no worse than a scratch—and the new field rank of major—beneath Reginald's scuffed red coat, his shirt clung sweat-soaked to his skin. Straggles of hair lay plastered to his temples in the midday heat. Yet his bones ached as though it was winter, and he a man three times his five-and-twenty years.

Earlier an officer had gone forth to hash out the particulars of the fort's surrender with the French general, the Marquis de Montcalm. Standing outside the hospital with his bundle, Reginald had the news of Montcalm's terms from Lieutenant Jones, one of the few fellow Welshmen in his battalion.

"No prisoners, sir. That's the word come down." Jones's eyes were bloodshot, his haggard face soot-blackened. "Every soul what can walk will be escorted safe under guard to Fort Edward, under parole . . ."

Jones went on detailing the articles of capitulation, but Reginald's mind latched on to the mention of Fort Edward, letting the rest stream past. Fort Edward, some fifteen miles by wilderness road, where General Webb commanded a garrison two thousand strong, troops he'd not seen fit to send to their defense, despite Colonel Monro's repeated pleas for aid—as it seemed the Almighty Himself had turned His back these past six days on the entreaties of the English. And those of Reginald Aubrey.

Why standest thou afar off, O LORD?

Ringing silence lengthened before Reginald realized Jones had ceased speaking. The lieutenant eyed the bundle Reginald cradled, speculation in his gaze. Hoarse from bellowing commands through the din of mortar and musket fire, Reginald's voice rasped like a saw through wood. "It might have gone worse for us, Lieutenant. Worse by far."

"He's letting us walk out of here with our heads high," Jones agreed, grudgingly. "I'll say that for Montcalm."

Overhead the white flag stirred in a sudden fit of breeze that threatened to clear the battle smoke but brought no relief from the heat.

I am feeble and sore broken: I have roared by reason of the disquietness of my heart—

Reginald said, "Do you go and form up your men, Jones. Make ready to march."

"Aye, sir." Jones saluted, gaze still fixed on Reginald's cradling arms. "Am I to be congratulating you, Capt—Major, sir? Is it a son?"

Reginald looked down at what he carried. A corner of its wrappings had shifted. He freed a hand to settle it back in place. "That it is."

All my desire is before thee; and my groaning is not hid from thee—

"Ah, that's good then. And your wife? She's well?"

"She is alive, God be thanked." The words all but choked him.

The lieutenant's mouth flattened. "For myself, I'd be more inclined toward thanking Providence had it seen fit to prod Webb off his backside."

It occurred to Reginald he ought to have reprimanded Jones for that remark, but not before the lieutenant had trudged off through the mill of

bloodied, filthy soldier-flesh to gather the men of his company in preparation for surrender.

Aye. It might have gone much worse. At least his men weren't fated to
rot in some fetid French prison, awaiting ransom or exchange. Or, worst of
terrors, given over to their Indians.

My heart panteth, my strength faileth me—

As for Major Reginald Aubrey of His Majesty's Royal Americans . . .
he and his wife were condemned to live, and to grieve. Turning to carry
out the sentence, he descended back into the casemate, in his arms the
body of his infant son, born as the last French cannon thundered, dead but
half an hour past.

The resounding silence brought on by the cease-fire gave way to a tide of
lesser noise as soldiers and civilians made ready to remove to the entrenched
encampment outside the fort, hard by the road to Fort Edward. There the
surviving garrison would wait out the night. Morning promised a French
escort and the chance to put the horrors of William Henry behind them.

All thy waves and thy billows are gone over me—

Reginald Aubrey ducked inside the subterranean hospital, forced to
step aside from the path of a surgeon spattered in gore. The balding, sweating man drew up, recognizing him. "Your wife, sir. Best wake her and
judge of her condition. If she cannot be moved . . . well, pray God she can
be. Those who cannot will be left under French care, but I'd not want a
wife of mine so left—not with the savages sure to rush in with the
officers."

"We neither of us shall stay behind." Reginald turned a shoulder when
the surgeon's gaze dropped to the still bundle.

He'd been alone with his son when it happened. Spent after twenty
hours of wrenching labor, Heledd had barely glimpsed the child before

succumbing to exhaustion. She'd slept since on the narrow cot, the babe she'd fought so long to birth nested in the curve of her arm. Craving the light his son had shed in that dark place, Reginald had returned to them, had come in softly, had bent to admire his offspring's tiny pinched face, only to find the precious light had flickered and gone out.

A hatchet to his chest could not have struck a deeper blow. He'd clapped a hand to his mouth, expecting his life's blood to gush forth from the wound. When it hadn't, he'd taken up the tiny body, still pliable in its wrappings, and left his sleeping wife to wander the shadowed casemate, gutted behind a mask of pleasantry as those he passed offered weary felicitations, until he'd met Lieutenant Jones outside.

How was he to tell Heledd? To speak words that would surely crush what remained of her will to go on? These last days, trapped inside a smoking, burning hell, had all but undone her. And it was his fault. He'd known . . . God forgive him, he'd known it the day they wed. She wasn't suited for a soldier's wife. He ought to have left her in Wales. Insisted upon it. But thought of being an ocean away from her, likely for years . . .

Born an only child on a prosperous Breconshire estate not far from his own, Heledd had been raised sheltered, privileged. Reginald had admired her from afar since he was a lad. She'd taken notice of him by the time she was seventeen. Six months later Reginald, twenty-three and newly possessed of a captain's commission, had proposed.

When it came time for them to part, Heledd had begged. She'd pleaded. She'd made all manner of promises. She *would* follow the drum as a soldier's wife. He would see how brave she could be.

She'd barely weathered the sea voyage. The sickness, the filth, the myriad indignities of cramped quarters had eaten away at her fragile soul, leaving behind a darkness that spread like a stain, until he barely recognized the suspicious, defensive, unreasoning creature that on occasion burst from beneath her delicate surface. Nor the weeping, broken one.

But always she would rally, come back to herself, beg him not to leave her somewhere billeted apart from him, love him passionately, sweetly, until he lost all reason and caved to her pleas.

Then had come the stresses of the campaign, the journey from Albany to Fort Edward, then to Fort William Henry, Heledd scrubbing laundry for the regiment, ruining her lovely hands to earn her ration. Brittle smiles. Assurances. Clinging to stability by her broken fingernails while his dread for her deepened, a slow poison taking hold.

Then she'd told him: she was again with child. After an early loss in the first months of their marriage, she'd waited long before informing him. By then they were out of Albany, heading into wilderness, she once more refusing to be left behind. Would that the babe had waited for this promised safe passage to Fort Edward. Maybe then . . .

How long shall I take counsel in my soul, having sorrow in my heart?

Why standest thou afar off, O LORD?

Providence had abandoned him. He alone must find the words to land what might be the final blow for Heledd, and he'd rather have stripped himself naked to face a gauntlet of Montcalm's Indians.

Shaking now, Reginald started for the stuffy timbered room where his wife had given birth—but was soon again halted, this time by sight of a woman. She lay in an alcove off the casemate's main passage. He might have overlooked her had not two ensigns been coming from thence supporting a third between them, dressed in bloodied linen. They muttered their *sirs* and shuffled toward the sunlit parade ground, leaving Reginald to peer within.

The alcove was dimly lantern-lit. Disheveled, malodorous pallets lined the walls, all vacated except for the one upon which the woman lay. A trade-cloth tunic and deerskin skirt edged with tattered fringe covered her slender frame. Her fair sleeping face was young, the thick braid fallen across her shoulder blond. No bandages or blood marked any injury. Reginald wondered at her presence until he saw beside her on the pallet a bundle much like the one he carried, save that it emitted soft kittenish mewls. Sounds *his* son would never make again.

He remembered the woman then. She'd been brought in by scouts just before Montcalm's forces descended and the siege began, liberated from a band of Indians a mile from the fort. For weeks such bands had streamed in from the west, tribes from the mountains and the lake country beyond, joining Montcalm's forces at Fort Carillon.

How long this white woman had been a captive of the savages there was no telling. She'd no civilized speech according to a scout who had claimed to understand the few words she'd uttered. One of the Iroquois dialects. She'd been big with child when they brought her in. Reginald vaguely recalled one of the women assisting Heledd telling him she'd gone into labor shortly before his wife.

Heledd's travail had been voluble, even with the pound and crash of mortars above their heads. But he hadn't heard this woman cry out. Had she survived it?

He looked along the corridor. Voices rose from deeper in the casemate, distracted with evacuating the wounded. Holding his dead son, Reginald Aubrey stepped into the alcove and bent a knee.

The woman's chest rose with breath, though her skin was ashen. A heap of blood-soaked linen shoved against the log wall attested to the cause. He started to wake her, thinking to see if she knew the fort had fallen—could he make himself understood. That was when he realized. The bundle beside her contained not a baby, but *babies*. One had just kicked aside the covering to bare two small faces, two pairs of shoulders.

Reginald glanced round, half expecting another woman to appear, come to claim one of the babes as her own. They couldn't both belong to this woman. They were as different as two newborns could be except—a peek beneath the blanket told him—both were male.

That was where resemblance ended, at least in that dimness. For while the infant on the left had a head of black hair and skin that foretold a tawny shade, the one on the right, capped in wisps of blond, was as fair and pink as Reginald's dead son.

The ringing in Reginald's head had become a roar as he bent over Heledd to wake her. His heart battered the walls of his chest like a thirty-two pounder set at point-blank range, waging internal war. Despite his mistakes with Heledd, he'd still considered himself a good man. An honorable man. For five-and-twenty years he'd had no indisputable cause to doubt it. Until now.

How could he do this thing?

With a groan, he backed from his wife. He would set this right, return things as the Almighty had—for whatever inscrutable reason— caused them to be. There was time to undo what ought never to have entered his thoughts.

Only there wasn't.

Heledd's eyes blinked open. A slender, reddened hand felt for the infant gone from her side. With a cry she heaved up from the cot, hair flowing dark across her crumpled shift.

"Where is he? My baby!" Panic pinched her voice, twisted her fine-boned face into a sharp mask.

Reginald's heart broke its pummeling rhythm, swelling with love, aching with shame. "He's here. I have him here."

With grasping hands Heledd took the swaddled babe. The child's features were scrunching to cry, but the instant it settled in Heledd's embrace, it calmed.

Reginald's hands shook as his wife stared at the child in her arms. She would know. Of course she would. What mother wouldn't? In another heartbeat she would raise those brown eyes that had claimed his heart, sear him with accusation, unleash the darkness that he knew bedeviled her, and he'd have lost more than a fort and a son and his honor this day.

Heledd's narrow shoulders heaved. Like a mirror of the babe's, her face calmed, softening in a manner Reginald had never seen. Not even on their wedding day when she'd looked at him as though he'd lit the moon. It was as though, in the face of the child in her arms, she'd found her sun.

"Oh . . . it is well he looks. When I saw him before I thought—was his color not a bit sickly? But do you look at him now, Reginald. Our son is *beautiful*." With a bubble of laughter she raised her face to him, joy shining from her porcelain features, her beautiful eyes alight in their bruised hollows.

He couldn't see the darkness.

For a fleeting moment Reginald was glad for the thing he had done. "He is—" The catch in his voice might have been for reasons purer than the truth. *He was beautiful, Heledd. As I lay him beside the dark child, I saw he had your eyes . . . my mouth . . . and I think my father's nose.*

"Major?" a hurried voice hailed from the doorway. "Ye've but moments to be on the parade ground, sir."

Reginald nodded without looking to see who spoke. Grief and guilt swallowed whole his gladness.

For mine iniquities are gone over mine head . . . neither is there any rest in my bones because of my sin—

As footsteps hurried away, he tore through his soul for refuge, even the most tenuous—and found it in Heledd and what he must now do to see her safe across fifteen miles of howling wilderness. He clenched his hands to stop their shaking. "Quickly," he told his wife. "Let me help you dress."

Heledd wrenched her gaze from the babe to echo vaguely, "Dress?"

"Aye. You must rise, and I am sorry for it, but we have lost this ground. We're returning to Fort Edward."

ood Voice of the Turtle Clan woke to the screams of wounded
men being slaughtered in their blankets. The fort had surrendered to the French. This much she knew, and for it she had given thanks
to the Master of Life, telling herself she need only gather strength, bide her
time. Soon she would be free to return to Stone Thrower, if he still lived.

None of the *a'sluni*—the whites—not the women who tended her
through the birthing, not the soldiers who questioned her, knew how
much she understood their talk. English traders came often through her
town. Many of her clan sisters spoke to them and passed on their words to
Good Voice. But since being hauled a prisoner into this fort, she'd let none
of those words pass her lips.

But now she had new reason to fear. She could hear that Montcalm's
Indians were already inside the fort, killing the English. Though in her
heart Good Voice was *Onyota'a:ka*—Oneida—with her light hair and
blue eyes she looked as English as any woman in the fort. More than some.
And now she had Stone Thrower's sons to protect.

On her knees, Good Voice yanked aside the blanket to lift the nearest
baby, the second-born—the brown one—alarmed by the weakness of her
arms. She'd lost much blood. Willing her bones to be like iron, she reached
for the firstborn, marveling afresh that her sons had not in the usual way
of two-born-together shared their parents' blood in equal measure, but one
taken more of hers, the other more of Stone Thrower's. It was a thing that
would be much talked of once they were all safe away, back home at
Kanowalohale.

A yipping shriek curdled down the corridor beyond the recess where Good Voice had pushed her sons into the world. It raised the hairs on her scalp, even as she felt against her cradling arm the light-skinned baby's stiffening chill.

A more visceral panic gripped her. Holding the brown child to her shoulder, warm and solid, she laid his brother on her thighs and bent over his tiny face. No breath! For a moment her own breathing ceased, her throat clutched by shock, then choking grief. She had let this happen—let Stone Thrower's firstborn slip away while she slept.

More screams rent the dank, earth-tanged air. Good Voice pressed the dead child to her shoulder. With the living clutched to the other shoulder, she staggered to her feet. The blood rushed out of her head and from her womb. Earthen walls and timber frames and lantern light spun. She braced herself with feet planted wide lest she spin, too, and fall.

Other feet pounded the earth. A warning shout rose in the passage behind her. She whirled as an Abenaki warrior fell across the bloodstained pallet where she'd lain, war club falling from open fingers, a hatchet buried in his back. The one who'd shouted came up behind the Abenaki, relief in his eyes as he looked at her. Lizotte, a Canadian *coureur de bois*—a woodsrunner, as the English named them. They served the French as interpreters for their Indian allies. Lizotte snatched the hatchet from the Abenaki's back and caught Good Voice as she staggered, nearly dropping her dead son.

Lizotte took the body and steadied her, eyes fierce in a face narrow and sharp like a bird's. "Stone Thrower sends me for you. He did not know whether the babe had come—two of them! Can you walk? Montcalm's Indians have slipped the leash, but I will take you out of this."

"I must walk," Good Voice said in his French language.

Sparing no more words, Lizotte swept her out of the recess, seeming not to notice the child he now held was dead. There was much else to demand his attention. Along a dark corridor, past scenes of slaughter, he led her, deeper into the earth, finally up again into daylight, where Good Voice blinked and squinted until her eyes could bear it.

Lizotte had spoken true. The fort's interior swarmed like an anthill kicked over. Indians were coming over the broken walls, through the gun embrasures, taking prisoners of the English left behind, stripping some of clothing, tomahawking any who resisted. They raced about, shrieking, angered to find so little baggage to pillage or rum to drink. As Lizotte pulled her along in the shadow of a barracks wall, she saw a big Huron pick up a broken barrel and hurl it in anger.

Lizotte made for the gate, hatchet ready to defend them both, though with his stocking cap and quilled leggings he looked too French to be mistaken for English. Halfway to the gate his stride faltered. He looked down at the child he carried, then at her. "Dead?"

Good Voice wanted to release the keening trapped within, but she had one son still living. For him she must be strong. "Yes. Dead."

Another Huron came loping past, lofting high a fresh scalp. A black-robe priest rushed into the fort, long skirts flapping, face pinched in fury at sight of the Huron's prize. Behind the black-robe more French came. Soldiers. More Indians. Good Voice couldn't tell who meant to join the slaughter and who—besides the black-robe—meant to stop it. She didn't think anyone could stop it. The warriors needed scalps and plunder, or who would believe their boasts of victory? But this . . . it was very bad.

Outside the fort, Indians were digging up the soldier graves so they could plunder them. There had been no time for the English to bury their battle dead. These were spotting-sickness graves. Could those warriors not see what horror they touched?

Spots danced in Good Voice's vision, a mockery of the sickness that had stalked the fort, an enemy within. She stumbled on, her insides raw, aching in protest. She should have spent this day in a birthing hut, cared for by the clan mothers—more days still, until her bleeding stopped.

They were nearly to the forested hills to the west when her arms sagged. At her cry, Lizotte turned back to take the living child, trading it for the dead one, which seemed to weigh nothing in her weakened arms, its spirit flown. Lizotte hurried on, but paused at the wood's edge to wait for her.

"Stone Thrower was wounded when you were captured. He was taken to the French at Fort Carillon to heal. He waits for you there."

Good Voice knew about the wounding. They had come with a party of Oneidas in answer to Montcalm's call for aid, but Stone Thrower had decided not to take up the hatchet for the French. They'd been heading home when the redcoat soldiers burst into their camp. Before she was dragged away from him, Good Voice had seen Stone Thrower take the thrust of a bayonet in his side, had feared he'd died of it.

She rejoiced that he lived, but what her eyes were telling her, now that she saw their dead baby in the light of day, wiped the gladness from her heart. This was not her child. She looked back in bewilderment at the detestable fort. Indians and woodsrunners poured from its gate, making for the entrenched camp into which the redcoats were marching.

"Good Voice! *Hanyo, hanyo.*" Hurry, hurry, in the tongue of her people.

She gaped at the dead baby she held, then at Lizotte. "I do not know this child. It is not mine."

Lizotte's sun-weathered hand splayed over her second-born, cupped to his shirt. "What are you saying? Did you not birth two?"

"Yes. *Tekawiláke'.*" Two babies. "But I would know the son out of my own body, even dead. This is not him!"

How could this be? Whose child was this? Where was *her* son? A scream of sheer panic swelled until it threatened to tear out her throat with the need for release.

She must have appeared ready to bolt, and not for the safety of the forest. Lizotte put himself between her and the fort. "What are you thinking? You cannot go back."

"I must find Stone Thrower's son!" But as she spoke, knowledge of what had been done burst inside her head like one of the big fort guns exploding.

Another woman in the fort had given birth. As Good Voice's sons raised their first cries, she'd heard that woman screaming, seen the two English women cleaning her babies wince, heard them speak of that woman's husband—how he worried for his fragile wife, for the babe taking long to come. Then one had given the other a sly look and their talk changed to how good that woman's husband was to look at, so tall in his officer's red coat.

In desperation, Good Voice latched onto the one bit of importance . . . *his officer's red coat.* That one whose wife had given birth was a redcoat officer. Had those women named him?

"Good Voice!"

Ignoring Lizotte, she closed her eyes, summoning memory of English words spoken heedlessly in her presence. *Aw-bree.* One of the women had called him that. She opened her eyes.

"I know who has done this." She hadn't heard anyone say that other woman's baby had died, but this child, newborn as her own, must belong to Redcoat Aw-bree. *He* had done this. She could see it in her mind. While she slept he'd come, taken her living baby, light-skinned like his, and left behind his dead one.

As certainty engulfed her, she almost flung the strange child to the ground. She wanted to do it. Meant to do it. But her arms would not obey.

Lizotte slid the hatchet into his belt and reached for her, strong fingers closing over her arm. "Save *this* son. Save him to place in Stone Thrower's hands. Then you will tell him of the one who has taken his brother. It is for Stone Thrower to make this right."

She didn't want to accept Lizotte's words, but what use was there in going back, trying to find one man in that chaos? One whose face she didn't know. Even if she found him, who would speak for her against a redcoat?

Turning her back on that fort was harder than being torn from Stone Thrower's side. Harder than the tearing of her body as her sons were born amidst strangers.

Good Voice's heart tore in two as she slipped into the forest, weeping at last for her firstborn. Each tear was a prayer to the Master of Life to guard that son and watch where he was taken, so that one day his father could be led to that place. And take him back.

3

August 10, 1757

From the edge of the fire's shrinking light the Indian watched him: a gleam of oiled flesh, bristling scalp-lock, silver glinting in stretched earlobes, eyes staring from a black-painted mask. Reginald clenched his musket, feeling keenly the want of ammunition and bayonet, relinquished upon surrender to Montcalm's Frenchmen. The Indian's gaze licked along the gun, pausing at Reginald's white-knuckled grip. Teeth gleamed in the blackened face.

Anyone who'd thought the walled encampment sufficient to keep the Indians at bay had been disabused of such thinking. Barely were the British within the palisade before hundreds of warriors surrounded the camp, the boldest pushing past the halfhearted French guards to stalk among them, pilfering whatever struck their fancy from wagon or person, striking down any who offered hindrance. Though Montcalm himself had come hurrying from his camp to wrangle his Indians into order, sporadic intrusions had continued throughout another sleepless night.

With darkness finally lifting and the march to Fort Edward tantalizingly near, Indians were slipping back into the camp to have another go at looting. From all quarters came sounds of helpless protest, but Reginald didn't take his eyes from the lone warrior confronting him. He tried to look menacing—he'd several inches on the Indian, a hatchet and knife belted beneath his coat to attract less notice—but he was wretched with fatigue and strain and knew it showed.

The Indian's gaze shifted to Heledd, asleep beneath one of the regiment's baggage wagons behind Reginald. Dread stabbed hot down his throat. *Do not punish her for my sin—*

As he moved to block the Indian's view of his wife, a new alarm gripped him, spinning a tangle of speculation. Was it the child the Indian had fixed upon? Could this be the father of the babe he'd taken? He hadn't seen the blond captive in the encampment. No reason he should with more than two thousand soldiers, women, children, and Negro slaves packed within. Had she died in the fort? escaped to the forest? What had become of his dead son, abandoned beside the dark infant?

Remorse and self-loathing battered from within, tempting him to open his coat and invite this bloody-minded heathen staring him down across the embers to try for his heart. Only knowledge of what would happen to Heledd afterward kept him from it. His hand went to his hatchet. The Indian's eyes gleamed, taunting him to raise the blade.

Suddenly Reginald sensed them there, a soldier on his left, two moving up on his right, no more armed than he yet giving the Indian back his menace. So quickly it left Reginald weak-kneed, the Indian slipped into the shadows, gone to harry another corner of the camp.

Reginald nearly tottered as he turned to see Heledd, awakened, eyes gaping shadows in her stricken face. In the faint glow thrown beneath the wagon by the dying fire's light, her mouth trembled.

"Reginald, where are my gowns?"

Gowns? He knelt and saw in her gaze the bewildered fear of a child woken from a nightmare. "They're above you, Heledd, in the wagon. They'll be safe until we—"

From somewhere outside the encampment shouts arose.

Heledd clutched his hand, hers icy despite the morning's muggy warmth. "What is happening?"

Reginald drew her from beneath the wagon. She came out clutching the babe she hadn't relinquished even in sleep.

Though dawn tinted the sky above the eastern hills, it was too dark to tell what was afoot beyond the palisade. On their feet at the first shout, a company of regulars ahead of their wagon lurched forward as if to begin the march, and as abruptly halted, stricken with confusion as more shouts rent the dawn. Children set to wailing, including the babe Heledd attempted to comfort. Reginald could smell his reeking clout.

As the ranks ahead shuffled forward again, the wagon's driver, who looked all of sixteen, clambered onto the seat. Before he could snap the lines across the horse's back, Reginald called, "Bide you! Let me see my wife to her place."

The lad peered down, face strained in the graying light. "Hurry, sir. I don't know what's afoot but don't mean to lose the column."

Shouts outside the palisade turned to screams. Were they under attack? Where was de la Corne, Montcalm's captain, left in charge of the camp? Where were the guards? Reginald took the babe and helped Heledd to the space provided her at the rear of the bed. As the wagon creaked forward, he handed the bawling infant into her care. His place for the march was with his men, but given the state into which circumstances had deteriorated, he wasn't about to let Heledd out of his sight. Let them punish him for it at Fort Edward, as long as he and Heledd made it there. He clung to the wagon, keeping pace alongside.

They were near the center of the column, most of the regulars ahead, a few companies behind, the colonials and their camp followers bringing up the rear. As they passed from the encampment, Reginald blanched. Indians crowded close in the burgeoning dawn, most observing the exodus in stony silence. But some were dragging wounded soldiers out of nearby huts and tomahawking them, while forty feet away Captain de la Corne leaned on his musket, his guards standing idle around him.

Reginald heard Colonel Monro shouting at the captain to halt the barbarity, to honor the terms of surrender. De la Corne turned a faint shrug toward the colonel's voice. "If you do not wish to give them your blood, then give them the baggage of the officers and men. Command your soldiers to throw down their packs!"

Some abandoned their packs forthwith, eager to part with them in lieu of their scalps. Indians snatched them off the ground. The wagon jolted over a rut, heading toward the forest still black with night, a wilderness pressing in so close it seemed to swallow the track and the red-coated ranks that trod it. Gut already heaving with pity and outrage for those dying behind him, Reginald felt his innards lurch again. More Indians lined the road ahead. Some lunged forward to snatch at the soldiers who hadn't dropped their packs. Scuffles broke out as men were tugged aside and stripped.

Above him in the wagon, Heledd's face blanched. She gave a strangled scream a second before Reginald was hit from behind. He staggered but kept his grip on the wagon. Behind him, an Indian yelped in triumph.

"Steady," he called to Heledd, a throb starting at the base of his neck where he'd been struck. "It was only my pack." And his musket. The weight of both were gone, the straps sliced clean and lifted away. His open coat hung loose.

Fresh uproar engulfed the rear of the column. The driver shot a backward look. "The Indians! They're taking the clothes off the provincials' backs. Sir—what do we do?"

Reginald, trotting now to match the wagon's pace, met Heledd's frantic gaze. "Drive on. Preserve the baggage if you can, but not at risk of your life."

Sunrise streaked the sky above the mountains a delicate coral, but the forest rose like a green-black wall. Reginald moved to the verge to look ahead. An advance guard of Canadian regulars, white-coated, marched ahead of the first British ranks, which remained in some semblance of order. Before veering back to the wagon, he glimpsed an Indian a dozen yards ahead, crouched in forest shadow. More crept out, flanking the first.

One broke from a thicket and rushed at him. With violent hands he grabbed a lapel of Reginald's coat and yanked.

Reginald shrugged out of the garment, letting the savage take it. He yanked his shirt free of his belt to cover his remaining weapons as more Indians picked their targets among the ranks, darting in from both sides of the track.

"Reginald!" Heledd and the wagon were yards ahead. He sprinted to catch them.

The provincial ranks behind them had dissolved in panic. He reached the wagon, as behind them rose an ululating war shriek, taken up by hundreds of trilling throats.

The natives lurking on the verge had been but the vanguard. Throngs poured into the open now. Arrows flew. Muskets barked. A woman was dragged, screeching, into the woods. The wagon lurched to a halt, jarring Heledd nearly over the side. Reginald caught the wailing babe out of her arms as the driver leapt down.

A painted warrior vaulted up in his place.

"Jump!" Reginald shouted, but Heledd sat gaping at the Indian tearing through the baggage within arm's reach.

Tucking the reeking, swaddled babe into his shoulder, Reginald clamped an arm around Heledd's waist and dragged her from the bed, tearing her petticoats over splintery wood. They fell together, Reginald to his knees, Heledd sprawled on the verge. She thrashed and scrambled, clawing at him with groping hands. "My baby! Be careful—be careful!"

"He's safe. I have him." Reginald scanned the brush along the track. Aside from the Indian busy with the baggage, there seemed no others in their immediate vicinity.

Holding the babe, he led Heledd at a crouch past the wagon's wheels, past the wild-eyed horse, then raced with a group of regulars toward the Canadian escort. Several British officers, having overtaken the guard, were demanding intervention. Heledd in tow, Reginald shouldered his way to the front in time to hear a Canadian officer declare his men had no intention of dying to save them.

"Your only choice," the officer shouted in thick-accented English, "is to leave this road and scatter to the wood. Look to your own safety, and try to reach your people at Fort Edward!"

Despite outcries of protest, Reginald feared the man was right. But Fort Edward was too far. They'd never make it by road, not with the length of it become a bloody gauntlet. Refugees streamed up the track, some barely clothed, some dazed and terror-stricken, some with faces set, gazes wild with calculation. The Canadians backed away as men and women chose conflicting directions of flight. Some fought back. Others cowered together while Indians picked off those at the edges, dragging away captives.

A wagon came careening down the track, its team panicked, four Indians clinging to it. British and Canadians threw themselves from its path.

Using the distraction as cover, Reginald pressed the babe to his shirt to muffle its noise, gripped Heledd's sweating hand, and made for the wood south of the road. He barreled through laurels, forcing a path, then turned along the narrow thicket. Deeper in, the trees soared in massive pillars, forming a canopied gloom. Yards away, two Indians flitted like shadows between them.

He yanked Heledd down behind a fallen tree, hitting the ground with her and the babe sprawled across him. He clamped a hand over her mouth, stifling her yelp, then rolled to the side, curving around her. The babe's fetid stench was a scream in his nostrils. With every breath he expected a tomahawk to split his head, but the Indians passed, too far off to smell a soiled clout or too intent on reaching the melee on the road to notice.

Hearing their shrieks as they joined in, Reginald cautiously sat up. A woman screamed, hair-raisingly close to where they hid, a few yards off the track. "Strip his clout," he hissed, scooping up handfuls of forest loam and rubbing it into his shirt.

Heledd gaped at him until he repeated the command. With shaking hands she obeyed, yanking aside the babe's swaddling to unwind the filthy clout. He took it from her and shoved it into the rotting tree-fall, then rubbed more dirt into his sleeves. "Get the back of me," he said.

Grasping at last what he intended, she steadied the babe on her knees and rubbed handfuls of dirt across Reginald's white garment. Her gown was dark enough in stripes of rust and blue not to stand out like a flag of surrender in the wood, so he let her be. She'd be begrimed soon enough. If they survived long enough.

"Must we go into that?" She seemed as frightened of the forest as of the slaughter beyond the laurels.

"Fort Edward is south," he said near her ear. "A little east."

"No." Heledd's eyes were huge with desperation as she wagged her head. "No."

"It will be hard. I'm sorry for it—"

"I cannot!"

He clamped his fingers over her mouth, pressing hard. She didn't take her hands from the babe to wrench free, but her eyes were wild above his hand. Tears spilled, trickling over his dirty fingers. "Look you, Heledd, I will help you. Every step of the way. But we cannot stay here. Do you understand?"

She nodded through her tears. He released her and staggered to his feet. Through a gap in the laurels he saw what had transpired while they hid. Most of the killing was happening back toward the fort, but just here on the road a woman lay slain, two men fallen near her. Over one an Indian crouched, knife in hand. Reginald motioned Heledd to stay down.

Finished with his work, the Indian kicked his victim into the weeds. Reginald stood unmoving as the warrior made off down the road, never noticing the baby tangled in the petticoats of the woman lying dead on the verge. The child flailed, freed itself, and set to wailing. It was older than the newborn, though doubtful it had seen its first year out. Gowned in a dirtied shift, it sat up amidst the carnage, ceased its crying, and looked about with wide, unblinking eyes.

But its noise had given it away. Another Indian, loping down the road toward the heart of the action, veered aside with hatchet raised, making for the child.

He'd Heledd to think of. It would be all he could do to bring her alive to Fort Edward. But at sight of that defenseless babe sitting there as death approached, for the second time in two days something within Reginald Aubrey snapped. He charged through the laurels, wrenching free his hatchet, and snatched up the child one-handed as the Indian took the low swing meant to crush its head.

The child—a heavier weight than the newborn—gave a startled squawk. Reginald jostled it, seeking firmer grip. The Indian caught himself and whirled with a panther's grace, took in the child Reginald clutched to his ribs, then pointed his blade at Reginald's head and shrieked as though the kill were a *fait accompli*.

They met beside the bodies of the dead, blade to blade. The clash jarred up Reginald's arm as he turned to protect the child. The warrior's blade grazed his cheekbone in a searing line. He feinted and turned with a wild backward stroke, felt his blade catch in flesh and bite deep.

Howling in rage and pain, the Indian fell upon him again. Staggering back to avoid the stroke, Reginald tripped. He rolled as he hit the earth, hand splayed protectively over the child's head. The warrior's blade bit the ground inches from his face.

Still gripping his hatchet, he wrenched to his knees, then stood to find the warrior swaying on his feet, hand clamped to a hideous gash that had nearly severed his arm. The hatchet fell from his grasp. Blood snaked through his fingers. As the warrior fell, Reginald shoved the hatchet into his belt and sprinted for the laurels with the child.

On her knees with the babe, Heledd greeted him with eyes as flat as stones, widening as she took in his gashed face, his bloodied shirt. The child—a girl, he thought it—was looking at him too, tiny hands pressed flat against his chest. He could feel the blood coursing down his cheek. "How bad is it? Can you see bone?"

Heledd shook her head, rocking the babe, dazed eyes staring as if at a stranger. "Blood and bone," she murmured, crooning as a lullaby. "Blood and bone . . ."

Wrenching his gaze away, Reginald scanned the track beyond the laurels, littered with corpses. Had that woman been the child's mother, one of those men her father? If not, perhaps at Fort Edward someone would claim her. If he could get them there.

A crashing in the wood made him look sharply round, fearing further attack. It was a pair of red-coated soldiers, blundering into the wood. Instinct urged him to herd up with them to make their way, but the pair was too far off. Shouting might draw more deadly attention. He reached for his wife, his hand sticky with blood. She recoiled from him.

"Heledd—" He fought the impulse to run like a rabbit into the wood, dragging her behind. "We will come through this, you and I. And our son."

Guilt caught like a bone in his throat, but at last Heledd suffered the grasp of his bloodied fingers.

With panic urging reckless haste, Reginald picked a path into the dismaying wood as, each carrying a stranger's child, they started for Fort Edward.

4

*S*he was a quiet one, the girl. Time and again Reginald glanced down, expecting her to be asleep against his chest, only to find her looking back at him with eyes too sober for a babe. Impossible to tell their color under the thick leaf canopy, until they passed into a birch grove. Dappled sunlight flashed across her eyes. Between her rapid blinks he saw they were a clear green-brown, no more one shade than the other.

Woodland eyes. It made no sense to reason, yet as he gazed into them, his fear lifted a small degree. Not so Heledd's. Every unwilling step she took was fraught with the horror of certain death lurking behind each tree and rock, waiting to spring. She went silently weeping, finding comfort only when they paused so she could nurse the boy.

She didn't offer to feed the girl. Thus far the child hadn't demanded to be fed—nor cried for her mother; perhaps she was in shock. Reginald didn't press the issue.

By afternoon they reached a stream. While the girl sat on a flat stone patting its cushioning moss, Heledd washed the newborn's nether regions, careful of the cord stump.

Reginald thought they'd made three miles, as the crow flew. Impossible to tell the position of the sun even if the thick forest allowed. Clouds had come boiling up, dark and ominous, muttering in the distance.

And if it rained, what then? Should he find them shelter? Even if they pressed on, it would take days at this rate to reach Fort Edward, if they didn't run up against swampland or other hindrance to force them out of their way. Such might have happened already. He'd shied from clearings for fear of making themselves targets to roving savages, but without the sun for guidance, the wood was as disorientating as a hedge maze.

One eye on the girl, he cupped his hands upstream from his wife and slaked his thirst. He could hear Heledd's belly complaining to be filled. Helplessness gnawed more fiercely at his own vitals as Heledd unpinned her bodice, loosened her stays, and put the boy to her breast. Reginald removed the girl's wet clout and set it in the runnel to rinse, leaving her bare beneath her shift. Despite being freed of the clout, she began to fret, looking about as if in expectation of a familiar face and not finding it.

When his wife finished with the boy, Reginald ventured, "What of the girl?"

Heledd had been cooing at the boy, playing with his toes, forgetting for a moment the horror of their situation. She raised her face. Disbelief, then repugnance, overcame her look of tenderness. That baffling shadow-self of hers—that dismaying stranger—rose in her eyes, coming between him and the woman he loved. He could *see* it.

Heledd curled her lip. "Put a stranger's child to my breasts? Reginald . . . I couldn't."

The words were barbed with his own guilt. "Heledd, the child must eat."

As if to underscore the statement, the girl's fretting escalated to a wail. Desperate to hush her, he scooped her up and brought her to his wife.

"Till we reach Fort Edward—for pity's sake, before she brings down worse upon us."

Heledd lay the boy on soft moss and, with evident aversion, took the girl into her arms. "But I shan't have her taking what our son needs. She eats second."

"Do what you can for her. That is all I ask." Reginald started to step away but hesitated when his gaze fell to the boy. While Heledd grudgingly fed the girl, whose hunger outstripped any shyness over suckling a woman strange to her, Reginald gathered up the milk-full babe and laid him on rags Heledd had torn from her petticoat. As he wrapped the boy, he looked at him—truly looked—for the first time since finding him. Looked to see had his eyes played him tricks in the dimness of the casemate.

The boy was still blond, fair. To outward appearance white.

With his back to his wife, he finished the swaddling, then retrieved the girl's clout, wrung it, and tucked it through his belt to dry. Above the stream's gurgling, thunder grumbled. When Heledd at last pinned her bodice and handed over the girl, she refused to look at him. He stood, bone-weary. "We should make another mile, at least."

Heledd groaned as she got to her feet. There were bloodstains on her petticoat but not so much as to alarm or convince him to stop for a longer rest. "Heledd . . . I am sorry."

The words ground up from the depths of him, broken shards dredged from a place deeper than regret. Still his wife didn't look at him. She gazed at the babe she carried, as if all her reason for pressing on began and ended in his sleeping face.

The girl slept in his arms as they followed the stream south. Thunder continued to grumble, sometimes cracking. Sheet lightning illuminated the surrounding wood in alarming flashes. The air pressed upon them like a wrapping of wet linen, soaking them through, clothing, skin, and hair. Almost Reginald longed for the rain, just to break the oppressive humidity.

They'd gone half the intended mile when Reginald halted, lifting a hand for silence. Heledd walked into the back of him. He steadied her, a finger to his lips. He'd heard voices downstream. As he looked for somewhere they could hide, the heavens rumbled, drowning the voices. When it quieted, they'd risen in volume. Relief overcame him.

"English," he said. "But let us go carefully. They could be Canadians."

They weren't. One wore a red coat. Two men on their feet were arguing, while a third lounged at the base of a tree, taking no part in the conversation, though by their gestures he was the topic of debate.

A stick cracked beneath Heledd's foot. The two broke off their argument, whirling to face them. The one in the red coat, filthy and bedraggled, was Lieutenant Jones.

"Major? Major Aubrey! It's grand to see you, sir."

"Lieutenant," Reginald said as Jones rushed forward. "My wife and I share your profound relief at the sight of a friendly face."

Jones's companions were both New Hampshire militia, among those who'd borne the brunt of the assault at the column's rear. The one on his feet, some fifteen years Reginald's senior, had a stubborn jaw and a bold gaze, and sported a bloodied knot on his brow. At odds with his tight-muscled frame, his hair was salted white, his face weathered.

"Ephraim Lang," Jones said, somewhat less than amicably. "Rank of captain. Militia." The other, Joshua Wells, a lad of seventeen or so, lay propped on a makeshift stretcher, the remains of his shirt binding his ribcage, blotched red. "Just now, sir, we were debating whether to press on or stop, and did we press on, exactly which direction it was we ought to be pressing."

"Ye needn't stop . . . on my account," came a thready voice from knee height.

"Hush, Wells," Captain Lang said, his accent the clipped twang of a New Englander. "You get no vote. You've not reached your majority, and I don't see your honored parents by to tell you your opinion on the matter."

Wells's grimace came near a grin. "Suppose I earned a few years today, Capt'n?"

Lang's eyes grew luminous. "You've a point there, son. But now the good major's stumbled upon us, I'm thinking he'll be the one deciding the matter—if *major* he is." The blue gaze scoured Reginald for any indication of rank, settling with a raised brow on the baby in his arms. "Only it's grown hard to judge of such things since commencement of the morning's festivities."

"You may argue that you outrank me, Captain," Jones snapped. "But I'll thank you to trust I know my commanding officer when—"

Thunder boomed, silencing Jones. Even Reginald jumped; this was much louder than any before. In fact . . .

Heledd clutched the babe as muffled echoes rolled, bouncing back from unseen ridges. "Are the French attacking again?"

"Was it thunder?" Helpless on the ground, Wells looked terrified.

"Ordnance," Reginald said. "But not French. Fort Edward. And," he pointed along the stream, "I make it in that direction."

Captain Ephraim Lang threw back his head in a soundless whoop. "Webb's guiding us in like a harbor light! Least he can do, eh, boys?"

Jones's relief was too great to bristle at being addressed so casually by a provincial. "The very least!"

Heledd gave a small sob. Reginald's chest ached at sight of her, all tangles and tatters. "Gentlemen, my wife can go no farther today, so neither shall I."

Heledd's exhaustion and distress settled the issue. They set a watch, Jones volunteering first. There was little to do toward bedding down but gather up a pallet of leaves—in abundant supply—for what Reginald hoped, but dared not pray, would be a peaceful night.

Lying with the boy asleep beside her and the girl next to the boy, Heledd raised her head and looked about her suddenly.

"Reginald, what has become of my gowns?"

"We lost your gowns," he reminded her in a whisper, chilled by the blankness of her gaze. "With the baggage." Nothing resembling memory stirred in her eyes. "If they don't turn up at Fort Edward, we . . ."

No longer listening, she stroked a fingertip along the babe's cheek. "I would call him William. After my father. William Llewellyn. Is that agreeable?"

Reginald's throat constricted. When he could breathe again, he did so until assured his voice would be steady. "Aye. If it pleases you."

"*He* pleases me." Through grime and forest shadow, her smile was an incongruous ray of light. "William . . . William."

Reginald spotted Jones, walking the perimeter of their tiny camp, then he lay down beside his wife, the babies now between them. The cannon at Fort Edward gave another muffled *boom*. The echo rolled across the wilderness, meant to console and guide those stumbling toward it.

To Reginald's ears it made an ominous underscore to the name bestowed on the changeling who had replaced their son: *William Llewellyn Aubrey*.

1759—1768
The Mohawk River Valley—
New York

*T*he dream has visited me so often since Fort William Henry, I know it now as once I knew myself—or the man I was before I set foot within those timbered walls. Not that the dream is the same each time. Though its end holds true, the means to that end shift like light on water. Often it is a blade that ends it. Other times an arrow. Sometimes a club, wickedly spiked. Once it was a stone clenched in a fist. A brown fist, strong-fingered and hard.

Now I make no claim to prophecy, but this I know: it is a matter of time before my waking eyes see that which haunts me in the night. I am in the forest, hard by the wilderness road. It is everlasting dim beneath trees so broad below and laced above I see but a few paces on. I had a musket, a blade, a hat, a coat. They are stripped from me, and I am naked. And he is there. I tell you I know this, though I see him not for the gloom. He hunts me. With painted face and shaven scalp, he hunts. And so as the hunted do, I run. Not fleet like the deer, for I clutch to my chest what he seeks to take from me. It slows me, grown heavier in my arms as the years have passed.

I've no love for an untamed wood. It is his home, see. Him it serves, while thwarting me. Brambles snake across my feet. Sinkholes open and suck me down, trammeled. He looms over me, a coppery Goliath murderous in his hate. Yet no move do I make to save myself, for in this there is also relief, and though foolish, there is hope—that it will be enough, a life *for a life. That it will satisfy a God who grinds even His darlings down to bone. "The thing which I greatly feared is come upon me." So said righteous Job. So think I, far from righteous, as the hatchet—arrow, club, stone—falls to cleave my skull. But as it falls I know it will not be enough. Death will be too swift.*

Then comes the lung-burn of waking, the stunning sanctuary of barred doors, stone walls, a pistol within reach. Beside me sleeps my wife, haunted by her own demons but unsuspecting of that which stalks me. I do not reach for her. She is no comfort to me. Nor am I to her. Because of what I did for her.

And if that is not an irony, then I know not the meaning of the word.

5

October 1759
Schenectady

*L*ife at fourteen was pure vexation. What else could it be for one caught in that limbo between girlhood and womanhood? It was like being a leaf snagged on driftwood, forced to pray for a pitying eddy to nudge one along life's river.

Lydia Eve McClaren, fourteen's latest victim, thought it intolerable that she should *look* as awkward as she felt. In the past twelvemonth her height had outstripped her weight. Her nose had surged ahead of the rest of her features. Her hands, once so biddable, now rebelled against whatever she set them to do. But never had she felt more keenly her body's betrayals than now, approaching the below-stairs chamber that contained Major Reginald Aubrey.

After two years of heroically fighting the French in Canada, the major had returned to the McClaren's household—with whom his wife and children had billeted in his absence—for a stint of convalescence of undetermined length.

"'Tis a stubborn wound," Papa had confided to Jacob van Bergen, his apprentice at the apothecary shop. Lydia hadn't managed to learn precisely what part of Major Aubrey had suffered the injury. Shoulder? Limb? Chest? Nor by what means. Bullet? Blade? Shrapnel? This hadn't prevented her rifling her mental catalog of the herbs she might use to poultice a wound labeled *stubborn*. Not that Papa would permit her to see the major's wound, much less treat it.

Pausing in the passage, Lydia took a firmer grip on the tray she'd carried from the kitchen, swallowing back a surge of nerves. Had she been wise to don her second-best gown—the dun wool brocaded in red—or merely ridiculous? *Possess yourself, Lydia. You're no longer twelve, prone to silly infatuations for officers in smart red coats. Not even tall, handsome officers with lilting Welsh accents who fight off cruel Indians to save orphaned babies.*

She reached the chamber near the back stairs without dropping the tray or spilling its contents, to find the door ajar. Beyond it rose a Scotch-burred rumble. Papa's voice. But here was a quandary. Should she free a hand to knock—and risk sending the tray tumbling to the floor in a catastrophe of tea and shattered cups—or call out and interrupt their conversation?

She was on the verge of applying the toe of her shoe to the door when the well-remembered cadence of Major Aubrey's voice, with its long vowels and nearly rolled *r*'s, washed over her.

"Heledd is looking well, she is. And the children. I cannot believe my eyes, so much have they grown."

The sadness in the major's tone caught at Lydia's heart, promptly melting it. And she'd yet to even set eyes upon him. That had been deliberate, of course. Even Mrs. Aubrey had kept to the kitchen with the children and Agnes McClaren, Lydia's mother, while the major undertook the halting journey from the wagon that had conveyed him from the army's general hospital in Albany into the house, assisted by the men of his regiment who'd escorted him to his family's present billet in Schenectady. Keeping Lydia at bay had preserved the major's dignity—she was sensible of it—yet it underscored the fact that Papa still thought it necessary to shield her from the grim realities of his profession.

"I ken 'tis hard, having missed these years with William," Papa said beyond the door. "He's a fine wee lad. What happened before, his taking on at sight o' ye . . ."

"He'll sort out who I am in time," the major said. "I am beyond thankful—to you and Mrs. McClaren—that you've sheltered my family these long months. It cannot have been easy."

Papa cleared his throat. "Aye, weel. Mrs. Aubrey makes no secret she pines for seeing Wales again."

"So I have heard." Weariness swamped the major's voice. It made Lydia wish they'd kept Mrs. Aubrey from him altogether, at least until he'd rested from the ordeal of travel.

Shame made her repent the thought. Naturally Mrs. Aubrey had wanted to see her husband. If only she hadn't launched at once upon her favorite theme—taking herself, her son, and preferably Major Aubrey as well, back to Wales. Forever.

Silence fell at last in the room beyond. Into it Lydia called, "Tea, Papa. For you and Major Aubrey."

"Ah, Lydia." Relief brightened her father's tone. "Bring it in, lass."

Contrary to her expectation, the major wasn't tucked up in the high-post bed dominating the room. Wrapped in a banyan, bareheaded, he sat in a wing chair pulled near the blazing hearth, across from Papa who occupied its twin. Curled asleep against an arm of Major Aubrey's chair, half in his lap, was Anna.

Lydia flushed with pleasure at the sight.

The major had changed in two years. The scar across his cheekbone was harder now to see, having healed from its livid red to a thin line the color of the surrounding skin. October sunlight slanting through the parted curtains showed pain etched at the corners of the major's slate-blue eyes. The strain of long enduring it bracketed his mouth. Both vanished briefly as he returned her smile.

"Now, George. Who is this young woman so kind to bring us our tea? Never tell me 'tis the little blue-eyed daughter of yours I recall."

Lydia's insides softened to a pudding. "Your hair is shorter," she blurted, and blushed from stem to stern. Her wrists began to ache for gripping the tray. Its contents gave an ominous rattle.

"Lydia," Papa said with mild alarm. "Set down the tray, there's a good lass."

She reached the table beside the major's chair without mishap. Hands free, she made the major a wobbly bob. "It's good to see you again Mister— Major—sir."

Lydia stifled a groan. Young woman? Pitiful child, more like.

"Your servant, Miss McClaren." Major Aubrey's smile broadened. "And 'tis a keen memory you have." He raised a hand to his hair, fingers mussing the short curls as they glided through. It was sun-bleached, almost blond. Black-haired as a raven herself, Lydia was envious. "Aye, I cropped it. At the advice of the Rangers, with whom some of the officers trained for woodland warfare."

Beside him Anna stirred. "Lydee!"

The child reached for her, squirming against Major Aubrey. His wince was slight, but Lydia noted it. "Shall I take her?"

"Do you, please." His eyes thanked her, though it seemed he'd rather have kept the girl near. Lydia hoped so. Oh, she hoped.

Hoisting the drowsy child onto her hip, she felt the warm cling of soft limbs, the small head drooping like a noonday flower into the curve of her neck. "Does *she* remember you? She wasn't much older than William when . . ."

Seeing him flinch at her words, her face flamed again.

"Whether she recalls me I cannot say," Major Aubrey replied. "I remember her well enough."

Lydia's gaze fell to his scar, reminded of those days after Fort William Henry's fall, the rumors of the massacre away north at Lake George. Reports at the time had been uniformly alarming, though wildly at variance. Ten thousand French—twenty thousand. Two thousand Indians—ten thousand. Overrunning the forts. Marching next for Albany, where the McClarens had then resided.

No such attack had come. What had come was the major, seeking billet for his traumatized wife and the babies he'd brought alive through it all—his newborn son and an orphan rescued from the side of her murdered parents, with no one found since to claim her. Lydia's parents, moved by the plight of Fort William Henry's survivors, had opened their Albany home to the officer's family. Major Aubrey gratefully accepted billet for his wife and children and, for a few memorable days, had remained with them before rejoining his regiment.

Beyond the window a cart rattled by, loud in a silence Lydia nervously filled. "And your wound, Major? Does it pain you greatly? Was it musket ball or—"

"Lydia." Papa all but rolled his eyes at the major. "I canna turn round these days without the lass peering into my receipt book, filling her head with needless remedies."

Needless remedies? With all her heart, Lydia wished the polished floorboards would part and swallow her whole.

"'Tis all right, her asking." Major Aubrey straightened in the chair, wincing again, but when he addressed her it was without condescension. "You'll have heard of Brigadier Wolfe? His capture of Quebec?"

"The British scaled the cliffs to the Plains of Abraham, outside the city. That's where the battle was fought—and won. Brigadier Wolfe died a hero there."

"That he did . . . though one nation's hero may be another's villain." Major Aubrey spoke as though he was thinking aloud. Recalling himself, he gave her a half smile. "Had I not taken injury already I should have been there with my battalion."

"The Royal Americans."

Major Aubrey nodded. "Over two hundred we lost that day—apart from Wolfe. But my campaign ended weeks before, at a place called Beauport, a few miles up the St. Lawrence from Quebec. We were meant to break the French defenses, entrenched on a height. I was barely out of the landing boat when I was hit. 'Twas come on to rain, see, a proper deluge, with neither side making headway and our powder wet and useless. So the attack was abandoned. I managed to haul myself back into the boat to be ferried away. The army surgeon removed the ball. Above my hip it was."

The right hip, Lydia judged, by the angle at which he sat. When the major spoke again he addressed Papa as well, who appeared to be hearing this for the first time—probably why he hadn't interrupted the major and sent her double-quick from the room. "But the wound has never healed proper. It tries to, only to green again and lay me low with fever—which is more than your father likely wished you to know of the matter, Miss McClaren."

Indeed, there went Papa's lowering brows, his firming mouth, the look he invariably donned before bidding her run along to the kitchen and mind her mama. Before he could do so she hurried to inquire, "Did the regimental surgeon try boiled sassafras root for a poultice? It's efficacious for drawing out impurities, according to—"

George McClaren's throat-clearing bordered on a growl. "Lydia, take the bairn to the kitchen, aye? The major and I have matters to discuss before he rests. I'll pour the tea."

Lydia left the door ajar but had hardly taken her hand from the latch when the major's voice halted her. "Well? Was she right in her remedy?"

"Aye, maybe so," came the grudging paternal reply. "Though I didna wish to say so in her hearing, ken."

Lydia's spirits sank. Silence elapsed, filled with the clink of tea service.

"She's a bright girl, George. I should think I would be proud, did Anna come into such focus, in time."

Lydia's spirits soared.

Her papa chuckled. "Tell me that again in ten years, lad, and I'll believe ye then."

Lydia fumed down the passage to the parlor. Hadn't she a brain in her head as sharp as Jacob van Bergen's? And stomach enough to face the infirmities he and Papa were called on to treat? For a fact, she did. How frustrating that *she* seemed the only one possessed of such conviction.

Anna's head popped up from her shoulder, as if the child sensed her turmoil. Or else Lydia had squeezed too tight. "Sorry, love. It's only—I doubt Papa sees me equal to tweezing out a splinter."

"Spinster?"

"*Splin*ter. Though I'm sure *spinster* is what Mama fears I'm destined to be." Sighing, Lydia buried her face in Anna's hair, which flowed past her shoulders—absurdly thick for a child of three—in a honeyed wave of blond-brown. It even smelled like honey, though Lydia had never reasoned why.

The instant she stepped into the kitchen, she was assaulted by questions.

"Is my husband pleased with the tea? The almond biscuits are his favorite. Did he mention that? I was so careful not to burn them."

Heledd Aubrey, the most delicately beautiful woman Lydia had ever seen, stood at the worktable, knife poised over turnips she'd been chopping for the stew Agnes McClaren stirred at the hearth.

Lydia avoided her gaze. "No, Mrs. Aubrey, he didn't. Papa ordered me away before I could serve."

William, the Aubreys' son, hunkered on the flagstones, pudgy knees poking from beneath his frock, fair head haloed in a shaft of sunlight from the south-facing window. At his feet an army of wooden soldiers, coats painted cochineal red, stood arrayed for battle. Seeing him, Anna squirmed in her arms. Lydia slid her to the floor.

Mrs. Aubrey watched the girl make a beeline for William.

Lydia held her breath as the boy, younger of the two by ten months, thrust his favorite soldier into Anna's hand. "Papa," he said.

Mrs. Aubrey beamed. "You see? He *does* remember Reginald."

Neither Lydia nor her mother mentioned that since William burst into tears at sight of the major limping into the house in civilian clothes, Heledd had hardly ceased explaining that his papa wore a red coat *just* like one of his prized toy soldiers, that the man in the room by the back stairs *was* his papa, and soon she would *show* William the red coat his papa wore.

Agnes McClaren, tucking a strand of graying hair beneath her cap, replaced the pot lid with a clank and swung the crane back over the flames. Unfortunately, the noise failed to mask Anna's voice as, still holding the red-coated soldier, she repeated, "Papa."

Mrs. Aubrey's smile vanished. She set down her knife, crossed to the children, took the soldier from Anna, and put it back into her son's hand. "He is not your papa. He is William's."

The little girl flinched, then stared at the soldier in William's hand, her rosebud mouth drooping.

Lydia drew a breath, caught her mother's warning glance, and exhaled it wordlessly.

Time and again her mother had admonished her. No matter how she might love the child, or think her unfairly treated, Anna was the Aubreys' charge. Not theirs.

Let it be different now. Lydia flung the prayer heavenward as she stalked to the hearth to check the herbs she'd left steeping, thankful Major Aubrey was returned. The child hadn't even had a name when the Aubreys came to them, fresh from the harrowing of Fort William Henry. Of course they couldn't know what her name had been, but to have come all the way from Fort Edward to Albany calling her nothing at all?

Lydia had taken one look at the girl and knew—just knew—her

name was Anna Catherine. Before the major departed she'd suggested the name. Mrs. Aubrey had shrugged, but the major . . . Lydia hadn't forgotten how his face had lit, like a candle flaming up behind it. "That's lovely, that is," he'd told her. "Aye, let's call her so."

"I regret she's such a bother," Mrs. Aubrey said into the kitchen's silence.

"She's no such thing," said Agnes. "She's a biddable child, and quiet with it."

"Now Reginald is here," Mrs. Aubrey went on, "he'll find a place for her to bide. She'll not be long underfoot."

Lydia, stooping over the clay jar she'd left on the hearth, straightened with a blazing face. "You would give her away after all this time? Like some unwanted kitten?"

Mrs. Aubrey stared, patently bewildered by the question. "Why not? She is nothing to me."

"But—"

"Lydia," her mother said. "The child isn't *ours*."

Lydia clamped her lips over what she wished to retort, that God—and Major Aubrey—would have the last word on Anna.

The clay jar in which she'd left calendula petals steeping at the edge of the embers had been pushed aside. Stooping again, she touched the lid with a finger. Cool. "Mama—you moved the jar?"

Her mother's petticoat swished past. "I need space on the hearth to cook, young lady. I cannot be concerned with your little diversions—"

"*Trials,* Mama. I'm attempting to ascertain if steeping calendula at a warmer temperature will enhance its efficacy for Jacob's blemishes. Now I'll have to begin over."

"Oh, Lydia. I'm not sure I even know what you just said." Her mother slid a pan of cornbread into the hearth oven. "Would that you showed such devotion to something of matter to a girl your age."

Lydia scooped up the jar.

"She's not our child either," Mrs. Aubrey cut in, reverting to the subject of Anna. "Yet Reginald chose to spend his first hour with *her*."

Lydia schooled herself to silence while Agnes reminded Mrs. Aubrey that the major would have spent that same hour with William, had attempting to do so not sent the boy running from the room in tears.

"The girl cannot remember him any better than does William," Mrs. Aubrey protested. "Reginald favors her. I cannot understand it."

Lydia ground her teeth. Rarely was it helpful to argue with Mrs. Aubrey once she fixed on a notion, and never on the subject of Anna. Or William. Or Wales. But to judge the major so, when for the past two years she'd showed complete indifference toward the child they rescued?

It was too much. Fearing she might erupt in an unseemly fit of temper if she didn't escape Mrs. Aubrey's presence, Lydia slipped from the kitchen while her mother's back was turned, gripping the clay jar fit to crush it.

6

*L*ydia hurried along the street outside the McClaren's gabled home. She'd left the house too precipitously to fetch her cloak but wasn't going far, and the afternoon was mild for October.

Nearing the center of Schenectady's stockade, private homes mingled with trade shops in an odorous clash of livestock, humanity, and the river curving round the town to the north and west, sending out marshy tendrils hither and yon. Passing a baker's shop, Lydia nodded to two of her mother's friends exiting with baskets on arms, a yeasty breath of air escaping with them. She hurried on before they could inquire after the McClarens' new houseguest.

Mrs. Aubrey made her blood boil. For two years their household had been afflicted by her dark moods, the bouts of weeping, the near hysterical fear of Indian attack. Then there were those days of hand-wringing when she nigh drove them mad insisting William was colicky, fevered, bilious, and a dozen other ailments the boy never suffered. Whereas if Anna should fall bleeding at her feet, no doubt the woman would step over her to offer William another biscuit.

"We must show her patience," George McClaren had explained. "We dinna ken the horrors she's endured. As for Anna . . . have ye nay thought the wee lass may be too sharp a reminder of Fort William Henry and what happened thereafter?"

Lydia tried to mind her father's admonition, but when Mrs. Aubrey's dislike of Anna bordered on the cruel, it made her suspect the child was less a reminder of a terrible ordeal than a source of jealousy, a rival for the major's paternal affection. As if a man couldn't love two children at once.

She'd reached the shop with the white shingle bearing the scripted letters *G. McClaren, Apothecary*. Huffing from anger more than exertion, she pushed the door open and stepped inside.

The shop was devoid of customers, but a rush of aromas greeted her like a clamor of voices—exotic voices from distant lands mingled with those from as nearby as Papa's physic garden and the woods and meadows surrounding Schenectady. The heady smells would soon recede from notice, but those first seconds were like walking into the embraces of friends.

Which wasn't what Jacob van Bergen—seventeen, gangly, big-eared, and pimply—could be called. Her papa's apprentice paused his work of rolling pills behind the dispensing counter as Lydia crossed the shop. He brushed aside a hank of coppery hair that had slipped its binding.

"Back so soon? Where's Mr. McClaren?"

"With the major, last I saw."

Jacob quirked a rusty brow at her glum inflection. "He didn't let you examine the wound?"

Lydia sighed. She'd borne such teasing for well over a year now, ever since Jacob discovered her interest in all things apothecarial. "What do *you* think, Mr. van Bergen?"

She rounded the counter, an eye to Jacob's work. He'd mixed the ingredients and rolled a thick paste into a slab on the tile, ready to be cut into uniform pills. A sniff identified the components, among them aloe, chicory, endive, rhubarb, agaric, and cinnamon.

"Why won't you call me Jacob?"

Lydia looked up to find the apprentice studying her as intently as she'd observed his work. She drew back, wary of further teasing. "Is that Angelic Pill you're making?" she asked, knowing the answer. "For Mrs. Stowe?"

"How did you guess?"

Guess? She shrugged, mistrusting her sharp tongue, and started to head for the distillation room.

Jacob's next question halted her. "Did you run all the way from the house to flush your cheeks so pink, or is it Mrs. Aubrey again?"

Lydia supposed she deserved the hot blush now prickling her cheeks. Obviously her annoyance with Heledd Aubrey was no secret. At least she'd a ready excuse so she didn't have to admit it. She held up the clay jar. "Mama ruined my decoction. I wish Papa would let me work here in the shop."

"Oh? What *work* might that be?"

Without dignifying that with an answer, Lydia pulled out a drawer in a vast bank of them lining the shop's back wall, seeking calendula. They were running low. Jacob would have to treat his pimples by some other means.

A customer entered the shop, requesting hawthorn for her husband's kidney stones. Jacob hesitated over where in all the shelves and crannies to find what the woman requested.

"I'm closer. I'll get it." Lydia extracted a bundle of dried flowering tops and berries, which she handed to Jacob to measure into the woman's leather wallet.

Alone again, Lydia asked, "Is there more calendula stashed away somewhere?"

"Let me see . . ." Jacob went to the account book and leafed back through a page. "No. Mr. Mayfield came in asking for it yesterday, just after you took that bit for your *work*."

Lydia heaved a sigh. "We're low on hawthorn as well. Calendula I can get from the garden, but I'll have to ask Papa to accompany me out to collect the hawthorn berries."

"With Major Aubrey to look after, as well as his other patients? He won't have the time."

"Well, I cannot go beyond the stockade alone, can I?"

The threat of Indian attack that so terrified Heledd Aubrey was un-likely now that the Six Nations—the Mohawks, Oneidas, Tuscaroras, Onondagas, Cayugas, even most of the fierce and distant Senecas—had come over to the English side of the conflict with the French. It was never-theless a concern to take seriously. There'd been that terrible attack last November, in German Flatts, an isolated settlement sixty miles upriver. But there was Fort Stanwix now at the head of the Mohawk River to keep the French and their Indians at bay. And she didn't like to let their stock of any herb run low if she could help it. Perhaps she could strike a bargain with Jacob . . .

"The calendula was for you," she said.

Jacob's brows shot high. "Me? Why? Oh . . ." Spots of red unlike his normal affliction stained his cheeks. "Think calendula might help, do you?"

"I thought it worth the undertaking. I'd be willing to brave Mama's ire for another try . . . if you'll accompany me tomorrow outside the stockade."

"Before work, you mean?"

"The early bird gets the hawthorn berry." She grinned at her attempt at cleverness—admittedly weak—but was surprised to see the appren-tice's expression soften. "Please, Jacob?"

She hadn't meant to call him by his Christian name, but it seemed to aid her cause. His dark blue eyes widened with pleasure before he said gruffly, "Long as we're straight back. No sidetracks. Just the hawthorn."

"Naturally." Lydia made for the door. "Though maybe some sassafras as well," she called over her shoulder as her hand touched the latch.

"Why do you need sassafras?"

"Never you mind," Lydia said and pushed her way out onto the street.

Heledd Aubrey's plaintive voice troubled the house as Lydia shut the front door: "But I do not understand it! Never return to Wales? How can he mean to stay in this godforsaken place?"

Lydia huffed. Schenectady godforsaken? They had *three* churches within the stockade—including their own Presbyterian meetinghouse. Avoiding the kitchen, she ducked down the passage that led to the back stairs, above which waited the sanctuary of her room under the gables. But the stairs were outside Major Aubrey's door, and it stood half open. The third stair creaked like a rusty hinge beneath her foot.

"Miss McClaren?" He said her name softly, but it froze Lydia on the stair. Except for her heart, which leapt beneath her stays and ran off at a gallop.

She descended the stairs and peered into the room.

Major Aubrey was abed, reclined upon pillows. The coverlet outlined his legs. He looked weaker than when she'd served him tea, his features pinched with fatigue, as if her papa had prescribed a stroll round the stockade during her absence. Then she saw the shirtsleeve rolled high. A linen strip, red-spotted, wrapped his arm below the elbow joint. The bleeding bowl and lancet had been removed, but Papa's medical case rested on the table beside the bed.

Lydia flushed but didn't lower her gaze, wanting to seem accustomed to the sight of a patient in bed. "You called me, Major?"

"I did." Major Aubrey raised a hand and worried the curls at the base of his neck. "Do you come in. But softly, see." He directed his gaze toward the hearth.

Lydia pushed the door wide to view the room. On a quilt between the wing chairs, guarded by a sentry of painted soldiers, William and Anna lay napping, mussed fair head to mussed fair head.

The major kept his voice low. "Seems he's over his fright of me."

Lydia forgot to be embarrassed. "Oh, I'm glad. He's a good boy—a handful at times, but sweet." And astonishingly unspoiled by his mother's constant doting, she didn't add. "Did Mrs. Aubrey show him your coat?"

"Aye. 'Tis what did the trick."

The woman had known what she was about, this time. Even so, mention of her creased the major's brow. Here at the end of the passage, his wife's complaints were muffled but audible still. Or was it physical pain that distressed the major? Sweat beaded his face. His fever was up. Ought she to get basin and rag, cool his brow?

"Can I fetch you anything, Major?"

"No. I have all I need." Major Aubrey's gaze went briefly to the children, then returned to her. "Your father has been telling me of you and Anna, though well do I remember how you cared for her from the start. I see that hasn't changed."

Lydia drew in a breath, unsure what to say. She'd known one day the major would return and take Anna away. She'd tried not to think of it. Or if she did, she imagined the Aubreys settling in Schenectady, where she could go on seeing Anna from time to time. Not across an ocean.

Never return to Wales. The import of Mrs. Aubrey's unhappy words struck her now not with annoyance but hope. "I know it isn't my place to ask but . . . shall you be keeping Anna?"

Some emotion Lydia couldn't read rippled across the major's ashen face. "I've every intention of it. She's the one pure thing—"

Lydia waited, but the major had bitten off whatever he'd meant to say. Or begun to say inadvertently. "And you've told Mrs. Aubrey."

"That I have—" His voice caught again. This time his unhappiness was plain.

"I wish Mama would gag her, so she'd *hush.* I'm sorry you must endure her senseless fretting."

On the heels of those blurted words, Lydia felt her face burn, as the major's look sharpened. "Never say that, Miss McClaren."

The words, though soft-spoken, were edged with disapproval. Lydia felt as though she'd been slapped—and deservedly so.

The major must have realized it. "It is only that you cannot begin to imagine . . ." He shut his eyes. "Do you be thankful, Miss McClaren, that you haven't endured what I and His Majesty's army have put my wife through these years past. And if you must complain of her, then do your complaining to God. Ask *Him* to grant her peace."

Lydia took a step toward the bed, her heart twisting at the major's bitter tone. She could barely get breath enough to say, "I'm sorry, Major. Of course I'll pray for her." And she had done, though not as often as she might have.

The major cleared his throat. "I have no doubt you will, dear girl. But let that bide. I called you in to say . . . 'twas about Anna, see. I realize Heledd . . ." He spread his fingers on the coverlet, then made them into fists. His lips compressed as though against a stab of pain. "Thank you—that is what I mean to say. Thank you, Miss McClaren, for the kindness you have shown my Anna."

My Anna. Lydia felt a thread of warmth enter her soul, even as his suffering constricted her throat. She'd added to it with her thoughtless words. Now he *thanked* her?

Tears burned her nose, which by now must be going hideously red and puffy. It did whenever she cried. She had no words. She could only nod at the major—who wasn't looking at her now—and beat a retreat up the stairs to weep her heart out in private.

7

July 1761

*P*erched on the cart's tail, hedged by sacks and barrels and what looked like part of a plow, Lydia watched Schenectady's stockade vanish behind a rise of piney meadowland and waves of humid heat. Summer grasses, seeding between the road's twin ruts, slapped her stockinged feet as they passed.

"A young woman of ten-and-six mustn't gad about shoeless," her mother had admonished weakly from her bed that morning. Though Lydia had no intention of presenting herself shoeless to the Aubreys, clinging wisps of the child within made her long to whip off her cap as well as her shoes, to feel the breeze on her scalp. But what sort of example would that be to Anna, for whose home upstream on the Mohawk River she was bound?

She hummed aloud, happily off-key, until the cart's driver detected the tune she was attempting to render and raised his pure tenor to join her.

"He breaks the power of canceled sin, He sets the prisoner free. His blood can make the foulest clean, His blood availed for me."

Lydia glanced behind her at the narrow, brown-coated back of the Irishman Major Aubrey had hired to oversee the planting of his new farm. Rowan Doyle, hair hanging in graying tendrils below his hat, turned a beaky profile to call over the cart's rumble, "'Tis right gladsome you are today, Miss Lydia."

"What's not to be glad about, Mr. Doyle? The sun is shining, the French are beaten, and the Aubreys have settled in Schenectady—or near enough."

"So it is. So they are. And so they have—to me own content as well."

Mr. Doyle chirruped to the horse to liven its pace. Lydia clung to her bouncing perch, a hand to the satchel at her side, which she planned to fill with gleanings from the woods that edged the Aubreys' new farm. The major told her he'd spotted a patch of ground holly. She hoped also to replenish the shop's supply of milkweed root. Who knew what else she might find?

Mr. Doyle fell to whistling in the bee-buzzing warmth. Fields and scattered dwellings fell behind. Patches of forest crept nearer the road. Lydia leaned against a sack and with eyes shut raised her face to the sun . . . and thought again of her mother. Though bedridden with a fevered cough—a malady that had plagued her since the spring—Agnes McClaren had insisted Lydia take this opportunity to visit the Aubreys' new home, knowing how she'd missed having Anna and William about their house the past month. Jacob had agreed to sit with her mother. Papa was down the street at the shop. It was a beautiful day. She was going to see Anna and William, and, should he return from town in time, perhaps the major as well.

The major. She still thought of Reginald Aubrey thus, though it was a year and more since he sold his army commission and hung up his red coat. The wound above his hip had proved slow to mend, but after a winter spent convalescing in the McClarens' home, he'd felt himself fit enough to rejoin his regiment—only to have the wound fester again on the eve of his departure for Albany.

About that time, across the sea in Wales, the major's father had died. Though the family estate there—near a village with the outlandish name of Crickhowell—went to his elder brother, the major received a small inheritance. Enough to enable the family to leave the McClarens' house for a home of their own.

"You'll want to slip those shoes back on," Mr. Doyle called, interrupting her thoughts. "Here we are to home."

Lydia buckled her shoes as the cart turned down a narrow track, passing through fields of corn beginning to tassel. Children's voices reached her before the cart rocked to a halt in the track that ran beside a two-storied, white-washed, stone farmhouse. She slid to her feet as Mr. Doyle climbed down.

"Lydia!" First to round the cart, a collie at her heels, Anna grappled Lydia's petticoat in a hug.

"Well met!" She hefted the child onto her hip. "Oof! You've grown an inch since last I saw you. And gained a stone!"

Anna put her nose to Lydia's. "I *am* four."

"That explains it." Lydia inhaled the smell of sunshine and grass and that inexplicable sweetness that was Anna. Feeling a tug, she looked down into William's lifted face, startled at how sun-browned he'd gotten in a month's time. "Well met to you too, Master William."

The boy gazed at her earnestly from under his mop of hair. "Next month *I* am four."

"Yes, William," Anna said from her perch in Lydia's arms. "But I will always be older."

William sucked in his bottom lip, thinking how to answer this irrefutable statement. His small face lit. "But one day I'll be bigger."

Lydia slid Anna to the ground and planted a kiss atop William's tousled hair. "I daresay you shall—if you take after your father." Like Anna, the boy smelled of sun and grass, and sweat and dog besides. His hair had begun to darken, making Lydia suspect he'd end up with his mother's coloring. Except for his eyes. They were the major's, though an even purer blue.

"And where is your cap, little miss?" she inquired of Anna, whose waist-length hair held a collection of leaves and grass bits that would have done a rolling filly proud.

"She never wears it," William said. "She's a little hoyden."

Recognizing his mother's sentiments—minus her critical tone— Lydia glanced at the steeply gabled house, behind which Mr. Doyle had disappeared. The farm was one of the valley's oldest steadings, its house and outbuildings Dutch-built in the previous century. Shifting her gaze to the tidy cottage set back beyond a picketed vegetable garden, she asked, "Where's your mother, William? And Mrs. Doyle?"

"Mama's in the house. Mrs. Doyle . . ." The boy glanced around, half-guiltily.

"Spreading wash on the bushes out back." Anna took her hand and tugged in that direction.

Lydia hesitated. "I best give my greetings to Mrs. Aubrey first."

"Mama has a sick head."

Lydia might have grinned at the boy's wording, if the reality of Heledd Aubrey's suffering—and the major's—wasn't so tragic. Only days after they'd settled in their new home, Mrs. Aubrey had birthed her second babe since the major's return from Quebec. Like the one before, born in the McClarens' house, ten months after the major joined their household, it had been another boy. And like the one before, it had lived only a few days.

"Has she taken the dogwood tea my father sent?" Such a feeble offering might mend a headache, but not a broken heart.

She'd taken a step toward the house when a familiar voice called from the cottage yard. "Lydia! 'Tis yourself then, is it? I thought I heard Rowan's cart."

Maura Doyle, faded red hair pinned under a cap, had come round the cottage, wiping her hands on her apron. With her husband in charge of the fields and stock, Mrs. Doyle had made herself indispensable as cook, housemaid, and second pair of eyes for Heledd Aubrey, who rarely set foot outside, Lydia had overheard her parents say.

She started toward the woman when the back door of the house opened and there stood Mrs. Aubrey, blinking like a mole in sunlight. A mole with reddened eyes. "Lydia? Oh . . . I'd forgotten your visit. I'm sure Mrs. Doyle reminded me, but . . ."

"Mrs. Aubrey." Lydia bobbed a greeting, her chest tight with pity at sight of the woman, whose beauty had worn to a brittleness as fragile as glass. "William says you've a headache. Is there anything I can do for you?"

"Headache?" Mrs. Aubrey looked confused. "But you must stay to tea now you've come all this way. Only might we take it a little later?"

Lydia glanced at Mrs. Doyle, who'd crossed the yard to join them. The invitation to spend the day at the farm had included dinner as well as tea. "Of course, Mrs. Aubrey. That would be fine."

Heledd Aubrey nodded. After an awkward pause she asked, "How is your mother?"

"Not yet recovered, I'm afraid. But she bid me come visit since she was feeling no worse at least."

"Ah." Mrs. Aubrey's gaze went to William, wrestling in the grass now with the collie, and Anna. "William, do you come into the house now."

The boy looked up, pouting. "Mama . . . Lydia is here."

Mrs. Aubrey's clouded face abruptly brightened, as did her voice. "But I've a treat for you, darling. Come and see. Come you, now."

William glanced at Lydia, uncertain. Then, unable to resist such a siren call, he followed his mother inside.

Anna watched him go. The hurt in her eyes, and the resigned acceptance of it, kindled an old blaze of anger in Lydia. Little enough had changed, at least in regard to Anna, with the major's return two years ago, save that he provided a buffer between his wife's indifference and the child's tender heart—when he was present to do so.

Lydia couldn't fathom it. It was understandable that the woman would cling as fiercely as she did to William, her only living child, but that she kept Anna at arm's length was inexplicable. Was there no room in the woman's heart for a child not born of her body?

"Anna, dearie," Mrs. Doyle said. "Run inside to your place and get that *thing* you wished to show Miss Lydia."

"All right." Anna raced across the yard, hair like tangled banners streaming behind her. She ran to the cottage. Not the house.

Mrs. Doyle saw Lydia's surprise. "It seemed for the best."

Mr. Doyle came from the cellar beneath the house, where he'd been stashing the goods brought home in the cart. He gave his wife's shoulder a pat and climbed onto the cart to drive down the track toward the barn, whistling as he went.

Maura looked after him, a faint smile on her lined face. "We were never blessed with children, Rowan and I. Though we're still all settlin' to the notion, we're happy the child should be called Anna Doyle. At least for now. Perhaps in time . . ." The woman glanced at the big house. "She's with child again, poor thing."

"So soon?" Barely a month since . . . Swallowing back dismay, Lydia turned to Mrs. Doyle. "But about Anna . . . the major agreed to it?"

"He'd have her under his own roof, sure . . ." Mrs. Doyle trailed off, for Anna was returning, holding out to Lydia a cardinal's feather, stunningly red. Heart aching, Lydia knelt and said she simply must be shown the exact spot such a treasure had been found.

"My favorite place," Anna began, when William burst into the yard, mouth ringed in crumbs, and slipped a sweet biscuit into Anna's hand. The little girl smiled in delight—then whipped the biscuit behind her back when Mrs. Aubrey appeared in the doorway, frowning.

William stepped in front of Anna and said in a rush, "Mama-can-we-show-Lydia-the-creek-and-footlog-and-dock-and-and-and-the-other-places?"

Mrs. Aubrey darted a wary look over the fields to the distant woods, as if they were a line of menacing storm clouds, but seemed helpless against her son's hopeful gaze. "Lydia . . . you'll not let William alone by the river? He is full of such spirit and heedless of his safety."

The woman looked in equal parts proud of her son and terrified for him.

"I'll watch them like a hawk," Lydia promised, including Anna in this covering though Mrs. Aubrey hadn't. Anna's small hand slipped into hers. The other was still tucked behind her back.

"*Do* keep watch and have a care." Mrs. Aubrey looked on the verge of tears. "And don't be gone overlong or I shall have to send Mrs. Doyle out to find William."

And should Anna fall in the river and drown, I suppose the woman would promptly forget she ever existed.

Kneeling on the creek bank beside the promised ground holly, in waxy-white bloom, Lydia put away the ungracious thought, bound to spoil the day if she let it. Breaking off a few leathery leaves, she folded them into the last leather scrap she'd brought and slipped it into her satchel, crowded with earlier gleanings.

Anna and William had showed her the barn—and the cow, oxen, pigs, and horses—the empty corn crib waiting to be filled, and every outbuilding the farm boasted, down to the springhouse and necessary. They hadn't paused at the old burying ground, fenced in wrought iron and studded with the markers of earlier families who'd owned the farm, and one heartbreakingly tiny new mound.

For the past half hour they'd explored the creek that came bounding down from the wooded hills stretching westward into a wilderness peopled mostly by deer and bear and Indians—with a few isolated farming settlements—winding its course to the river, which bordered the farm for several acres. They'd waited while she harvested ragwort along its bank, finally coming to a place where a young poplar had fallen across the creek, making dry-footed crossing possible. Beyond the footlog, a path gave access to a wide stand of beeches and a clearing beyond, sweet with birdsong and the hum of insects, then a breathless climb up a rock-strewn knoll where the creek reappeared; Anna's favorite spot on the farm.

"My waterfall!" the girl exulted once Lydia reached the level shelf in the largely treeless hillside.

"Lovely," Lydia exclaimed, brushing down her petticoat and settling on a nearby shelf of rock. While it *was* lovely, it was hardly a proper fall. Just a spill where the creek dropped over a broad, mossy stone, then tumbled down the hillside to wind toward the river beyond.

"*Our* waterfall," William corrected, springing up the hill lastly, trailing his collie-shadow. Above the spill was the creek's spring-fed source, issuing from a thicket of rhododendron choking the narrow spaces between massive rocks.

"We're never to go farther into the wood than this." Anna, hunkered beside Lydia, watched a wren flit at the base of a nearby shrub.

Already clambering the rocks above them, William scooted down on his bottom and landed with a thump that frightened off the wren. "Mama says Indians will steal us away unless we take care."

Heledd Aubrey had more excuse than most to fear such a thing, but Lydia thought her anxiety unreasonable in its intensity, after all this time.

Sir William Johnson, superintendent of Indian affairs at Fort Johnson, across the river, lived with a Mohawk woman, Molly Brant, as his wife. His influence over the Mohawks, at least, held strong. And the Oneidas were peaceful neighbors. There would be no uprisings, not with Sir William in charge. Besides, Indians often came into Schenectady for trade. A Mohawk sachem from Canajoharie Town favored her father's apothecary, arriving yearly with herbs harvested from forest and mountain to trade for simples her father purchased from eastern cities or London.

"It's not a *wholly* unfounded concern," she'd told the children, trying to be fair-minded. "Not all Indians are friendly." Nor were all Indians their neighbors. But there was a treaty of sorts, called the Covenant Chain, between the Six Nations and the English king. The Mohawks or Oneidas would warn Sir William of any impending threat from the west. Surely they would do that much.

She hoped so. It had surprised Lydia to learn—from their visiting sachem—just how much autonomy Indian men had. They were more or less free to do as they chose, holding to a chief's rule only so long as that man proved worthy of leadership. Which meant, Lydia was forced to conclude, one could never know for certain what might be brewing beyond the peaceful wood's edge the children were forbidden to pass.

But how irresistible it must be to be young in the world with such a place as this to be explored!

With her satchel full, Lydia admired the spot anew. From the height of the little fall, the distant farmhouse could just be glimpsed through the summer-leafed trees lining the creek, white and tall beyond the green fields of corn. It was perfect, a place that felt wild and remote, with the security of home within sight.

She cupped her hands beneath the tumbling creek and splashed her face, reveling in the coolness. Even in the wood the day was beginning to swelter.

"Tadpoles!"

Lydia looked downhill. At its base, the children leaned over a shaded pool. William poked a stick into the water as if he meant to spear one of the tiny creatures.

Anna shaded her eyes, looking up at her. "Lydia, are you done?"

William tossed his stick aside. "Let's show her the river!"

Grabbing Anna's hand, he looked to see Lydia descending the slope, then made off across the clearing and through the beeches, back along the path to the footlog.

Smiling at the boy's enthusiasm—as if she'd never seen the river before—Lydia followed along its bank until they reached a dock set on pilings braced with stones. William trotted to the end of it, plopped down, and dangled his feet in the river. "*My* favorite place."

"Will you put your feet in the water?" barefooted Anna asked her.

Lydia's feet were hot and clammy in her shoes. The river looked inviting, flowing smooth along this stretch. "Why not?"

She removed her shoes and hose and sat between the children on the dock's downstream side. The river made a bend beyond; still she might have seen quite a ways were it not for an old maple with a massive branch overhanging the bank, like a green-clad arm dipping for a drink.

Schenectady, several miles downstream, was the farthest east one could travel by boat on the Mohawk because of the Cohoes Falls. On the Binne Kill, the town's waterfront, carpenters did thriving business crafting flat-bottomed bateaux for transporting goods—brought overland from Albany—upriver to supply the forts, and for trade with settlers and Indians. Some of those bateaux went beyond the Mohawk River, portaged over the Oneidas' Carrying Place between the river and Wood Creek, then on to the lake country far to the west.

Major Aubrey was at work on the Binne Kill.

While recovering from his wound, the major had met old Mr. Boswell, a bateau-maker, and taken an interest in the craft. Mr. Boswell hired the major upon his leaving the army, then made him a partner as time proved him an able carpenter and businessman. Though sometimes he was gone for weeks at a time on his trading journeys upriver—when he went farther than the Little Falls Carry, a closer portage manned by a German farmer called Herkimer—it pleased Lydia to see the Aubreys prospering. The major was liked and respected in Schenectady. His farm was situated on some of the richest acres within a day's ride of the stockade. He'd found a good man in Rowan Doyle to help farm it.

If only their babies would live. If only Mrs. Aubrey would let Anna, as well as William, assuage that grief . . .

Determined not to spoil the day with such thinking, Lydia tilted back her head, feeling the sun on her face, the river's cool on her feet . . . and the collie's tongue wet across her mouth. "Impudent dog!" she scolded, wiping her lips as the children howled with laughter. "Stealing kisses is a sign of bad breeding, you know."

The collie trotted to William's side and sat, grinning at its cheek.

Lydia poked William in the ribs. "So, Farmer Billy, have you taken up fishing on this fine river yet?"

"He means to," Anna said. "But Pa . . . Mr. Aubrey doesn't fish."

William kicked his feet, spraying water. "I want to catch a wally. Mr. Doyle said he'd teach me."

"A wally? Oh, a walleye." Lydia just managed not to laugh. "I daresay Mr. Doyle will keep his word. Summer is a busy time for farmers."

"In autumn?" William asked. "I'll be four by then."

"I'll be *five*," Anna said.

Lydia did laugh at that. "There's the harvest . . . After that there should be time for taking up the life of a gentleman fisherman."

On her left William giggled.

On her right Anna gasped and pointed. "A canoe!"

Indeed it was, its single occupant laboring to paddle upstream.

Indians came in canoes. Lydia scrambled to her feet, only to realize the man in shirtsleeves had hair too light for an Indian's.

"It's Papa," William said.

Lydia's heartbeat quickened. The children stood beside her as Major Aubrey, rowing hard against the current, brought the canoe past the leaning maple and pushed on to the dock, swinging around and bumping against the pilings. As he tied the canoe fast, the children clamored questions at him, but it was Lydia his gaze sought. Though she couldn't help noting how his shirt clung to his broad chest, the glow of exertion coloring his face, his eyes were what gripped her. They were deeply pained.

"Major? What is it?"

Still breathing hard, he looked at the children. "Do you two run up to the house. Tell Mrs. Doyle I've come for Lydia."

They went unhappily, after Lydia hugged them and thanked them for

showing her their new home. Feeling as tousled and stained as they—and
caught barefoot—she faced the major. "Please, I see something's amiss.
Tell me."

"Lydia." Reginald Aubrey took her by the shoulders. "Jacob came to
the boatyard to tell me. I'm so very sorry."

His touch surprised all thought from her head. Then his words struck
comprehension through her. Her mother. *No.* Numbness descended over
her face, her lips. She couldn't feel them as she said in a small, breathless
voice, "She told me I should go . . . that she'd be all right. How? So
quickly?"

He offered no answers. Only a canoe to bear her home.

Dazed and stricken, she clambered into it and stared, bewildered,
when he held out her satchel, shoes, and hose, forgotten on the dock. She
took them onto her lap, uncaring that a man—he of all men—had han-
dled them. The canoe rocked as he settled behind her. He pushed off with
a paddle, finding the river's flow.

Lydia looked steadfastly ahead, willing the river to carry them faster.
"When?"

"Two hours ago I make it. She wasn't alone. Jacob and your father
were with her."

"But I wasn't!" Aching tears blurred the river, touching her lips with
salt. Behind her the canoe's paddle rested. The major's hand fell again on
her shoulder.

"I know," said Reginald Aubrey, who'd not only put two babies in the
ground but had lost a father and hadn't been there to comfort him in his
passing. Or to be comforted. Lydia reached up to touch his hand but
found no voice to say now what she hadn't known to say then.

"I do know," he said and gave her shoulder a squeeze before he dipped
the paddle again and sped them on.

8

Harvest Moon 1761
Kanowalohale

Gripping the hands supporting her, Good Voice bore down as pain ground through her hips and back and taut, swollen belly. With the corner of her mind not consumed with birthing the child, she asked the Master of Life to make it another son. A son to fill the void He-Is-Taken had left in the heart of his father, who was somewhere outside the birth hut getting drunk and starting to be loud about it.

The clan women helping her cast disapproving looks toward the door hide. Good Voice knew it, though everything beyond the burning cradle of her hips felt remote, separated from her by a curtain of red.

Between the pains, the curtain thinned. The door hide moved inward with a puff of chill breeze, and the small hand of Two Hawks, her son of four summers, who waited for this hard thing to be over.

He should not be so near the birthing hut. Already his father was too full of trader's rum to care for him.

She heard Stone Thrower's distant bellowing as one of the women, a Turtle Clan grandmother who sat in the women's council, said to Bright Leaf, Good Voice's aunt, "Someone should send that man farther away. He is no good for her now."

To which Bright Leaf muttered back, "Is that one ever good for her?"

Good Voice felt her heart break for her husband, even as her body bled to birth his child. She took firmer grip of the women's hands as the urge to push gathered in her thighs and back, sparing breath to say, "Do not send him away," before she pushed, grunting through the cleaving pain. Suddenly the women were busy around her, Stone Thrower forgotten.

Good Voice reached down. The baby's head had crowned.

Come, my son, and heal the pain of your father. Heal all our pain.

Stone Thrower stopped shouting long before the morning her bleeding stopped and she emerged from the birth hut to walk to her lodge at the edge of the village on Oneida Creek, but Good Voice did not see him until later in the day, when he poked his head inside the lodge. Bloodshot eyes squinting in the dimness, he reached for something near the doorway. Their son. With a hand on the boy's slender neck he pushed Two Hawks in ahead of him.

Two Hawks scurried to his sleeping bench across the central fire and perched there like a wary owl, knees drawn to his chest. The marks of crying streaked his face. Good Voice wanted to gather him to her but waited, watching his father. So did Bright Leaf, who had a pot of hominy boiling over the fire. Good Voice sat up on her sleeping bench and gave her aunt an imploring look. Bright Leaf firmed her mouth and glared at Stone Thrower.

"I would see my wife," he said, defensive in the face of her silent rebuke. The feathers in his scalp-lock were crumpled. Grease spotted his wrinkled shirt. But he didn't slur his words.

Even on the day of the child's birth, Good Voice had known his drunken shouting had been to do with his fear for her—and the memory of the terrible thing that happened at her last childbed, which he hadn't been there to prevent. More and more often these days he tried to wash away those memories, and the guilt he carried, with trader's rum. It didn't seem to be working for him.

"They tell me it was a son." Grief made his voice ragged. The same grief that skewered her like arrows through the heart and womb.

"It was."

Emotion flickered in Stone Thrower's reddened eyes, but the lodge shadows obscured it. "He cried. I heard him."

He'd uttered one plaintive mewl, that tiny boy, then before the cord that bound them could be severed he'd gone back to where he'd been before, as though the world—or the mother—he was born to was too great a disappointment to bear.

It was wrong to think so. Good Voice knew this. That one's death was not a rejection of her. But she'd put such hope in the child. Hope that he would bring wholeness to his father, to their family. She never once thought she would lose another son, not while she was looking right at him, holding his warm, slippery flesh.

She waited for her husband to say something more.

Stone Thrower folded his lean-muscled legs to crouch beside her, his handsome face twisted with grief, haggard with drinking. He put his hand against her cheek. "You are well?"

His rum breath made her belly churn, but the tender gesture brought tears rushing. She was well enough, in the way he meant, but she couldn't say the words.

Stone Thrower bent his brow to hers. "This was not your fault."

But the other was. He didn't say it—had never said it and maybe never thought it, she couldn't know—but as he drew back, other dark thoughts slid across his eyes, pushing out the tenderness. He was thinking of He-Is-Taken. He was curling around that pain that gnawed him with viper's fangs and flooded his soul with venom. He was adding to it now this new loss.

Stone Thrower's gaze fell on Two Hawks, crouched on his sleeping bench, watching. The boy asked, nervous but hopeful, "Will we shoot arrows today, now my mother is home?"

Her son had his first bow—a slender curve of hickory that Stone Thrower had made in the weeks before the birthing, and a quiver for his little arrows she had made from a gray fox's pelt, the pieces laid across her belly while she sewed them. How they'd laughed together, she and her son, when the baby kicked and the little pelt moved on her belly like it still had life . . .

The bow was Two Hawks's prized possession. He was determined to master it and make his father proud.

Stone Thrower was in no frame of mind for it now. He grunted a sound no one could mistake for anything but *No,* then rose and stalked out of the lodge, smacking the door hide aside as he went. The disappointment on Two Hawks's face left her spirit folded up in grief.

She had seen Stone Thrower like this before, when the memories grew sharp, when he couldn't go on with things as though one of their sons wasn't missing from their fire, their hearts. What would follow was as predictable as night after day. Stone Thrower would leave them, go off to search for He-Is-Taken, for Redcoat Aw-bree who stole him. *If* he managed to get beyond the village before he found another jug of rum. Either way, he was lost to her for many sleeps.

"At least he stayed to see it through. That is something." Bright Leaf, whose sad duty it had been to bury the dead child in the forest, pushed a lock of graying hair from her lined face as she checked the boiling hominy.

Bright Leaf was tired, her patience thin. She had been working to glean Good Voice's part of the fields too, while Good Voice had been confined to the birthing hut. Tomorrow she would rise and be of help. There was no babe to suckle, no new life to tend like the spark from struck flint. But there were crops to bring in and store, hides to be worked, corn to be ground. Life would go on around its circle. She would heal. And next time she would do better.

She had sent the wrong plea to the Master of Life. Better to have asked for a living child, son or daughter, than demanding one over the other. She would not let Stone Thrower know she'd prayed such a prayer. She couldn't bear him to know it. He might think she deserved what she got. Even though he loved her, he might have that thought, and she might see it in his eyes before he could hide it.

"Now we will see him no more, until he crawls back stinking of vomit to tell you he is sorry and will change his ways." Bright Leaf's disdain filled the cabin like the stench of rotting meat. "That is what an old woman thinks—if anyone should ask."

"He is remembering last time, when I was in the fort," Good Voice said in dull defense of her husband. *And he is dreaming again.* She didn't say that. It would only make her aunt more ill-at-ease. But Good Voice knew. Even when the dreams didn't make her husband thrash beside her in his sleep, or bolt upright with a war cry on his lips, there were signs. The restlessness, the drinking, the hard light in his eyes. "There is nothing to be done, and it makes him angry."

"When is that one not angry?" Bright Leaf countered, bending over the pot. "When he has rum he is loud and angry. When he has no rum he is silent and angry."

It wasn't quite true, the bitter words her aunt pronounced. At times Good Voice glimpsed the man she loved, the kind, strong, good man she'd been eager to call husband, those years before the French and English went to war, back when the Haudenosaunee, the Longhouse People, stood strong between them, making those great *a'sluni* nations vie for their favor, their furs, their friendship, their warriors' strong arms in battle. That man was still there, buried beneath the hate and grief. Few agreed with her. Some of the *kutiyanéshu*—the clan mothers—Bright Leaf chief among them, thought it time she put Stone Thrower's belongings outside their lodge and tell him to go back to his mother's Bear Clan people.

Good Voice couldn't bring herself to do it. She had no brothers to teach and train her son, as was their custom. With her own father and mother dead, Two Hawks and his father had only each other.

"I will go downriver to Fort Johnson!" Stone Thrower shouted outside the lodge, startling them. "This time I will go. If anyone can help me it is

Warraghiyagey. He will tell the English king to find that redcoat, make him give back my son!"

Stone Thrower was talking to someone, not shouting to himself as he sometimes did when the dream-need was on him and no one would listen. Good Voice waited to hear who it was, gazing around the lodge at hanging strings of beans and onions, and the first dried rounds of squash, at woven storage baskets pushed under benches along the walls, at stacks of deer hides to be traded, others needing work, at the fire in the earthen floor sending up smoke to curl beneath the roof hole.

"You might do that," said a voice unruffled by her husband's temper. "But will the great William Johnson give you his ear? Are you too drunk to make your words to him sensible?"

Good Voice breathed out a sigh. It was Clear Day, her husband's uncle—his mother's brother—the one man who could still sway Stone Thrower with his counsel, who could curb his thirst—for liquor and vengeance—long enough to be sure he hunted for them in the months when autumn's crops were depleted, or went to the fish camp to catch their share when that time came. Only Clear Day could shame Stone Thrower into remembering he still had a son who needed to learn what it was to be *ukwehu-wé*, an Indian person, a man of the People.

Bright Leaf called Two Hawks to the fire and gave him hominy in a gourd bowl. The boy ate it with his fingers, watching the door hide.

Good Voice watched her son. Two Hawks was a lively boy, good-natured, athletic, fond of games like snow snakes and *Tewaarathon*, the little-brother-of-war game played with webbed sticks and deer-hide ball. Anything that called for physical skill—most of all shooting those arrows. Yet he could make himself still and quiet too. He was a good son, rarely naughty like other boys.

She waited until he finished eating, then beckoned him to her bench. He was no longer a baby, but sometimes he would still crawl into the blankets and snuggle close. She hoped he wanted it now.

Two Hawks put down the bowl and came to her, mouth smeared with hominy, and cuddled beside her with a care for her sore flesh wise beyond his years. Tears still dampened his hair. Two Hawks had wanted this brother.

"Did he look like me?" the boy asked.

Bright Leaf looked up from the pot she still tended, brow creased as though she thought of shooing Two Hawks from the lodge to let her rest. Good Voice shook her head at her aunt. She needed this closeness as much as her son needed it. She breathed in the smell of him, his hair, his skin, and in answer to his question said, "He was not as brown as you."

The infant had looked as Good Voice expected her babies would look. Dark of hair, skin a shade between hers and his father's, though still flushed pink from birth. She clenched her teeth, remembering him—separate from the oneness they had been until that moment, distinct among every other person who had lived. She'd known an instant of pure wonder and joy . . .

"But there was something of you in his face." Good Voice gazed down at Two Hawks, who Bright Leaf said was starting to look like her despite his coloring. What Bright Leaf saw was in the shape of his head and the set of his eyes. How his wide mouth angled up at the corners even when he wasn't smiling.

Sometimes when she looked at Two Hawks, Good Voice tried to picture him with lighter skin. She recalled thinking, even in that place underground like an animal's den, that her firstborn would have eyes like hers, eyes Stone Thrower once told her were like the Harvest Moon sky. Did her firstborn still look white, as he had at his birth? Did the redcoat treat him kindly, or had he made of him a slave?

Where *was* he?

Good Voice drifted on the edge of sleep, while outside the lodge voices rose and fell. Sometimes Stone Thrower railed. Or complained. Or pleaded. Once, in a snarl of rage, he shouted, "I will find the redcoat and do as I have dreamed—but not before he sees I have taken back my son from him!"

It was silence that finally roused her, to find Two Hawks napping on his bench, Bright Leaf still puttering about the lodge.

A knock sounded on the door frame.

"Clear Day would speak with you," Bright Leaf said, having gone to see who wished to enter. "I told him you are tired."

Outside was quiet. Stone Thrower had gone. "He may come in."

Clear Day of the Bear Clan, her husband's uncle, wasn't an old man, but neither was he young. He still wore his graying hair in a scalp-lock, and his body was that of a warrior, though one past his prime. Grunting, he folded himself to sit on a mat beside her. The spotting sickness had long ago pitted his cheeks, and his features were blunter and broader than Stone Thrower's, who took after his father's Wolf Clan men in looks.

Two Hawks sat up, pleased his father's uncle had come to call. "Will you come and watch me shoot my arrows, Uncle?"

"I would be happy to do that later," Clear Day told him. "You must be getting good with that bow your father made."

Two Hawks nodded with unabashed pride.

"He is ready to be a hunter, that one," Good Voice said, beaming at her son.

After food was offered and tasted, Clear Day grew sober. "I must speak with you about your husband."

Clear Day glanced at Bright Leaf, who took his meaning and called Two Hawks to her. "I will have him in the fields with me."

Two Hawks's face fell—the fields were a woman's place—but he brightened as he asked, "Can I take my bow?"

Bright Leaf chuckled. "Yes, yes. Bring it. Only do not be shooting arrows at my pumpkins!"

When they went out, Good Voice gazed at her hands in her lap, waiting for Clear Day to speak.

"Maybe you heard what my nephew had to say to me?"

"All of Kanowalohale heard, I think."

"He dreams again?"

Good Voice nodded.

"I thought they had stopped."

They had stopped, those terrible night dreams, once her belly began to grow, as if the life inside her had absorbed the darkness of its father's spirit. Could *that* be what made the child unable to live in the light?

The thought was too painful to hold under scrutiny.

Stone Thrower hadn't recounted those dreams for her in a long time, but she didn't need him to. During that first year after He-Is-Taken was lost, Stone Thrower had told her how, in his dreams, he hunted for Redcoat Aw-bree, through forest and shadow. The details of the hunt were rarely ever the same, but its ending never varied. Stone Thrower stood over the redcoat, ready to kill him.

"And our son?" she once asked him, back when she believed they must see the dream fulfilled. "Do you get him back?"

But Stone Thrower hadn't wanted to answer that.

Night dreams weren't meant to be ignored. They were the expression of a person's true heart and deepest desires. If they could be fulfilled, they should be, else a person might not prosper in his ways. At first Stone Thrower had found warriors willing to go out with him, men of his mother's Bear Clan, though he had no way to find the redcoat he longed to kill, no notion where to look for their lost son.

After a time the other warriors grew weary of his obsession with his dream, until now he couldn't find a single one to go with him on his fruitless searches eastward. They hunted with him, fished with him, let him play *Tewaarathon,* but they had drawn back from him in their hearts about the dreams. So Stone Thrower had begun looking elsewhere to see them fulfilled, their son restored.

"You know I have refused to go with him to Warraghiyagey," Clear Day said. "You have never questioned this." He paused, searching her face. "Do you understand why I refuse?"

Good Voice took a moment to order her thoughts. "You do not want him to go because you believe Sir William would know my husband wants more than to get our son back. He wants to kill the man who took him, as his dreams tell him to do. You do not want Stone Thrower to bring back the white man's violence on us all if he should find Redcoat Aw-bree and kill him for taking our son."

Clear Day raised his eyebrows. "All those things are true. I wish it was not so. All this time I have had in my possession three strands of white beads. Stone Thrower will not receive them. This you know."

Clear Day spoke of the condolence ceremony, the giving of white wampum and the speaking of good words to wipe away tears, to clear hearts of grief, to help the people heal and go on with living. The ceremony had been given to the Haudenosaunee generations ago in The Great Law of Peace that held their clans and nations together and made them strong.

Their firstborn wasn't dead, Stone Thrower argued, and Good Voice had forbidden him to bring her a captive to replace him. That was another thing that might have been done.

Good Voice had been too small to remember when warriors stole her from a farm many sleeps away. Had the woman who birthed her, whose name and face were lost to Good Voice of the Turtle Clan, felt this anguish at the loss of *her*? Knowing now that terrible grief, she could never cause another woman, red or white, to bear it.

So they were trapped, unable to move on from that moment she held a stranger's dead baby and looked back at Fort William Henry with a shattering heart.

"I have given him time to stop the drinking," Clear Day said. "To remember he is blessed with a good wife and a son who need him to be a man. He has yet to hear my words. So I tell you, who carry the same pain but have not forgotten how to be a woman of the People . . . I tell you I will go myself to Warraghiyagey and plead the cause of my nephew."

Good Voice felt a brush of pleasure at the praise from her husband's uncle, before that last thing he said came clear. "You will go?"

"Yes. But I do not mean to tell my nephew of it."

"Why will you not tell him?"

Clear Day's mouth tightened, but he didn't let his disappointment in his nephew show on his features. "*Atahuhsiyost*—Listen, daughter. I want you to have back what was taken from you. But I also want my nephew to find his way. Killing that redcoat is not a good path for him, no matter what his dreams tell him to do. This is something I sense in my heart. So I will go to Sir William and see what comes of it. We may find a better way than blood-spilling to make this right again."

Tears blurred Good Voice's vision. "I wish you were wrong about that. Thought of killing that redcoat has many times crossed my mind."

How could it not, in the dark hours she'd wept for He-Is-Taken? Yet she too sensed spilling that redcoat's blood wouldn't cover their sorrow. She wasn't certain why this should be. She only knew that Clear Day was right. It wasn't a straight path through that dark valley, but one that would lead in circles of pain. Sometimes, awake in the night, she could almost glimpse another path. A shining path, like the stars across the heavens. But when she tried to trace its course, it shifted like forest shadows and was lost.

"As much as I want my son found," she said, "I do not want my husband lost. Or anyone else."

Clear Day put his scarred brown hand over hers. "If there is a way to do both, we will look until we find it. We—"

A fierce cry, trilled from somewhere in the town, locked their gazes in alarm. Clear Day's hand gripped hers as another voice took it up.

"What is happening? Who—"

"Traders. They came a while ago, from the Carrying Place." Clear Day wrenched himself off the ground and hurried to the door hide. "They must have opened their rum and given it to the warriors."

Good Voice's empty belly clenched. "Is that where Stone Thrower has gone?"

She needed no answer.

Clear Day was looking out into the falling dusk. "I see fire glow, from the council ground, I think."

Good Voice was on her feet now, propelled by fear. Two Hawks and Bright Leaf had gone to the fields. Soon the warriors would be crazy with the rum. It happened sometimes when the traders came. Men, sometimes women too, would get drunk and hurt each other, break belongings and heads, then wake up sick, in pain and shame, with no memory of the bad things they'd done to each other. Bloody wounds. Broken bones. Waste and ruin.

Scalp prickling as more voices shouted, Good Voice pushed her way past Clear Day into the yard. She saw the glow for herself. A big fire. She hoped it wasn't a lodge burning. "I must find my son!"

Clear Day came out with her. "Go to the field. Keep him and your aunt with you. Do not come back into the town until I come for you. I will get Stone Thrower out of this if he is not too drunk."

Good Voice was already running for the fields.

It was full dark when Clear Day found them, two dozen women and children who had found each other amongst the dry cornstalks and late-ripening pumpkins. Two Hawks knelt beside Good Voice, brandishing his little bow, though Good Voice felt him shudder when screams or musket fire—shot into the air, she hoped—came close. There was crying, women's voices soothing, low moans from an old woman who rocked herself and would not be consoled.

The tumult was still going on when she heard Clear Day's approach. He called out before he neared, knowing some of them would be armed. The moon was up and full. Its light revealed a gash on Clear Day's scalp. Blood had made rivulets down over his ear, dark and colorless in the moonlight.

"Stone Thrower?"

She felt the breath of her husband's uncle warm on her face. "I was too late. But he is not hurt."

Bright Leaf clutched her arm. "Who *is* hurt?"

"No one badly," Clear Day said. "A trader kept back some rum, refusing to sell it. The warriors found it out. They tried to stake him and burn him for it, but some of the sachems got that man away out of the town. He is probably halfway to German Flatts by now."

"My husband? Did he do this to you?" She touched Clear Day's face, but he drew back.

"He did not know what he was doing, swinging a club at anything within reach. I got in the way."

Rage filled Good Voice, coiling in her legs, urging them to spring her up, to race her off to find her husband and . . . she didn't know what. Wring his neck, if she could.

"*I* would like to do some head smashing," Bright Leaf hissed.

There were grunts of agreement, a few whimpers from children, then the huddlers in the cornfield fell quiet, listening to the chirps of crickets, the wind moving through rustling stalks. Now and then a trill, or a moan, or whoop from the town's ravaged center. Good Voice held her son close as night enclosed them in its chill.

They waited until the warriors had all passed out on the ground and it was safe to make their way back to their homes.

9

April 1762

*S*hawl-wrapped against the threat of chilling rain, basket in hand, Lydia pushed open the apothecary door, walked into its scented embrace, and drew up short. On the near side of the dispensing counter, opposite her papa and Jacob, stood a man with black hair that reached halfway down his back.

Hanging Kettle, the Mohawk sachem, turned at the tinkle of the bell above the door but didn't smile. Hanging Kettle rarely smiled, even when he shook with silent laughter. "*Sekoh,* McClaren's daughter."

"*Sekoh,* Mr. Hanging Kettle." The address, used at their first meeting, still made humor dance in the dark eyes set above cheeks patterned with tattoos.

Beneath a long shirt Hanging Kettle wore a breechclout and leggings—quilled like his moccasins—but his hair was full, not plucked nearly bald like that of the other Indian standing off to the side, fingering an arrangement of lavender-scented soap on a shelf. An older man than Hanging Kettle, he took no part in the conversation at the counter spread with a deerskin arranged with the plants Hanging Kettle had brought to trade.

Jacob manned the scale while her papa and Hanging Kettle haggled. Lydia caught his glance and lifted the basket, mouthing the word *dinner* before ducking into the distilling room. It was warm in the back where the fire was kept burning for the various distillations in progress. Sight of them caused a pang of longing. There'd been little time to spare for experimentation since the responsibility of house and garden had fallen on her shoulders.

Lydia pushed aside a drying rack on the worktable and emptied the basket of bread, cheese, and half a pie made with the last winter apples. By habit she checked the pots on the hearth. More often now, her papa left the medicinal preparation to Jacob, while he chatted with customers or dispensed to them at their homes. She replaced a lid as Papa's voice carried from the shop. Since her mother's death, he'd dropped a stone in weight. His hair had thinned and whitened.

Lydia decided to linger until Hanging Kettle departed, to be sure Papa ate his share of dinner. He needed to be reminded these days.

She stepped back into the shop in time to see the strange Indian put a piece of soap to his nose, then jerk it away, grimacing. Lydia grinned—right as the Indian turned his head to look at her. His weathered face was slightly pitted; he'd suffered smallpox, probably as a child.

Her papa cleared his throat. "Lydia, ye havena met Clear Day, of the Oneidas. Clear Day, my daughter, Lydia."

Surprise flickered across the Oneida's face when Lydia made him a polite curtsy.

The shop bell tinkled. Lydia turned as Rowan Doyle came in, so tall his hat brushed the drying herbs hanging from the ceiling beams. His eyes widened at sight of the Indians. George McClaren nodded to him but continued sorting herbs with Hanging Kettle, jotting each transaction in his ledger with a quill, while Jacob weighed and measured.

The Oneida turned to finger more displays of toiletries. Lydia stepped past him to greet Mr. Doyle. "I haven't been down to the Binne Kill in days for news. How are Anna and William?"

"Gone feral, Miss Lydia, and happily so." Long face clouding, Mr. Doyle took off his hat. "Or would be happy but for what brings me to town. The major's to home with his old war wound festered."

This was dismaying news. "*That* wound? But Major Aubrey has been in such good health these last years."

Mr. Doyle hesitated. "Not as good as he'd have ye think. 'Tisn't the first time the wound's troubled him these six months past, but he'd never have us tell Mr. McClaren. It'd come right on its own, sure. But this time he's taken to his bed, so by his leave or no, I've come."

Lydia's frustration and worry mirrored Mr. Doyle's. "What do you mean by 'it'd come right on its own'? What has Major Aubrey done for—" She broke off the question when, his face stiffening, Mr. Doyle put a hand to her shoulder.

Behind her, in broken English, another voice spoke. "Who is Aw-bree with wound?"

Startled, she turned to find the Oneida, Clear Day, standing close behind her. Lydia's gaze traveled over the feathers tied in his graying scalplock, the silver loops in his ears. The intensity of his eyes.

"You say name, Aw-bree?"

"Yes. Major Aubrey. My father's friend." And her own, she thought, her mind still a roil of worry and distraction.

"He redcoat soldier?" Clear Day asked.

Lydia looked closer at the Indian, bewildered by his interest. "He used to be. Why do you ask?"

Clear Day ignored the question. "Where fire?"

Lydia shook her head. Fire? Did he mean the infected wound? She glanced at Mr. Doyle, but he seemed as mystified as she, and none too happy with the Indian's queries.

The Oneida tried again. "Where Aw-bree lodge?"

The man must be a healer after all. Did he wish to see Major Aubrey to treat his wound? Lydia could think of no other explanation for his interest. Yet something a shade too urgent in the man's gaze kindled her unease. Before she could decide what to say, Hanging Kettle turned and spoke to the man in Mohawk. Clear Day stepped back from her, ending the conversation. Papa instructed Jacob to finish transactions with Hanging Kettle and beckoned Mr. Doyle into the back room. With a frown at Clear Day, Lydia followed.

". . . a mild fever as yet," Mr. Doyle was saying. "But a bad case of pigheadedness, you might say, has confounded matters." The major, it followed, had saddled his horse that morning to ride to the Binne Kill, concealing the state of his troublesome wound. He'd barely made it to the road before tumbling from the saddle. "Maura caught the gelding wanderin' back and ran up the lane to find the major pickin' himself up off the verge. He admitted the wound's been threatenin' to break for days. So it has done."

Lydia listened as her papa asked for details, knowing he'd set himself to go to the farm. "May I ride with you, Papa, and help with the major?"

Her father shook his head. "Och, Lydia. There's nay need. Ye've enough to keep ye busy to home, aye?"

Both the Indians, Mr. Doyle, and Papa had left the shop, which Lydia minded while Jacob ate the dinner she'd brought. Papa had grabbed no more than a morsel on his way out to the farm. She hoped Mrs. Doyle would offer him something and see that he ate it.

"Hope you didn't want any of that pie." Jacob came out of the back, wiping his mouth with a sleeve. He grinned as he went to the ledger at the end of the counter. "I'm afraid I demolished it."

"Naturally." Lydia tried to match his mood, but her thoughts were miles to the west. Or most of her thoughts. "You did that well, you know."

Jacob's burnished head, bent over the figures jotted earlier, lifted. "What? Eat pie?"

Lydia rolled her eyes. "*That* never fails to amaze. I meant Hanging Kettle. You'd never dealt with him alone before, had you?"

Jacob's brows rose. "I was nervous. Think he noticed?"

"I think that gift you made of the soap pleased him. Amused him too. Did you see the way that Oneida grimaced at its smell?"

Jacob's eyes twinkled. "That's what gave me the notion."

"Indians hold generosity in high regard—so Hanging Kettle reminds Papa over and again. It was well done." It had been an offhand remark. The change that came over Jacob's features surprised Lydia. He was looking at her as intently as that Oneida had done, but in a different manner.

Maybe it was down to how the window-light fell, but for the first time it struck Lydia that Jacob van Bergen was a man grown. And not a bad-looking one. When had his blemishes cleared? His jaw grown so firm? His shoulders so wide? It was as if she was seeing him for the first time in years. And something else was happening. The air between them had taken on the crackling weightiness it sometimes did before a thunderstorm came rolling down the valley. A little unnerved by it, she hurried to say, "Did Hanging Kettle say who Clear Day was? A friend of his?"

Jacob hesitated, still staring at her. "It was my impression they knew each other but slightly." A flush rose from his neckcloth, staining his lean cheeks. "Lydia . . . next time I'm called to tend a patient, you'd be welcome to accompany me."

Lydia was surprised by the offer, even touched, until it occurred to her to wonder how much it could mean. Jacob was barely past his apprenticeship. The denizens of Schenectady wouldn't often call on him while Papa was available. As he would be, surely, for years yet.

Still it was kindly meant, and she thanked him for it.

Two weeks later, Lydia snatched a few moments to hurry down to the Binne Kill and learned from Mr. Boswell that Reginald Aubrey hadn't been to work in all that time. Alarmed by the news, she longed to go out to the farm, but no one was free to escort her. Jacob and Papa were busy caring for two families south of town fallen victim to the smallpox, which meant she was the one on hand when Mr. Doyle returned in urgent need of an apothecary.

The major's wound had worsened.

"The pox is spreading," Lydia explained. "The town physicians have been called out as well. I'll leave a note for Papa," she hurried to add as Mr. Doyle's face registered dismay. "He or Jacob will come after us as soon as they're able."

She'd fished out a scrap of foolscap from a drawer and begun writing before Mr. Doyle registered her intention. "Come after us? If you mean what I think—"

"At the least," Lydia said, refusing to acknowledge the protest, "I can sit with the major and give Heledd and Mrs. Doyle a rest."

She thought it worrisome that Mr. Doyle barely hesitated. "Have you a horse I could be saddlin'?"

"Papa has it." She dipped the quill and finished her note. "I'll be out directly. I need but a moment and a quick stop at the house."

Lydia left the note on the counter, then filled her satchel with oil, flannel, linen bandaging, and every herb she could think of to poultice a wound so reluctant to heal. At the last she took a small, elongated case from a window display. Whether she'd have the nerve to use what it contained—should it prove needful—she couldn't say, but she'd every intention of doing *something* more for the major than sitting by cooling his brow.

Maura Doyle was nigh to losing her self-possession in the kitchen of the Aubreys' farmhouse. Confronted with Lydia instead of her papa or Jacob, she raised her hands in surrender. "He's after treatin' smallpox? Heaven help us—with the major fevered and that wound a suppuratin' mess, us two nigh to keelin' over, and Rowan with the fields and stock to tend."

She grabbed a breath as Lydia came farther into the kitchen to see Heledd, looking days—if not minutes—away from giving birth again, sitting on a stool with William clasped to her bosom. She rocked them both as his small body shook, sobs muffled in her gown. Anna stood alone by the hearth, white-faced with fear. Lydia reached out an arm. The little girl flew to her, wrapping her with skinny arms.

Lydia met Mrs. Doyle's haggard gaze and repeated what she'd told her husband in the shop. "I can sit with Major Aubrey and let you rest."

"What would your father say did I let you? A girl of sixteen—"

"Seventeen," Lydia cut in. By the space of three days.

"—not to mention *where* the wound is."

"I know where it is." Lydia squeezed Anna's thin shoulder and smiled encouragement to the lot of them. "I may as well continue with whatever you've been doing for him."

Refusal was gathering on Mrs. Doyle's lined countenance when Heledd's head reared up. "For mercy's sake, let her tend him if she's willing." Her lilting voice was hoarse with exhaustion and weeping, but her brown eyes made an eloquent plea as her gaze fell to the satchel slung at Lydia's shoulder. "If there's aught you can do till Mr. McClaren arrives . . . please, I wish you to try. I cannot lose him, see? Not here in this wretched wilderness."

Drawn curtains dimmed the major's room. A fire in the hearth warmed it. Before her eyes adjusted to show her the bed and the major's fretful form within it, Lydia was struck by the rank smell of fever-sweat and purulence.

"Here be rags, a clean batch." Mrs. Doyle set a basin on a stand beside the bed, filled from a bucket by the door. "Cool his brow, his neck maybe . . ." *But no more,* her tightened lips added.

The major was unclothed beneath the covers. In his fevered thrashing he'd bared himself to the waist. Mrs. Doyle pulled the linen up to his unshaven chin, leaving the heavier quilt turned back. The major's head moved restlessly, though no sound escaped his lips.

Lydia set the satchel on the bed. A chair was drawn close by. She took a seat in it. "Would you light a candle for me?"

Mrs. Doyle lit two, leaving both on the stand. Lydia noted a small pot on the hearth and thought, *good.*

Mrs. Doyle hovered, gazing with pitying eyes at the major, uncertain eyes at Lydia.

Thinking she required some demonstration of competence, Lydia took a rag, dipped and wrung it, and placed it across the major's brow. The touch of him was startlingly hot.

"Is there aught else you're after needin'?" Mrs. Doyle inquired.

"Yes," Lydia said firmly. "You and Heledd resting while you may. And your prayers for the major."

"He's had those—for days," Mrs. Doyle snapped, then sighed as Lydia flinched. "You're right. I'm done in. I'll leave you to watch and thank you for it."

Upon touching the major's flesh, the cool of the rags vanished like water on a heated griddle. Still Lydia ran them over his face and neck, every breath a prayer for his well-being, save those she spared in wonderment. Not in the five years she'd known him had she been granted such liberty to simply look at the man. He'd lost all trace of what youthfulness he'd possessed at five-and-twenty, the angles of his face grown leaner with the years, the bones beneath more prominent. The thin scar along his cheekbone hadn't changed, but the lines webbing the corners of his eyes had deepened, visible now even by candlelight. Fever had pared away his flesh, yet even now she thought him the handsomest man of her acquaintance.

Her regard for him—as one above the cut of other men—was a part of her now, part of the weft of her soul, the more so since the day of her mother's death. With a few spoken words of understanding, the major had rescued her that day on the river, drowning in guilt and grief, a rescue as viable as his snatching Anna from death on a wilderness road.

The major groaned as she drew back to wet the cloth again. He freed an arm and flung it across his torso, dragging aside the sheet. A hiss of pain escaped his lips.

"I'm hit. Jones . . . *help me.*"

He was back in Canada with his regiment. At war.

Lydia grasped his flailing arm. "Major, hush now. You're safe at home, with those who love you."

Love you. Her face flamed. That was a thought she'd no right to entertain.

Then something more pertinent caught her eye. His thrashing had revealed the edge of the poultice on his hip. Had he disturbed it?

She'd all but promised Mrs. Doyle to do nothing Papa might find objectionable, but the remembered appeal in Heledd's eyes proved the stronger compelling force.

"Father in Heaven," she whispered. Preserving his dignity as best she could, she folded back the sweat-soured linen to expose his lean hip and a little of his muscular thigh.

"Father in Heaven," the major muttered, a startling echo of her prayer. "Not the babe . . ."

Lydia waited, uncertain where the major's mind had wandered now. Rescuing Anna?

While the fire snapped at her back and a bead of sweat rolled down her temple, she eased away the poultice. *A suppurating mess* well described it. Pus came away with the pad of oil-soaked linen, exposing the wound—larger than she'd expected, with red lips as mangled as an ulcerated mouth.

Lydia swallowed, then rose and put the fouled poultice in the fire.

First to heat water in the little pot. Then boil the sassafras root she'd brought in her satchel. It would make a decent dressing, as she'd once told the major. While water heated, she steeled herself to clean the wound, gently sponging away the oozing matter and the sticky residue of the honey Mrs. Doyle had smeared on as a dressing.

Lydia approved a honey dressing, but the wound required more drastic measures. With the curtains parted and both candles brought near, she spied deep, whitish pockets of infection beneath the wound's surface. And thought she saw something else. Major Aubrey's legs jerked. Lydia held the bedclothes in place while her face burned and her heart thudded. He muttered again about a baby and stilled.

Lydia brought a candle close, bending low to the odorous wound. There *was* something there, dark at the center of one pocket of suppuration.

She straightened, her mind in a spin. Was she seeing a fragment of lead the army surgeon had failed years ago to remove, having worked its way to the surface? Musket balls weren't known to shatter. Flatten maybe. Perhaps there'd been shrapnel or splinters driven in?

Whatever it was, ought *she* to attempt its removal?

She didn't let herself debate the question but launched into motion as though it was a thing she'd done a hundred times. From the satchel she withdrew the case taken from the shop window, containing a set of surgical knives and, more to the present purpose, tweezers.

With the wound as clean as she could render it without a thorough debriding—something Papa would do as soon as he arrived—she took the smallest knife, passed it through flame, then with the candle set by to guide her, used the blade to expose what she'd seen—the tip of something brownish, slender as thread and wide as her thumb, extending down into the wound.

A scrap of cloth, forced into the wound by the musket ball?

Excitement and dread throbbed at her temples. *Guide my hands, help me . . .*

When she had enough of the foreign body exposed she grasped it with the tweezers and pulled, gently, fearing to tear whatever it was and leave the bulk of it unreachable. The wound clung to its prize. Perspiration beaded her brow as she applied the blade, cleaning away more suppuration. The major's thigh muscles quivered. She tried again with the tweezers, still with measured force.

Major Aubrey's body jerked as the thing slid forth, a piece of cloth not only as wide as her thumb but as long, brown beneath its coat of glistening matter. Once, she was certain, it had been red.

She dressed the wound, adding bruised parsley leaves to the pulp of sassafras root, binding it with honey she found in a jar by the hearth. She rinsed the pot in which she'd boiled the roots and brewed a tea of sassafras leaves—with chickweed for fever and dogwood bark for pain—for when the major woke. The cloth fragment taken from the wound she'd wrapped in oiled linen. She'd covered the major decently again and gone back to cooling his flesh, having no qualms now about running the cloth over his chest as well as his face. With a hand resting on his shoulder, she paused to push a straggle of hair behind her ear.

Reginald Aubrey opened his eyes and groped for her hand. "Heledd . . . forgive me."

"Major?" He'd given her a jolt, but she recovered and leaned close, thinking her face too shadowed to tell she wasn't his wife. "It's Lyd—"

"Do not despise me for it." His voice cut over hers, roughened by fever, weak but determined. "I couldn't bring myself to tell you he was dead. Our son . . ."

Shock surged through Lydia as visions of William drowned, murdered by Indians, a dozen other calamities his mother habitually fretted over, raced through her mind, until she recalled William whole, if distressed, in the kitchen when she arrived.

Did the major mean one of their babies born since?

In her leaning forward, the band of light from between the curtains had fallen past her and across the major's face, his rigid jaw and clenched lips, his glassy eyes staring . . . but not truly seeing her. He was still in the fever's grip. Dreaming.

What was she to say? do? Before she could decide, his grip on her hand tightened. "Two babies she had, and ours . . . dead in my arms. I was wrong to do it. All my thinking was wrong. But she'd *two* babies. I took the white one . . ."

Lydia was imprisoned by his grip. His stare. His words. *The white one?*

A spasm wracked the major's face, as though another wound long festered in secret was breaking open, oozing guilt and shame. "I have lived with this every moment since that wretched fort fell. I tell you I cannot bear it if you despise me. I did it for you. And he *is* our son . . . whatever his blood. Has he not become so?"

Were it not for the major's grasp on her hand, Lydia would have felt outside herself, watching this scene unfold from a distance. Was he saying William wasn't their son? And Heledd didn't know?

There was no sense in it. It was the fever talking. Yet the naked plea for mercy in his eyes tightened her throat. She must answer that soul-suffering—to end this terrible confession, if such it was, and ease him back into healing sleep.

"Reginald." She'd never addressed him by his Christian name, did so now only because he thought her his wife—who ought to have heard these terrible things in her stead. Or ought Heledd Aubrey never to hear them? "Reginald, please . . . say no more."

He wasn't content with that. "You've no love for Anna, I know . . . but do you not love *him* as if he were our blood?"

That, at least, Lydia could answer in Heledd's place. With utter conviction. "Yes, Reginald. I love William. With all my heart."

Raving or not, it was what he'd needed to hear. He raised her hand, trembling, to his lips. As the heat of them brushed her skin, Lydia shut her eyes. When she opened them, whatever remained of the major's fever had pulled him fathoms deep again.

10

Hunting Moon 1763

When the Ottawa chief, Pontiac, took up the hatchet against the British at their lake forts, along with the tribes of those places, the Senecas, keepers of the Great Longhouse's western door, went to fight with them. The Oneida sachems spoke against the war, calling on their warriors to keep out of it. Though most of the warriors heeded their words, a few from Kanowalohale went to fight. One of those was Stone Thrower, who left in summer after the deer hunting.

In the moons since, Good Voice had busied herself tending and harvesting the corn, beans, and squash, gleaning nuts and berries and every edible thing to fill their hungry bellies.

Now the first snow was on the ground. It was time for the hunters to leave for their winter camps, but Stone Thrower hadn't returned. Good Voice had preserved some deerskins to trade for cloth and blankets, powder and lead, all those needful things that came from white traders, but should Stone Thrower fail to provide the thick winter furs the British craved, she foresaw a lean time for their family.

"Come with me to my camp," Bear Tooth said when she met him sitting outside his lodge, testing his new metal traps.

Bear Tooth was a Turtle Clan brother, not yet married, a few years younger than Good Voice. Over the summer he'd taken to checking on her to be sure she had wood for the fire or meat for the pot. She was grateful, but seeing the young man at her lodge door sometimes made her feel like a woman whose husband had fallen in battle, leaving her and Two Hawks to the kindness of relations for their sustenance.

Perhaps that was what she was.

"My uncle's sons are gone to Oriska Town with their wives, so it is us two alone this season." With a stick, Bear Tooth sprung the trap he was testing. Good Voice flinched as the jaws snapped the wood with a crack like breaking bone.

Bear Tooth looked up at her, smiling. "Tend our fire and I will share with you what furs I take. It is better than none."

Not knowing what else to do, Good Voice packed her carrying basket and her snowshoes, bundled her son in furs, and set out with Bear Tooth to the winter camp he shared with his uncle.

Outside the bark hut, Bear Tooth said something that made Two Hawks laugh like a loon. Good Voice smiled as she inspected the fox pelt she'd finished working, keeping one eye on the *ola:ná,* corn soup, bubbling over the small cook-fire, filling the hut with its wholesome smell. As her chapped hands joyed in the lavish fur, she was thinking how rarely she heard Two Hawks's laughter these days. He had grown too solemn for a boy of six.

It should be his father who makes him laugh. Like many thoughts about Stone Thrower, worries clung to that one like ticks to a dog. Had he come to Kanowalohale and found her gone, Bright Leaf would have told him where she was. But the Hunting Moon was passing with no sign of her husband.

Good Voice set about dishing up soup for the men outside.

Bear Tooth reminded her of Stone Thrower that first year of their marriage, before Fort William Henry: hard-working, easy to be with—as was Stands-To-The-Side, his uncle, a quiet man of middle years whose wife had died in the spring. They were good hunters and kept her busy. Good Voice admired the curing furs lining the walls: martin, mink, otter, fox, raccoon, wolf, and beaver pelts stretched on hoops. Though the men did most of the skinning and helped build the drying frames, it was demanding work to stretch and cure so many furs coming in, tanning them as time allowed, all while feeding the hunters and repairing their winter moccasins and clothing.

Two Hawks was a help. He minded snowmelt over the outside fire or fetched downed wood to dry. All in all, it was peaceful being with these Turtle Clan men and her son. Only it wouldn't be peaceful long if she didn't give them the corn soup they were waiting to eat so they could put on their snowshoes and head into the forest.

She'd put chestnuts in the soup. It pleased Stands-To-The-Side, who remarked that his wife had made it that way. Bear Tooth smacked his lips loudly and said, "My aunt was a good cook."

Two Hawks smacked his lips, dribbling corn soup down the front of his wool shirt. "My mother is the best cook of all."

He glanced at her, and it struck Good Voice that this boy of hers was a helper not only with his hands but also with his heart. "That is a good thing for a mother to hear," she said, letting him know she appreciated it.

While they ate their soup and the ground corn cakes she'd made to go with it, Good Voice settled by the outside fire. It was good to see her son filling his belly. Good to see men eating her food, knowing it would warm them while they crossed snowy ridges and frozen streams where their net of traps and snares had been cast. *If only it could be . . .*

Good Voice shut her eyes. Below the surface of every small joy lay the ache. She longed for Stone Thrower, longed sometimes simply to hold him, feel the warmth and strength of him, while at the same time she dreaded his return. Maybe he would never return and that would be an end to it. The end of their love that started out bright and whole but was

tattered now, gnawed by grief, that rabid dog that chased her thoughts in
fruitless circles.

Two Hawks was asking the men to bring in a bear so he could see it,
touch its claws and big cold nose.

"Bears sleep in their winter houses now," Bear Tooth told him.

Two Hawks pondered this, then said, "Maybe a bear has to get up in
the middle of his sleep and go out to make water, like a boy does. Maybe
you will find one doing that?"

The men laughed. It wasn't a mocking sound but one of amusement
and, Good Voice thought, appreciation. She opened her eyes and smiled at
her son, wondering if one day they would be changing his name to something like He-Clears-The-Way. He had a way of circling a thing in his
mind until he found a path to reach it. They'd called him Two Hawks for
the pair of hunting red-tails she'd seen over Fort Carillon when she stepped
from the trees, carrying her living son, one of a pair . . .

But she didn't want to think about that. She filled her lungs with the
sharp morning cold, clearing her mind.

Bear Tooth's camp, ringed by hemlock and birch, lay two sleeps from
Kanowalohale. It was a small camp, only three huts—one for the men,
one for her and Two Hawks, one standing empty—and a shelter for Bear
Tooth's two horses. When the wind was right, the fires of other camps
could be seen drifting low against the sky. Now and then, women from
those camps visited, or a hunter wandered by and was given a portion of
whatever she had cooking. It was a good place.

As she thought it, a kingfisher swooped by, making its dry rattle.
Good Voice watched its choppy flight. When it was gone into the forest,
she said, "The wolf pelt you brought in . . . I will work that next. It is beautiful. The best I have seen."

"It is yours, that one," Bear Tooth said as he scraped the last of the
ola:ná from his bowl. His uncle got up to get his snowshoes.

Good Voice was touched. "The wolf? You give that to me?"

Bear Tooth licked his fingers and held out the empty bowl. She came around the fire to take it, but Bear Tooth didn't release his hold when she grasped it. With a quick look toward the lodge where his uncle had gone, he pulled her closer by the bowl they held. "You *are* the best cook of all. Do not tell my uncle I said so."

Their faces were close. Close enough that she could lean forward a little more and plant a kiss on his brow without toppling over. This she did. "You are good to us, Brother."

With the bowl released into her hands, she straightened and looked across the clearing. Stone Thrower stood at the forest's edge, his handsome features contorted in disbelief.

He'd done some trapping on his way back from fighting but had left those furs curing in their lodge in Kanowalohale. "Did you think I would stay away all winter, neglect you and our son? Is that why you have taken up with these men?"

Good Voice looked to see that Bear Tooth and his uncle had gone into the forest and hadn't heard those words. The hemlock boughs no longer swayed in the wake of their going.

Two Hawks sat by the fire, staring at his long-absent father, come abruptly into their midst with his face suffused with anger.

Heart pounding, Good Voice put down the bowls, walked to her husband, and put her arms around him. "I am relieved to see you. I feared you might be dead—"

As her voice caught, she felt the tenseness of his body ease. He put her from him, shrugged out of his pack, and sat at the fire to unlace his snow-shoes. With shaking hands, Good Voice bent to pick up the bowls. Stone Thrower glanced at them. "Is there food?"

For *him,* his tone implied. Was she still willing to feed him, or only those other men? It cut her, but she smiled and ducked inside the hut. When she returned with the last of the corn soup, Stone Thrower was telling their son about a battle he'd fought.

"It happened at a place the redcoats call Devil's Hole. There is a wooded ravine there. Near it we waited to ambush some wagons going to the fort at Niagara."

"Did the wagons make it through?" Two Hawks scooted across the log to sit nearer his father. His eyes were big.

Stone Thrower laughed, low in his throat. "Three hundred Senecas— and I with them—made sure they did not. We surprised them with muskets and made their animals stampede and drag the wagons into that ravine, then we moved in to kill the British with hatchets. If any got away I did not see. I was busy taking scalps."

British scalps. Blood on the Covenant Chain.

Two Hawks looked wide-eyed at the hatchet thrust through his father's belt sash. "Do you have them now? Those scalps?"

"I brought one to show you." He took from his pack a scalp with hair shiny blond, like Good Voice's after a washing, before she darkened it with grease. It gave her a queer feeling in her belly.

"Redcoats came running from a camp not far away," Stone Thrower said, continuing his story. "Too late to do anything about those wagon men, but not too late to join them in death. We cut them off from their retreat to the fort. We killed most of them and lost none but one man wounded, and he lived when I last saw him."

Good Voice had been looking her husband over. Silently she thanked the Master of Life that he was whole, then set the bowl of corn soup into his hands. He glanced up to acknowledge her, not pausing in his boasting of battle exploits. Two Hawks listened with ears for nothing else. Stone Thrower had charmed their son but seemed to have no charm left for her. She went inside the bark hut to start on the wolf fur.

Her husband lounged around the fire that day, talking to Two Hawks while she worked inside, but Good Voice didn't speak to him of anything that mattered until Bear Tooth and his uncle returned, ate the food she'd made without their usual talk, and everyone went to their beds for the cold night. Then it was their bodies that spoke, coming together for the first time since the summer.

Good Voice had had time to think. She knew Stone Thrower was shamed to find another man taking care of his family while he'd been to war. His anger and suspicion were only covering that shame. Now in the darkness, Stone Thrower spoke sweeter words into her hair, against the skin of her neck. Lying with her warm beneath a buffalo robe, he said, "I did not see my things put out of your lodge. Does this mean I am still your husband?"

His voice held no teasing, but she forced it into hers. "After what we just did you must ask such a thing?"

It was too dark even with the glow of embers to see his face. "A man should hunt for his family and for furs to trade for things they need. But sometimes a man must go to war."

"Sometimes." But not always was it needful. She heard that implication in her voice and hurried to say, "These words were spoken before you left. Now you are back. Let us not speak them again."

Stone Thrower pulled his arm away and rolled over, putting his back to her.

Outside the lodge next morning, Good Voice sensed no overt hostility between her husband and Bear Tooth. Stands-To-The-Side seemed uneasy. He wolfed down his food and left to check one line of traps. Bear Tooth lingered, talking little though he listened with interest when Two Hawks begged his father to tell the story of Devil's Hole again. Still, Good

Voice was surprised when Stone Thrower asked if he might go with Bear
Tooth and set a few snares of his own. Bear Tooth, hesitating only a moment, agreed.

Though this was his uncle's camp, Bear Tooth had made every effort
to give place to Stone Thrower. He knew Stone Thrower had seen that
tender moment between them. His eyes had asked her at first glance that
morning if all was well. She had tried with her eyes to reassure him.

She was inside the bark lodge with Two Hawks when the sound of
men's voices reached her. It was early for them to be back. She'd barely
started the venison stew she'd planned to feed them. And they didn't
sound like men coming in tired from a day of fur harvesting. Their voices
were sharp, urgent. She shot a look at Two Hawks, then pushed past the
buffalo hide in time to see Stands-To-The-Side and Stone Thrower, supporting Bear Tooth between them, stagger along the beaten path into
camp, leaving a trail like bright red petals dropped in the snow.

They lowered Bear Tooth to sit by the fire. Good Voice, hurrying to
him, saw his heavy winter moccasin had been removed, his left leg and
foot wrapped in torn linen, soaked in red. She unwound the bloody strips,
and gasped.

The flesh above Bear Tooth's ankle was mangled, punctured as
though an animal had tried to bite off his foot. Bones were clearly broken.
What had done this? A bear? Had he tried to take a bear out of its den, for
her son to see?

Cold swept down her face and limbs, for with her next breath she
knew what teeth had done this damage. Not the teeth of a bear. "You
stepped into one of your traps?"

Bear Tooth's face was gray and clenched. "Yes," he said through gritted teeth but wouldn't meet her gaze.

"No!" It was a startling sound, that word bursting out of Bear Tooth's
quiet uncle. Stands-To-The-Side glared at Stone Thrower, clouds of furious breath shooting from his nostrils. "My nephew did not step into his

trap. He was pushed. With my own eyes I saw this as I came upon them quarreling. This man, your husband, pushed him, and you see the result!"

Stone Thrower took a step back, staring at them each in turn. Then his eyes dropped to her hands, stained with blood. His face went as gray as Bear Tooth's.

He didn't deny the accusation. He didn't say he never meant to do such a thing, that it had been an accident. He lunged toward their bark hut, thrusting aside the hide. Seconds later he was out again with his pack and snowshoes.

Good Voice stared, stunned, as Stone Thrower shrugged into his pack and, without looking at her, headed off across the clearing toward the setting sun, snowshoes in hand.

Stands-To-The-Side moved to follow, but Good Voice caught his wrist. With a terrible effort she said, "Let him go. I need you here. Please . . . let him go."

11

Snow Moon 1764

tone Thrower didn't return to Kanowalohale during the Long Night Moon. Had he done so, Good Voice knew he wouldn't have been pleased that she'd taken Bear Tooth into her lodge to care for him. The bones of Bear Tooth's ankle hadn't knit straight. A few places where the trap's teeth had punctured were still prone to fester.

Clear Day came to her lodge on a snowy morning with a man Good Voice didn't know—a Mohawk sachem from Canajoharie, a town in the east surrounded by white settlements. Hanging Kettle, he was called. "This man knows the white man's medicine," Clear Day explained. "He goes into their place of trade for such medicine and is known there by a healer called McClaren. Maybe he will know something that will help."

Hanging Kettle was a younger man than Clear Day, but there was wisdom in his gaze, and kindness. Good Voice, desperate enough to let a white man help Bear Tooth had one offered, had no qualms about a Mohawk with white medicine trying. Maybe his blended medicine would be strong enough to make her clan brother's leg heal so he could walk again and hunt.

She welcomed them into her home, fed them, then took her son out into the falling snow to Bright Leaf's lodge, one in a straggle of Turtle Clan homes on a bend in the frozen creek. Snow sifted down, big as feathers. When she returned through the flurry, Clear Day, wrapped in a buffalo hide, occupied the bench beneath a pole arbor built against her lodge. She could hear Hanging Kettle chanting on the other side of the door hide.

"Uncle, did you go all the way to Canajoharie for that healer?"

Clear Day nodded, seeming preoccupied with other thoughts. Good Voice sat beside him with her blanket-shawl held close. The snow slanted down. Their breath rose in white clouds beneath the arbor's shelter.

"Has my nephew gone to look for that redcoat?" he asked.

Clear Day had asked that question when she returned to Kanowalohale without Stone Thrower. Why did he ask it again? The answer hadn't changed. She didn't know.

Good Voice looked out through the snow that obscured the nearby lodges. Many of the people were still at their hunting camps, but the elders and mothers with sickly children had stayed. "Better he do that than running up to the Carrying Place."

Some men made provision for their families by helping white traders portage their bateaux from the Mohawk River to Wood Creek, to continue their journey west to the lake country. No one traveled so now, with the streams and rivers frozen, but many still gathered to trade—or drink their earnings away with corn liquor and rum. When Stone Thrower went to the Carry, he rarely brought anything back but a bruised and reeling head.

"Maybe," Clear Day said. "But listen, my daughter. I have a thing to say to you."

Good Voice's heart sank. Did even Clear Day think it was time to put his nephew's belongings out of her lodge? "What is it, Uncle?"

He glanced at her, frowning at her tone of resignation. "You remember how I said I learned nothing from Warraghiyagey about that redcoat or the son he stole from you?"

Good Voice's thoughts flew back to spring nearly two years ago, to the crushing disappointment she'd felt at the news. She'd tried not to think about it since. "I remember. Why do you speak of it now?"

"Because I did not tell you that the reason I learned nothing is because I never spoke to Warraghiyagey. I never saw him." Clear Day didn't look at her. He watched the snow fall, the breath flowing from his mouth as if his words were ghosts, each one a haunting to Good Voice's heart. "I had gone as far as Canajoharie, on my way to see him. There I met the man who is inside your lodge now. That man was preparing to go to the place where they build the boats they carry between the waters—Schenectady. He meant to visit a place inside their stockade called *apothecary*."

Good Voice understood much English, but *apothecary* was a new word. "What sort of place is that?"

"A place where medicine is made, where that one called McClaren does his trade. They call it a *shop*. There are many shops in that town, each making and trading its own things. It is a noisy, stinking place. Still I went with Hanging Kettle to this *apothecary* because I was curious to see it, but I still meant to go across the river to Warraghiyagey."

Good Voice nodded, trying to be patient, waiting for him to get to the important part—why he hadn't sought the help of Sir William Johnson in finding He-Is-Taken.

"It was there I heard a girl with black hair speak to a man who came in after us, ringing the little bell McClaren keeps above the door to let him know when someone has come through it. He was a tall man—not Mc-Claren, this other who came in—thin like a stalk of corn. One of the Irish, like Warraghiyagey, except he wore the clothes of a farmer and he had a farmer's smell—like what comes out of the backsides of horses."

Good Voice restrained herself from saying *hanyo, hanyo*—get to the part about her son.

"Black-Hair-Girl spoke to that man. She said a name to him. One that made my ears stretch to hear their talk. It was the name you once told me. Aubrey."

Good Voice drew in a searing breath. The cold leached from her lungs into her heart. *Aw-bree.* She sat with frozen lips, felt one crack in a tiny split of pain when finally she said, "Was it that man who came into the shop? The man who stole my son from my side?"

Clear Day shook his head. "That was not the man. But as I listened

I thought he knew this Aubrey the girl had named. It seemed by their talk this Aubrey was sick or wounded. That was why the farmer came to that shop. For the healer, McClaren."

Clear Day paused, gathering his thoughts, while Good Voice screamed in silence for him to say it all quickly else she couldn't bear it.

"I spoke to Black-Hair-Girl. I got her to say that this Aubrey was once a British officer. Major Aubrey. That is his name. And that is all I learned then. But when the tall farmer left the shop, I also went. Out of that town I followed him, though he rode a horse and I was on my feet. He did not cross the river, so I did not cross either. I knew I could do so later, go to Johnson, if following the farmer came to nothing."

It was a dangerous thing to do, following a strange white man through settled country. Good Voice was glad she hadn't known about it at the time, but now her whole being was with Clear Day, flitting between whatever cover he could find along a wagon track, dodging the farms and the dogs and the watching eyes—the muskets—trying to keep the farmer in sight to see where he went.

"All the way to his farm I followed him. It is some ways west of the town, with thick woods nearby. I hid in those woods and watched that place, a big stone house, a small stone house, a barn, much fields. And the people there. A woman who worked in the yard. Another woman who never left the doorway of the big house. And two children."

Good Voice had let the blanket fall open. She pressed a hand to her mouth. Clear Day looked into her eyes, where she saw the truth before the words left his lips. "One of those children was male. From a distance he might have been Two Hawks. Two Hawks in *a'sluni* clothing, though his hair and face were not so dark. He was too distant for me to tell how much he resembled your son."

Chills prickled up Good Voice's arms, over her scalp and face, chills that had nothing to do with the cold. "He was very white, that first son born to me. He might look nothing like his brother."

"One twin brown, one twin white. I thought of that as I watched that boy." Clear Day gripped her hand, his gaze earnest. "If you wish it, I will go back to that farm and find out more, if I can."

Good Voice put her hand over her mouth again. Tears ran warm over her fingers. She wiped them away, leaving her skin chilled in the gusting snow-breeze. "He looked strong and happy? He was allowed to go where he wished?"

"He had a girl and a dog with him. They ran free over the fields and down to the river like a son and daughter together. That is how they were as I watched."

For a time all Good Voice could do was sit there, fist pressed to her heart, seeing in her mind this boy who looked like Two Hawks, but white, see him running free. Gradually those good thoughts ebbed, letting others in. Thoughts as sharp as blades.

"Do you know what words I spoke when I put Two Hawks into his father's hands, there at the French fort on the lake? I said, 'This is half of the son I bore you. A redcoat stole the other half. But you will get him back for me and take the scalp off that redcoat for what he did.' I have had many nights lying awake to regret those words."

"It was your right to ask him to do that thing," Clear Day told her.

Somewhere, beyond the veil of snow, children shouted. The voice of a grandmother cracked as she called to them. Good Voice swallowed and said, "That may be, Uncle. But I think sometimes to claim a right is the wrong thing to do."

Clear Day's mouth curved sadly. "That is a wise thing for someone to have learned."

If it was wisdom, then it was learned in a way that made a young woman feel old in her bones. "Why did you never tell me what truly happened? And why tell me now?"

Looking pained, Clear Day went back to the beginning, how Stone Thrower was away to the Carry when he returned from seeing the boy who was probably He-Is-Taken. Already he'd had doubts about telling his nephew what he'd seen. "But when I saw Stone Thrower again, it was clear there was something still broken in him, something that taking revenge on the redcoat might not make whole. Still I nearly had the words out, more than once. Each time it seemed a hand covered my mouth. I could not speak. As for why I did not tell *you* . . . it was not because I thought you would send my nephew to kill those people on that farm, stirring up a nest of white hornets to follow him back and kill some of us. I did not want you to live with knowing where your son might be, and not know how to get to him in a way that would not bring more grief than you already bear. If I was wrong to keep this from you, I will do what I can to make amends."

Good Voice let go of Clear Day's hand. Inside the lodge, Hanging Kettle had stopped chanting. She hoped he was helping Bear Tooth with his medicine.

Medicine from the place where first they'd crossed the faint trail of He-Is-Taken. That thought gripped her with its power. What sort of place was this *apothecary*? Did it have medicine for the soul as well as for the body? That's what she needed. What Stone Thrower needed. A healer for the soul.

"He will not know me," she said. "He will call that redcoat *father*. Maybe he calls one of those women you saw *mother*."

Clear Day said, "We could tell my nephew what I have told you. Maybe I am wrong. Maybe he only needs to find He-Is-Taken to be made whole again."

But Good Voice couldn't decide, and Clear Day didn't press her to do so.

Three sleeps after Hanging Kettle's visit, when it was clear Bear Tooth's ankle was at last going to heal enough that he would not die of the wounding, Stone Thrower returned. He came with a bundle of furs so big Good Voice knew hunting was all he'd been doing, not getting drunk at the Carry or roaming the settled borders looking for their son.

Bear Tooth, on his feet with the aid of a stick crutch, all but bolted from the lodge after Stone Thrower entered. Two Hawks hesitated, then ran out after Bear Tooth, calling his name.

"Is he to be your husband now, even if he is your clan brother?" Stone Thrower sneered at the swaying door hide. "A father to my son? Should I find some other fire to sleep at?"

No greeting. No words of concern for her or their son or the man he had—according to Stands-To-The-Side — pushed into the trap that nearly cost him his foot. "Bear Tooth needed my help," she began, but Stone Thrower cut her off.

"You are always helping! Everyone but me. *Me* you help not at all."

"Those are not true words," Good Voice said, wounded. "I give you food from my fields, a roof over your head, a fire to warm you—*when* you return to it. A wife should have to remind a man of these things?"

Stone Thrower waved aside her question, his face set hard against her. "All these years that redcoat goes about living and breathing and calling our son his own, or his slave, or maybe he's sold him to someone else and forgotten him. But no one does anything to help me kill that man!"

Killing. Killing. Were they back to this again? Good Voice longed for Clear Day and his white strings of wampum, longed to hang those strings before her husband's face and plead until he took them. "And if you killed that man, what then? Do you think his people, whoever they are, will do nothing about it?"

Stone Thrower snorted. "Let them try. They will never find me."

"Do not speak foolish words," she snapped. "You know when whites are angry with us, they do not care which Indians they kill. They find Indians who have done nothing to them, and those they kill in vengeance. Is that what you want?"

Stone Thrower closed the distance between them, looming over her with fists clenched. "So my wife thinks I am a fool. She would rather have another at her fire."

As often as she'd seen him drunk and raging, getting into quarrels and fights with other warriors, he'd never tried to intimidate *her* with his size and strength. For the first time, fear of her husband coiled like a river eel in her belly, cold and slithering, making sweat mist up on her flesh. But indignation was a burning in her throat. She took her strength from that and stood before him, refusing to cower.

"If that is what you think, then you are a fool. Bear Tooth will never be a husband to me. But if I want him to live in my lodge, that is my right."

Stone Thrower blinked down his nose, the look in his eyes shifting from anger to puzzlement, as if he couldn't understand how they had come to this ugly place.

Good Voice pressed on. "Especially if you pushed Bear Tooth into that trap on purpose. Did you? Is that why you ran from the hunting camp? Did you mean to do it?"

The instant she saw his flinch, she knew. He had lost his temper that day, but he had never meant to hurt Bear Tooth so badly. She could see it in her mind now, as though she stood in the forest with them. Stone Thrower letting jealousy become his master, accusing Bear Tooth, shoving Bear Tooth, not seeing the trap until it was too late . . . Bear Tooth stumbling backward in the snow . . .

Shame and regret rippled the fire-shadowed contours of her husband's face. "You think I *meant* to do it?"

"That is not what I think." It was the truth, but it came too late. Still she pointed at the venison simmering in a pot. "Come. Eat. There is stew . . ."

Stone Thrower paid no mind. Shaking off regret like a horse shedding flies, he stalked around the lodge, snatching up a pair of leggings, some lead and powder, a ruffled trade cloth shirt. He stuffed the belongings into his pack and pushed past the door hide.

Outside the lodge came a woman's startled cry. The hide swung inward and Bright Leaf entered, her face showing displeasure and a hint of fear. "He is back and gone in the same day? Did you tell him of the baby?"

At first Good Voice thought her aunt knew what she talked about days ago with Clear Day, but Bright Leaf was looking at her belly. She meant the new baby, started at the hunting camp the night she and Stone Thrower were together. She'd already missed a time in the women's hut. She sat down on her sleeping bench, wondering if the life inside her had heard the bad words its parents had said. "There was no time."

Nor had she told him about the farm near Schenectady, the boy, and Aubrey. Perhaps she should have blurted one of those things as he was stepping out of the lodge. Perhaps . . .

"If you do not put that man's things outside for him to see when he comes back—if he comes back—I will never understand it," Bright Leaf said. "And you had better tend that stew."

Her aunt went out abruptly, leaving Good Voice alone with a bubbled-over stew burning in the embers.

Long after Stone Thrower left, Bear Tooth came to say his uncle had asked him to come home. Good Voice hated seeing him go this unhappy way but made no protest. She wished she'd never followed Bear Tooth to his hunting camp. It hadn't been necessary after all, and it had brought such harm.

Deep in the night, while Two Hawks slept, she rose from her bench, put wood on the fire to drive back the shadows, gathered up every piece of clothing and weaponry, every tool and adornment she could find that was Stone Thrower's, and piled them beside the door hide.

Standing cold in the fire-glow, Good Voice stared at the pile and could not find a thread of hope to cling to, even knowing that, at long last, He-Is-Taken was probably found. She took a step toward the pile, intending to shove the whole of it past the door hide and into the packed snow outside.

A voice stopped her. Not a voice one could hear with the ears. But something *like* a voice—in the silence of her mind—told her to go back to sleep. That was all. *Sleep.*

Too drained to do anything else, Good Voice turned her back on the pile beside the doorway. Perhaps morning would tell her on which side of the door hide it belonged.

12

Late September 1765

Down the track between the Aubreys' browning cornfields Lydia rode, bearing news that oughtn't to be delivered on such a brooding day, with sagging clouds and arrowheads of geese passing overhead like mournful heralds. Such news should have been attended by a sky so blue it hurt the eye, air so clear it brought the low hills looming near enough to kiss.

She didn't pause at the big house but rode to the cottage beyond. For all that she'd tried to befriend Heledd Aubrey in years past, the woman's indifference and discontent had finally outmatched Lydia's resolve—which hadn't prevented her visiting Anna, William, and the Doyles whenever time allowed.

Poor Heledd. The burying ground now held four of her and the major's babies, all carried full term, all dead within their first few days. Except the last. That little boy had lived three months, long enough to give his parents hope and doubly break their hearts.

Lydia smelled the hot tallow before rounding the cottage to find Maura Doyle and Anna in the yard, dipping candles over a warming fire. Anna, half her mass of honeyed hair escaped from its plait, pink-cheeked from the fire's heat, held aloft a stick of freshly dipped tapers. "Lydia!"

Maura straightened from hanging another rack on a drying frame. "Careful, child. Knock those tapers against the rim and you'll be strippin' them to start again."

Anna dipped the tapers, giving them a critical stare. "Done?"

"Done." Maura took the candles from Anna, pausing to greet Lydia before she took them to the drying rack.

Lydia dismounted. Brushing down the striped skirt of her riding gown, she walked the horse near. "I come bearing news." Her stomach fluttered at the words.

Maura caught her eye with a knowing look. Surprised, Lydia realized the major must have already heard her news and told the Doyles. Lydia slid a querying glance at Anna, but Maura shook her head. "Dip you the one more stick, Anna, then go have your visit with Miss Lydia."

A fortnight shy of nine, coltish in homespun petticoat and jacket, Anna grinned with mischief in her eyes. "What of the washing? That's next and you need my help. You said so."

"Is it arguin' for more chores you're after?" Maura said in mock reproof. "Fetch that last stick and be done."

The gelding tossed its head as the girl dashed to retrieve the rack draped with twisted wicks. Lydia slipped an arm beneath the horse's neck, giving its broad cheek a caress. "Is William at his studies?"

Maura nodded, with a glance at the big house's ivy-framed windows. For the past two years, the Aubreys had employed an English tutor for William. "The lad's at it four hours a day now."

"*Six* on Fridays." Anna gave a pitying shake of head that resulted in a further unraveling of her braid.

"Do you mind so much having learnt to read and write?" Lydia asked her.

Anna held the wicks over the steaming pot, making sure each hung straight before dipping. "No, but I couldn't sit to it as William does. So much reading will cross his eyes."

Holding the gelding's reins in one gloved hand, Lydia peered inward at her nose. "I've read dozens of books and nothing of the sort has happened to me." Anna dissolved in giggles. The half-dipped tapers swung on their stick and a chunk of her hair slid into the tallow pot. "Persinette, Persinette, put up your hair!"

"I've a mind to crop it to her ears." Maura swept the half-braided sheaf behind Anna's shoulders, holding it there. "Keep amusin' her so and she'll be dipped for a candle herself."

Lydia relented. "I promise to be dull as porridge the rest of the day. Come find me when you're through, Anna." She turned the gelding toward the stable. "And bring a hairbrush!"

Perched beside the spill of creek water at the wood's edge, Lydia glided the brush through Anna's abundant hair, working out tangles and stiffened tallow. It was a sumptuous blend of shades, from fawn brown at her nape lightening through every shade of gold imaginable to streaks of pale wheat at the crown. It was longer than Lydia's would ever be, already skimming the child's hips. "You'll never have need of a shawl, my girl. Just loose all this hair and you'll be set."

Anna bent her head as Lydia sectioned her hair and began weaving a thick braid. "Is it bad news you bring?"

"Not at all." Behind her back, Lydia bit her lip. "I'm going to be married. In a month, after the banns are read."

Anna's slender shoulders stiffened. "Married to whom?"

"Jacob . . . Mr. van Bergen."

The girl slipped from Lydia's hold and stood, snagging the brush out of her hand. It dangled, caught in the mass of her hair. "You're *marrying* him? Why?"

The child's distress was plain, yet bewildering.

"For one thing, he's done me the honor of asking me." It wasn't the most satisfying of answers, even to Lydia's ears. Jacob van Bergen was a good man, and he loved her—had loved her, he'd confessed, for years. But along with his name and his heart, he offered her something else of price-less value—Papa's shop, which he all but ran himself now, and in which he'd agreed to her working alongside him. And she *liked* Jacob. Admired him. Even cared for him. He knew that was as far as her feelings went but wanted her regardless.

Feelings. Heat prickled Lydia's face. She'd been careful over the years to conceal what she felt for Major Aubrey, feelings she'd never been able to fully banish, not for all her trying.

If anyone had noticed how rattled she'd been that day, three years past, when she extracted the bit of fabric that had long festered the major's wound, such was explained by her reckless treatment—an attempt that caused George McClaren equal parts pride and consternation.

What she'd risked in treating the major had been nothing to discover-ing her long-esteemed hero possessed feet of clay like other men, and, like other men, had sinned. Grievously. At first her mind had rebelled against the notion that this man she'd adored since girlhood could be capable of stealing a baby, deceiving his wife into thinking it was their own. But as she brooded over—and over—what the major had said, adding every passing observation she'd made of William's person, she became con-vinced of its verity, despite the many questions it had raised. Then in crushing, bitter waves had come the disillusionment, the indignation, the grief. How she'd pitied Heledd in those days.

Weeks later, recovered at last, the major had come to the shop to com-mend her, clearly with no recollection of his confession. Only then, seeing him face to face, had she recalled the brokenness and guilt that had at-tended that devastating utterance. For a time then, the suffering his sin, borne so long in secret, had caused his soul—perhaps Heledd's too—was all she could fix upon.

It was too great a burden to bear. She began to pray about who she might tell. Papa? The Doyles? Heledd? For weeks she prayed, seeking the Almighty with an intensity heretofore unknown, until one thing grew clear. God had placed upon her a restraining hand. She was to share the major's confession with no one. Yet in that time of seeking, God had granted her strength to bear the knowledge in silence. She'd learned to bring her questions to her Heavenly Father, to seek solace and clarity from Him and no other. Through it all, her girlish infatuation for the major had been remade, its rough edges smoothed, its shallow waters deepened into a compassion that transcended failings.

As for those romantic notions—she was self-aware enough to admit they still existed—she'd learned to bring them to God as well, whenever they flamed up. And if the notion of marriage apart from the major felt at times ill-fitted, like a gown donned before its final sizing . . . what was she to do? Refuse to live her life because the one she wanted to share it with was forever out of reach?

"Anna," she said now. "Don't you like Mr. van Bergen? He likes you a great deal."

Tears gathered in Anna's eyes. "I like him."

"Then why has this upset you so?"

"Because—I'm going to lose you!"

Anna flung herself at Lydia, who held her as the child cried in her arms. "What? Why would you lose me?"

Anna's words came like hiccups between sobs. "If you—have a husband—to care for—you won't—have time—for *me.*"

"Of course I'll have time for you, goose. It's not as though so much will change." Lydia blushed as she spoke, though the girl couldn't see her face. "I've cooked and cleaned and mended for Jacob and Papa for years. I shall go on doing so. It's mainly my name will change."

Anna pulled back from her, eyes brimming pools. "Like mine was changed when Papa saved me from the bad Indian?"

Lydia touched the girl's wet cheek. "A little like that."

"Anna! Lydia!" At the breathless shout, they looked to see William starting the climb up the hill. He reached them in a scrabble of tumbling stones, panting. "I asked Mr. Blakeley to release me early. He wouldn't—the old toad."

"Poor William." Lydia refrained from tousling his hair, knowing he felt himself too old for it. "Mewed like a hawk while we've been free as the southbound geese."

William looked up at the dark skein even now crossing from north of the river, honking as they went. "Still I'd rather be a hawk than—" Noticing Anna, tear-streaked and runny-nosed, William broke off. A crease appeared between his brows. "What's the matter?"

Lydia took a kerchief from her sleeve and gave it to Anna, who tidied herself while Lydia shared the news of her impending marriage. "Anna took it to mean I'd no longer be able to visit you."

"Anna." William rolled his eyes. "Lydia would no more marry a man who wouldn't let her do as she pleased than would *you*. And you've a brush stuck in your hair. Did you know?"

Anna sniffled. "I know."

He plunged his hands into Anna's hair and worked the bristles free of the strands entangling it. "Turn around."

Anna complied, and William set to brushing out the snarls, working at a stubborn knot with such delicacy that Lydia knew he'd done it before.

"Glad I'm not a girl. This is too much hair to bother with . . . even if it's pretty."

When Anna turned, she was smiling. Before he could dodge away, she wrapped her arms around the boy. "I love you, William."

Over her shoulder, he pulled a comical face. "That's because I'm lovable. Everyone says so."

"Not Mr. Blakeley!" Anna sprang away. William started after her but caught Lydia's eye and checked, handing her the brush.

"Sit down, Anna. Let me finish with that braid." Lydia had known since the two had toddled about the McClarens' home that Heledd's dislike of Anna hadn't soured William's heart toward the girl. If anything, it had sweetened it. She'd seen the pair grow closer as, one by one, William's brothers had failed to thrive. But she'd never seen such a demonstration of tenderness between them as moments ago.

Now she was the one blinking back tears.

To distract herself, she asked after William's studies. He plunked down on the damp hillside, heedless of his breeches, and grew animated as he talked about English history, Welsh myths, Latin, and mathematics. Though he still tore about the fields and woods with Anna when chance offered, William was proving an apt pupil, no doubt destined for some eastern college. He wouldn't be a warrior, or a sachem . . . whatever he might have become in another place, with other parents.

William's eyes were as blue at eight as they'd been at four. His hair had darkened but still might have been a blend of Heledd's rich brown and the major's fairer shade. But other than in coloring—even that couldn't be said at the height of summer, when every exposed inch of him deepened to a startling brown—William didn't remotely resemble the major or his wife.

Three years on, much of that fevered confession still puzzled. Lydia knew Heledd had given birth during the siege of Fort William Henry. By the major's admission, that son had died, and he'd taken—stolen—a replacement from another woman.

Two babies. Had William been a twin?

The white one. A child of mixed blood, white enough to pass as his and Heledd's? And the other darker of complexion? Indian?

Yes. She could see it in him. Or thought she could.

It had taken months to draw even such incomplete conclusions, longer still to come to terms with what had prompted the major to such a terrible act.

I did it for you. For Heledd.

Lydia often ached with wondering what the major thought about that now, for while William had brought Heledd undeniable consolation in an otherwise unhappy existence, the major's deception had—Lydia strongly suspected—contributed to the widening gulf between the Aubreys she'd witnessed over the years. Perhaps it had been the root of it.

Lydia walked up the track from the barn, leading her saddled horse. Anna clutched her hand. William trailed behind. Near the cottage they halted, as Heledd's voice drifted through the open back door of the house: "'Tis a wilderness infested with savages! Maura saw a canoe full passing on the river just this morn. And you mean to go upriver and leave us?"

"Look you, Heledd." Reginald's reply was weary. "I promised I'd not go so far as the Oneida Carry. I'm only going to Herkimer's, and I'm sure those Indians Maura saw were about their own business and no threat to any."

"How is it you can be so easy about them? Would you let *wolves* over-run our yard?"

"Do I own the river? Whoever wills is free to use it."

Having no other way to go but forward, Lydia continued on. They passed the cottage, but Maura didn't appear. *Gone to earth till the storm blows over,* Lydia thought, and wished for a similar escape. The clop of hooves had drowned a portion of the argument. She paused the horse but felt unable to abandon the children.

"I tell you I have no intention of returning to Breconshire," Reginald was saying. "Our future is not in Wales, but here."

"*Our* future? Never did you ask me where I wished to live!"

Anna's small hand tightened its grasp. The girl exchanged a glance with William, who frowned and rubbed the toe of his shoe in the dirt. He didn't look at either of them again.

"Have I not provided well for you? This house, acres of land, the Doyles to serve you. A tutor for William. I've promised he'd go on with his schooling."

"I wish him to be schooled in England. Mr. Blakeley says—"

"And I've told you there are colleges he may attend without putting an ocean between us."

William stiffened, his head rearing erect.

"Reginald, your brother would take us in. He would, I know it."

"You'd have us live by my brother's charity? That I will not do. Not when I've built a life here. For you *and* William. 'Tis a good life, Heledd. If you cannot see that by now, then I despair of you!"

A sob. A door slamming. Silence, ringing and sharp.

Lydia breathed out in relief, thinking that the end of it. Only it wasn't quite. Major Aubrey lunged through the open back door, still dressed for work at the Binne Kill in a coat the color of buckskin—the better to hide wood shavings, he'd once quipped to her.

His sudden appearance startled the horse. Lydia gave her attention to the animal, assuring it didn't sidestep onto tender toes. When she'd attention to spare the major, she found him staring with stricken eyes at William, whose summer-brown face echoed the look. The major took a step toward the boy. William spun on his heel and sprinted for the nearest cornfield. The major didn't call him back or follow.

Anna did both, after squeezing Lydia's hand and wistfully confiding, "I wish *you* were his mother. And mine."

That left Lydia and the major standing in the yard with the horse—the only one not awash in mortification. The major scrubbed a hand down his face. "Lydia. I didn't know you were here . . . and now you're going?"

She attempted a smile. "As you see. And you're bound upriver? I'm sorry. I didn't mean to overhear."

"Tomorrow, aye. Just to the Little Falls." Major Aubrey crossed the yard, the permanent limp his wound had bequeathed him more pronounced than usual. "I'll help you to the saddle, shall I?"

Lydia thought he meant to give her a boost. Instead he encircled her waist with his hands and lifted her easily. His strength was reassuring, but the warmth and pressure of his hands made the blood warm her cheeks. She took more time than needed to arrange her skirts, then donned her gloves and took the reins from his hands.

"Thank you, Major." Her voice at least was steady.

He was looking up at her, his eyes the slate of the clouded sky, one hand on the horse's neck. The hand of a craftsman now, scarred and callused. "I hope . . ." He glanced away. "I hope young van Bergen knows what he's getting."

Lydia quirked a brow. "I daresay he's forewarned."

He looked abashed at her wry tone. "It was kindly meant, that was."

"I know it was, Major."

She watched his expression ease, then his brows twitched together. "You've taken to calling Mrs. Doyle by her given name. And my wife by hers. Why do you not call me Reginald?"

He seemed to consider his motives for asking the question only after he'd spoken it. As their gazes held, in his eyes rose something like surprise, mingled with appreciation—as a man might have for a woman. It left her feeling that the thirteen-year gap in their ages had just melted away.

"May I call you so?"

The major stepped back, letting his hand fall. "I'd like if you did."

"Then when next we meet—at my wedding—I shall." Summoning self-possession, she shut away what dwelled in the secret chambers of her heart, the awareness of his unhappiness, his loneliness. Most of all, her desire to assuage both. She gave the horse a heel tap and didn't look to see if he watched her away down the track.

She prayed for him, for Heledd, and for the children he called his own, until Schenectady's stockade came into view. Then she turned her thoughts ahead to the good man she'd agreed to marry. If she regretted what couldn't be, she yet knew herself a woman blessed, with more cause for contentment than not.

13

Thunder Moon 1768

*G*ood Voice had come to the fields to decide which portion of her allotment would be planted that season, a hard thing to do when hunger lived in the belly. Last year's sickly crops hadn't stretched to feed the People until wild foods could be gathered again. The face of her son had grown lean, the blades of his cheekbones sharp. She'd ground some of the seed corn to feed him over the past moon, which was why it had come down to choosing what part of the field to sow and what to let rest.

Some said the hunger was their own fault for allowing whites to come among them. They didn't mean the settlers pushing up against Oneida lands, with their farms and ranging hogs and cattle. They didn't mean the traders who'd come among the People since before the grandmothers were born. What the sachems grumbled against now was new. For the past two years white men had walked the paths of Kanowalohale, had put up houses, and called it home. They called themselves *missionaries*.

One of these was Samuel Kirkland, who'd come to them after being driven away from the Seneca, where he tried to live for a time. Few Senecas had welcomed him. Good Voice thought she knew why. He had with him a holy book. It was said the book talked much about peace, but in truth it brought division, when already there was division enough over land and hunting and white ways of living thrusting in like spades to uproot their traditions.

Kirkland's book said there was one God and His name was Jesus. The book said no man could be happy in the Life After unless he confessed *sin* and got this Jesus in his heart. Good Voice had never heard Kirkland say such things because she kept out of his path. Her lodge stood at the opposite edge of the sprawling village from the missionary's, so this wasn't difficult to do. Until today.

With her mind on what she was going to give Two Hawks to eat that day, she nearly stumbled over an older boy sitting at the back of a crowd gathered outside a lodge not far from the fields. Good Voice froze. Kirkland stood under the lodge's arbor. She'd stepped into view around the side of a neighboring lodge as he started to talk. She stepped back behind it and looked around. If she didn't want to cross an open space in full view of the missionary, she would have to backtrack and take another way.

Good Voice hesitated, her ear caught by something the missionary said. He had a strong voice, loud enough to reach the back of the gathering, and though sometimes his words were clumsy, he'd learned her language well enough to make himself understood.

"There was a certain man who lived, long time back," Kirkland was saying, "in the city where Jesus taught the people about His Father in Heaven. This man was a sachem called Nicodemus. Though he was curious about Jesus, he feared what other sachems who hated Jesus and His words of Heavenly Father would think of his interest. Nicodemus thought, 'I will go to Jesus in the middle of the night, when no eyes will see me go, no ears hear the talk I mean to make.'"

Good Voice lingered, curious to hear what happened next to the sachem planning to sneak about in the dark.

"Nicodemus went at night to Jesus and said, 'Teacher, we know You come from Creator, for no one can do the great things You do unless Creator is with him.' He said this because Jesus had made the blind to see and the lame to walk and had done other things impossible for a man to do without the help of Almighty God."

Kirkland paused at that moment. In that pause, a rumble rose among his listeners, the sound of many throats expelling breath in an *ahhh* of surprise and intrigue. Good Voice was startled to hear the sound from her throat. Jesus had made the lame walk? Her mind went to Bear Tooth, who'd found a Cayuga woman willing to marry him even though he still limped badly. He and his uncle had gone to live with her people at Oquaga Town, far to the south.

Since the day he left her lodge, Bear Tooth had not spoken to Good Voice again. Perhaps he blamed her, as well as Stone Thrower, for his misfortune. She blamed herself.

Would Jesus have made it so his ankle had healed better than Hanging Kettle and the Oneida healers had managed? Good Voice peeked around the lodge, looking out with one eye at Kirkland. The missionary was not impressive to look at in the way white men could be. Still she fixed her attention on the man in his drab coat, with a cloth wound tight around his neck and a hat with corners on his head, the book open in his hand.

Kirkland looked out across the heads of his listeners—some glossy black in the spring sun shining down, some plucked to a scalp-lock tied with feathers that fluttered on the breeze—and, still speaking about Nicodemus, locked his gaze with hers. Absorbed in listening, Good Voice had stepped out from the corner of the lodge, and now for a choking beat of her heart . . . two beats . . . three . . . there might not have been all those heads between them. No space at all.

Good Voice ducked behind the lodge and hurried away until she could hear the sound of Kirkland's voice no more.

"I found a patch of nettle growing," Bright Leaf said. "And fern tops, and here—some dried squash I set aside. It is not much . . ."

"A beginning." Good Voice put happiness in her tone as she added the meager gleanings to the water heating in the pot. Her happiness wasn't all feigned. Much had changed for her family since the night she piled Stone Thrower's belongings beside the door.

In the end it wasn't Stone Thrower's belongings she cast, but the child he didn't know about. She'd lain for a time afterward, heart on the ground and body fevered, certain it was the last time her womb would ever try to grow a child. That had been a bad time, but something good had come of it. Returning at last to find she'd nearly died had worked on Stone Thrower like a hand shoving him off the bad path he'd followed since Fort William Henry. He stopped going to the Carry where liquor was easy to come by. He stopped talking about the dreams, or the red-coat, or their missing son.

It was the son who'd always been there that Stone Thrower finally took under his wing, near to his heart. He'd made Two Hawks a new bow, one big enough and strong enough for a man to shoot, and though Two Hawks was a better shot than most boys twice his age, he practiced daily, growing strong. He didn't have his own musket yet but was learning to fire Stone Thrower's. They were out hunting together even now.

It gladdened Good Voice to see her husband acting like a man again, but later when the pair pushed aside the door hide and came into the lodge, she knew the hunting hadn't gone well. Two Hawks's face was a careful mask. Stone Thrower must have given him the shot, but whatever game the boy had aimed the musket at, he'd missed.

Maybe next time he would use the bow, but she knew her son. He pushed himself too hard. Expected more from himself than anyone else expected.

"We are not empty-handed." Stone Thrower gave their son a small push toward the fire. In his hands Two Hawks held a grass nest. Inside were six speckled quail eggs. One had cracked and leaked part of its contents, but the other five were whole. Two Hawks's eyes shone with tears he fought to banish. "I held it too tight. One is broken."

"But not empty," Good Voice pointed out. "Most of it can be saved."

While Two Hawks held the nest, she extracted the broken egg and slipped what remained of its contents into the simmering soup. It bloomed yellow and white, hardening into lumps. One by one she broke the eggs. It wasn't enough to feed them all.

Stone Thrower had crossed to their sleeping bench to clean his musket. Good Voice met his gaze and saw the worry there. "I will go out again," he said, as if sensing she needed to hear it.

Good Voice nodded, pretending that the goodness between them didn't feel as fragile as those quail eggs.

"What else is in that pot?" Stone Thrower asked.

"My aunt brought squash and nettles. And fiddleheads."

"Fiddleheads?" Stone Thrower repeated the English word. "What are *fiddleheads,* and where did you hear such a word?"

"My aunt said your uncle called them that, those curled tops of ferns. You have seen a fiddle played? At the Carrying Place maybe?"

Understanding lit his eyes. "That thing they take a stick to and make sounds like wildcats quarreling?" He raised his head and emitted a ghastly, high-pitched screeching.

Two Hawks laughed, forgetting his disappointment. "Fiddleheads!"

As if her mention of him had called him to her lodge, Clear Day knocked on the doorpost, entering when she called out. Her husband's uncle carried a sack of something Good Voice hoped was edible. He held it up, looking around at their grinning faces. "I have this cornmeal for you. A gift. From Kirkland."

While Good Voice made ash cakes from the meal to eat with the watery soup, Clear Day and Stone Thrower lit their pipes and fell to talking of Kirkland, the good and the bad of him.

This was good: the man was adamant against traders' rum. He'd made deputies of some warriors, charging them with seizing any liquor that came into the town and spilling it on the ground before anyone could drink it. There was much less disturbance now from men and women getting drunk and breaking things, and each other.

Also the man had a generous heart. He lived no better than they in a simple log lodge. Any clothing or tools or food he got from his important friends back east he shared. He gave them a voice with those friends, like Warraghiyagey did for the Mohawks. The *Onyota'a:ka* needed that voice. Not only were the whites taking the game from the forest, their crops had spread new diseases, causing the People's harvests to fail.

Kirkland and those assisting him had begun teaching some of the People to read white men's words, which was in part a good thing, but also something that was bad about Kirkland. He wanted to change them too much. He wanted their warriors to dig the ground, not understanding that this was the women's birthright. He wanted them to forget the traditions of their fathers. That was why the sachems spoke against those in Kanowalohale who called Kirkland *brother*.

"Not all of the sachems," Clear Day said as he sat near the fire, watching the smoke of his pipe drift toward the roof hole. "Those in Old Oneida Town are angry about it. But some of the sachems here are listening to Kirkland's words."

Stone Thrower nearly choked on a draw of his pipe. Clear Day had been one of those who stood against Kirkland. Now he came bearing food for his nephew's family given by Kirkland, admitting that the man had some good qualities.

"Did you go and listen to his talk?"

Good Voice, waiting for the ash cakes to need turning, watched her husband's uncle, who shifted, looking uncomfortable.

"I decided to stop listening to what people say Kirkland says and hear it for myself. Today seemed a good day to do that."

Good Voice hadn't noticed Clear Day among the people gathered to hear Kirkland teach. Had he been hiding too?

Clear Day went on, "Among those who were listening were Grasshopper and Skenandoah, that great warrior with his fine house here. Because he listens to Kirkland's path for our people, more are listening."

Good Voice turned the cakes. She served the men, then made sure her son had enough before she took what remained. Watching them fall upon the cakes and soup in their bowls like half-starved wolves, Good Voice found herself able to put aside her unease long enough to be grateful for Kirkland's generosity.

But at what cost was it given? Did the man expect something in return?

In a quiet moment when they were concentrating on their food, Two Hawks said a thing that made his mother's heart pound.

"I want to learn English. I want to go with the boys who are learning at Kirkland's *school*."

Every mouth in the lodge stopped chewing. Every eye stared at Two Hawks.

"Stay away from that missionary," Stone Thrower told him. "He will confuse your thoughts."

"But you said he is not all bad. I heard you. And you, Uncle." The boy turned pleading eyes to Clear Day. "You said it too."

"I said so," Clear Day affirmed, but warily, as though he sensed a trap about to spring. "Why do you wish to know English?"

"We can teach you," Good Voice said before her son could answer. "We know enough to speak to traders."

Two Hawks's brow puckered. "I want to know all their words."

"But why?" three adults asked together.

Her son opened wide his eyes, clearly surprised they needed to ask. "My brother will speak it. Someone should know how to talk to him when we find him."

Three sets of brows rose high. Three mouths hung a little slack.

"That is a wise thought," Stone Thrower finally said. "But I do not want you going near that missionary. Not until we know he can be trusted. That is all I have to say about it."

Far from showing disappointment at this pronouncement, Two Hawks grinned. "It is not the missionary who teaches the boys. It is his *ah-sis-tent*. The one called Fowler. He's not even a white man. He will teach me."

David Fowler, the man who'd come with Kirkland to help him, was of the Montauk people, an eastern nation much overcome by white ways and religion, which made him not much better. Still . . . Good Voice's heart was no longer pounding. She thought this idea of her son's was a good one.

"We will see," said his father.

The boy dropped his head, but Good Voice saw the smile lingering at the corners of his mouth before he raised his bowl to hide it. She knew what he was doing. He was circling this thing in his mind, confident he would find the clear path to it eventually.

He was patient, her son.

Stone Thrower beckoned her from the fire. By the door he leaned close, his head tilting toward their son. "When that one's belly is full, I will take him hunting again. We may take a few days to find where the deer have gone. Will you be well?"

"I have enough to get by."

"Because of Kirkland." Stone Thrower sounded unhappy to say it. "When I get back, we will go to the fish camp."

"*Iyo,*" she said. Good. "But after . . . Will you let him go to *school*?"

"If he wants it still, I will not speak against it. But only with Fowler."

"Yes," Good Voice agreed. "Only him." And she put it from her mind. They had enough to eat this day. Her son, though thin, wasn't sickly with hunger as some had become but was still strong and lively. They had the hope of a new crop to put into the ground and the fishing yet to come. No one was making war on them or threatening to burn their town. Stone Thrower was caring for them, doing his best in a hard time.

So why did she mistrust the good path that lay before her feet? Its smoothness felt deceptive, as if some danger lay coiled beyond its next bend, waiting to strike them as they passed.

14

*T*wilight had crept in from the forest, thickening shadows between the lodges. In one of those shadows Clear Day paused, looked around, then turned onto the path that led through a stand of white pine to the missionary's house. He didn't see Good Voice, on her way back from taking a gourd of the missionary's cornmeal to a couple too old to hunt or grow crops. Seeing those elders with their bones like birds', eyes lost in smiling wrinkles as they thanked her for the meager offering, had pained her. Now here was Clear Day making for Kirkland's house.

Astonishment washed over Good Voice like a cold plunge in the creek. Had she stepped into that story Kirkland told, about the sachem going to Jesus at night because he feared what the people would say?

Hooding her blanket-shawl over her head, she followed her husband's uncle up the path, pausing at the edge of the clearing in which the missionary had his lodge. Clear Day stood at the door, which was open and filled with the flicker-light of fire, except where Kirkland's thin figure shadowed it. Good Voice hid herself in shadow as Kirkland stood aside and motioned Clear Day into his lodge. After a hesitation, Clear Day went in. The door closed.

Good Voice knew she should leave, but her feet crossed the trodden yard to the window. Unlike a few of the frame houses in Kanowalohale—Skenandoah's being the grandest—the missionary didn't have the stuff called glass but thin oiled hide across his window. It wasn't yet tacked down for the night.

Crouched below it, Good Voice peered back through the trees separating the house from the rest of the town. Voices reached her, sounds of people finishing up work and turning to their cook-fires. It was almost dark. Stars lit the sky with milky light. Dampness filled the chilling air. Inside the men were talking. Kirkland was telling Clear Day how he'd seen him at the meeting where he spoke to the people, listening like someone with a question in his mind.

"Have you come to ask me that question?"

It was rude to come so straight at a thing or presume to know what was in the mind of another before he revealed it. Maybe Clear Day thought so too. When he spoke, he sounded uncertain he'd done right in coming to the missionary. "It is about my sister's son. A warrior called Stone Thrower."

Alarm raced over Good Voice's face like crawling insects. What was Clear Day doing? She'd been right to creep in close to listen.

"I have heard of this warrior," Kirkland said. "He is one who went against the sachems' counsel and fought with Pontiac, and left his wife and child to be tended by others. And he is one who indulged in that devil's rum. He has been a drunkard and a troublemaker."

Good Voice felt shame and anger at these words against Stone Thrower. Shame because they were true. Anger because this white man said them.

If he felt the same, Clear Day kept it from his voice. "Those things you say of my nephew are true. But listen now to my words. As one who knows him well will tell you, lately he has tried to walk a better path, to put the needs of his wife and son before his own."

A mouse skittered across the toes of Good Voice's moccasins. She started, clapping a hand across her mouth to keep silent. The mouse scurried away through rustling leaves. Good Voice composed herself, taking heart at Clear Day's defense of her husband. But the mouse had made her miss some of Kirkland's response.

". . . good to think of others, to love our neighbors, to give to those in need. But it is not in doing good that we find peace with Heavenly Father, our Creator. There is only one way, through being born again—being born of the Spirit into Heavenly Father's family by believing that His Son, Jesus, shed His innocent blood to cleanse all mankind of the sin in their hearts. To cleanse you of sin, and me. It is in confession of sin and acceptance of God's cleansing that we are set on a good path—for this life and the one after."

There was silence. Clear Day was waiting to be sure Kirkland had said all he meant to say. Then the older man cleared his throat. "Maybe you brush aside the efforts of my sister's son to follow a good path because you do not know the bad thing that happened to set him on that crooked path and hold him there with its power."

Good Voice listened as Clear Day told the story of Fort William Henry and her sons born there. He took his time, putting in every detail she'd ever shared with him. All he kept back from Kirkland was the name of the redcoat who stole her son.

"I am telling you these things because I think you have some wisdom, though much you say is hard to understand. I think you have a heart for our people, whether or not your path for us is best. And you are a white man. You understand white men's thinking. That is why I have come to talk of a thing that happened before you came among us. It is to do with Stone Thrower and his son that was taken."

On the cold ground below the window, Good Voice rocked herself in darkness, hugging her knees. She knew what Clear Day was going to say before he confessed to knowing where He-Is-Taken could be found. Then he said it, and there was no taking back the words.

"I want to know," Clear Day concluded, "whether it is wise now for me to tell my nephew where to find the child we think is his son."

"You have not done so?"

"I came to know these things when my nephew was on that bad path.

Even after he left it, I did not trust he would stay off it if he knew about his son. He has dreamed of killing that redcoat, and the dream is strong in him still, though he fights it. I feared he might let that dream win the fight, that he would go to where his son is and kill all the whites there. Then other whites would come killing more of us. He might get his son back only to see us all dead."

Kirkland was silent for a time. The waiting made Good Voice's heart drum with the beat of a war dance, so loud she feared the men would hear it.

"Does the mother know?"

Good Voice gripped the blanket-shawl, fingernails digging into the fibers. "She has kept the secret with me, thinking as I do," Clear Day said.

Good Voice bowed her head against her knees, hoping so fiercely it hurt that the missionary would have something wise to say. Some way for what was broken in her family to be made whole.

What Kirkland said was, "Vengeance belongs to God. He will repay. No man's sin is overlooked. If he does not ask forgiveness through the blood of Jesus, then he will spend eternity paying for it himself."

Good Voice put a hand across her mouth, afraid for her husband, of what he might do, what he might suffer for doing it.

"Do you want me to tell Stone Thrower about his son?" Kirkland asked. "Is that what you are asking?"

"I do not think," Clear Day said, "that he would stand still and listen long enough for you to get the words out."

It sounded like the missionary chuckled at that. "You have given this much thought."

"Years of thinking. And prayer smoke to Creator."

Good Voice waited, wondering what Kirkland with his differing ideas about God and prayer would say to this.

"You have been open with me," he said. "I will be so with you. I do not know whether to say *tell him* or *do not tell him*." Good Voice's heart plunged to the ground, only to rise again when Kirkland continued. "But it is not my wisdom you need."

Through the window came a rustling like dry leaves in a wind, before Kirkland's talking voice changed to his reading voice. " 'If any of you lack wisdom, let him ask of God, that giveth to all men liberally, and upbraideth not; and it shall be given him.' Are you willing to ask God for wisdom in this matter of Stone Thrower's son?"

Clear Day made a sound in his throat that could be taken as consent.

If any of you lack wisdom . . . ask . . . it shall be given . . . Good Voice ran the words over in her head, clutching them like a drowning woman would a passing canoe.

"Heavenly Father," Kirkland said, dropping into his prayer voice. "God of all creation, who sent Your Son to earth to live a sinless life and die to satisfy Your just indignation over men's sin, we come before You, this man Clear Day and I, to ask for wisdom in this matter of a great wrong done, a son stolen at his birth."

And me, a woman called Good Voice. I am the mother of that son. I am here.

She'd joined in the prayer before she knew she meant to do it. She'd heard Kirkland talk to his God as she passed by his gatherings. He didn't use a prayer pipe, only words. She couldn't be sure she'd done it right, keeping her words inside her head, but she couldn't speak or her presence would be known.

"You know the outcome of either decision we make on this matter," Kirkland prayed, "as You see the end of every path Your children choose, for good or ill. We cannot see that far with human eyes, but You have a path planned for all Your children, white and red."

My skin is white. My heart is red. Does the God of white men have a path for one like me to walk? For my husband, my children?

"Heavenly Father," Kirkland prayed, "we ask as children who don't know which path to take, show us what to do about Stone Thrower's son. Show us whether now is the time to tell him where to find this child, how to see this son restored."

That man praying to You calls You Father. He says You have a Son called Jesus. He says this Son went away from You and died in a distant place. Do You know the pain of my husband? Do You know my pain?

Something was cracking open in Good Voice's soul. Like the quail egg Two Hawks had brought home, the one that broke and spilled its running insides.

"For the man who did this terrible thing, I ask You to awaken repentance in his heart so he may seek Your forgiveness, so his heart will be soft toward You and the family of the son he stole. May there also be forgiveness in the hearts of Stone Thrower and Good Voice. 'Forgive us our debts, as we forgive our debtors.'"

Good Voice put her hands over her face. Forgive Redcoat Aubrey? Before her son was even restored? Not knowing if he ever would be? It was too much to ask . . . but had demanding her husband take vengeance on Aubrey brought peace? Had it covered her grief or eased her pain? It had made everything worse. What if one day Stone Thrower carried out that demand she regretted? What if he obeyed his dreams?

The missionary paused in his prayer, as if he sensed her outside, fighting against the words he'd uttered to his God. The silence tugged like hands pulling, urging her to do this hard thing. She resisted and found they were gentle hands, ready to release her if she struggled.

That terrified her more.

"I forgive Redcoat Aubrey for the harm he did me," she whispered aloud. "To my husband. To my sons. Will you forgive me through-Jesus-blood-amen?"

Kirkland's voice drifted through the window. "You are the Good Shepherd who leaves the sheep safe in the pen and goes to find the lost one.

We wait for You to tell us what to do and when to do it, and we ask all these things in the name of Your Son, Jesus, that He be glorified in them . . ."

Good Voice no longer heard the words of the missionary, though it seemed she floated on the river of his voice. She hadn't meant to ask his God to forgive *her,* but having done it, that breaking-open feeling had passed. Now she felt empty and spilled, yet . . . somehow full. And not alone. No one from beyond the trees had come near. The men inside hadn't noticed her. She blinked into the darkness. Tears coursed along her nose, over lips that were smiling now.

Is it You?

She realized it was quiet. Were they still inside, Clear Day and the missionary, waiting for God to speak? As He had spoken to her? Not in words. He was simply there, where He hadn't been before. He'd heard the words of a woman called Good Voice and let her know they were important to Him. *She* was important to Him. Like a daughter. *Heavenly Father.*

Inside Kirkland's lodge, Clear Day asked, "Have you heard your God speak?"

Good Voice waited with anticipation, with wonder, still with a little fear—but that was fading like the darkness lifts at the coming of dawn.

"I will tell you what is in my heart, and you may do with it as you think best," Kirkland said. "I believe it is time to tell Stone Thrower the truth about his son."

15

May 1768

*L*ydia smoothed the gown laid across the Doyles' bed. It was the brocaded wool she'd worn the day Reginald returned wounded from the campaign in Quebec. How small the garment seemed, yet how grown-up she'd fancied herself that day she brought tea to the major—until she'd opened her mouth and disabused even herself of the notion. She smiled forbearingly at her fourteen-year-old self from the amused detachment of three-and-twenty.

"Look at this one, Anna." Across the bed Maura Doyle held up a striped gown, all blue and cream and girlish bows.

"That one's agreeable," Anna said, peering at the gown cascading across the coverlet. Her voice held but a trace of the enthusiasm Lydia had hoped to elicit by the gift of her girlhood gowns. At eleven, Anna was nearly as tall as Lydia had been at fourteen, far prettier, and every bit as spindly. The gowns would require little altering. Some taking in at the shoulders, a few fresh ruffles . . .

Anna's brows, darker than the wealth of hair restrained beneath her cap, tightened above eyes that reflected pain like glints of sun on water. A few new gowns wouldn't fill the emptiness William had left behind, any more than they'd have assuaged Lydia's grief at the loss of her father the previous year.

As though he'd only waited for Lydia to be settled, three months after she and Jacob van Bergen wed, George McClaren went to his bed one night and never rose from it.

As had been the case when her mother passed and, far away in Wales, his father, Lydia and Reginald Aubrey were destined to lose a significant family member within the same year. This time it was the major's brother.

That distant death brought about a significant alteration in the Aubreys' lives. Because his brother hadn't married, the family estate in Breconshire passed to Reginald, whereupon Heledd Aubrey redoubled her efforts to persuade her husband it was long past time to return to it.

Instead, a flurry of letters ensued between Reginald and the family's factor, centered on the topic of keeping the estate running *in absentia*. For now.

Forever, Lydia had prayed, relieved the major refused to abandon his farm and business on the Mohawk, each prospering with the continued stream of settlers moving upriver, needing provisions and a means of transporting them.

Thus it was with no little dismay that she'd received word the previous autumn that Heledd had at last prevailed upon Reginald to allow William's education to continue in England. Heledd would accompany him and reside at the Aubreys' Breconshire estate.

That winter Heledd was like a creature reborn, the steadiest of temper Lydia had ever known her; she was going home, and there would be no snatching back such a long-deferred hope, not once her hands had closed upon it.

And so the following spring, ten-year-old William journeyed with his mother by sloop from Albany down the Hudson River, took ship from New York, and left behind the only home he'd known, the only father, and a distraught girl who'd been to him a sister, who now went about the farm alone, the seams of her heart unraveling behind her.

Lydia put an arm around the girl.

To her credit, Anna made an effort to show appreciation for the gowns. "Thank you, Lydia. They're lovely and . . ."

"And the child's in dire need o' them," Maura finished with a firmness to make up for Anna's lack. "Sproutin' like a garden weed whenever I turn my back." Maura's face was lined with worry over Anna, yet there was a lightness about her these days Lydia hadn't noticed for years. If William's absence left them lonely, Heledd's made life decidedly less taxing.

"Will Papa be home to supper?" Anna asked, calling the major what he'd always been to her, now there was no one willing to deny her the comfort of expressing it aloud.

"I'm after fixin' it for him, so if he isn't to home when 'tis served I'll be knowin' the reason." Maura's mock severity elicited a lackluster smile from Anna. Over her head the women exchanged a look.

"Why don't I bundle these," Maura said, reaching for the blue-striped gown. "And you two can oblige me by gettin' out from underfoot while I start that supper."

"Shall we go walking?" Lydia pulled Anna close to plant a kiss atop her head, thinking it wouldn't be long before that head stood too tall for it. "Out to the creek, perhaps?"

"All right. I'll find my shoes." Anna pulled away and left the room.

When she was out of earshot, Lydia said, "Oh dear."

"Poor lamb. 'Tis like watchin' someone fade o' the wastin' sickness." Maura lowered her voice. "Rowan and I . . . we're after having her move into the house with the major, into William's room."

Lydia gripped the bedpost, searching Maura's face. "But what of you and Mr. Doyle?"

Maura sighed. "I'll miss her under our roof, but she's always been his daughter. We've known that. And won't she be right across the garden and me seeing as much o' her as ever?" The older woman sighed again. "Such sadness and discord has attended that house. May those two together find a happier content."

Hearing Anna coming down the ladder steps from her loft room, Lydia whispered, "Does she know?"

"'Twas settled only this morn. The major thought you might like to tell her."

They sat on the creek bank, not far from the footlog. The day was warm for May. As the westering sun thrust golden spears of light through the trees, Anna leaned over to trail her fingers in the creek's burbling flow. Her silence made Lydia's chest feel heaped with small round stones, like those littering the creek bed. The child bent so low her cap slid askew. Lydia caught it before it fell into the water.

"I'm sure William misses you, too."

Anna sat up, clutching a smooth gray stone. It dripped in her lap, darkening her petticoat to match her soaked sleeve. Her braided hair, pinned round her head like a many-shaded crown, looked too heavy for her slender neck. "He wanted to go. He told me so."

There'd been no denying William's excitement for the adventure of weeks aboard ship, then taking up residence at the Aubreys' estate in the border hills of Wales, where he would be tutored before attending university.

Yet Lydia had heard the boy promise to write—a dozen times if she'd heard it once. "Never think it was easy for him to leave you."

A tear rolled down Anna's cheek. "Is that supposed to make it easier for *me*?"

"Would you fancy having his room?" She hadn't meant to blurt it out but was desperate to comfort the girl.

Anna's fingers tightened around the stone in her lap. She looked at Lydia, uncomprehending. "His room?"

"Major Aubrey and the Doyles thought you might be happier sleeping in the big house now—in William's old room."

Anna's face fell as though Lydia had told her William would never
write her a single letter. Not one. "I don't want William's room—I want
William!"

On her feet, Anna hurled the stone into the creek, then darted away
along its bank, leaving Lydia clutching her abandoned cap. "Anna!"

Half-blinded by tears and streaks of sunlight, Anna ignored Lydia's call
and sped across the footlog. She raced through the beech grove, all her
heart set on that special place she and William had found together. It was
there she would feel near to him. Not his room, in which she'd hardly ever
set foot. Besides, moving into his room would be like admitting he was
never coming back. He'd told her he would come back. She didn't want his
room touched until *he* walked through its door again.

She broke from the beeches into the clearing where so many summer
days she'd picked daisies and wove them into chains for her hair. For William's hair too, when he'd suffer it.

He'd be too old for daisy chains when he came back.

The pain in her chest was as blinding as the sunlight that hit her full
in the face. She didn't need to see. She knew every tussock and molehill in
the clearing and ran on, her steps sure, glimpsing through the sun blots in
her vision the hill where the creek tumbled down.

At the base of the hill, speared by sunlight, a boy stood.

William. He was *here.* Not on a ship. Not leaving her. He'd changed
his mind. He'd run away from his mother. The surprise of it sent a shock
down to her toes, yet she didn't hesitate. "William!"

The boy at the clearing's edge started like a deer at the sound of her
voice and bounded away. The dappling shadows hid him.

Anna staggered to a halt. Her braid broke free of its pins and tumbled down, falling around her shoulders, unraveling to skim her hips. Tresses blew across her eyes. Panting, she whipped them away and looked desperately for William.

At last she spotted him—in the shade of a big hickory.

She ran for him again, crying now for relief, afraid somehow, too, because she knew if William had come back he wouldn't be skulking in the forest, waiting for her to find him. He'd have found *her*. At the house.

Still obscured by shadow, the boy she desperately wanted to be William turned as if to run away again.

"No—wait!"

He stopped. And faced her. His height, the turn of his head, were so like William that her heart leapt again with unreasoning joy—but he wasn't William. She could see that now. This boy's hair was black and long, straighter than William's. His face and hands were browner than William's got by summer's end, though it was only spring.

She slowed. Just within the shade of the hickory tree, she halted, feeling round nuts roll beneath her shoes. The boy looked at her, not moving a muscle. Such stillness wasn't at all like William, who almost never stopped moving unless he was reading a book. Not even a lock of this boy's hair lifted to the breeze.

It felt like one of them should say something, not go on staring at each other like a pair of stumps. Since he didn't, she did. "Are you real?"

That made the boy smile. "Are you?"

Anna gasped. For the first time she'd noticed what he wore—breechclout and leggings and fringed shirt. Hanging against that shirt from a cord looped round his neck was a knife sheath, decorated in bright quills in a design she was too far away to make out.

"You're an Indian!"

"Onyota'a:ka," the boy said. When she frowned at the strange word, he said, "Standing Stone People . . . Oneida."

Oneida. They lived west of their nearest Indian neighbors, the Mohawks, beyond the treaty line. The way he spoke English sounded like the man called Hanging Kettle, who she once talked to in the shop that used to be McClaren's but was now van Bergen's. Jacob and Lydia's shop.

Lydia. Anna looked back, expecting to see Lydia coming through the beeches after her. But she wasn't. She didn't hear her calling either.

Another voice, deeper than the boy's, spoke words Anna didn't understand. She whipped her head around, searching for the source. Beyond the boy, on the other side of the hickory, two more Indians stood. These were both grown, though one was bigger than the other. His hair was plucked on the sides and front, his chest and arms tattooed. The rest of him was all feathers and beads and gleaming bronze skin. The other Indian had gray in his hair. His cheeks were pitted with scars. The big Indian was looking straight at her as if he wanted to *eat* her. The older one had hold of his arm.

Fear froze Anna where she stood. The menacing Indian spoke something harsh to the boy, who flinched and looked at his elders. The Indian thrust his chin toward her, his mouth set in a scowl. The boy turned back to her. Fear was in his eyes. He spoke his next words with care. "Who live in house of stones?"

Anna dropped her mouth open to say, "*I* do now," when at last she heard Lydia calling from the other side of the beeches.

"Anna—Catherine—Doyle!"

The boy's eyes went round. "A-nuh-Cath-run?"

She couldn't afterward say why, but she didn't want Lydia to see this boy. "My name," she said, and like a frightened rabbit she bolted, leaving the Indians standing beneath the hickory.

She half expected them to chase her down. They didn't.

Back across the clearing and through the beeches she ran, nearly colliding with Lydia at the edge of the grove. Clutching her forgotten cap, Lydia grasped her as Anna tried to catch her breath.

"Anna! Did something frighten you?"

"No. I just—don't want—to be there now." She gulped a breath and looked away from Lydia's face, where concern was melting into understanding. *Mis*understanding.

"Oh, Anna. It will grow easier to bear, I promise. Especially when William's letters start arriving. I'm sorry I upset you."

Anna's heart was slamming hard. "I'm all right. Can we go home?"

"Of course." Lydia took her hand. "We'll try on those gowns, shall we?"

She nodded and set the pace, hurrying Lydia along, eager to put the creek and fields between them and the Indians. She looked back only once, while Lydia was crossing the footlog.

There was no sign of them. Not the big warrior. Not the older one. Not the boy that for one gloriously perfect moment she'd believed was William.

1770–1775
The Mohawk River Valley—
New York

I have a son born to me. A son I have never seen. A son his mother
has not seen since she pushed him into this world. There were two
sons—two-born-together—one with skin brown like mine, the other
white, like his mother. That is what she tells me. I have wished in my heart
that she never told me, that I knew of only the one. That my heart was
whole. It was the white one taken, snatched from the side of his brother as
an egg is stolen from a nest. Now he walks this earth far from the land of
his people and does not know what he is.

Listen, and hear me. I am going to tell you what he is. He is the empty
place at our fire. He is the hole in the lodge where the bark has rotted, letting in the wind, rain, and snow. We are left exposed in the place where
he should stand. Bad things have come into our lodge through that place.
Bitterness. Hate. Dreams. The drink the traders are eager to thrust into
my hands. I grasp these things, floating twigs to a drowning man. Under
me is a black lake going down. In dreams I sink under the flood . . . Then
in my hand is a war hatchet. I am hunting. I am strong. The earth beneath my feet speeds me on. The paint is black on my face. It is blood I
want. The blood of him who traded his dead son for my living son and left
us to bear it in brokenness. My feet run to spill it. My hands long to drench
themselves in it.

Round and round the circle of seasons I have pursued him who bears
my son away from me. But at long last I have caught him. He is on the

ground before me, on his knees and at my mercy. At last his eyes see me, wide with fear. I have no mercy.

My blade is sharp and bright. My heart leaps. My ears hunger for the sound of his skull splitting like a pumpkin dashed to the ground. But even in such visions I have yet to hear it.

To carry a dream this long is a hard thing. But who is there to help me see it fulfilled? I bear it alone, a stone I cannot put down.

16

October 11, 1770

*A*nna slipped her hand beneath the table, feeling through layers of linen the satisfying crinkle of paper in her pocket. By force of will she'd read the letter but thrice since Papa brought it home last night, though soon enough it would be creased and memorized like the rest of William's letters.

This one had been sent in remembrance of her birthday—or the day Papa called her birthday. He'd reckoned her about ten months old when he rescued her on the road from Fort William Henry, which meant she'd been born in October. He'd chosen to mark her birth when the hills were ablaze with color—today, in fact, which made William's letter more like a present than ever. She reached for it again, as if it might have vanished from her pocket in the past few seconds.

"Finish your breakfast, Anna. Then take yourself off someplace quiet with that letter."

Papa was watching her across the table, his mouth a knowing curve. She sprang from the chair and grabbed her plate. "I'll clear up."

His amusement grew less veiled as she hovered at his shoulder, eyeing his nearly empty porridge bowl. Papa was home today to help with the harvest. He'd dressed for it in shirt and nankeen breeches, over which he'd don a coarse frock for the dusty work of bringing in the stalk-dried corn. Placing a hand over hers he said, "You needn't today. You've the morning free of chores."

She bent and brushed a kiss across the scar he'd taken saving her—
and snatched his bowl from under his nose.

"Imp!" he said, reaching to swat her and missing. "Mind you, I'd like
to read his letter as well—when you can bear the parting." Papa pushed
back his chair, standing stiffly on account of his hip that pained him of a
morning. "A most blessed birthday to you, my girl."

He kissed her forehead and went out to the day's work.

Frost lingered in patches in the yard. Over the river, mist hung in drifting
bands. Anna grabbed a shawl and set off for the wood that beckoned beyond the fields, where Rowan Doyle was filling a cart with corn in the
husk. So were several of Papa's crewmen from the Binne Kill, among them
Captain Ephraim Lang.

The Yankee captain had fetched up in Schenectady two years back, a
river man for hire, amazed to find his old wartime acquaintance—
Papa—in the business of shipping goods up and down the Mohawk. He
and Papa had renewed their friendship, forged that harrowing day she
became Papa's ward. Before long they were partners in the business, old
Mr. Boswell having gone to glory years ago. Papa, who once made trading
trips upriver, now stayed moored in Schenectady, overseeing the boat-
building and account-keeping, while Captain Lang managed the shipping
and crew.

Standing in the wagon's bed, the captain saw her passing along the
field's edge and hailed her, wishing her a happy natal day with such exu-
berance every gaze was drawn to her. Face flaming to rival the scarlet ma-
ples, Anna waved and hurried toward the creek.

Beyond the footlog, the beeches enfolded her, wide of trunk, soaring
to a golden canopy. Leaves lay scattered like coins underfoot. The scent of
smoke and wet earth spiced the chilly air with a smell faintly melancholy

as she climbed the hill beyond the clearing. She settled on the stone that jutted in a little shelf beside the spill that she persisted in calling a waterfall. Though the rising sun slanted warmth now through the misty trees, cold seeped from the stone beneath her. She kept the shawl pulled close as she freed the letter from her pocket and unfolded its pages.

"Anna Catherine," a voice said above the purl of creek water.

She yelped, nearly dropping the precious letter. Leaping to her feet, she spotted him standing above her on the rocks, the boy she'd once mistaken for William. Her heart slowed its gallop, but a small thrill raced through her. "Two Hawks!"

Looking smug for having startled her, he descended, slender as a colt in leggings and breechclout, a blue shirt rolled at the elbows baring skinny brown arms. His black hair swung free as he descended nimbly over the rocks, moccasined feet landing with a thump beside her.

"*Shekoli,*" he said, his word for greeting.

"*Shekoli.*" Anna looked him up and down. He had his bow and quiver and wore the familiar quilled sheath knife against his chest—worked in a bird design, two tiny hawks with red tails—but its placement was a good deal higher up than it had been. "You're taller than I am!"

She could see the observation pleased him. "It six moons since I see you. I grow."

Nearly an inch for each of them. "How old are you, Two Hawks? You've never told me."

"I count thirteen summers. How many you?"

"I mark ten-and-four today."

Surprise flashed in his brown eyes. "Good I come this day."

She regarded him, taking in other changes half a year had wrought. He was becoming handsome with his strong-bladed cheekbones and smooth skin of a light copper-brown. His nose was straight, and his mouth well molded, curving up at the corners in a way that seemed vaguely familiar.

Anna was glad Two Hawks didn't mind her staring. She'd learned to bear his steady gaze in return. He seemed as fascinated by the way she looked as she did him. He settled on the rock she'd vacated. "You not run from me this time."

Anna sat beside him, holding William's letter. "Nor last, remember?"

"True. First time only you run—scared little *a'sluni* girl."

Anna twisted her mouth but supposed she had been a scared little white girl—then. "*And* the second."

The day after that first encounter, she'd summoned the courage to return to the clearing. She'd waited, heart pounding . . . until out of the forest the boy she would come to know as Two Hawks had stepped. Alone. She'd suspected the other Indians were nearby, though they didn't show themselves.

She and Two Hawks hadn't said much to each other. His English wasn't good. She'd asked him simple questions, learned his name and that the other Indians were his father and his father's uncle. Then Two Hawks had repeated the question from the day before: who lived in the big house across the fields?

Knowing no reason why she shouldn't, she'd told him about Papa and the Doyles. And William. At first his eyes had seemed to burn with excitement when she mentioned William. He'd looked toward the wood, revealing where the grown Indians hid. But his gaze cooled when she told him William was gone with his mother across the sea to Wales. Perhaps because she cried in the telling, the pain of it still raw, Two Hawks had looked crestfallen too. He'd asked if William would come back—sounding as if he cared about the answer.

"He promised to," she'd said, wiping her tears. "Someday."

A voice had called from the wood, startling them.

Anna had nearly wet herself when the big Indian, Two Hawks's father, came rushing out of the brush toward her, but he was stopped again by the older Indian, who moved quick for a man with gray hair. He caught Two

Hawks's father and jammed a fist into the center of his chest. In his fist were beads, three strings of them hanging down, all white. He seemed to want Two Hawks's father to take them, but he wouldn't. He gestured their way, uttering guttural, angry words. The older Indian said firm, harsh words. Two Hawks said pleading words. His father sent a glance of anger—or was it anguish?—toward the farm. He shoved the white beads away and stalked off into the forest.

Two Hawks had looked at her with eyes full of alarm and whispered, "Run."

She'd run.

"Good you not run this time," Two Hawks told her now, his eyes teasing. "I like see your face, not only back, all that hair swinging."

She'd braided her hair properly that morning, though she'd forgotten her cap. As far as she could remember, she'd had it braided last time too, back in spring, when he and his father had lingered in the woods for days before she happened across the creek to find them waiting. It had frightened her to see his father, especially since the older Indian hadn't been with them. But the man had behaved himself, even spoken to her civilly, though he'd remained tense and forbidding. She'd learned his name was Stone Thrower.

She'd asked how often they came there to the little creek, how long they waited to see her, and did they ever give up and go away again? Two Hawks admitted to having waited in vain one time only, but she'd vowed to be more diligent in visiting her favorite place. Even though Stone Thrower still unnerved her, she liked seeing Two Hawks.

Their village, a place called Kanowalohale—it meant *head on a pole*, Two Hawks told her—lay far to the west, not many miles from the portage trail between the Mohawk River and Wood Creek, where the old fort called Stanwix stood moldering. Papa had been there many times, though she'd no idea how long it took to travel there on foot. Days, she imagined. Nor was she sure why Two Hawks and his father came so far to talk with her. She was no one special. Just a girl on a farm. But she was terribly curious about them.

She looked beyond Two Hawks, to the forest skirting the hill. "Where is your father?"

Teasing fled the boy's eyes. Dark lashes swept his cheekbones as he lowered his gaze. "I come alone."

Anna chewed her lip, wondering. The last time she'd seen Stone Thrower had been brief. He'd asked one question—had William come home? When she'd explained that it would be a long time—years—before that day arrived, Stone Thrower had grown sullen and gone away.

Two Hawks had stayed behind, looking upset. When she'd pressed him for why his father seemed so unhappy, he'd said, "It not for me to tell," but looked at her with longing, as if he wanted to tell. "He drinks the trader's rum again. My mother unhappy."

Distracted by this first mention of a mother, she'd asked about her. His mother's name was Good Voice. No more was said that day of his father.

Anna wished now she'd been more persistent. It seemed things with Stone Thrower hadn't improved. Two Hawks kept his eyes on the forest spreading out from the hill in clumps of gold and scarlet. A breeze kicked up, making the leaves of oak and maple, beech and hickory flutter on their stems or let go to drift on the air like sparks.

"My father's uncle has new name," Two Hawks said abruptly. "He is Daniel now. Daniel Clear Day. He did this for Jesus."

Anna stared, slow to comprehend. "You mean he's a Christian?"

Two Hawks picked at the colorful quillwork someone—probably his mother—had sewn onto his legging. "There is a man with us. Kirkland. He talks Jesus. All the time."

"The Reverend Samuel Kirkland?" Anna had heard of the Presbyterian missionary. He was getting to be known in the way Sir William Johnson was known, as a man who spoke for the Indians. The Oneidas, anyway. Two Hawks didn't sound pleased about him. "What does Mr. Kirkland say?"

Two Hawks gripped his knees, scowling. "He say no person is good, even if they do no stealing or falling down drunk. He say only Jesus lived good. He say the way to have good heart is through Jesus who is Savior and Shepherd and Vine—and other names I forgot."

Nothing he'd said sounded wrong to Anna, however strangely worded. "What do you think about it?"

Two Hawks made a noise of dismissal. "The Master of Life has watched over us always. Is he the same as Kirkland's Jesus? If so, why do we not know of him? Why do we not have the book?"

"The Bible? I don't know." Anna wished for better answers, or any answer at all. Mrs. Doyle had made sure she said her prayers every night as a girl. The Doyles still took her to meeting with them every Sabbath; Papa stopped going when Mrs. Aubrey and William left. Though she put herself to bed in her own room in Papa's house now, she still prayed every night. For William and Papa, the Doyles, Lydia . . .

If anyone talked of the Almighty as though He were truly listening it was Lydia, who often prayed for someone sick in the shop, for neighbors, for William and his mother far away in Wales, for Papa, for *her*.

"What of Aubrey?" Two Hawks asked, turning to look her in the eye. "Is he Christian, like Kirkland?"

Anna felt a twinge of unease. Whenever Two Hawks or Stone Thrower mentioned Papa, their voices took on an edge, sharp as a hatchet blade. She'd yet to find the courage to ask why. She wanted to say that of course Papa was a Christian. But had Papa ever talked to the Almighty in her hearing? Anna couldn't think of a time, not even at meals. She knew he had a Bible; once she'd gone into William's room, opened an old chest, and found it there. Papa's name was inscribed inside it, but she'd never seen him read it, though many of its pages were marked as though he once had.

She sometimes wondered if something bad had happened to Papa.

Something that hurt him. Not like his hip, where that musket ball had hurt him. In his heart. Sometimes it seemed to her as if a weight dragged at Papa's soul, the way his hip slowed his stride.

"He must be," she said, banishing her doubts. "He just doesn't talk about it all the time, like Reverend Kirkland."

"I saw a warrior always drunk on trader's rum, his wife and children hungry, give his heart to Kirkland's Jesus and become a man again. His children eat now—but he plows *dirt* to feed them." Two Hawks's mouth puckered like he'd tasted soured milk.

Anna frowned at his obvious disdain. "What's wrong with that?"

"Scraping dirt for planting is women's work, given to them to do. Man's work is hunting, fighting enemies. Protecting the people."

The insult stung. "Mr. Doyle is a farmer. So is Papa. They're both men. And Papa builds boats. Is that also wrong for a man to do?"

"A man may build a canoe without shame." Two Hawks glanced at her. "Aubrey does this?"

"They're called bateaux. Some of your men—Oneida men—make wages portaging bateaux and supplies, at the Carrying Place."

For a moment Two Hawks had looked interested, but at her mention of the Carrying Place he firmed his mouth again. "*Bateaux* come there with trader's rum."

"And other things," she hurried to add. "Good things. Kettles and knives, blankets, mirrors, beads—"

"Trinkets," Two Hawks cut her off, dismissive.

Anna didn't like the contention that had crept into their exchange. It had never happened before. "Isn't it better to be a farmer who feeds his family than a warrior who lets them starve?"

She wished those words back instantly, certain they would wound. But Two Hawks pulled his brows tight in thought, then said, "Anna Catherine . . . best is a warrior who does not drink demon-rum. That is Kirkland word for it. That one thing he say true."

"Maybe other things he says are true?" Anna put her hand over his and did what she hoped Lydia would do had she been sitting there. "Would you mind if I prayed for Stone Thrower?"

The hand beneath hers twitched. It occurred to Anna this was the first time she'd ever touched him. She slid her hand away.

"Pray if you will." Perhaps so she wouldn't do it right then, Two Hawks pointed to her other hand. "You have letter?"

Anna grinned—she couldn't do otherwise. "It came yesterday."

Two Hawks pulled his bottom lip between his teeth, suddenly shy. "You say marks for me?"

She'd read from one of William's letters last time she'd seen Two Hawks. He'd seemed fascinated by it. "William wishes me well on my birthday," she said. "He misses me—so he says—but I think he misses the horses more because he asks more about them than about me." She scanned the letter. "He doesn't know what university he'll attend once his tutoring is complete, but he'd like it to be Oxford. That's in England. He's learned to read Greek and a little Hebrew. And he talks about the factor's two dogs . . . bigger than our wolves here, he says."

"That is big dogs," Two Hawks murmured.

Anna smiled, her gaze still on the letter. "Here's a part I think you'll like: 'Mr. Davies'—that's the factor—'is accomplished with the ancient Welsh war Bow and has taken to showing me the Art of shooting it several days out of the week, and though he may be speaking to my Vanity says I show some natural Inclination. In any case 'tis a Grand Diversion from dusty Tomes and lures me out into the Hills . . .'"

Anna glanced at the bow and quiver slung across Two Hawks's back. He saw where her gaze had gone. "This Welsh bow . . . it like my bow?"

"I'll ask William if you'd like. Maybe he'll make a likeness of it for you."

"Yes," he said, before wariness leapt to his gaze. "You put me in marks?"

She wrote to William about everything that happened on the farm but had never mentioned Two Hawks or his father, as she'd never mentioned them to Lydia, Papa, or the Doyles. She'd started to tell Lydia once but found she couldn't bring herself to do it. What if Lydia was afraid or objected to their friendship? What if she told Papa and Papa made her stop coming to the wood?

"I never have," she said, and the set of Two Hawks's shoulders eased.

"Is more?" He brushed a fingertip over the letter resting on her lap. She felt his touch through the paper. Disconcerted, she dropped her gaze and began reading before realizing it was a portion she'd meant to keep to herself.

" 'Mama is happy. 'Tis as though for her the years in New York never were. I wish it was not so. I wish more she had treated you kindly. She is as much your Mother as Papa is your father, or she should have been. I hope it hurts less now. And you know you might have taken my old room instead of that Cupboard of a space next to—' "

"What means?" Two Hawks cut in. "Mother not kind to you?"

William might hope otherwise, but whenever Anna thought of the woman, there still rose up that puzzled shame she'd always felt when she failed to please Mrs. Aubrey.

"William's mother. She and Papa couldn't agree about me." Two Hawks tilted his head, clearly no better enlightened. "Papa wanted to keep me. Mrs. Aubrey didn't. So I lived with the Doyles in their cottage—the little house behind the big one—until William and his mother left. Then Papa said I should come sleep under his roof."

She could see Two Hawks still didn't understand, but he asked, "William want to leave you? Or no?"

"No . . . Yes." She faltered as a memory rose up sharp in her mind. *"I hate him!"*

William's jaw was clenched so tight, Anna barely heard the words he'd hissed over the chatter of the creek slipping over the stone beside them.

It was the last time they would sit together in her favorite place, and he was spoiling it. Spoiling this last memory with his shocking words. "William . . . don't say that."

William made his hands into fists. "Why won't he go with me and Mama? Why cannot the Doyles look after things here the way that factor does in Wales?"

Anna opened her mouth to tell him why but couldn't find the words. Instead she said, "The Binne Kill . . ."

Anger twisted William's mouth. "I hate those boats!"

"Do you hate me?"

"What? No . . ." His face blanked, then his brows pulled together in a flinch. There it was. He understood at last why Papa was staying. Not just for the life he'd built in New York, the Binne Kill, his boats.

William gazed at her, stricken. "Is this how you've felt all these years? About Mama? But you don't hate her, do you?"

"No."

"Why not?"

Anna's heart wrenched, watching William struggling to understand, struggling not to hate Papa, who he felt was rejecting him in letting him go, the way his mother had rejected her by refusing her a place beneath their roof. Or in her heart. "How can I hate someone who loves you?"

A single tear rolled down William's cheek. Anna wanted to touch it, for it seemed a precious thing. But William brushed it away roughly, and afterward there was no more to say.

Two Hawks was quiet, his smooth brows drawn. Anna waited, wondering what trail his thoughts had taken while hers had wandered back to the last time William sat where he did now. After a moment he looked at her, still frowning. "Aubrey's woman not want you for daughter? But wanted He—William—for son?"

Anna's heart squeezed with the old pain. "William *is* her son." The only one who'd lived.

Two Hawks's expression blanked, leaving him looking for an instant like a boy carved of wood. Then the frown returned. "You not born to her?"

"No."

"Born to Aubrey?"

"I'm his ward."

Two Hawks shook his head. "I not know *ward*."

Anna started at the beginning and told him how she came to be the daughter of Major Reginald Aubrey. Two Hawks was attentive—intensely so—as she talked of Fort William Henry's fall. She enjoyed seeing people hear the story for the first time, watching their gazes slide with admiration to the scar on Papa's cheek. Papa wasn't there to be admired, still . . . Two Hawks's reaction was different from any she'd ever witnessed. As she spoke, his color blanched as much as his tawny skin allowed.

"He *is* the one."

"One what?" Anna asked. But Two Hawks's face closed up, and she knew she wouldn't get an answer. Two Hawks wasn't like William, who'd told her everything in his head almost as fast as it came into it.

Hearing the lowing of a cow, she peered through the trees fringing the creek. The mist on the river had burned away. The sun was high, the morning wearing on. "I promised to help Mrs. Doyle ready dinner for the men." On impulse she added, "Come with me. Meet Papa. See where I live."

Two Hawks stood. "No. My father . . . He not hunt now as we need. I must hunt."

He was only thirteen, yet it sounded as if the care of his family had fallen on his narrow shoulders. Or was it just an excuse to leave her? She wished his visit had ended better.

"Good-bye then," she said, hoping it wasn't the last.

"*O-kee-wa'h.* Good-bye for now."

Two Hawks smiled, and the restraint between them lifted. She wanted suddenly to touch him again, but like a deer he sprang back up the rocky slope. Anna watched him vanish among the rhododendron, then folded William's letter and started home.

Warm under quilts, Anna stared at the shadows of her room—cupboard, William called it—no nearer sleep than she'd been hours ago. She'd have lit a candle to read his letter again, but she'd given the missive to Papa before retiring to bed. Surely *he* was asleep by now. Might he have left it lying somewhere?

She rose and donned a shawl over her shift. Moonlight shown bright enough through the windows to forgo a candle. Below stairs, Papa's door was open. Anna tiptoed past it, only to spy the flicker of firelight in the front room.

Papa sat in his wing chair near the hearth. In his hand was William's letter, but he wasn't reading it. He held it limply, elbows on his knees, shoulders bent. She crossed the room and knelt beside him. "Papa? Is that William's letter?" She'd doubted it for a moment—there was nothing upsetting in the letter. But as Papa straightened in surprise, she saw it was the letter.

"Anna. Awake at this hour? Even birthdays must come to an ending, my girl."

She lay her head against his knee, hair spilling on the floor. After a moment his hand rested on the crown of her head.

"I love you, Anna. You know that, do you not?"

His voice was thick with emotion. She raised her face to see something like anguish in his eyes and remembered what William had written about Mrs. Aubrey. Was Papa upset about that? She was too far away to kiss his scar, but she looked at it and he smiled as though she'd done it.

"You were mine, see. From the moment I picked you up off that road. My daughter, as much as if you were born to me."

"As much as William is your son?"

Papa's voice cracked as he said, "More so."

She hadn't meant to ask that, was mortified it slipped out—as mortified as Papa looked now.

"How can I be more? Oh . . . because I'm here and William isn't?" She rose and settled on his lap so she could twine her arms around his neck. "You must miss him more than I do."

Strong arms encircled her. A gentle hand stroked her hair, fallen in a tangle over both their laps. He snagged his fingers in it. She said *ouch* and then giggled at his look of dismay. She kissed the crown of his head. The thick, curly hair he still kept cropped unfashionably short tickled her nose. He smelled like corn chaff.

"I love you, too, Papa."

A smile reached his eyes at last. "You're all the brightness in the world to me, my girl. Now get you to bed before that blazing moon has our rooster rashly commencing the morn."

"You, too, Papa. You had a long day."

She left him the letter. He seemed to need it more than she.

17

Storing Moon 1770

*T*he sun was bright, the sky a radiant blue. Good Voice straightened her back, raised the smoothed wooden pestle, and thumped it into the stump bowl, crushing parched corn into meal.

While she filled the cool autumn air with rhythmic pounding, Two Hawks sat beneath the lodge arbor attaching some of his hoarded metal arrow points to new shafts. Each of those points had killed rabbits, squirrels, and pheasants, now and then a turkey. He was turning out to be as good a hunter as his early skill with the bow had promised, though he longed for a musket like his father's—better still a rifle—which wasn't being put to best use since . . .

Do not think the worst, she admonished herself. Stone Thrower had taken the summer's deerskins to the traders at the Carry and was long in returning, but *maybe* he wouldn't drink or gamble them away and return with nothing to show but an aching head.

Clear Day still hunted, but Clear Day's eyes weren't sharp now and he often came back empty-handed. Two Hawks was taking up the slack. Or trying to. The more his father forgot his place as a man of the People, the more Two Hawks seemed determined to assume the role.

Pausing the grinding to rest her shoulders—she was just past two-and-thirty summers now and did not feel as young as she once had—she looked at her skinny, big-kneed son. He spent less time these days with the teacher, Fowler, though he'd gone to him that morning.

"You learn much words from the teacher?"

She'd asked the question in English. He looked up, but she couldn't read his expression for the arbor's shade. "Some," he said and dropped his gaze to his work.

Usually he was eager to tell her all his new words, trying them out in his voice that lately would crack, plunging without warning, then soar again, circling the edges of manhood like the hawks for which he was named. "Tell me," she prompted.

Two Hawks's hands stilled on the shaft he'd been tipping. He raised a troubled brow. "That one who is wife to the missionary, she asked about you today."

Good Voice raised the pestle and slammed it down again. Some moons ago, Samuel Kirkland had gone back east and returned with a wife called Jerusha. Good Voice found herself torn about it.

Two Hawks had obeyed his father in this one thing: he stayed away from the missionary, only learning English so he could speak it—to his brother one day, he said. Good Voice thought it was also so he could speak to the redcoat's daughter, whom she suspected he was still going to visit from time to time, though in this he did not obey his father. She was careful not to ask him about it.

When Two Hawks, Clear Day, and Stone Thrower returned the first time from Aubrey's farm to tell her they'd been too late, that He-Is-Taken was gone out of their reach again, she'd thought the guilt and disappointment would crush her. She had been glad she'd chosen to wait for them in Kanowalohale, once the decision was made to follow Kirkland's advice and tell Stone Thrower that Clear Day had seen their son.

Only one thing to come from that encounter with the girl, Anna Catherine, was good. Stone Thrower hadn't killed anyone. He'd wanted to, but Clear Day had made Stone Thrower promise he would do no violence before he agreed to show him the farm where He-Is-Taken lived.

Clear Day had wanted Kirkland to go along, to speak for them if it came to speaking, but Stone Thrower had refused to have him. Stone

Thrower's plan had been to go to that place and watch it, wait until those children Clear Day had seen came out to play. When they strayed near enough the wood's edge, Stone Thrower meant to dart out and take the boy, get him away so he could see his brother, see he had a twin called Two Hawks, see what he truly was, then bring him back to Good Voice.

But they'd found only the girl. Stone Thrower had wanted to take her instead, but Clear Day hadn't let him do it. Clear Day had brought along the white beads. What he hoped to do with them Good Voice hadn't known. If Stone Thrower wouldn't take them and be consoled about their missing son, did Clear Day think his nephew would offer them in peace to the redcoat who took that son?

To her surprise, Stone Thrower hadn't blamed her, or Clear Day, for not telling him where their son could be found sooner than they had. He blamed the missionary for how it had turned out. No amount of reasoning that Kirkland had nothing to do with Aubrey's wife taking their son across the sea could soften his heart against the man.

"If not Kirkland," Stone Thrower flung back, "then his god has done this bad thing. What sort of god keeps taking a son from the parents who want him back?"

Maybe Two Hawks felt the same. He spoke no bitter words, but he had no interest in hearing words of Heavenly Father. He was a watchful boy. Surely he could see the division Kirkland was causing between those who followed Jesus and those who clung to the old beliefs. A division Good Voice thought needless in some ways.

Kirkland seemed to think that following a Jesus path meant one had to follow a white path as well. She wished she had words to speak her heart about such matters, because she didn't agree. Why couldn't they have their Green Corn Festival, and their Giving Thanks Festival, and all the other ceremonies around the circle of the year, and give their thanks to Heavenly Father? Why couldn't they dance to Him, or beat the drums, or send their prayers up with pipe smoke?

Or maybe Two Hawks sensed the division in their own family—light
and darkness dwelling under the same roof—though of the two of them
who'd given their hearts to Heavenly Father, only Clear Day had confessed
to it.

That had been an ugly scene between Stone Thrower and his uncle—
one that happened soon after they returned with their bad news of He-Is-
Taken. The two had spoken little since then, so Good Voice dared not
admit her own heart's change.

Nor did she dare follow her heart about Jerusha Kirkland.

She'd watched the woman from afar, seen how she adapted to many
of their ways as her husband had before her. How those women who wor-
shiped Heavenly Father were welcomed into her home. Good Voice ached
to be among them. To know a woman who understood what it meant to
have faith and *walk in the light* and *wait on the Lord* and other stirring
words she'd heard Kirkland use those times she contrived to pass near
when he taught the people.

Now the woman was asking about her.

"What does that one say of me?" Good Voice asked, breathing hard
around the words as she went on with the grinding.

"She has asked more than one time—she catches me as I am leaving
Fowler's lodge—whether you are born of the People or . . . ?"

Good Voice brought the pestle down crooked but caught it before it
bounced out of her grip. That wasn't good, that question. Maybe it was
best she stay away. Maybe the woman would prove more meddler than
friend. "What do you tell her?"

"Nothing." He'd spoken of Jerusha in a defensive tone. Now curiosity
replaced it. "*Were* you born of the People?"

"I was not." She'd assumed he must have realized it long since,
though the fact she was born to whites wasn't a thing anyone mentioned. Perhaps, like most children with their mothers, he'd never seen

her as a person unto herself, with a history that started long before his own began.

He was waiting for her to say more.

"I do not know the people to whom I was born." She'd no memory of that mother and father, not their faces or their names, or the name they had called her. She'd been taken in a raid from the place the whites called Penn's Wood when she was two summers, maybe three, and given to a couple whose warrior sons had all been slain by settlers and themselves driven from their home on the Susquehanna, to live in Kanowalohale. They'd had a daughter too, one who died a girl. She'd been given the name of that girl, Good Voice. Her memories started there.

Those parents died soon after she and Stone Thrower married, leaving her with Bright Leaf, her mother's sister, who was also her mother in the way of the Haudenosaunee.

"I am sad my brother is being raised white," Two Hawks said after she finished her story.

"I thought you liked that *a'sluni* girl."

Two Hawks's expression softened. "She is good to see and talk to."

Good Voice was surprised by her son's unguarded words. Stone Thrower had made it clear his visits to Aubrey's land were done. Good Voice knew it drove daggers into his heart and brain to see that girl and listen to her talk of their son. He'd forbidden Two Hawks to go there without him.

This was the first her son had openly acknowledged his visits. She was glad he trusted her with the knowledge, but in truth it worried her, his sneaking off alone all that long way, three days of travel—maybe less for Two Hawks, who probably ran most of it—through wilderness with farms and settlements springing up like mushrooms after rain.

"Is that why you still learn English, to talk better with her?" Speaking openly of the girl reminded her that He-Is-Taken was unimaginably far away. *William.* That was how her firstborn was called among the whites. Was it a good name? Strong? Maybe, now that it was made open, she should get her son to repeat what that girl told him. Maybe it would be good for her heart to know about this *William.* Her son.

"It is one reason." Two Hawks looked at her, perhaps to see whether she was angry with him for disobeying his father. It could take a little coaxing now to get out of him what he was thinking. Not like when he was small.

Good Voice missed those days, wished she'd had more babies after the last one born too soon. But it was long since she'd wanted to share Stone Thrower's bed in that way. He lived in her lodge, ate at her fire, but was hardly a husband anymore.

Two Hawks got to his feet. "I am going hunting," he told her.

"Alone?" She suspected he hunted alone when he meant to see the girl.

"With someone. He is waiting."

"Ah?" When he didn't say who was waiting, Good Voice decided not to ask, though it was hard. "Good hunting then."

Her son smiled and went into the lodge for his bow.

After Two Hawks went off to meet whoever he was hunting with, Good Voice stopped grinding corn, overtaken by an impulse. She didn't pause to question it, knowing she'd talk herself out of it if she did. She put the meal she'd ground into a hide bag and set off toward the missionary's lodge.

Not since she crouched in darkness beneath the window two years past had she been back there. The heart that cracked open then was banging now as she came boldly in daylight and knocked on the door. Ten heartbeats later, Jerusha Kirkland opened the door. She was a small woman, young, with brown hair and eyes that widened at seeing who was at her door.

"It is you," said the missionary's wife, in careful Oneida. "Two Hawks's mother."

"I am that one's mother." Feeling heat wash through her, Good Voice thrust out the bag of meal and in English said, "I bring—this—you." She shook her head, frustrated. "My English much bad." It was better than that poor attempt, but she was rattled.

"Thank you, Good Voice," Jerusha Kirkland said, taking the gift of meal and answering in her native tongue. "And your English is fine, much better than my Oneida." She laughed, a pleasant sound. It made something tight inside Good Voice uncoil.

Other women's voices reached her. The missionary's wife already had visitors. Good Voice started to step away, but Jerusha put a hand to her arm. A very white hand.

The woman hesitated but only until Good Voice raised her eyes again. These the other woman searched. What did she see? The longing that had come over Good Voice, strong enough to drive her across the village to do this frightening thing? To offer trust.

"Some of the women are here," Jerusha said. "We're talking about the book of Proverbs, and I'm entertaining one and all with my attempts to speak your language. Will you join us?" She opened her door wide.

Good Voice hadn't caught every word the woman just said, but it was clear she was being invited to enter. With a look over her shoulder at the pines that secluded the cabin, and a heart pounding again like the pestle that had ground the meal in Jerusha Kirkland's grasp, Good Voice stepped across the threshold.

Two Hawks admired the rifle his new friend was aiming at a yellow leaf clinging to the lowest branch of a chestnut, some fifty paces away. The long leaf danced and fluttered in a chill breeze, smaller than the white tail of a deer. Tames-His-Horse lowered the rifle without firing. Shooting a target when they needed meat would warn every animal within hearing there were hunters in the wood. Grinning at the other boy, Two Hawks raised his bow and sent an arrow flying. It took the yellow leaf with it in its passage deeper into the wood.

"You are good with that bow," the other boy said. "But you should get yourself a rifle. Bring home bigger game than rabbits, eh?"

Tames-His-Horse was a Wolf Clan Mohawk from up north on the St. Lawrence River. Though barely sixteen summers, he was the tallest Indian Two Hawks had ever seen but so skinny he looked like a giant stick bug walking around. He'd come to Kanowalohale to be with his father's people for a while. Two Hawks had met him while learning English with Fowler.

"I could get a deer with this bow." Two Hawks tried not to sound boastful because it was a thing he'd yet to do. Maybe hunting with Tames-His-Horse would bring him that lucky kill. The Mohawk was a good hunter and didn't mind hunting with a younger boy. But there was another reason Two Hawks had asked him to go hunting.

Since coming to Kanowalohale, Tames-His-Horse had been having dreams—dreams that were coming true, with no help from him or anyone else. Like that dream he'd had of a flood overtaking the town. Sometime later beavers—an animal so hunted it hadn't been seen nearby for years—moved in and dammed Oneida Creek, and a heavy summer rain caused it to overrun its banks in the night, near some low-lying lodges on the outskirts. One of those had flooded, but the woman whose lodge it was got her food stores and belongings out in time because she'd heeded the dream and watched the creek.

Not all Tames-His-Horse's dreams warned of bad things. Once he dreamed that a woman in his father's clan had born a girl child. This woman had been married three times, with no babies to show for it, and was almost past the age she could expect to have a child. But sometime after that dream was told to her, she discovered that at last a child was on the way. No one knew if it would be a girl, but many were laying wagers on it.

Two Hawks wanted to talk about his father's dreams.

They'd been stalking deer for two days, following game trails to watering holes they both knew. Neither had yet to kill a deer, but they were enjoying the hunt. Two Hawks had shot a rabbit the evening before, which they'd shared over a companionable fire.

They walked together down the arrow's path, hoping to recover it, and since the sun was high in the sky and the chances of finding deer before evening low, Two Hawks decided now was the time to bring up that other matter.

"If I tell you a thing, can you keep it to yourself?"

Tames-His-Horse, who'd been scuffing a moccasin through leaves, searching the place where they thought the arrow must have landed, looked over at him. "I can do that."

"It is about dreams."

The Mohawk's brows rose. "Mine? Or yours?"

"Neither. I have dreams, but I never remember them. Not like you."

"Be glad you do not."

Two Hawks wasn't sure what to say. Did Tames-His-Horse not like having dreams that came true? They brought him attention, but maybe that wasn't always a good thing.

"My father has dreams. Ones no one wants to help him see come true."

Tames-His-Horse hadn't heard the story of Fort William Henry. It wasn't much talked about now, only sometimes when people shook their heads at his father's bad behavior, giving the tired old excuse.

"My father dreams of killing that redcoat," he said, after finishing the story of his lost twin. "All these years later he is still dreaming it." Two Hawks frowned over memories of his father shouting in the night, waking from the dream to seethe and rant about it. But that redcoat wasn't just a monster from a dream now. Two Hawks's mouth went dry at what he was about to ask. "Do *you* think my father's dream should be made to come true?"

His heart beat heavy as he thought of Anna Catherine.

Tames-His-Horse frowned, looking as if he was going to think about it for a while before he answered.

Stifling impatience, Two Hawks busied himself scouring the surrounding wood. Leaves lay scattered bright on the ground, yellow, ochre . . . red as spilled blood. Maybe it hadn't been good to ask this Mohawk. Yes, he had dreams that came true, but he wasn't an old man, not a sachem wise with years. He'd half decided the older boy didn't intend to answer at all when Tames-His-Horse spoke.

"Our people say it is wrong for dreams to go unrealized. Not good for the dreamer. Not lucky. But others have things to say about dreams."

"Others? You mean Fowler and Kirkland?"

"And the book Kirkland has. That book has a lot to say about dreams."

"Does it?" Two Hawks had heard some of what was supposedly in that book—he hadn't yet learned to read a word of it; perhaps he ought to—but he hadn't heard anything about dreams.

In the dappled forest light, Tames-His-Horse's eyes were bright. "There is one in the book who had dreams sent by his god. He was a slave, but he had power. He could also tell others what their dreams meant. When those dreams came to pass as he said they would, the people made him a chief, and that way his own dreams came true. That one was called Joseph."

"Huh," Two Hawks said. "Do you think my father's dreams of killing the redcoat are sent by Kirkland's god?"

Tames-His-Horse thought about that, but not for long. "There is something else in that book, something about thoughts—and dreams are a kind of thoughts, yes? It says all thoughts must be held up to Heavenly Father's words in the book to know if they are from Him or are only bad thoughts from our own spirits."

Two Hawks felt his lip pull back. "Are you one of them? a Christian?"

"No," Tames-His-Horse said. "I am thinking about such things. That is all."

"I don't want to think about them." Two Hawks heard the anger in his voice. "I want my father to be at peace and my brother returned to us."

Tames-His-Horse looked at him searchingly. "Little Brother, do *you* want your father to kill the redcoat?"

He didn't. For then he would have to see Anna Catherine cry. He would have to see her warm gaze turn cold. Turn to hate. What else would she feel if his father killed her father?

"Ha," Tames-His-Horse said. "Your arrow!" The Mohawk snatched it from a mossy bank and held it out, its shaft still piercing the yellow leaf.

Two Hawks took it but didn't answer the question.

Good Voice found it easier to knock on Jerusha Kirkland's cabin door the second time. She'd found the woman alone, and together they'd found their way through each other's language to something that might one day be friendship. Jerusha didn't ask how Good Voice came to be Oneida—the question she had asked Two Hawks—but before it was time to return to her work, Good Voice offered the story.

"Thank you," Jerusha said as Good Voice was leaving her lodge.

"For what?"

"For telling me your story. Will you tell me another thing?"

Good Voice lingered on the doorstep, wary. "What thing?"

"Are you happy with your life?"

Good Voice knew what Jerusha was asking. Often it was hard for whites to believe someone of their kind adopted and raised one of the People might want to remain as they were, and though there were reasons she could say *no* to the question, none of them had to do with who she was—Good Voice of the Turtle Clan. "I am much happy as *Onyota'a:ka.*"

This had satisfied Jerusha, Good Voice thought, as she passed through the pines near the lodge, but it had stirred up troubling thoughts in her own mind. She was content—aside from the trouble Stone Thrower caused, aside from the ache of her lost son. But what about that son, living across an ocean? Was *he* content with what he was becoming? Did he ever feel a lack, a longing? Did he sense there was a mother who—

The bruising grip on her forearm yanked her nearly off her feet.

She cried out, assaulted by the reek of spirits and musky unwashed male before her eyes could focus on the face of her husband, looking at her in disbelief.

"What were you doing in the missionary's lodge?"

Not waiting for an answer, Stone Thrower hauled on her arm, pulling her out of sight of the cabin where her friend had already shut the door. Good Voice went without struggle. She didn't want Jerusha Kirkland to see her husband drunk.

She'd let him tow her back to her lodge, where their argument went back and forth and ended in her enduring his many excuses for why once again he'd little to show for the hides taken to the Carry. "But see—I have brought you a deer." Stone Thrower's words slurred as he pointed at the butchered carcass lying by the fire. "Already skinned, ready to cook. And I am hungry."

She set about the work of a wife, put some of the venison over the fire to roast, before she saw to the hide and the rest of the meat. Her arm where he'd grabbed her throbbed. She could smell him more in the closeness of the lodge, wanted to tell him to go to the creek and clean himself, but didn't.

She tried to talk to Heavenly Father about him, tried to pray in the way Jerusha had demonstrated to her. Her mind was a turmoil.

"Where is my son? Not gone to see that *a'sluni* girl, has he?"

Good Voice's stomach clenched. "He is away hunting with a friend. Three days now."

Stone Thrower made a scoffing noise. "What good will that do anyone? Those boys will scare off the game and make it harder for the men to find anything."

That boy has been doing the work of a man I could name, Good Voice thought, but the smarting of her arm warned her to silence. He'd bruised her so once before, too drunk to know his strength. She didn't think he would do worse, but . . . *Heavenly Father, I do not know how to be at peace with this man anymore. Can You do anything with him?*

Stone Thrower went out. Moments later he came back in. She heard his stomach gurgling. "Is that meat done?"

He was eating some of it half-raw when the door hide shifted and Two Hawks came in with his bow and a brace of rabbits. Good Voice saw his face stiffen at sight of his father at the fire.

Stone Thrower turned toward the door, venison grease shiny on his chin. "Rabbits again? Maybe one day you will get a deer, eh? Like the one I have brought home. A good deer."

Two Hawks laid the rabbits beside the door. He made for his sleeping bench to hang up his bow. "Maybe if I had a rifle I might be a better hunter."

"A boy has no need of a rifle." Stone Thrower took another bite of venison and chewed, not looking at the son who was looking at him, angry and hurt, and longing.

"I am not a boy," he said, sounding half-strangled. "And you—" He stopped himself, catching Good Voice's warning look. They spoke behind Stone Thrower's back with their eyes, hers pleading. *Let him be the one who knows it all. This will pass.* But for a while it would be like trying to walk on clacking beach stones in silence.

Good Voice offered her son some of the meat. As he reached for it, his gaze fell to her arm. Too quick to stop him, he turned over the white underside where the bruises were starting to darken.

"I am going to the creek." Stone Thrower got up and went out. He didn't see Two Hawks's eyes following him. When the hide fell shut, her son's gaze met hers.

"He did this?"

She pulled away. "He did not mean to. I went to the missionary's lodge, and he saw me. He was upset. Now . . . eat."

Two Hawks wouldn't take the meat. Wouldn't even look at it. "Has he ever hit you?"

For the first time in his life, she couldn't hold her child's gaze. "Never."

"Are you telling me the truth?"

She looked at him, a skinny boy with the eyes of a man, resolute and angry, and in her mind one thought screamed. *Do not get between us. You would be like a reed before a trampling horse.*

"I am telling you the truth." She put all the conviction she could summon behind the words, more frightened by her son's hard gaze turned toward the swaying door hide than she'd ever been of his father.

18

Green Corn Moon 1771

*I*t happened in a place called Crickhowell, near where my brother lives. The young men of that place wanted to see who could shoot an arrow farthest from one of their grandfathers' war bows. Many tried, but William's arrow went the farthest. That is what he put in a letter to Anna Catherine."

Two Hawks, fresh from seeing the girl who called He-Is-Taken *brother,* had been talking since he stepped from the forest near the field where Good Voice picked beans from the vines coiling up around the cornstalks. She dropped a handful into the basket he now held for her. The corn, beans, and squash spread around them in the heat-shimmered air, giving privacy for this talk neither meant other ears to hear.

It was Bright Leaf's portion of the field she gleaned. Bright Leaf was unwell, too tired to pick what she planted in spring. It was a worry at the back of Good Voice's mind as she stepped over squash vines to the next hillock. In the front of her mind were the feelings that always tangled inside her when Two Hawks had been to see that girl.

"My brother has decided on what he means to do. *Read law at Oxford.*" Two Hawks spoke the phrase in careful English. It sent a shiver up Good Voice's spine, despite the day's heavy warmth. Was that how He-Is-Taken sounded when he spoke?

She cast a look at her son. "Oxford?"

"It is a place of learning they have in England."

Good Voice snapped off another handful of beans and motioned her son to bring the basket near. "Is he not in a place called Wales?"

"Yes, but England is close by. Like Onondaga land is to us." Two Hawks grinned, baring straight white teeth. "Anna Catherine asked to shoot an arrow with *my* bow. She said if William and I could do it, she ought to be able." He laughed, as if the memory amused him.

"Bring the basket closer," Good Voice said. "Did she shoot an arrow?"

"All of them." Two Hawks picked his way through the vines to her side, the planes of his face gleaming in the sun's warmth.

He was growing very handsome, her son.

"The bow was hard for her to draw. She said how strong I must be to pull it back as far as I do," he added, with a look of pleasure his mother didn't miss. "I laughed when she tried. I could not help it! My laughing made her more determined, and before we stopped she hit the target I made. Though if it had been a deer, it would have been its tail. Ha!"

Speaking of deer made her wonder if her son had pulled himself away from this girl long enough to kill a deer and bring her the meat and hide. Good Voice observed the flush under his skin—a flush not put there by the summer heat.

Once she'd asked him whether seeing that girl was a hard thing to do. Two Hawks had held her gaze for a moment; she'd seen in his eyes the same tangle of feeling that lived in her. He had simply made a different choice about it. "Do you never wish to go and talk to her yourself?" he'd asked. "You would not need to tell her who you are—that much my father is right to forbid—only that you are my mother."

"It is a thing I might do, if I thought it would not bring a pain so great that . . ." But she hadn't been able even to speak of it. And that was only one reason—the pain talking to that girl about her son would bring her. There were others.

It was one thing for Two Hawks to disobey his father. One day he would leave them, be his own person, a warrior who decided for himself. It could be said that she might do likewise, risk angering Stone Thrower—to a point where he did her harm—by going to see the girl. She had the right to do that. And perhaps he wouldn't harm her. Perhaps it would only be the thing that ended their marriage.

But she didn't want to see even that happen, not if she could help it. She'd decided it was best this way, to let Two Hawks use the need for hunting to cover his coming and going to see that girl. She still got to hear, in much detail, everything she told him. Though lately he was talking more and more about the girl herself.

"Is she pretty, this girl?"

She spoke as though inquiring whether it might soon rain. Despite her seeming indifference, Two Hawks hesitated. Then, as if he couldn't hold his peace he said, "She has this hair, long and thick. Like dark honey from a bee tree. Honey with the sun shining through it."

Good Voice blinked, taken aback. She'd thought white women kept their hair covered. Even white girls. "You have seen her hair all down?"

"The first time I saw her, when we were small. But sometimes her braid hangs down. It is thick as my arm."

Good Voice cut another look at her son. Two Hawks had just marked fourteen summers, and his bones were growing fast again. He was taller now than she, though not as tall as his father. Not many moons from now he would be.

When had Two Hawks stopped being her little boy and become the young man standing there telling her about people she didn't know, about that other son she'd carried nine moons in her belly, fourteen years in her heart? That was how it was with children. In the mind they stayed small, their heads down around your knees, your hips. Then one day you turned around to find they'd stretched toward the sky like cornstalks.

He-Is-Taken would be as tall now. Then she thought, *My son in a white man's school, learning white man's law!*

"William says in his letters he misses Anna Catherine," Two Hawks said, picking up on her change of mood as he was wont to do. "He says . . ."

Good Voice paused in her picking. Hard as it was to be separated from her firstborn, to depend on others who had no right to it for these scraps of him, she was greedy for those scraps. "What does he say?"

Two Hawks looked away. "He misses Aubrey. He calls him *Father*."

Good Voice felt the breath rush out of her, as if a weight had hit her in the back. Maybe that was one thing she needn't have known. She turned her attention to the beans.

"Why do you think it happened this way?" Two Hawks asked. "That just when we found him he was taken away again."

Good Voice dropped the beans she held into the basket and met her son's searching gaze. For many moons she'd wrestled in prayer with that very question. *Why.* She wanted to speak comforting words to her son about trusting God's path for them. Trusting His goodness. But how was she to begin when she'd never told anyone about her choice to follow the Jesus path? Not even Jerusha Kirkland. Before she could find words, Two Hawks spoke again.

"Clear Day says if we let Jesus give us new hearts, He will work all things out for good. Even bad things."

Good Voice's mouth dropped open in surprise. It was as if her son had read her mind. "You have spoken to Clear Day about such things?"

Two Hawks shrugged. "He is like you."

"What do you mean, like me?"

"He does not mind talking about William, so . . . sometimes we do." Two Hawks averted his gaze. "It is good to have a man to talk to. He knows I see Anna Catherine. He thinks it good that I do so, that I make a friend of her."

"That is what my Jesus-praying uncle thinks?" said a voice from the edge of the cornfield.

Good Voice's belly made a sickening drop as Stone Thrower strode toward them, staggering a little, heedless of the squash vines he trampled. The smell of rum and sour sweat hit Good Voice like a wall.

Stone Thrower settled his glare on Two Hawks. "You have gone back to see that girl when I said we were finished with it. Do not lie and say you have not done so."

Good Voice stepped forward, touching Two Hawks's rigid arm. "It is my fault. I let him go and said nothing—"

Stone Thrower raised his hand. "Let this son of mine talk for himself."

Still clutching the gathering basket, face as rigid as his limbs, Two Hawks said, "I was not going to lie. I have been to see her."

Stone Thrower's eyes narrowed. "Has your brother returned?"

"No."

"Then why do you go?"

Color crept into Two Hawks's face. "I want to know about William. Anna Catherine reads his letters to me."

"*William.*" Stone Thrower spat the name. "Is it only for news of your brother you go? Or do you wish to see that girl?"

Other women in the field, those within hearing, had stopped working to look their way.

"Husband," Good Voice began.

Stone Thrower silenced her with a look. "You will have your chance to explain why you kept this from me. Let *him* speak now."

Two Hawks gripped the gathering basket. "Anna Catherine is my friend."

"She is nothing to you!" Stone Thrower shouted in an explosion of stinking breath. "Or am I to lose another son to these thieving whites? Look at you," his lip curled in derision, "picking beans like a woman!"

He struck the basket from Two Hawks's grasp. Beans rained over the ground as the basket tumbled into the vines. Murmurs of disapproval rose among the women looking on, but none came nearer. This was a family quarrel. They would not interfere unless things got out of hand.

"You will go no more to that girl," Stone Thrower said. "I heard it from her mouth that it would be years before He-Is-Taken returns. You have no business with her now."

Two Hawks held his peace, but Good Voice saw the defiance in his face. So did his father. "Tell me you will obey me in this!"

Two Hawks said nothing. Stone Thrower lunged forward and shoved their son. Caught off guard, Two Hawks staggered back but didn't fall.

"Answer me!"

Shock froze Good Voice where she stood. As often as her husband had been angry-drunk, he had never laid a hand on their son. She ground her teeth as something fierce came writhing up from the center of her, pushing back the shock.

Two Hawks stood straight. "It is not your place anymore to tell me *stay* or *go*. I am a man now."

"You are a foolish boy!" Stone Thrower made to lunge past Good Voice, fist pulled back to strike. That fierceness writhing inside her burst forth in a scream as she stepped between them.

There were two blows. One from Stone Thrower's fist in her face, the other from the ground when her head hit it. Then all was spinning, corn and sky, sky and corn, moccasined feet and faces . . . all spinning into darkness.

The sun that had shone upon his father's shame had set, but the long summer twilight lingered. There was light for Two Hawks to follow his father through the town. Light, but little color. Color had leached from the world like the happiness that had leached from Two Hawks's heart. He burned with the image of his mother's battered face. That blow had been meant for him. He wished he'd taken it. With all his heart he wished it.

Stone Thrower walked away through the town, past lodges where women scowled after him and children stopped playing to watch him pass. Old men shook their heads. Two Hawks wanted to scream at them to look away but did not. He followed, the scene in the field repeating in his mind. His mother crumpled on the ground among the squash vines. His father standing over her, breathing hard, bewilderment on his face, as if he couldn't fathom how she came to be lying at his feet. Rage had filled Two Hawks, but before he could unlock his frozen limbs to attack his father, Stone Thrower had fallen to his knees.

"Good Voice—open your eyes! Good Voice!" His mother only moaned and fluttered her eyelids.

Stone Thrower had risen with her in his arms while the women came running to hover and scold and tell him not to move her. Ignoring them, he'd carried Good Voice to their lodge, leaving Two Hawks to trail behind with the rage banked within his heart.

Near sunset Good Voice regained her senses—enough to stand on her feet and gather his father's things and put them outside the door hide. Stone Thrower stood outside and watched her do it.

Two Hawks had watched his father, seen the desolation on his face. It satisfied some of the rage inside him, but not enough. Not nearly enough. So he followed his father now. Straight to the lodge of the missionary.

In the years since Samuel Kirkland came among them, he'd proved himself a man strong-minded, convinced his God was the only way to happiness in the Time After, that apart from Jesus there would be something called hell-and-damnation, which to hear Kirkland talk sounded like being pushed into a fire and held there screaming. Two Hawks had asked Clear Day how the missionary knew this, having never died.

"It says it in the book," Clear Day said. That seemed to be all the answer Kirkland needed to believe a thing. If it was in the book, it was true.

Two Hawks was less sure.

But Kirkland had proved he cared what happened to them in *this* life too. He cared that their crops failed, that game was gone from the forests and there was never enough to eat, that their kin on the southern border were murdered by settlers greedy for land. He did what he could about it, sharing all that was given him from his friends in the east, writing to those people to try to make the bad things better. He was a good man, in his sometimes prickly way. Many of the people loved him.

Stone Thrower wasn't one of those. That was why Two Hawks expected his father was going to the missionary now to do him harm. But the missionary wasn't at his lodge. Two Hawks watched from the pines as his father pounded on the door, calling out to him.

The light had not yet faded, though stars were in the sky, when his father headed off into the woods, down a path that led toward a little stream that ran into Oneida Creek. There on the path he met Kirkland coming up from the stream with a bucket.

Stone Thrower didn't pull the hatchet from his sash and raise it against the missionary, as Two Hawks had expected. He only raised his voice. He had just lost everything that mattered to him in this life, his father told the missionary. Now he wanted to know how to go back and start over. Was there a way to do that?

Hunkered in the brush along the path, Two Hawks couldn't see his father's face, only Kirkland's. The man stood with creek water dripping on his shoes and started doing that thing called *preaching,* only he did it in a voice like a man would use to talk to another man. He told his father about the consequences of *sin,* that the only way to walk a right path from that point was to repent of sin—to be sorry for it and resolve to stop doing it—ask for Heavenly Father's forgiveness through the blood of Jesus-on-the-cross. Then go and do his best to sin no more. If sin happened anyway—as it would because no man except Jesus was perfect—then ask for Heavenly

Father's forgiveness again and be glad the blood of Jesus covered that new sin too.

"That is what God's mercy does. But it does not mean a man can go on sinning and never suffer consequences," Kirkland cautioned. "Like what has happened to you and the woman who was your wife—yes, already I have heard what happened in the field today. I am sorry for it, but I am not surprised. I have watched you and seen how you have struggled in your own strength to be a good man. But the grief of the past has hardened your heart and crippled your soul. You need the strength of Jesus in you, the power of His Spirit, to be the man you want to be, the man your family needs you to be."

Looking like the one who had been struck in the head, Stone Thrower left the missionary and went back to Good Voice's lodge. Two Hawks followed again, ready to defend his mother if his father made more trouble. But his father only gathered his things and went away. That was the last Two Hawks saw of him that day. And many days after.

Later he learned Stone Thrower had built himself a bark hut at the edge of the village. He stopped drinking rum, as far as Two Hawks could tell. When he had meat, he left it outside their lodge. For a time it seemed he was seeking that good path he'd walked in the years before they learned Two Hawks's brother had again been taken away. That he would do the one thing needful to make Good Voice want him back as husband.

Two Hawks learned what that thing was in late summer, before his mother's face fully healed. The day Bright Leaf died. They were with her when it happened, Two Hawks and Good Voice, and some of their Turtle Clan kin, gathered to say good-bye, to see Bright Leaf on her journey.

"You must forget that man," Bright Leaf labored to say from her pallet by the fire. She reached a shaking hand to touch Two Hawks's bony wrist. "He who gave you this good son . . . gives you nothing else but grief. Find . . . a better . . . husband."

Good Voice told her dying aunt she wanted no other husband. She didn't want Stone Thrower either unless he did what Clear Day had done, what she herself had done.

That was how Two Hawks learned his mother was a Jesus follower.

Soon after, Bright Leaf died.

His father didn't embrace the missionary's God. Sometime when the leaves began to color, he abandoned his bark hut and went to live with his friends among the Seneca, those he'd fought beside years ago when Pontiac had his war.

"To clear his head of too much talk." That was how Clear Day told them his father explained his going. "He took the white beads I have kept for his condolence," the old man said, and for a moment Good Voice looked hopeful. But Clear Day shook his head. "To bury them out of sight where they will never again be found. That is what he told me."

Stone Thrower never meant to forgive or forget.

Neither now did Two Hawks.

19

March 1772

*M*ary Margaret Tiller entered the world with less fuss and bother than most firstborns, Lydia confided afterward. Anna, who couldn't stop her hands shaking as she wrung soiled rags in a water bucket, asked, "How many births have you attended now?"

It was the latest in a string of questions begun when a messenger had arrived at Lydia's door with news of Mrs. Tiller's confinement.

Lydia paused in returning supplies to a wooden medical case to gaze at a wall sconce flickering in the passage near the bedroom where the drama had unfolded, her brows drawn in thought. "This will have been my twelfth. And by far the easiest."

"Easy?" Anna dropped her voice. "I was terrified for Mrs. Tiller."

And yet, now the labor was past, she wasn't shaking with fear so much as wonder. And excitement. It had been the most thrilling experience of her life—excepting the day she met Two Hawks.

"If you were afraid, you hid it well, though I've never seen your eyes so big as when the baby's head crowned." Lydia smiled as they worked, seeming as buoyed as Anna by the happy murmurs from the room beyond. "Be glad you weren't with me at the first birth I attended."

"I am," Anna replied. "Although . . . it turned out all right in the end."

She knew the story well, how on a summer evening two years past a pair of children burst into the apothecary where Lydia had been rolling pills—Jacob had been out with a homebound patient. The near hysterical children, who'd recognized the apothecary's shingle above the door, had begged her to come help their dying mama.

They'd led her to a rickety structure on the outskirts of town, long since sprawled beyond the stockade. Lydia had wondered if anyone knew the fatherless family was living in what amounted to an abandoned cow shed, but that hadn't mattered at the time. The mother—in travail and exhausted from the fruitless effort—*had* seemed near death.

Lydia sent the oldest child after the nearest midwife, hoping she'd be found to home. Meanwhile she determined the baby was trying to be born feet first. It was too far along in the process to think of turning the child—had Lydia known how. By God's grace she'd delivered the baby alive and whole, kept the mother this side of heaven as well, in time for the midwife to arrive and help clean up, quiz Lydia as to the baby's presentation and her actions, and welcome her into the exclusive company of midwives, should she wish to practice the trade.

"Either you're blessed with the luck of angels," the midwife told her frankly, "or you've found your calling."

Lydia had known which it was. While the birth was unnerving, attending it had fulfilled that incessant, lifelong hunger to heal, to make whole. The next several births she'd attended as a midwife's apprentice had sealed the decision. Not until the fifth had she seen a baby die. Though hopelessly premature, Lydia had grieved the tiny girl.

But not as deeply as she grieved now.

It was barely a fortnight since Jacob van Bergen, carried off by an acute wasting sickness that had taken him in a matter of months, had left Lydia widowed at twenty-six.

And childless, Anna couldn't help thinking while they bid farewell to tiny Mary Margaret and stepped into the afternoon, hoods thrown back to welcome the weak sunlight. That Lydia's brief marriage had produced no children while she'd helped so many into the world pierced Anna's heart even as the March air stung her cheeks.

Melting snow lay in dingy piles in front of shops and homes. The Til-lers' house was two streets over from Lydia's. Between them lay the apoth-ecary. As the shingle bearing her late husband's name came into view, Lydia cast the shop a glance of longing but passed it without speaking.

What would happen to the shop, now there was no apothecary? Though Lydia hadn't spoken of it, she was surely thinking of it. Anna often heard her up and about in the night, though such nocturnal stirring wasn't always for worry or grief. Anna was surprised to learn how often women called on Lydia for remedies for ailing children and husbands, or advice on issues too delicate to mention to a physician. All of which Lydia now dispensed from her kitchen, trading simples and receipts for the oc-casional small coin, foodstuffs, or words of condolence.

Papa had been the one to suggest Anna stay with Lydia for a few weeks after Jacob's burial. Though she'd found herself intrigued by all Lydia knew of herbs and tinctures and decoctions, and was eager to set her hands to any practical task to be of help, Anna longed to be of consolation as well. But what did she know of grief? She still had a father—the only one she could remember. And if William's absence was a perpetual ache, she had the comfort of his letters. And she had Two Hawks.

In the entryway of the house, they shed cloaks and pattens, then trooped to the kitchen to tidy away supplies. Lydia immediately restocked her midwifery case and then pronounced, "I could do with some tea," and set about stoking the fire and putting the kettle over it.

Anna cut slices from a loaf and set the bread on a plate. They took their meals in the kitchen since most of their time was spent near the hearth.

"I remember this kitchen from when we lived here," Anna said, com-ing back from a pantry shelf with a jar of apple butter. "My very first memory is a puddle of sunlight and William sitting in it with those sol-diers of his. He let me hold one."

Lydia looked up from arranging cups and tea leaves. "That was the day Reginald returned from the war. You would've been . . . three years old?"

"I mostly remember the soldiers." And William's mother taking the one out of her hand, but she didn't mention that. "Will you see Mrs. Tiller and her baby again?"

She hoped so, and that Lydia might let her go along.

The fire cracked. Sparks sifted over the hearth bricks. Lydia grabbed a twig broom and swept them back, then straightened with a faraway look in her eyes. "I'll stop by tomorrow, as often after that as seems needful. Sometimes . . ."

"Sometimes?" Anna prompted.

Lydia blinked, giving her a rueful smile. "I must be tired. My thoughts have scattered."

More likely other thoughts were demanding her attention. "You sit down. Let me finish."

The kettle was aboil. Anna took a cloth to grasp it and poured steaming water for the tea. Lydia spread apple butter on a slice of bread, raised it to her mouth, then put it down without taking a bite and looked across the table at Anna. "I mean to sell the shop."

Anna set down the kettle on a tail of the cloth. "Oh, Lydia. Must you?"

"What else can I do? I cannot be an apothecary—not with a shingle." Lydia glanced at the shelves, cupboards, and chests crowding the kitchen, overflowing with the shop's former medicinal stock. Fragrant herbs hung from ceiling beams. Jars and crocks and corked glass bottles adorned every sill and surface. "I'll treat any of Jacob's patients who'll let me, along with the midwifing, but I'll do the work from here. I can manage if I sell the shop and the lot on which it stands." Lydia's eyes gleamed. "But it will be like losing Papa again."

"And Mr. van Bergen," Anna said before thinking.

Lydia's eyes softened. "And Jacob." Her mouth trembled briefly, then steadied, as if by an effort of will. She looked at Anna, and her gaze cleared. "You owned that what you experienced today unnerved you. 'Tis perfectly natural it would."

"It was overwhelming," Anna admitted. "But not in a *bad* way. I don't know if I can find words to adequately explain it."

"You may never find them," Lydia said, as if she knew. "But then again, you might. I'm wondering, Anna . . . how adverse would you be to experiencing it again?"

"I—experiencing it again? You'd want that? My helping you?"

"I would," Lydia said. "Very much. If you want it."

Anna didn't know why she was so surprised. It felt as though part of her had been anticipating the question since they left the Tillers' home. And yet . . . it felt a little like that birth had felt. Thrilling *and* terrifying. Anna felt herself poised, as though come abruptly to a chasm in her path, a divide she hadn't expected. Looking across, she measured the distance. A prodigious leap, but on the other side stood Lydia, holding out a hand. How often had she run into Lydia's arms and found safety there. Solace. Love.

She met Lydia's gaze, a host of feelings welling. Curiosity. Fear. But growing stronger all the while . . . eagerness.

"I wouldn't be at all adverse to that."

For the first time since Jacob's burial, a heaviness seemed to lift from Lydia. The smile she gave Anna was like the sun peeking through grim clouds. "It's what I hoped you'd say, my girl. Finish your tea, then we'll go down to the Binne Kill and talk to your father about it."

The river ice had thawed, sending the floes that jammed the current downstream to the falls above the Hudson. Despite the lingering snow on its banks, the smell of the river was strong along the quay where several bateaux were being loaded for the season's first trip upriver. With a bursting energy at odds with his white hair, Captain Lang paced the quay near Papa's boatyard, cargo list in hand, checking poles and rigging, overseeing the crewmen stowing crates and barrels into the flat-bottomed, shallow-draft bateaux.

One crewman was a young man, no more than eighteen, a stranger to Anna. Pink-cheeked from exertion and the brisk air, he'd a longish face, blond hair tailed back, and a smile he flashed at Anna over a hefted crate as she and Lydia passed on their way to Papa's warehouse.

Warmth bloomed in Anna's cheeks as Lydia, with a narrowed glance at the young man, hustled her inside.

The front portion of the warehouse contained the rooms where Papa conducted business, while the larger, rear portion was given to storage and the workshop with its broad doors opening onto the waterfront, where he built his boats. While any skilled carpenter could cobble together a serviceable bateau, Papa was a true craftsman. His bateaux were prized for their clean lines and durability.

As they entered, he was talking to a tradesman Anna recognized from their church meeting. She and Lydia waited for the man to conclude his business. After he left, lifting his hat in passing, Lydia said, "Have we come at an inopportune time, Reginald?"

"Not at all." Papa came to greet them, his gaze on Lydia soft with sympathy. "They were lined up deep this morning, the merchants. I'm sending only two boats, in case the river is still blocked. But canoes have come down, and from what I hear 'tis clear to Herkimer's Carry." Dismissing matters of business, he asked, "To what do I owe this pleasure, ladies?"

"I—" Grinning sidelong at Anna, Lydia amended, "*We* have come with a proposal to present to you."

After the heaviness of Jacob's passing, it was good to see Lydia's smile. Papa's face lit at the sight. "A proposal, is it? Come you back to the sitting room then, where a fire's on the grate, and tell me of it."

Seated in the snug, green-paneled room behind the office, Lydia came to the point. "I propose taking on Anna as my apprentice. Provided we have your blessing, of course."

Anna stared, along with Papa. Then she leapt to her feet. "I thought you only meant I should accompany you if I happened to be in town during a confinement. You want me for an *apprentice*?"

"If I'm not being too precipitous?" Lydia asked, her smile dimming just a bit. "I meant soon to find a younger woman to train beside me, but I confess for a while now I've hoped it could be you."

That Lydia should place such confidence in her left her struggling for words. "I—I want to be, but I don't know whether I've the passion for it you do. I wouldn't want to disappoint . . ."

Lydia reached for her hand. "Dear girl, you could never do that. But is this something you'd like to try, at least?"

"I do want to try." She turned at last to Papa, sitting in his chair like one stunned. "Papa, may I? Please?"

His mouth moved, but at first no words came.

"You've taken me quite unawares, the two of you." His gaze sought Lydia's. "I take it you'd wish her to live in town with you."

Anna drew a sharpened breath. Live in town? Away from the farm?

Two Hawks. She'd gone to the woods frequently the previous year, hoping he would be there, but had seen him only twice. Both times without his father. She'd hoped with spring's coming to once again find him waiting for her across the creek. She'd missed him.

"We hadn't discussed that detail," Lydia said, noting her hesitation. "I wanted to know your mind on the matter first."

"I see," Papa said.

Their gazes shifted to Anna, who found herself in turmoil. All she could see in that moment was Two Hawks waiting for her at the wood's edge, never knowing why she didn't come, giving up on her. Never coming back . . .

"Lydia . . . might I be your apprentice and still live at the farm? I could ride in with Papa when he comes to work and go home with him at day's ending."

Papa stood and put an arm around her, drawing her to his side. "I'd determined to put a brave face on it, but I own the thought of you no longer under my roof wasn't going down easy. I'm touched you feel the same."

Smiling at the two of them, Lydia rose. Anna couldn't meet their gazes. Truly she didn't want to live away from Papa, but thought of never seeing Two Hawks again had filled her with an alarming desperation—near to what she'd felt at William's leaving.

Papa gave her shoulders a squeeze. "Well now, what say you? Shall we give the arrangement a trial? Say, three days in the week to begin with?"

Lydia agreed. "It suits splendidly for a beginning."

Papa's eyes shone down at Anna. "However did you grow up without my noticing?"

Breathing easier, Anna tried to suppress a smile. "I'm not *so* grown."

"Fifteen." Papa said it as if he mistrusted the number.

"There's another matter I meant to discuss with you, Reginald," Lydia said. "If you've a moment more to spare."

Sensing she wasn't vital to whatever that discussion entailed, Anna—content to speculate happily on all that was to come—left them to it and drifted to the outer office. A window fronted the quay. She found a place where she could see Captain Lang and his crew loading the last of their cargo and found herself watching the blond-haired young man who'd smiled at her so boldly. Behind her in the sitting room, Lydia was telling Papa about her decision to sell the shop.

"Look you, Lydia . . . would you permit me to buy it?" Papa replied. "Not just from you, but for you?"

Anna turned her back on the window, more interested in this development than the scene out on the quay.

"Reginald . . . I didn't mean to ask that of you."

"Nor have you, see. I know what that shop means to you. One day, when you're able, you may buy it back from me. If you wish to."

A beat of silence passed before Lydia responded. "You'll never know how touched I am by your kindness, but I mean to let it go. That is my choice."

There was no bell above the office door, but Anna heard its opening. Captain Lang entered with a gust of cold, dank air. "Miss Anna," he said, and stepped to the sitting room door.

"Ready?" she heard Papa say.

"Squared away." The captain moved inside the sitting room, out of Anna's view. Standing by the office counter, she jumped at the sound of an indrawn breath behind her.

"I'm told your name is Anna," said a brisk New England voice.

She whirled to find the young blond crewman, dressed in a coat of sturdy plain cloth. He wasn't tall, barely taller than she. She raised her chin, not wanting him to see he'd startled her.

"I saw my chance at meeting you and had to take it," he said, though in apology for his familiarity or in defense of it, Anna couldn't tell. He doffed his hat and made her a bow. "Sam Reagan, from Connecticut. Your most obedient servant, Miss Aubrey."

She made him a slight curtsy. "Actually, my name is Anna Doyle."

That ruffled his smoothness. "I thought . . . Capt'n says you're Major Aubrey's daughter."

"I am." Anna was smiling at the young man's confusion when Captain Lang emerged and fixed him with a glare she was thankful wasn't aimed at her.

"Reagan. Let's go." There was warning enough in those snapped syllables, yet Sam Reagan didn't heed it directly. Recovering his aplomb, he cast her a lingering grin that lit his hazel eyes.

"Charmed to make your acquaintance, Miss *Doyle*." He sketched another bow, replaced his hat, and followed Captain Lang onto the quay.

Though put off by such brash Yankee manners—as Papa would doubtless wish her to be—Anna moved to the front glass to watch young Mr. Reagan board the lead bateau and, with the rest of the crew, push off with his pole to begin the tedious trip upriver. Mr. Reagan looked straight at her—and freed a hand to wave.

Anna drew back from the glass. Only then did she realize Papa and Lydia hadn't emerged as well. She made to return to the sitting room but stopped upon hearing her name uttered.

". . . good for Anna, spending more time in town." Papa's voice was pitched so low she knew she wasn't meant to hear. "But I don't want her mingling with the rougher sort who come through this office, see. I know you'll look after my girl."

"As if she were my own."

Papa's voice warmed. "I remember . . . You were hardly more than a child yourself, but you loved her from the start. A thing we've always had in common."

"Yes." Lydia imbued the word with such affection that Anna felt her heart swell. How blessed she was to have Papa and Lydia. And Mr. and Mrs. Doyle, who were like the grandparents she'd never known. And William . . . though far away. And Two Hawks.

"You'd have made a wonderful mother," Papa said. Silence fell, awkward and startled. "Lydia . . . look you, that was thoughtless of me. That was—"

"The single loveliest thing anyone has ever said to me," Lydia cut in, the words thick with pain and sincerity. "Don't wish it unsaid. Please."

As she waited for whatever would be said next, Anna had the strangest feeling—a disconcerting loss of bearing, as if a path she'd followed all her life had just vanished in a sweeping fog and she didn't know where next to place her foot. Strangest of all, she sensed Papa and Lydia felt it too.

She held her breath.

"I won't then. And I thank you, for all your care of Anna these many years." There was a tenderness in Papa's voice she'd never heard him use with anyone but her, and maybe that was why the thought went through her head that if only Papa wasn't married to Mrs. Aubrey far away in Wales, Lydia might become not just her mentor, but her *mother* . . .

She clapped a hand to her mouth, as if the selfish notion—appallingly disloyal to Mrs. Aubrey *and* Jacob van Bergen in his grave—might leap off her tongue and horrify Papa and Lydia.

20

Thunder Moon 1772

Since his father's leaving, it had fallen to Two Hawks to provide meat for his mother and to trap for winter furs. Now spring had come, and he must bring in deerskins for trade as well as meat. That was why he woke on a mist-shrouded, rain-dampened morning in the hunting camp he'd made for himself, instead of in the woods near the Aubrey farm, where he wanted to be.

It made his chest tight, thinking of Anna Catherine coming across the creek to look for him, so he tried to put her from his mind. He thought instead of his empty belly and what he must do to fill it. He thought of his mother waiting. He thought of the new rifle he'd gotten by trading some of the furs his mother prepared that winter past. At last he could hunt with something besides arrows; Stone Thrower had taken his gun with him when he left Kanowalohale. Game was so scarce even so, they rarely had any meat, and once again the summer crops hadn't produced enough to see them through the winter.

His rage against his father had cooled to ashes. If he could, he would go and find his father and beg him to return. But he couldn't go. He had to get a deer while he still had strength left to do it.

He began a prayer, soft as the mist draping the budding forest sloping away in tangled aisles from his camp. He prayed for good hunting and steady hands so his dwindling supply of lead and powder wouldn't be wasted. He prayed for there to be something to kill. He'd take a turkey and be glad, never mind he needed deerskins almost as much as he needed meat.

Two Hawks was no longer certain to whom he prayed. It was a muddle now, which god was the true Great Spirit and how a man ought to pray. As the mist drifted and his nose ran with the chill, he said the words a brave hunter should say, but the heart in him was curled up cold and afraid.

He broke his camp in the lee of a downed tree. He still had a little parched cornmeal in a pouch. He ate a handful standing by the place he'd slept, wanting to gulp it all. He drank from a nearby spring, much water to make himself feel full. As he wiped his mouth, he thought of his mother praying for his success. Praying to Jesus. He didn't know if it would help, but the thought gave him a spark of warmth. Enough to face the day.

He made sure he'd taken up all he'd lain down with—shot bag, blanket, bow, quiver—then gripped the rifle and started out.

Dogwoods showered white petals among the dripping trees Two Hawks trudged beneath, the spark in him grown fainter than the trail he followed. The days had blurred together. He remembered crouching in a thicket along a deer trail, near where it crossed a creek. Two does had come along it, one early, one when the sun was higher. He'd shot at both and missed both. The heavy rifle had wavered in his hand. He was worn down with hunger, though he'd found a few new cattail shoots, some cress . . . that morning? yesterday?

One lead ball remained to him, loaded in the rifle's barrel. He was almost sure he was going to use it soon. Not to kill a deer but to save himself from the hunter stalking him.

What made him look back when he had, he couldn't say. There'd been no sound beyond the *rat-tat-tat* of a woodpecker's knocking and the creak of wind-rubbed branches. But he had looked back, just before the trail dropped into a bowl-like hollow, and seen the great tawny cat slinking after him through the brush.

With his heart a gourd rattle in his chest, he'd plunged down the trail and sprinted to the center of the hollow where the trees were old and wide-spaced. He raised the rifle back toward the place where the trail crested and waited.

The panther appeared above the rise.

Two Hawks gulped a breath, willed his trembling arms still, then squeezed the rifle's trigger and fired his last shot. The flash in the pan . . . the roar . . . the cloud of stinking smoke . . . the kick . . . and far beyond it the panther falling down the incline into the hollow, twisting, rolling, crumpled.

Too weak to hold the rifle, he planted the stock in the springy turf and leaned against the weapon. He hadn't missed. But he'd have to hunt with his bow now, and an arrow didn't always bring down a deer, only wounded it, making a hunter trail it far before it finally fell, whereas a ball made a wound more likely to . . .

Two Hawks stiffened. Had the panther's tail twitched?

The tail rose again. Higher. The panther rolled onto its side, got to its feet, and came toward him. Two Hawks threw down the rifle, dug his feet into the leaves, and ran like the wounded deer he'd been imagining.

As he ran, the futility of it crashed down on him. Why run? Why fight so hard to live when all the forces of the spirit world and this one combined seemed bent on snuffing him out? Why not let the cat kill and eat him? If he couldn't get meat, let him *be* meat.

Two Hawks stopped and turned, heaving in what would be his final breaths. The panther stopped, lowering into its crouch, wary of him as a man, a hunter, not knowing yet that he was neither. Dropping to the ground, Two Hawks crossed his legs. At his knee he laid his hatchet, his quiver and bow, while the cat began its stalk, gaze fixed on him. It was very big.

When it was within an arrow's shot, Two Hawks thought about singing a death song. He had no exploits to sing about. He'd never plucked his hair for war. Never fought to protect the People. He hadn't even been a good son. He hadn't stood between his father and his mother when she needed him to.

Into his mind poured the image of his mother, wailing with ashes on her face when she learned she'd lost another son. Would she be ashamed to know he'd given up the life she counted precious?

Another thought shot like a spear through his vitals. *I will never see Anna Catherine again.*

Then he knew. He was going to have to do the harder thing and live. Or try to live. He had seconds before the panther made its rush and the decision would be made for him.

With one hand he snatched up the bow, still strung taut, and with the other swiped an arrow from its quiver. His hands knew this weapon. He didn't have to think about all the little steps, as with the rifle, leaving room for the memory of Anna Catherine praising his strength to flicker like new-breathed flame behind his eyes. He set the arrow, drew, and let it fly. It struck the cat through the neck as it made its leap. The heavy creature clawed dark furrows through the leaf mold as it writhed, giving out a gargled scream through its pierced throat.

Two Hawks had another arrow in hand, with no memory of grasping it. His thoughts were still of Anna Catherine. Her hair that he wanted to see unbraided again. Her green-brown forest eyes. How she treasured his brother's letters . . .

He sent the second arrow into the panther's heart. In its thrashing, it came near enough for him to touch before it died. Two Hawks could feel the warmth of its hide, smell its blood, see its spirit fly from its eyes.

"There, Brother," he said to the twin he knew only through words on paper. "Let me hear you boast of doing *that*."

On the heels of those words a sound came out of him, one he'd not heard from his mouth in many moons.

He laughed.

And then he couldn't stop. Soon he was crying tears with the laughter. Then it was no longer laughter but wrenching sobs that hurt his ribs. The bow tumbled from his hand, which shook now. All his limbs shook. His teeth chattered. He'd almost let that panther eat him. Where would his soul have gone if he had? Kirkland's burning hell?

He had no strength. Not even to stand. After all he would sit there and wait to die, and it would be a long death instead of the quick one he might have had.

Covered over in defeat, he sat by the dead panther, enveloped in the tang of its musk and blood. He drew his knees to his chest and put his head on his arms, too ashamed to sing.

He was still waiting to die, some moments later, when the rustle of moccasins passing through leaves reached his ears. His head snapped up, and he reached for his rifle. It was nowhere to hand. He'd dropped it when he ran.

A man was coming through the hollow, winding between the trees. A warrior with a crested scalp-lock, shouldering a burden—and carrying Two Hawks's rifle. The man had a limp. He neared, frowning at the panther, at Two Hawks sitting beside it. He studied Two Hawks's face as if trying to see in it another face, or a younger version of the same face.

The instant the limping man's brows shot high, recognition sparked in Two Hawks's mind. This was the man who looked after them when his father went away to fight with Pontiac. The man his father pushed into one of his own traps and crippled.

It was Bear Tooth.

"I heard your rifle fire and came to see who else was in these hills hunting."
Bear Tooth looked down at Two Hawks, sitting beside the dead panther.
"I never thought it would be you."

Two Hawks's heart beat dull and heavy, hurting with a mixture of
relief and humiliation. But all he could think about was the deer meat Bear
Tooth carried, freshly butchered and wrapped in its hide, tied high on his
shoulders with straps. "It is good to see you . . . brother."

An expression Two Hawks couldn't read flinched across Bear Tooth's
face before his lips drew back in a smile. "You have grown into a hunter,"
he said, black eyes assessing the panther. "You killed it with arrows? Sitting
there like that, you killed it?"

Pride in the accomplishment flickered. Two Hawks was glad someone
who had been important to him had come to witness what he'd done. But
why did Bear Tooth just stand looking at him?

"I shot it first with lead," he admitted. "But it did not die of it. That is
my rifle you carry. I dropped it when the panther chased me."

So many words left him exhausted, dry-mouthed. Bear Tooth didn't
seem to notice. He raised the rifle in his grip, admiring it. "A hunter should
not throw away a rifle like this. They are hard to come by."

"I did not throw it away . . ." Or he had not meant to. Two Hawks
tried to remember how it had been. He'd fired it. The panther had fallen.
There'd been no time to load again. Nothing to load had there been time.
He couldn't make the words to say all that come together on his tongue.

Bear Tooth peered down at him, frowning. "You do not look well."

Two Hawks could smell the deer meat. His mouth watered. His belly
writhed. Loudly. "I am hungry. You have a deer . . . ?"

"I can hunt for myself again now. Though not like before." Bear
Tooth's eyes grew hard. A shadow passed across his face. "Where is your
father? Why is that one not hunting with you?"

Two Hawks's empty belly twisted. He searched Bear Tooth's face to know what he was thinking, then dropped his gaze to the man's foot. There was still a noticeable twist to it. It looked like it must cause pain.

"He is gone. Not dead," he added when Bear Tooth's eyes flared wide with what must have been surprise. It couldn't have been joy. "He went to live with the Senecas."

"Did he?" Bear Tooth smiled. "Can you stand to your feet?"

Two Hawks's bones felt weak as water. Why must he stand? Did Bear Tooth wish him to show courage before he would offer food? Another test to fail?

His voice broke as he said, "I do not know."

Bear Tooth's smile vanished. He stepped closer as if preparing to bend down at last and help him. But as he did so, the shadow that had flickered on his face loomed like a cloud settling over his features. A dark and ugly cloud. "Good," he said, then raised his twisted foot and brought it down hard on Two Hawks's ankle.

Pain blinded Two Hawks, but it was the shock of it as much as the hurting that made him cry out. His vision swam in darkness. He heard the leaves rustle but could only lie there waiting for his eyes to clear. When they did, he was alone with his bow and the panther.

Bear Tooth had taken his rifle.

Two Hawks had wept like a child into the dead leaves, wounded more deeply by betrayal than the physical pain of what Bear Tooth had done to him. Bear Tooth's twisted foot might allow him to hunt, but it had lacked the strength to break Two Hawks's bones. The other pain . . . that only grew and grew.

He sat up and brushed leaves from his hair and face. Gingerly he moved his ankle back and forth. He winced, then curled his toes inside his moccasin. Nothing broken, not down there. But something in him felt snapped in two.

He sat with his arms curled around his knees, while his ankle throbbed, remembering the darkness that had stared from Bear Tooth's eyes. That man hated his father, and for that Two Hawks could not blame him. But why had he taken it out on Two Hawks, who'd never harmed him?

He raised his head and looked at the dead cat. Right there was meat. Not meat he would normally want to eat . . . but he decided not to die.

He built a small fire where he sat, cut strips of meat from the cat's shoulder, stuck them on a stick, held them to the flames, and ate them barely cooked. It took little to fill him, so small was his stomach shrunken. After a time, when he felt strength flowing into his limbs, he skinned the panther. Only after he'd done all that did he stand and test his swollen ankle. He could bear some weight, but it would be a long path home. He took more meat and the rolled up fur, and left the carcass lying where it had fallen.

This was his father's fault. All of it. Stone Thrower had pushed Bear Tooth into the trap and crippled him. Stone Thrower had hit his mother, making her put him out of the lodge. *Then he left me alone to feed us both.*

Or was it all the fault of Anna Catherine's father? *He* had done the terrible thing that made *his* father do terrible things to his mother and Bear Tooth and . . .

A shadow flit across his path. Startled, he limped to a halt and stared round at the dripping forest. Passing clouds overhead hid the sun, shadowing the budding ridges and hollows. But that wasn't where the shadow had come from. It was inside him.

He recognized the darkness. It was hatred. A cup his father had drunk from deeply, then passed on to Bear Tooth, who'd passed it on to him. He'd taken a swallow, and it was bitter in his belly.

Was he going to blame Bear Tooth and hate him, and hate his father, and Anna Catherine's father? Was he going to become another man with a soul like a twisted root inside? He didn't want to become that man, but he didn't know how to stop it from happening.

His mother would know. She wasn't like that in her heart, yet she suffered as much as anyone. Why wasn't she passing on the hurt to everyone around her? He knew only one thing different about his mother. She believed the words of Kirkland, the words from his book.

"You need the strength of Jesus in you." Those were the last words of Kirkland he'd heard for himself, spoken to his father. *"To be the man you want to be, the man your family needs you to be."*

What strength was going to help *him* be the man his people, his mother, his own heart, needed him to be?

As Two Hawks started forward again, weak from the long hunger and pain, he called out in his mind to Kirkland's god. *If You are there and can make me a man not like my father or Bear Tooth, but a man with a good heart, then that is what I want from You. A good heart. Maybe a new heart.*

And a new rifle, he added but wasn't sure that had been a wise thing to ask for and so he prayed to his mother as well. *Talk to Jesus for me. I do not know what to say, but I am coming home. Pray for me.*

Green Corn Moon

The Reverend Samuel Kirkland stood where the creek was deep, the cold water flowing past his hips. Good Voice stood before him, skirt pressed against her thighs, bare toes curling in the sandy creek bottom. Her tall son, just turned fifteen summers, stood to the side, ready to profess repentance of bad works called sin and his embracing of Jesus as Savior, Heavenly Father as God. The sky above shifted in a patchwork of white and blue. The leaves on the trees spreading up from the creek rustled in the breeze.

The faces of the people lining the bank shone, mostly with approval. Their garments were a riot of colors—stroud cloth, ruffled linen, deerskin, beads, quills. Their hair and ears and arms glinted with silver in the sunlight that darted through the clouds like firelight through a circle of dancing feet. Among them was Daniel Clear Day, beside him her son's friend. Tames-His-Horse, the dreamer, would go under the water, too, before returning to his Mohawk people in the north. All wore their best and brightest, for there was always a celebration after a baptism, with food and dancing.

Kirkland frowned upon such indulgence, but this they chose to overlook in him.

Good Voice had celebrated in her soul since Two Hawks, returned from his hunting with a limp he refused to explain and a mind so preoccupied he'd barely spoken to her during the days it had taken the mysterious wound to heal, finally came to her and said he wished to go under the water and come up again with Jesus in his heart.

I have no greater joy, she thought, remembering words from the book, *than to hear that my children walk in truth.* And one day . . . *May I know my firstborn also walks Your bright path.* That was the prayer of Good Voice's heart as Kirkland lowered her beneath the cold water and raised her up again, streaming wet and with a new name. Elizabeth.

Unless it was an old name, the name she had been called before she became Good Voice. It wasn't something she thought about often, but on this day she wondered . . . had her white parents shared this faith? Would she see their faces in the Life After? Would they welcome her, their lost daughter, with arms flung open?

There was murmuring among the men, trills from the women, despite Kirkland's admonition that this was a solemn occasion. He and they didn't always see with the same eyes how they should worship their Creator. Kirkland was a white man, even if he was a brother in Jesus. White men often had strange and inflexible ideas about unimportant things. It was what was in the heart that mattered most.

As she stood aside so Two Hawks could take her place before the missionary, Good Voice believed the good feelings in her heart couldn't possibly be stronger. But about that one thing at least, she was wrong.

Of those gathered in the water, it was she who first noticed the disturbance happening on the bank while Kirkland talked to her son about the meaning of baptism. Voices lifted in surprise as those nearest the water moved aside for a man carving a path through the gathering. The man didn't stop when he reached the creek but came on, walking straight into the water. The man was Stone Thrower.

Good Voice felt the shock of it course through her as though the creek water had indeed washed deep into her flesh, her bones. Kirkland saw him too. Good Voice knew it though she never took her gaze off the man who had been her husband. The missionary's words faltered. Now they were all just standing there in the flow, Good Voice, Two Hawks, and Kirkland, watching Stone Thrower wading out to them.

Almost a year had passed since Good Voice last saw him. Somewhere he'd shed his clothes and wore nothing now but a breechclout. His limbs were brown and sinewy, his chest full and broad. His belly was still firm and flat like a young man's, though his face looked older, the lines around his eyes grown deeper. Those high-boned, handsome features of his were set in determined lines, all too familiar.

Good Voice felt the first twinge of unease. Had Stone Thrower come there thinking to prevent this baptism? It was too late for her—it wasn't a thing that could be undone—but what of Two Hawks?

He is my child. He will do this thing if he wishes it. No man can say otherwise.

Stone Thrower's gaze met hers as she thought these things. As it did, his face softened with a tenderness more startling than his dramatic appearance. His eyes had a reaching power that made her breath catch, the way it had the first time he ever looked at her. But Stone Thrower didn't speak. Not to her. He turned his face to the missionary who still had his hand on Two Hawks's shoulder.

If Kirkland was unsettled by this intrusion into one of his most sacred rituals, he hid it.

"From whence do you come?" he asked Stone Thrower, his voice raised to carry above the creek's chatter, to the people crowding close to the bank to watch this turn of events.

"I come from Ganundasaga," Stone Thrower said, "and the lodge of your Seneca friend, who sought me out there. He was hungry for word of you."

Kirkland's face relaxed. He'd once lived in Ganundasaga, before he came to the Oneida. Few of the Senecas, that nation who guarded the western door of the Great Longhouse, had embraced his God. But those who did had loved him well. "How fares my Seneca brother and his family?"

"He has not forgotten you." Stone Thrower paused, drawing in a breath that expanded his chest. "Nor has he forgotten the God you preached among them. I bring greetings from your brothers and sisters among the Senecas . . . who are now my brothers and sisters."

The gazes of his son, the missionary, and everyone standing on the creek bank were fixed on Stone Thrower in astonishment. He raised his voice with the strength of a warrior, of a man unashamed of his words. "I am here to say I am ready to be forgiven my sins, and with the help of Jesus to be the husband and father I have failed to be. I know Creator will have me, for He will turn away no one who comes with a true heart. I have been told this many times, by you, by my uncle, by others from here to Ganundasaga. Now I believe it. My heart is true."

At last he set his gaze on Good Voice, who was clutching the hand of her son, trying to take in what she'd heard. Stone Thrower's face softened as it had moments ago. He spoke softly too, only for her ears. "Heavenly Father will not turn me away, but will you? Or can you find it in your heart to have me back? Not the man you knew, but one I am becoming?"

She let go of Two Hawks's hand, for the world had narrowed. It no longer included the people on the bank, the missionary, or even her son. She searched the brown eyes fixed on her and saw in them what she had never seen, not even in that first sweet year before Fort William Henry. *Death unto life.* That was what she saw in the eyes of her husband.

She hadn't bidden the word into her mind—*husband*—but it was there in her thoughts. And it was true.

"I will have you back," she said. The world widened again. She was startled to see Kirkland, still standing with his hand on her son's shoulder. The heart inside her chest had been leaping like a spring-happy fawn. Now uncertainty bloomed, but the joy in Stone Thrower's face rivaled the sun that broke from the clouds and dazzled their eyes with its dance upon the creek.

"Will you put me under the water, here with my family?" he asked the missionary.

Good Voice clasped her lip between her teeth, tasting the water still trickling from her hair. It wasn't Kirkland's way to permit baptism upon a man's or woman's first word of desiring it. His way would be to watch Stone Thrower for a time, talk with him often, see if the way he lived proved what he said had happened in his heart. Only when he was satisfied would he consent to baptism. It was one of those things he was stubborn about, and she could see on his face these thoughts were going through his head.

Kirkland looked at Two Hawks, whose eyes pleaded, full of hope. Then he looked at Good Voice. He seemed to be asking her was she certain about this man who had caused them such trouble and grief.

Through a warm rush of tears, Good Voice nodded.

"Very well." Kirkland squeezed her son's shoulder and moved him gently aside. "You will have your turn right after. In this case I think it fitting your father should be first."

21

April 1773

*A*nna went often to the woods bordering the farm the year she became Lydia's apprentice. Helping stock Lydia's pharmacopoeia was proving one of her favorite aspects of her training, but while she gleaned, she also hoped to see a familiar, lithe figure coming through the trees toward her or standing still in shadow, waiting for her to spy him.

Summer waned. Leaves blazed and swirled away like sparks, baring limbs to receive the season's first snow. But Two Hawks never came.

His absence left Anna cloaked in disappointment as bleak as the winter that ushered in 1773. Were it not for the companionable hours spent in Lydia's kitchen drying herbs, preparing tinctures and pills, the visits made to those who needed them—and William's letters—her spirits might have sunk pitiably low.

The winter passed in a patchwork of lonely days at the farm, busy days in town. Snow melted, and the river ice vanished. Trees along the creek sent out a mist of green, and tender plants shot forth again, begging for harvest.

"'Tis wash day," Mrs. Doyle reminded her as, breakfast over, Anna took a shawl from a peg, intending to check several favorite spots for harvesting across the creek. "My poor back cannot take that chore alone anymore."

"It's too chilly to begin now. Why don't you put your feet up by the fire—spend a while with that new novel of Papa's I've seen you eyeing."

Mrs. Doyle wasn't quick enough to hide her brightening at the reminder of Papa's copy of *The Vicar of Wakefield,* though she tried to douse it with a stern look.

"Stuff and nonsense—novels."

Grinning at the unconvincing censure, Anna reached for her gathering basket. Mrs. Doyle eyed it dangling from her arm.

"I *am* after gettin' through that laundry today, so don't dawdle." She set a plate on a rack in the hutch as Anna opened the door. "And be watchful. Rowan's seen a fair number of Indians on the river of late."

Though doubtless meant as a mild caution, Anna felt hope stir. She managed not to sound too eager as she said, "Perhaps Sir William is back from his travels."

William Johnson had sailed for England last July, hoping to impress upon His Majesty, King George, the importance of the Six Nations to the Crown's future interest in the colony—a colony crowding hard against its Indian neighbors despite edicts to prevent settler encroachment. Or so Anna gathered from snatches of conversation overheard in town. Nor was it possible these days to keep from overhearing the bitter grumblings over Parliament's high-handed treatment of the colonies since the war with France ended. Or the arguments for self-government springing up like weeds wherever she turned.

"Back from England is he? And the Indians flockin' to Johnson Hall to hear what the king had to say, no doubt." Mrs. Doyle set the last plate in its place. "Well, never mind Sir William. Just you have a care and don't stray far."

Anna hurried down the rutted track that crossed the fields toward the forest, noting the columns of chimney smoke that marked the distant farms of neighbors, cleared over the past few years. Papa's land was no longer as isolated as when Mrs. Aubrey cowered within the house and she and William had run wild about the place.

The thought stirred the old pang of longing for William, only now it was mingled with longing for Two Hawks. It had been a year and a six-month—no, a bit longer than that—since she'd seen her Oneida friend. If something terrible were to happen away in Wales—God forbid—she'd hear about it eventually. If something happened to Two Hawks, she'd be left to wonder forever.

Rowan Doyle was in the field near the creek, sowing corn from a bag slung at his waist. Past sixty now, his tall frame was stooped, his hair white across his scalp. He tamped down a handful of kernels with a sturdy boot. When he saw her across the open field, Anna waved. Mr. Doyle returned the salute but seemed to watch her more intently than was needful. He couldn't know her thoughts or who she hoped to find beyond the beech grove.

Still, cheeks prickling in the chilly air, she kept her feet from hurrying the last few yards to the old footlog—in case Mr. Doyle watched.

"What will you do with those?"

The voice that spoke behind her had deepened since last she'd heard it, but still she knew it, and the knowing sent a shiver up her arms. Anna pushed up off the ground at the clearing's edge where she'd knelt to gather fiddleheads, an irrepressible smile pulling at her mouth. The smile froze as she took in Two Hawks, standing in dappled shade, dressed in a long hunting shirt above leggings gartered with red wool. He'd a blanket roll tied across his back, a rifle slung at his shoulder, his bow in hand.

This wasn't the Two Hawks of her memory. Still lean and long-limbed, he'd a man's wide shoulders now, a man's strong jaw and nose. Yet the boy she remembered lingered in the brown eyes drinking her in, the wide mouth curled at the corners in a smile as frozen as hers felt.

Abandoning shawl and basket on the ground, she went several paces into the wood to stand before him. He was taller than Papa now.

"Two Hawks . . . you look so much older."

His gaze dropped to the braid she'd left unpinned that morning, following it down her shoulder, over her breast, to the curve of her waist. "You . . . you look so much beautiful."

What foolishness—if anyone was beautiful it was *him*. Flustered, overwhelmed by his presence, she reached to touch him. Dirt and plant matter stained her hand, but he took it and pressed it to his chest. His hand covering hers was big and warm. A man's hand.

Until that moment he'd seemed half dream. A thrill shot through her at the touch of him, and she stepped back. "Why have you stayed so long away? I thought you might never . . ." Flustered again, she couldn't finish.

"Never come see you again?" he asked, so gently the tears came.

"Yes!" She turned away to hide them, surprised how deeply she'd missed him, even mourned his unexplained absence. Her nose was cold and running. She wanted to look at him, but the easy freedom they'd known as children had vanished. It was like meeting him all over again. She didn't know what to say. How to behave.

At length he asked, "You missed me, all this time?"

She didn't turn around. "Of course."

"I also missed you."

"Then why did you stay away?" She faced him again.

"It was not by choice. I was needed for the hunting. It has been a . . . hard time for my family."

He was needed? Had something happened to his father? Dared she ask?

He spoke again before she could. "You gather ferns?"

"Fiddleheads, yes." The ferns were for the table—they made a nice addition to salads, young and unfurled. It wasn't what she wished to speak of, but the innocuous question eased the tension between them. She talked about Lydia and what she was learning of herb-craft and midwifery, but couldn't meet his gaze.

When at last she ran out of words and dared to raise her eyes to his, *he* looked away.

"It is good," he said, "these things you learn. They will make you a woman of status."

"I don't know about status, but I enjoy it . . ." Her stomach twisted when he wouldn't look at her. He must feel it too, this painful restraint. Where was the teasing boy she'd known? She'd thought seeing him again would be the most joyful thing—next to William's return. Hadn't she been joyful but a moment ago?

"I too have learned new things." Two Hawks shrugged off his rifle and leaned it against a nearby tree, alongside his bow.

"What new things?"

He hesitated, darting a look at her. "How to love my neighbor as myself."

Heat leapt to her face before she recognized the words. Her mouth dropped open. "You're a Christian?"

"I follow a Jesus path now."

Was that the same thing? She thought it must be. "But I thought . . . You seemed unhappy about Reverend Kirkland living in your village."

A smile tugged at his mouth. "You said you would pray for my family. Did you?" She had and told him so. "Did you think your prayers would not be heard?"

He was teasing her now, like old times, yet she found it hard to collect her thoughts with him standing there looking so grown-up and handsome, and his English so much improved, and those laughing eyes doing strange things to her insides.

"Will you let me help pick ferns?" he asked.

"Of course, if you want." She retrieved her shawl, though she was flushed and didn't feel the coolness of the woods now. She picked up her basket. He took up his weapons. As if by consent, they moved deeper into the trees, leaving the clearing behind.

They wandered the wood without picking a single fiddlehead or any other useful thing. Anna was too absorbed in listening to Two Hawks tell about his family. How Stone Thrower's drinking got so bad his mother finally put his belongings outside her lodge, which Anna took to be the Oneida way of ending a marriage. He told her how Stone Thrower left Kanowalohale to get away from his pain and from Samuel Kirkland. He told her of the burden he'd shouldered afterward, of their hunger, and the panther, and someone called Bear Tooth who'd been unkind to him.

"Believing in Kirkland's God seemed the only way to keep off the path my father traveled, or one as bad. But since . . . I have come to know Heavenly Father for more than His help. I know *Him*."

An unexpected pang of longing shot through Anna's happiness. Two Hawks spoke of the Almighty like a man did a friend. It reminded her of Lydia. She wanted to understand how both could talk so, coming from such different lives, but didn't know how to put that question into words.

"Did your father ever come back?" she asked him, steering clear of the subject of Kirkland and God.

"He did. At summer's end. I wanted to see you . . ." She could feel his gaze on her as they walked. "Autumn and winter were hard for us. If my father had not come back when he did, you might not have seen me again ever."

Anna wanted to take his hand in reassurance but couldn't. He didn't say it outright, but as he explained how far they'd had to travel to find game to hunt, she understood it was in part because of white settlers invading their land, pushing westward.

"But Heavenly Father brought us through." Two Hawks caught her gaze and smiled, and she felt a disconcerting sensation low in her belly. They walked on in silence for a stretch, then Two Hawks picked up the thread of conversation they—or she—had dropped. "Some in Kanowalohale still speak against Kirkland for the many ways he wishes us to change. But I see it this way: if knowing God in my heart means losing a little of what it means to be Oneida—I do not think it means losing everything, as the sachems fear—I think it is only what must be remade in every man who comes to Creator through His Son, Jesus. White, black, red, and any other sort of man. If I have lost anything, what I have gained is a trade in my favor."

Anna watched his face as he spoke, sensing that in some vital way he'd made a leap beyond her. One she couldn't follow. "Are things still hard for you, for your people?"

"It is hard to find food to eat. Hard to know who is enemy and who friend. I do not think the traders are friends. Not when they get our warriors drunk to do foolish things. That is why some warriors are embracing Kirkland's teaching. But many still waste their furs on rum to help them forget how hard it is to keep their little ones fed."

"Like your father?"

To her surprise, Two Hawks hesitated. "My father had other things to make his heart bad. Some things are hard for a man to forgive."

He looked away from her without explaining, leaving her to wonder what Stone Thrower couldn't forgive. She moved ahead of him, picking a path through a thicket, noting the stems with their blossoms that would in months be blueberries.

"But your father came back. Is it better with him now?"

"His things are in my mother's lodge again." Her petticoat snagged in the thicket. Two Hawks bent to free it. Straightening, he added, "He has a new name. My mother also has a new name."

"A baptismal name? Like Stone Thrower's uncle?"

"Yes." He followed her out of the thicket, adding in a tone both shy and proud, "I have a new name."

She paused beneath a chestnut tree that grew in a hollow between slopes covered in berry bushes. Morning sunlight fell in slanting shafts around them. "It's nothing awful, is it?"

"What name would be awful?"

She laughed, for he looked suddenly worried. "Oh, I don't know . . . Abimelech or Shamgar?"

That made *him* laugh. "Shamgar is a good name. Strong. But no. I was baptized Jonathan."

"King David's friend." Hiding the depth of her approval, Anna set the basket on the ground and studied him. "Jonathan . . . Acceptable, I suppose."

She noticed how white and straight were his teeth when he grinned, aware that she teased him. "I like to hear you say it. Call me so—if you wish."

"I'll have to see which name suits you now."

"Both, I think. I am still Two Hawks." With a deft motion he slid an arrow from the quiver at his back and raised his bow as if to shoot it. Anna thought he was playing along with her teasing. Then he stepped back and set the arrow so quickly she barely followed the smooth motion. He was scanning the forest.

"What is it?" Then she heard it, a steady stride through leaves approaching, with no effort made at concealment. Seconds later, Stone Thrower came over a rise to the west, tall and broad-shouldered, as she remembered him.

Two Hawks bent to her. "Have you a letter from William?"

"I do. It came a week ago." She usually carried them around for a fortnight, reading and rereading them, before putting them away.

"He is not returned?"

"No. He—"

"Speak of him later."

It was unlike Two Hawks to interrupt. But as he returned the arrow to the quiver, Stone Thrower was upon them, a rifle carried loose in his grip. His hair, always plucked before as Two Hawks's had never been, had grown out several inches all over his head. It made him look less fierce. A very little less.

"*Shekoli,* Aubrey's daughter," he said. "Before dawn my son runs from camp to this place, hoping to find you."

Stone Thrower's English had improved, but not as much as Two Hawks's, who appeared to be blushing. "He ran fast," she said. "He's told me a great deal that has happened to you all. But he hasn't told me your new name yet."

"I am Caleb. A great warrior name in the Book." Stone Thrower set the butt of his rifle against the earth. "It is good for a man to settle his soul about these things. I have peace with Creator, through Jesus-who-walked-the-earth-as-man, who died and lives again so the red blanket of His goodness is thrown over us as a cover."

The red blanket of His goodness. Anna had never heard such terms used to talk about God but hastened to say, "Amen."

She'd assumed Two Hawks looked more like his mother than he did Stone Thrower, but as the pair smiled at her now, she marked the resemblance between them, howbeit faint.

That was when the thought popped into her head.

"Would you come back to the house with me? We could wait there until Papa comes home. I'm sure you'd be welcome . . ." Looking into their faces, she knew Stone Thrower was far less certain than she.

"Aubrey is not Indian hater?"

"Indian hater? What makes you say that? Oh . . . because of the old French war?"

Two Hawks cut an uneasy look at his father. Stone Thrower, whose eyes had lost their earlier warmth, merely grunted assent.

"That was long ago. Papa isn't a soldier now. He builds bateaux. He's been to the Carrying Place and beyond, though he doesn't go anymore. He leaves that to Captain Lang—Papa can tell you this himself."

"Lang," Stone Thrower said. "He is strong man, loud voice, white hair?"

"You know him?"

"I see at Canajoharie. He is known."

Encouraged, Anna pressed, "Why not come with me? I'll tell the Doyles I've known you for years."

Stone Thrower looked at Two Hawks, who shook his head as if in reply to a question asked—though not in words. Stone Thrower's gaze held a struggle of impulses Anna didn't understand. He spoke to his son in Oneida. Two Hawks replied, his tone wary, as if he expected his father to do or say something unpleasant.

He didn't. He turned stiffly to her and said, "*O-kee-wa'h,* Aubrey's daughter."

Stone Thrower was moving away with his rifle and blanket tied on his back before she found her voice. "*O-kee-wa'h,* Mr. Caleb!"

At that he pivoted, and in his face was the struggle she'd seen moments ago, only now it was unguarded. She read sorrow and longing, but also something darker. It made her want to whirl and run like a rabbit through the wood.

Stone Thrower turned and kept walking. Two Hawks watched in silence as his father disappeared over the rise to the west.

"I—I should get back," Anna said. "Mrs. Doyle expects my help with the wash. Unless . . . Will *you* come to the house?"

He looked down at her, regret washing his features, and a heaviness that hadn't been there before. "I must go with my father." Disappointment flooded her until he added, "But I am fast. I will catch him after I walk back with you."

At the clearing Two Hawks hesitated. "You said you have a letter from William?"

Anna had been silent as they walked back, troubled about Stone Thrower and, when she'd asked, by Two Hawks's refusal to explain his father's behavior. It made her want to leave him, and it made her want to stay in hopes this sense of restraint between them would pass, that all would be as it once had been. *A few more minutes . . .*

They climbed to the stone shelf by the fall. Anna peered through the trees, relieved to see Mr. Doyle still in the field. She fished William's letter from her pocket. "Shall I read it to you?" Her eyes sought William's salutation, and she drew breath to start.

"No."

She looked up, puzzled. Two Hawks reached for the letter. He held it to the sunlight, staring at the densely written page. Haltingly, he began to read it for himself. "'Dear Anna . . . It is long past mid . . . midnight as I write this, but I find I am in such a state of nerves I cannot poss . . . possibly close my eyes, much less my mind, to sleep—'"

"Two Hawks! When did you learn to read?"

"You are kind to call it reading." He spoke with diffidence but couldn't hide his pleasure in her reaction. "Over the winter I learned, when I was not busy hunting. Shall I try more? Do you wish to keep parts from me?"

"Yes. I mean, no. Please, go on." Cheeks warming at the notion of William's letters being of an intimate nature, she nodded for him to continue.

"'I am in Oxford! Mother and I obtained a room in Town with time enough to spare us the chance to walk the more spacious of these cobbled Streets and to see something of the City, though at present the East End is under improvement (our landlady assures us 'tis much needed, it having been a Mean Section of the City heretofore). We strolled along the High Street, passing many a begowned Denizen of the various Colleges going in and out of the Coffee and Ale Houses, fair boisterous in conversation. I confess my heart leapt to think of being soon counted among their Ranks. We took a turn through the Physic Garden, which lies opposite Magdalen College, and though the Yew trees were impressive, pruned into the shapes of . . . I've forgotten what, will give them careful study next time, but by and large the garden gives the impression of having gone a bit leggy. Lydia would disapprove . . .'"

Anna couldn't look away from Two Hawks as he labored over William's words, reveling in the chance to watch him without his looking back at her.

"'Oxford is a towery sort of City, full of spires, but also trees, and beyond it much Heath and Wood and the encircling River. I am of course back in our hired room as I write this, having had Supper brought to us. Mother is worn from the day, already abed. Oh, Anna. I fear I shall wax effusive of this Place. I have yet to see Queens College—Yes, I am settled on Queens! And it is a year before I shall mat . . . muh . . .'"

"Matriculate." Anna leaned close as she sounded it out for him, though there was no need to see the page. She had it memorized.

"Matriculate." He flashed her a smile and read on, and she was dizzied by a sense that it was William sitting there telling her about Oxford and its charms, not Two Hawks reading his letter. She leaned back, staring at his face in profile, his black hair hanging long, his eyes so much darker than William's. Or were they?

She searched her memory of William's ten-year-old face and felt a clutch of panic when it blurred, blending with the face of the young man who turned to her with his brows drawn in puzzlement.

"You frown? Why?"

"I was thinking of William. I—I cannot remember his face." She blinked away sudden tears to find Two Hawks staring fixedly at the letter.

"I thought I read so poorly I displeased you."

He appeared so crestfallen that Anna started to reassure him with further praise of his reading skill—until she caught the twitch of his mouth.

"You're doing fine and you know it." She gave him a shove with her elbow. He pretended to fall off the ledge. She laughed, then looked toward the distant field. Mr. Doyle had paused in his work and was looking toward the creek. Had the sound of her laughter carried so far? She knew he couldn't see them through the trees, still she wanted to hide, and hide Two Hawks.

It seemed foolish now, asking him to come to the house. "Let me finish reading before someone comes to fetch me home."

Two Hawks handed the letter over, the humor in his eyes replaced by something deeper, searching and intent. "Then we must say *O-kee-wa'h.*"

"For now?" she couldn't keep from asking or stem the rush of reassurance when his dark eyes warmed.

"Always it is *for now.*"

22

July 1774

*P*reoccupied as she was with learning the art and mystery of midwifery, Anna was aware of the passage of the Tea Act and the backlash of upset across the colonies it produced. Merchants protesting the restrictive tax—disguised outlandishly as Indians—had boarded ships in Boston and dumped their cargoes of tea into the harbor. In response, Parliament closed the city's port, curtailed Massachusetts's government, and forced citizens to quarter British soldiers in their homes. Outraged voices clamored for a Continental Congress, with delegates from each colony to meet and address these grievances against the Crown.

To settlers in the Mohawk Valley, these events seemed of less threat than did the uprising of the Ohio Valley tribes that spring of 1774. In retribution for violence committed by Pennsylvania and Virginia settlers, Shawnees and Mingos struck back, appealing to the Six Nations for assistance. Sir William Johnson convened a council with the Indians at Johnson Hall to deal with the crises.

During the swelter of early July, Anna found her thoughts straying to that council, wondering if Two Hawks or Stone Thrower was in attendance. Wondering would Sir William find the force of will and eloquence to keep the Six Nations peaceful and settle the fearful ripples flowing eastward from the Ohio, threatening to engulf them.

On the muggy afternoon she and Lydia arrived at the Binne Kill, tired but elated after a morning spent ushering Schenectady's newest resident into his mother's welcoming arms, Captain Lang and his crew were just returned from German Flatts. They came with bundled deerskins. And news.

"... Seneca chiefs and most of the rest of 'em flat-out told Johnson the Stanwix Treaty back in '68 was rubbish. The boundaries set betwixt their hunting ground and settlement land were never honored, and if the *friends* of the English—meaning themselves—were treated with such contempt, how should they believe anything Johnson promised them on the king's behalf?"

Sam Reagan was relating the news of the council at Johnson Hall to Papa, who'd come out onto the quay, shirtsleeves dusted in wood shavings, to greet his returning crewmen. Captain Lang watched the cargo being unloaded, but his glance, when he spared it, glittered with amusement at Sam's blatant sense of drama.

Anna was about to announce their presence when Lydia put a hand to her arm. "Let's hear this out."

Other men—boatmen, traders, town merchants—drew near in twos and threes to hear as well.

"What it came down to," Sam told his swelling audience, "was Johnson telling the chiefs to keep their little brothers the Shawnees and Mingos under control, and the chiefs telling Johnson to keep his settlers under control, and neither admitting both demands were beyond anyone's control."

Two years of river work had filled Sam out in the shoulders and bleached his tailed hair to flaxen. Face sheened with sweat in the high sun, he looked past the ring of male listeners and caught her gaze. Beneath her wide straw bonnet, a dew sprang up across her brow. Though she'd long since realized nothing of a serious nature lay behind Sam's occasional flirtations, there was a glint at the back of those lively hazel eyes she didn't quite trust.

"Finally, this very morn," he said, all presage and portent, "for you know there's always feasting and smoking and then more feasting at these

Indian councils before they get down to business—this very morn John-son stood up to speak again and collapsed under that arbor—had to be supported inside the house to rest."

"Collapsed?" The shock on Papa's sweating face mirrored that of every man within earshot.

"How fairs Johnson now?" someone inquired. "Does the council proceed?"

"It hardly could," Sam Reagan replied, nimbly recapturing attention as he turned to address the questioner. "Not with Sir William gone on to glory."

"Náhte' asilu . . . lots of berries?" Anna asked, raising the basket she car-ried on her arm, half-full of the blueberries ripening over the slopes. How would you say *lots of berries*?

She and Two Hawks had reached the chestnut beneath which she'd last spoken to his father, over a year ago. The shade was welcome for the coolness it afforded. Sweltering July had given way to sweltering August. Two Hawks had discarded his shirt back at the clearing and wore only breechclout, moccasins, and the weapons he was never without, while she perspired beneath shift, stays, stockings, cap, gown, and petticoat. It hardly seemed fair.

"Yotahyú:ni," Two Hawks replied, making a grab for the berry bas-ket, which she whisked out of reach. He'd learned to speak English well, but until recently she'd learned very little of his language. She was rectify-ing that now.

"Náhte' asilu . . ." Her gaze fell on the weapons slung at his back. "Bow?"

"A'ʌ:ná."

"Náhte' asilu . . . arrow?"

"*Kayu:kwíle'.*"

"Knife?"

"*Ashale'.*" Two Hawks grabbed for the basket again. Again she snatched it from his grasp.

"*Náhte' asilu* . . . greedy boy?"

Two Hawks took exception to that. "I am not a *boy*. I am as many summers as you," he added, inordinately pleased that for the next two months they would both be seventeen.

"Only till October. Then I'll be your elder again and you'll have to mind what I say."

"But for now I need not?" Two Hawks grinned down at her, dark eyes teasing in the forest gloom.

"That depends."

"On what?" He snatched a berry from the basket and popped it into his mouth, too quick this time to prevent.

"On whether you wish to see me again after today." He made another try for a berry, but she moved too quickly, heading for the thicket spreading up the slope beyond the chestnut. "You're supposed to put them *in* the basket, not take them out."

"I thought Creator made them to go into the mouths of His children."

"They will, eventually. Mrs. Doyle wants these for pies."

Two Hawks followed her into the berry thicket, picking as diligently as she, though he ate as many berries as he added to her basket. *Greedy boy.*

When Anna glanced at him again, Two Hawks said, "I will always mind what you say. That is what a wise man does. He listens to his sisters, his mother, his aunts."

Thinking he still teased, she narrowed her eyes. "Truly?"

"Only a fool fails to heed the women of his clan. It is the women who choose which men will lead, after all."

Intrigued, she asked, "What clan are you?"

"*A'no:wál.* Turtle Clan. There is also Wolf and Bear. When I marry, it will be a woman from one of those clans or maybe . . ." He glanced at her, then looked at his hands, busy among leafy stems. "Just not someone who is Turtle Clan. The women of that clan, my mother's clan, are counted as sisters."

"All of them?"

"Yes. All."

She wasn't Turtle Clan. Had he meant to include *her* in the category of women he could marry? Flushed at the very notion—hastily dismissing it—Anna crouched to reach the berries on a low shrub, thinking about his words concerning Oneida women, how they were the ones to choose their leaders. To her knowing, there was no English colony in which women had a say in who became their governors, or part of this new thing happening now, Congress.

She stood, taking up the basket to move to another thicket where sunlight fell in patches and insects danced like motes in the slanting beams. "It's not so among us. The part about men listening to women. Not generally."

Two Hawks came up the slope behind her. "I know."

"You do?" He stood in sunlight, brows drawn against the glare. Sweat made a sheen across his brow. It was impossible not to admire him, standing there bare-chested. "Do you know many white women . . . besides me?"

"The wife of Kirkland lived among us for a time. That is mostly how I know, from watching her—them. I did not watch *her.*" His color deepened. "I saw how they were when I happened to see them."

Anna stifled a giggle at the discomfort he'd caused himself, not wanting her to think he'd spied on Mrs. Kirkland. "I didn't know Reverend Kirkland had a wife." She hesitated, uncertain how he would interpret her next question. "You said she *used* to live among you. Did she not like living in Kanowalohale?"

Two Hawks, back to picking berries, explained that Mrs. Kirkland had returned to the place Kirkland came from, back east, because of the unrest with the Ohio tribes and Sir William Johnson's death. "My mother was sad to see her go."

"Good Voice," Anna said. She pictured his mother, pretty and brown-skinned, with the same melting dark eyes of her son, who'd turned his attention to the bushes, the look on his face guarded. Or was it preoccupied? Though she'd grown almost as comfortable with him as she'd once been with William, there was much about Two Hawks she didn't fathom. Not like William, whose every thought had been as graspable as her own, and freely shared—still shared in his letters. She had a new letter in her pocket, a troubling one she meant to share with Two Hawks when the berry picking was done.

Thinking about William, the nearest to a brother she'd ever had, made her break the insect-humming quiet. "Am I like a sister to you then, that you intend to mind what I say?"

The stillness behind her made her turn. Two Hawks was looking at her with an arresting intensity. "Is that what you want to be? My sister?"

She opened her mouth to reply, then clamped it shut as a snatch of another conversation wafted to them on the breeze, muffled by distance. Footsteps were coming through the wood. Alarm sang through her.

Two Hawks flung out his hand. Then she was following him up the slope and into the nearest pine thicket. There was a declivity at its center where the hillside dipped behind a stone outcrop. They hunkered behind the stone, hemmed by poking branches. The tang of resin filled Anna's nose. She strained to listen, heart banging as footsteps came crackling through the berry shrubs. Voices resolved into words, though the stone that hid them prevented her seeing who they belonged to.

"This patch looks picked over."

"We're near the Aubrey farm. Anna Doyle will have been over this slope."

She recognized the voices—their neighbors to the south. A girl near her own age and a younger brother. Had she been alone, Anna would have welcomed them to pick with her.

That was when she realized her blunder. Two Hawks, huddled close at her back, must have felt her tensing. His whisper brushed her ear. "What is it?"

She swiveled her head to look at him. With his face inches from hers, she mouthed, *the basket*. He squeezed her arm. The heat of his hand seared through her sleeve. What would her neighbors think if they came across the basket abandoned on the slope?

"Come on, Sissy. It's too hot for this. Let's go to the river."

Anna waited for their footsteps to diminish, breathing out relief that her basket had gone unspotted.

Something prickly dropped onto the back of her neck. Hoping it was pine straw and not a spider, she raised her shoulders to dislodge it, but still it prickled.

Two Hawks brushed whatever it was away. The touch, so gentle it almost felt like a feathery kiss, raised gooseflesh down her arms.

Sweat sprang up fresh at every point their bodies touched.

The voices of her neighbors faded. Two Hawks's hand was on her shoulder, heavy and hot. "They are gone," he said in that soft baritone that still could catch her by surprise. It was deeper than ever just now, husky even, and so near her ear it made her shiver again, despite the heat.

Turning to face him, she lost her balance on the slope. His arm snaked around her and held her fast. Then it tightened, pulling her in to him. Grabbing for the rock behind which they'd hid, she used it to scramble to her feet.

She made as much racket as a moose getting out of the pines, snapping dead twigs, snagging her cap, having to retrieve it from the needled limbs. She was struggling to fit it back over her braided hair, tucking up sweaty strands as she reached the basket, before she heard Two Hawks coming more quietly behind her.

"I know another place to pick. Away from the river." She led the way up and over the slope, her heart skipping too hurriedly for the climb to account for.

"Anna Catherine?"

She pressed on, gathering her scattered composure. "It's not far."

It had been dim beneath those pines. Surely she hadn't seen in his eyes what she thought she'd seen, when he caught and held her. He hadn't been about to *kiss* her?

She didn't know. One thing she *did* know; she wasn't—and never wanted to be—his sister.

23

*T*wo Hawks followed her up through the berry bushes, gaze roving the forest lest others catch them unawares—this place wasn't as thinly settled as it had been—but his eyes were ever drawn back to Anna Catherine's slender neck, to that smooth spot where the hair coiled in wisps below her cap, that place he'd briefly touched, brushing away the pine needles. Before she fled the thicket.

"I've a letter from William." She'd come to a draw between low hills, choked with berry shrubs. She set the basket on a stone, fished the letter from her pocket, and all but thrust it at him. Two Hawks took the letter, careful to prevent his fingers brushing hers, not liking that what he'd nearly done under the pines had upset her. Had she not felt it too, with their bodies touching, that stab of wanting?

"Why don't you sit here and read?" She took her basket off the stone. "I shan't be long."

Almost he decided to go, to start for Kanowalohale without reading his brother's words. But he didn't want to leave her in the woods so far from her people. Or with this unsettledness between them.

He unfolded the creased pages, watching Anna Catherine, slender and graceful as a doe among the bushes, wishing he could give her words she would take into her heart and cherish as she did his brother's. What would she think of William if she knew the truth? What would she think of *him*?

He scanned the letter's first line, smiling faintly at Anna Catherine's recent determination to learn his language as he had hers, a thing that pleased him. Then he read,

Dear Anna,

I am matriculated! Where to begin? With my Tutor, I suppose. He is called Mr. Haviland. I think we shall get on tolerably for he is not so very old and seems to take a fatherly sort of interest in the Freshmen in his charge. Next of importance is my Room. I should say Rooms, for I have obtained two of them, a bedchamber, admittedly cramped, and a sitting room where I shall study and, once I've collected a few, entertain Friends. The furnishings are sparse, but my Allowance (from the Estate, though it is Mr. Haviland who doles it out) shall stretch to adding what is lacking if I am prudent. Best of all my Little Kingdom is neither stuffed up under a garret nor buried in a cellar but is on the second floor—with a view of St. Peter's Church, no less. A respectable Accommodation for a commoner, I am told. Yes, I am considered a commoner here. Does that sound strange to you, with your American Sensibilities? Yet do not take "commoner" to mean the lowest sort of Undergraduate. Those would be the servitors, who must work to afford tuition and the cost of College living, as well as seeing to their Studies. Above me are the Gentlemen-commoners, with the sons of the Nobility above them. A carousing, idle bunch in the main those latter, and as I do intend to learn a thing or two while mewed in Oxford, I'm just as glad to not be admitted to their Company, or their Senior Common Room.

Two Hawks looked up. Anna Catherine had moved deeper into the thicket. He rose and followed her, wading into the bushes. "He writes of this college where he studies. Have you seen such a place? Maybe in the east, in one of those big cities?"

"Philadelphia, you mean? Or New York?" She was hunkered down, picking berries low to the ground. "I've never been anywhere but our farm and Schenectady, and once to Albany." She waved away a swarm of gnats, adding, "Except as a baby."

Fort William Henry. How strange to think they had both been there as infants. His mother had not mingled with the white women at that fort after he and his brother came into the world, except for those that helped in the birthing. Had Anna Catherine's mother been one of those? Had their mothers touched? Looked at each other?

Her voice, a sound long since rooted in his heart, came from the thicket. "Read to me while I pick."

He shot her a wry look. "Could you not tell me all he says without looking?"

"Probably. But I'd like to hear how you're coming along with the reading."

Though he wished she'd denied it, she sounded more herself. He found where he had stopped reading before.

> *"Simply having these two small rooms to myself is heady stuff. Independence! No Mother or Mr. Davies or Cook or anyone telling me how to come and go—except the bells for morning Chapel and dinner of an afternoon, which reminds me to mention that we must all turn out at dinner with our hair most grievously coiffured, powdered, AND curled, else shorn and wigged out, or suffer the consternation of our Heads of House. Barbers are provided for this Necessity, though a Neighbor across the stair is passing good at arranging hair. You would laugh to see me, though I confess I am not sure how long*

*I may bear with the Practice before I dispense with powder
and tail my hair in its Primitive State and shock the entire
Hall."*

Two Hawks raised his head to ask what his brother meant about hair
and heads in houses, but Anna Catherine spoke first. "Your reading is
much improved."

Pride didn't let him admit that half his brother's words were beyond
his understanding. "I spent the winter again studying. I am reading a book
one of Kirkland's assistants loaned me. *The Vicar of Wakefield.*"

Anna Catherine looked at him, eyes bright with surprise. "Papa has a
copy. When you're finished, you must tell me what you think of it. I've yet
to read it."

Two Hawks stared at the letter, not seeing the words for his gladness.
She expected there to be another meeting between them. He hadn't dis-
gusted her with his embrace.

He wished he dared to try it again.

But what was he thinking? The issue of a stolen brother between them
aside, they lived in different worlds, ones that—if what they were hearing
in Kanowalohale was true—might soon collide in open conflict again,
with two sides of white men killing each other for the Haudenosaunee to
choose between, with no Warraghiyagey to keep the Covenant Chain
bright and unbroken.

And what of the chain of friendship between him and Anna Catherine? He could speak her words, and she understood some of his, but did
they truly understand each other? How could they, when they never met
in either of their worlds but in this place between? There was so much
about him she didn't know. So much he'd kept from her.

With an ache in his chest, Two Hawks went back to reading the letter.
And there was his brother, from across the water in England, writing of

one of the things he'd been thinking about. As if William stood there in the berry patch speaking to him face to face.

> *I have written to Father concerning his Worries over who*
> *will step into Sir William's shoes . . . or Moccasins, as the case*
> *may be. I doubt it shall be his son, Sir John, who—if what*
> *Father writes is true—seems little inclined for the Position,*
> *lacking even a scrap of his father's Diplomacy or Empathy with*
> *the needs of the savages. Nor Joseph Brant, who Father seems to*
> *think grasps Sir William's vision and might make a passable*
> *Superintendent of Indian Affairs if he was not, alas, an Indian.*
> *I suppose that leaves Colonel Guy Johnson, Sir William's*
> *nephew, to maintain the Covenant Chain and, it is to be*
> *hoped, keep the savages neutral in the event of Hostilities . . .*

Two Hawks lowered the letter and stared unseeing along the draw. It was no new thing to hear himself described a savage. Even Kirkland used the word in his letters, alongside such words as *tawny brethren*. But this was his own brother calling him so.

His brother thought like a white man. In all ways but one, he *was* a white man.

The thought made his belly roil. It was wrong that a son of the People didn't know what he was, that his mind had been formed by living among whites. Resentment against the man Anna Catherine called Papa surged up as it hadn't done in years. It coiled like poisonous vines around his tongue and set it in motion.

"William writes of who will take Warraghiyagey's place and hold the ends of the Covenant Chain between our peoples. But it is not as simple as another man like Warraghiyagey—if one exists—keeping the nations from taking sides in this quarrel brewing between the English father and his children. Not all Haudenosaunee will hold to what the British tell us, even for the sake of Sir William's memory. There are other men, like Kirkland, who say the king has treated his children as no father should and it is time for the children to stand on their own. He tells us his friends in the east prepare for war."

Anna Catherine was no longer picking berries. She stood a few paces off, waist-deep in the shrubs, looking pale and pinched. "Papa and Mr. Doyle and Captain Lang talk about these things. And William. Now you too. Do *you* think war is coming?"

"Many of my people see its black birds circling."

He regretted the harshness of those words, seeing her slender neck work as she swallowed. "And your people would fight in it?"

"If it comes to choosing sides," he said, striving to conceal his emotion, "not all will go with the British. The *Onyota'a:ka* will probably listen to Kirkland, the *Kanien'kehá:ka* will listen to Brant, and that makes me think there can be no consensus between all the nations over what to do if war comes. We will divide like the whites and turn on each other as enemies. As it was long ago, before the Great Binding Law was given and brought us peace."

Anna Catherine's eyes were round with the enormity of what he'd said. "Jonathan . . . could it truly come to that?"

Her use of his Christian name filled him with conflicting feelings—pleasure, longing, confusion. The warm air seemed to press on him, making it hard to breathe, as if a thunderstorm was gathering over their heads. But no cloud marred the summer sky. No black bird of war.

He didn't want to talk about such things anymore. He folded his brother's letter. "Put this away now."

She waded through the bushes and took the letter, searching his face. "You haven't finished."

"Later." He took the quiver and bow case from around his neck as she slipped the letter through the slit in her skirt. "Let us rest from words—and berries. Show me whether your shooting has improved as much as my reading."

"I have my answer," Two Hawks said, plainly striving not to laugh outright as they tramped through brush to find the arrow she'd shot wildly off among the trees.

"I haven't practiced. I haven't a bow and—there it is." Anna pointed to the arrow's feathered shaft bristling just short of a clump of rhododendron.

Two Hawks strode ahead, reaching it first. "I can make a bow for you. One better suited."

She bit her lip as he straightened, arrow knocked in the bowstring, resting against his bare thigh. The sight of him was distracting; it was hard to keep thinking of words to say when she wanted simply to look at him. "I'd like that, but how would I explain to Papa and the Doyles where I came by it? I should have to hide it in a tree stump." Unless he agreed to come to the house and . . .

She didn't finish the thought. It puzzled her that after so many years he still refused to make Papa's acquaintance. Knowing he would evade the question if she asked, she said, "I'd like to see *you* take care of a woman in her childbed."

Two Hawks spoke with a smug self-assurance. "That will never happen."

"And why is that?"

"I am a man." Oneida women, Two Hawks explained, retreated to a lodge at the edge of town to give birth, with only women to help, and remained there for days after the baby was born. "Until the bleeding stops."

Mildly disconcerted that he knew about such bleeding, Anna wrinkled her nose. "I shouldn't like to leave my home to give birth. I'd rather be in my own room, with my things around me. And Lydia. And Mrs. Doyle."

Two Hawks's eyes gleamed with humor and something deeper. "The women of my people see it as a time of rest from the fields and cook-fires . . . and from their husbands."

Anna's cheeks flamed as though the sun had burned them. What would Mrs. Doyle, or Lydia, think of her discussing such a delicate subject with a young man—a barely clothed one perfectly at ease in talking about it? She tried not to look at the bronzed planes of his chest, gleaming in the sun, but her face burned the more for wanting to look.

Perhaps he sensed her discomfort, for he raised the bow, the arrow still set in the string, only now she was mesmerized by the long muscles of his arms and the round muscles of his shoulders, the way his skin moved across them, supple and firm, as he drew back the bowstring twice as far as she'd ever managed. His hands were steady, his features fixed like an eagle sighting prey. The tension of the drawn bow seemed a part of him, seemed to pass from him to her, until she felt poised like the arrow, trembling on the verge of being cast far and fast by the strength of those sinewy hands.

Had he meant to kiss her before, in the pines? What would it have meant to him had she let him? That she was his woman? His *wife*? Would he have expected her to leave her life, go back with him to Kanowalohale and tend his cook-fire, share his bed, birth his babies at the edge of the village?

I would do it. If he wanted me, I would do that for him. My heart is that arrow, bound to fly where he aims it . . .

"There. Between those hickories. See the clump of sumac?"

His question snapped her free of the spell of his taut muscles, the drawn bow, the heat and power of him. Her heart wasn't the arrow. She wasn't his woman—or anyone else's—and she was supremely glad he was too busy sighting for his shot to have looked at her while she was thinking such outrageous things. "Sumac? I barely see it. You can shoot that far?"

In answer to her breathless query, he released the arrow, which arced past the hickories and disappeared among the far-off sumac. He glanced down at her, mouth slanted in a grin of satisfaction. The sight sent an arrow of another sort arcing low through her belly, a shivering ache and a warming pleasure that collided and spun her thoughts, but because he looked so smug she blurted, "Race you to it!" and sprinted for the sumac, leaving the berry basket and her confusion behind.

She glanced back to see him sling his rifle into a carrying grip and come leaping like a deer after her, bow clenched in his other hand. She strained with all her might to reach the sumac first, barely aware of a thrashing in the brush ahead, beyond the hickory trees.

Two Hawks's arm snaked hard around her ribs and jerked her off her feet. They stumbled sideways, scattering nuts and twigs and the bow that went skittering away through leaves. Two Hawks slammed against a hickory trunk, cradling her against his heaving chest, still clutching his rifle.

She struggled for breath, started to gasp out, "That was cheat—" but his fingers came around her mouth, cutting off her words, as out of the sumac a dozen paces away burst a massive, black-furred bear, writhing and twisting on itself to reach the arrow bristling from its haunch.

Stepping away from the tree, Two Hawks thrust her behind him. He raised the rifle but didn't fire. The arrow had barely wounded the bear, having lost its impetus before it struck. A swipe of a paw dislodged it. Then the bear swung its gaze toward them. With nothing between but a few yards of open ground, the force of its presence was immense and terrifying. Facing them on all fours, it grunted deep in its throat.

Time seemed to slow, catching Anna and Two Hawks and the bear in some suspended pocket where every thunderous heartbeat was a suffocating eternity, every breath an endless gasp. They were going to die—unless Two Hawks took his shot—and thus she gaped in horrified disbelief as he lowered the rifle, pointing its muzzle at the sky and, instead of shooting the bear, spoke to it.

His voice was calm, reasoning, yet Anna's stunned mind could make no sense of his words. She caught the name for bear—*ohkwa:lí*. That was all. Her heart beat like the wings of a trapped bird. Her gaze fixed on the bear's small eyes, every instinct screaming *run*.

She couldn't move.

Two Hawks stopped talking. The bear's black nostrils flared, smelling them. It gave another grunt, then heaved its bulk sideways, crashing back into the sumac scrub.

Anna's knees banged together as the sumac shivered and stilled. The sound of the bear's passage faded. She felt a squeeze on her fingers and looked down. She was gripping Two Hawks's hand with all her might. She looked up to find him grinning as though what had just transpired left him filled with awe. Not the sheer terror gripping *her* in its maw.

She burst into tears.

Two Hawks must have set down his rifle and pulled her against him, or maybe she flung herself at him. She didn't know, only that she was in his arms, muffling her sobs against his salty skin. After a time, the steady rhythm of the heart beneath her cheek calmed her. Two Hawks had a hand on her back, his other arm curved around her waist. It was stifling hot, but . . . oh, it was blissful comfort.

"It is gone." He sounded as if he'd been saying those words for some time. She felt his lips press against the top of her head. Her cap had gone missing, her braid come unpinned, hanging heavy against her back. Her cheek was slick with sweat where it touched his chest. She was drenched from running, and from fear, but didn't want to stop holding him. Didn't want to face what had just happened.

"Wha—what did you say to make it go?"

She felt his chest move with laughter. "No one makes *ohkwa:lí* go or do what he does not want to do. You trick him or ask nicely. I told this one

I was sorry my arrow hit him, that I was glad I had not hurt him badly, that I did not mean to hunt him today. I asked him to forgive me and go in peace and let us do the same."

Anna marveled. How could he have had the presence of mind to stand before that angry, injured bear and say such things? "Weren't you afraid?"

"Not for myself. But beneath the words I was saying to *ohkwa:lí,* I was praying to Heavenly Father. I did not want *you* to be hurt because I did a foolish thing in shooting an arrow farther than I could see to make you think much of me."

Anna felt a shudder go through him. It brought on a fresh eruption of tears, and she cried against his chest. "I would have run smack into that bear if you hadn't caught me. I was sure—sure I was about—to die!"

Two Hawks put her from him, far enough to look into her eyes. "Anna Catherine, do you not know Creator has us in His hand? Nothing can separate us from Him. Not even death."

Anna shook her head. "I don't think I know God the way you do." It was a frightful thing to admit, as terrifying in its way as that bear coming out of the sumac. "How are you so certain about God—and death? About everything?"

There was a look in his eyes of pain, almost anguish. Then it was gone, replaced by tenderness. "I am not certain about even most things. But I know Heavenly Father is with me because I asked Him to be. I have the blood of Jesus covering me."

"The red blanket of His goodness?" She surprised herself, recalling those words of Stone Thrower's, spoken long ago.

Two Hawks smiled his broad, beautiful smile. "Yes, covering all my sin. And when Heavenly Father looks at me, what do you think He sees?"

"The goodness?"

"His own goodness, yes. The blood of His Son, who died in our place so we can live forever with Him, after we pass from this life—when that day comes." *But not today,* his eyes reassured her.

She closed hers. "That's what I want."

He waited until she opened her eyes, and what she saw in his gaze left her feeling as though his arms were still around her. His arms and, strangely, Papa's too. Was that what God's arms felt like? Like the arms of a man who was friend and father and . . . maybe lover, all in one?

"Pray with me," Two Hawks said. "We will settle this for you. You need not walk your path another day in fear. Not of bears, or war, or men like Warraghiyagey dying and leaving none to take their place." His brows tightened. There was something going on inside him too, a wrestling his words to her had stirred. "Whatever may come, we do not have to fear."

He knelt beneath the hickory, brushed away the nuts and twigs on the ground before him, and reached for her hand. "Will you pray?"

He might have been on his knees asking her to marry him, if that was a thing Oneidas did. Then it dashed across her mind that what he *was* asking would link them forever, in a different way.

Breathless with the intimacy of it, Anna put her hand in his and knelt.

24

Harvest Moon 1775

Lying wakeful on his sleeping bench, Two Hawks listened to the rain outside, pounding the earth, drumming on the roof of his mother's lodge, muffling the murmurs across the dying fire. These he paid little mind to until he caught the name his parents still used when referring to his brother. He-Is-Taken.

It was no surprise William was heavy on their minds. Just three days ago, Two Hawks had returned from seeing Anna Catherine again, and told them what he learned from her, that it would not be many more seasons before William was done with Oxford. Then he would return to them.

"What will we do then?" his mother asked his father in the dark of the lodge. It was a question everyone was asking these days—not because of Two Hawks's brother; because blood had been spilled at a place called Bunker Hill, and the birds of war wheeled over the land for all who had eyes to see.

Back in spring, Samuel Kirkland had been removed as their missionary by Colonel Guy Johnson, who resented Kirkland's loyalty to the new Congress of the colonials and threatened him should he return to Kanowalohale. Though Colonel Johnson had since fled to Canada, the Congress Kirkland supported kept him traveling far and wide to councils and gatherings. Now, when they most needed guidance, when staying neutral in this conflict between the colonials and their king was becoming hard to do, when some prominent Oneidas, like the war chief at Oriska Town, Honyery Doxtader, had made their choice and joined up with the farmer-soldiers of a militia chief called Nicholas Herkimer, putting their names on his papers, promising to scout for the Americans. Now, when it seemed their prayers about William might soon be answered.

Two Hawks eased himself over on his bench and stared at the cookfire embers, thinking about those Oneidas who'd agreed to be scouts, feeling his own blood stir in answer to that call. But it wasn't himself acting as scout he saw by the embers' glow. It was Anna Catherine, filling his head and heart.

Looking back, Two Hawks knew he'd loved her long before he understood what could exist between a man and woman—like it was between his parents, a bond so strong it had weathered grief and separation, disappointment, blame, hurt. A thing tempered now like pounded iron. Perhaps he'd loved her since that first time he saw her bounding toward him across the clearing, hair streaming behind her, fleeing the pain of losing William. He'd known for certain he loved her since the day more than a year past when he shot the bear and she wept in his arms.

"Bear's Heart." He'd spoken the name over her as they rose from praying, seeing those green-brown eyes of hers luminous with tears and joy and question. "When an Oneida goes under the water," he'd explained, "he gets a new name. A Christian name. You should have a new name."

"But I haven't been baptized," she'd said. "Not yet."

"You were baptized in courage today. You have a bear's heart now." She'd smiled at him, and he'd thought his heart would burst with joy.

His heart still rejoiced that Heavenly Father let him be the one to put her hand in His, and since that day the sun hadn't moved a finger's length across the sky without his thinking of her, longing for her with as much anguish as joy.

He was feeling that anguish now, for across the whispering embers his father wasn't talking of love but vengeance, how he still struggled with the need of it. How the dream of killing Reginald Aubrey still ruled his heart in the night.

Two Hawks recalled, all too painfully, the last time it had done so. His father's inarticulate shouting, his mother's calming voice, his own frantic heart slowing as he stared into the lodge's shadows, realizing it was the dream again. His parents' voices:

"What about the white beads? If you would only—"

"No."

"If you buried them when you left us—dig them up now."

Two Hawks had waited, breath held, only to hear his father's choked reply, "I cannot!" and the sound of him struggling out of the furs, stumbling out of the lodge into the night.

That big warrior who once frightened and embittered Two Hawks with his drunkenness and anger, but filled his chest now with pride for how he'd let Creator remake him, had wept over his struggle with those old dark impulses and the dream that would not release him. He was a warrior fighting an unseen battle.

Two Hawks's belly cramped with dread. Surely his father would win it, with Creator's help. He *must*. If he didn't, if one day he killed Reginald Aubrey in his attempt to take William back, surely it would be the end of . . . whatever it was between him and Anna Catherine. Whatever it might have become.

If William never returns . . . none of us need find out. The pain in his belly tightened, cinched by guilt. He wanted to believe Anna Catherine's feelings for him were as deep as those she held for William, that she wanted him in her life as much as she wanted his brother, but already he feared she was pushing him away.

"They grow suspicious," she'd told him days ago. "Mrs. Doyle asked me this morning was I meeting a neighbor lad in the woods, since I still go so often. I said of course I wasn't. You aren't our neighbor. Not like she meant."

It had felt like a lie to her, what she told the Irishwoman. Her troubled face told him so. And he'd known with a sinking heart that he must cease coming to see her so frequently so she would stop expecting it, stop slipping away so often to look for him.

Or should he defy his father and make himself known to *her* father? Force everything into the open now . . .

Even as he turned the idea over with a fearful longing, he knew he wouldn't do it. His parents had endured enough sorrow over his brother to last many lifetimes. He couldn't add to it by risking their hope of seeing William again, even if not doing so was stealing his hope.

His parents had quieted. Two Hawks turned on his bench, the weight in his chest like a stone shifting. He would wait before journeying to see Anna Catherine again. Through the winter would be best. Let those who suspected she went to the forest for anything but berries and herbs conclude otherwise. *Wait until spring.*

An eternity! He'd never survive it.

A few moons then. One, at the least . . .

Two Hawks breathed out in defeat, knowing he couldn't wait even that long. His heart gave a thump, as if it leapt for joy at having won out over reason. He smiled in the darkness, anticipation flooding him. At last he let the drumming of the rain lull him toward sleep, knowing he would see Bear's Heart again soon.

It was so reckless a thing for Two Hawks to have done, Anna feared her heart was going to beat out of her chest. Seconds after she'd come down from the house to visit Papa's foal, born in late summer to his favorite riding mare, Two Hawks had crept behind her into the chilly, dawn-shadowed barn. She'd sputtered a few incoherent words before the trill of a whistled tune had him diving under a pile of sacking in the neighboring empty stall. Anna kicked sacks over him and whirled toward the graying rectangle of the barn door as Mr. Doyle stepped within, took up a pitchfork, then spotted her standing, frozen and dry-mouthed, by the brood stall.

"Anna," he exclaimed. Then a somber cloak fell across his voice, like Mrs. Doyle's had worn earlier. "You're up early this morn."

"I came down to see the filly. What—what are you doing?"

Perhaps he'd taken the strain in her voice as evidence of the tears she'd shed last night. She read sympathy in his searching eyes. "Aimin' to muck out some stalls before Maura has the porridge warm."

Anna lowered her gaze. Saddened as she was by the terrible news that had come yesterday, via William's letter, her heart still fluttered as though it meant to take flight. Everyone was saddened, including Mr. Doyle, who set about the work of cleaning stalls with a face preoccupied and subdued, forking ripe manure into a cart.

A nearby rustling jangled Anna's nerves, but it was only the foal, come to thrust her muzzle between the slats. "Good morning, pretty girl." Anna's hand shook as she ran it along the filly's neck. "So bright-eyed this early morn . . ."

There was nothing for it but to count the seconds and keep up a running chatter to cover any noise Two Hawks might inadvertently make, while behind her Mr. Doyle forked stale hay and droppings into the cart. What had come over Two Hawks? Did he have it in mind to finally meet Papa? He couldn't have chosen a worse time for it, if so.

She glanced across the aisle. Finished with one stall, Mr. Doyle moved to the next, bending to the work. He was directly across from the pile of sacking now. Anna risked a glance. A patch of blue-striped linen peeked between two sacks. Two Hawks had a new shirt, the cloth still bright from dying.

She nearly yelped when Mrs. Doyle's distant voice drifted through the open barn door, calling them to breakfast. Mr. Doyle leaned the pitchfork against the stall. Leaving the cart in the aisle, he started for the door but paused when she didn't follow. "Aren't you comin' then?"

"I've eaten," she said, hoping the morning shadows hid her blush as she compounded the lie. "I had toast."

Mr. Doyle's craggy face showed his doubt. "That's hardly fittin' breakfast."

"I know. I . . . don't feel much like eating just now." Truer words couldn't have been said, though not for the reason Mr. Doyle supposed.

"All right, Anna."

She didn't breathe until his footsteps scuffed along the track toward the house. "It's safe," she hissed.

The sacking erupted as Two Hawks scrambled to his feet, brushing at himself with frantic motions. "There was a mouse in there with me. It ran up my shirt and out at my neck."

"Never mind *mice*. What are you doing here?"

"I had to see you again."

The longing in his gaze sent surges of joy and fear clashing within her. She grabbed his arm and hauled him toward the barn door. "I'm glad. I've something to tell you, but we have to get you out of here while they're to breakfast."

"Will they miss you?"

Anna peered out. Mist curtained the river, chill and dank. She couldn't see the house. The track was clear. All they need do was dart across it and be into the tall corn, which stretched nigh to the creek. "We'll have to hurry."

Linking hands, they made a dash for it.

Through the cornfield and across the creek he followed her without speaking. At the base of the hill where the little waterfall spilled, Anna Catherine halted and faced him. The tip of her nose was pink with the autumn chill, her breath a cloud on the misted air. But what caught at his heart were her eyes. They were red and swollen—like his mother's eyes so many mornings of his childhood.

"You have been weeping." He started to raise his hand to her face but stopped. "Is it to do with William?"

Tears pooled in her eyes. "How did you know?"

Guilt stabbed him clean between the ribs, remembering that bad thought he'd had about William, wanting him to stay away. Then Anna Catherine was talking again, saying it wasn't really about William so much as the woman who took him away. The woman he called *mother.*

"She's dead. A sudden illness. William tried to make it home in time, but she died alone, with none by but a few servants Papa has kept on there."

Two Hawks drew in breath, searching Anna Catherine's face. "I am sorry for it." The woman had treated her badly. But now . . . it wasn't right to speak ill of her. Anna Catherine seemed to read his thoughts.

"I know she didn't love me. She didn't even like me. But she *did* love William, and he her."

"And you love William." His throat tightened when she nodded, wiping at a tear.

"By now Mrs. Aubrey is buried and William's back at Oxford, but I wish I could be with him."

Two Hawks swallowed past the ache. He was sorry for his brother's pain, but his belly twisted with that too-familiar agony. What was going to happen when William returned? Even if Stone Thrower didn't kill Reginald Aubrey, what would William do when he learned the truth? If he turned against Aubrey, would Anna Catherine lose her brother? If he turned against his Oneida family, would *he* lose his Bear's Heart? Would she feel he had lied to her, betrayed her, all this time?

"Do you have the letter?" he asked her.

"Papa has it." Her brows pulled together. "He's been sitting in his chair like someone came along and knocked him on the head. It's been so many years since he's even seen Mrs. Aubrey, I honestly don't know how he's feeling. He hasn't wanted to talk about it."

Two Hawks didn't know what to say about Aubrey, so he asked, "What will William do?" thinking perhaps this death would bring other changes, ones his parents would be anxious to know about.

"Finish out his studies, I suppose. Go home to that empty house in Wales between terms." Her eyes took on the sheen of tears again, but for the first time since he walked into that barn with his heart banging, desperate to see her, she seemed to fully take in the fact that he was there. "Why ever you came back so soon, I'm glad. I needed you."

It was sunlight after rain, her words. They filled him, driving every shadowed thought from his mind. "Come," he said, basking in their warmth. "I want to show you something."

The cave opening was a stone's easy toss above the waterfall, hidden by the leading edge of the rhododendron thicket that grew up the rocky slope to the hill's crest. They had to crouch to enter, but once inside it was spacious enough to stand. Anna Catherine's cap didn't quite brush the smoke-blackened ceiling, though Two Hawks had to duck his head.

"How did William and I never find this?" She turned around in the shadowed space thick with the smell of damp stone, her face catching glimmers of light from fissures in the roof. He watched her, enjoying her delight.

"I found it the summer I was fourteen. It is where I hide when I wait for you to look for me." He squatted near the blackened remains of fires built over the years, next to the rifle, blanket, and provisions he'd left there before crossing the cornfield.

She crouched beside him, tucking her petticoat up off the cave floor. Her face caught the light streaming in from the low entrance. "I cannot stay long. I wish I could."

"It may be spring before I see you again." It would soon be time for trapping fur game, and he must help with that. When Anna Catherine started to rise, he grasped her wrist. "Wait. I want to see . . ."

"What?" she asked when he hesitated.

"Your hair."

Time stretched while she stared at him. From deep in the little cave, in some recess near the spring's source, came the sound of water dripping.

"My hair?"

"As it was when I first saw you. Remember?"

Even in the dimness he could tell her face had turned a dusky shade. "I do, but—"

"Please, Bear's Heart. Then I will go."

She wavered, lip tucked between her pretty teeth, pleasure in the name he'd given her a light in her eyes. Then, wordless, she reached up and removed her cap and set it at her knee. With quick, deft movements she plucked out pin after pin, setting each inside the cap, until the heavy, gold-streaked coil of her braid tumbled to her waist.

She questioned him with her eyes. He nodded.

Now her fingers were unraveling the long plait. Now they were shaking out its sections. Now her hair was unbound, rippling in waves, all its honeyed streaks aglow even in the meager light seeping into the cave.

What man should ever need a fire if he had this woman?

He'd only meant to look, but as the thought sang through him he leaned close and put his hand to the flame. He ran his fingers gently down the waving length of her hair, all the way to where it pooled on the floor of the cave. He took up a strand across his palm, golden at the end where it curled a little, darkening up its length to her face all but swallowed in its mass.

She was utterly still, her gaze fixed on his. He felt her breath on his neck as she said softly, "Jonathan . . . I must go."

He longed to kiss her mouth, but boldness failed him. He settled for her brow. A brother's kiss. "Go now. I will think of you. And pray for you."

"For Papa and William too?"

"Yes." More than she could know. He trembled with the urge to take her in his arms. "Go now. Quickly."

She snatched up her cap and pins and ducked out of the cave, twisting that glorious hair over her shoulder to prevent it snagging in the thicket that guarded the opening. He didn't follow her out but stayed alone in the cave for a time, fingers tingling with memory, staring at a solitary pin abandoned on the ground.

The day after Two Hawks showed Anna the cave, Papa came into her room where she sat by the window, penning a reply to William's letter, and said he needed to speak to her. Every nerve in her twanged with dread at the resolution on his face. Despite no one having said a word about her absence yesterday at breakfast, she and Two Hawks had been seen.

Anna jammed the quill into its stand to hide the shaking of her hand.

But that wasn't what Papa wanted to talk about, and it quickly grew apparent he hadn't the slightest suspicion that an Indian from Kanowalohale had befriended her years ago, had talked with her, picked berries with her, taught her to shoot arrows, stood between her and a bear, prayed with her to be forgiven her sins, renamed her Bear's Heart, and yesterday had taken her into a cave and asked her to unpin her hair for him—he'd touched her hair and looked with such longing at her mouth that she thought surely this time he would kiss her.

So he had—on her forehead. Leaving her thoroughly confused.

Papa settled on the edge of her bed and told her of a decision he'd made. Now that Heledd, God rest her, was dead, it was his intention to divest himself of the estate in Wales, to cut his ties there. He meant to inform William that if he wished to continue his education, he would do it an ocean nearer to home.

"We're at war now, see. Every olive branch the colonies have extended to the Crown has been slapped aside. 'Tis independence for us, my girl, or subjugation, and I would have my family under my roof, together and accounted for."

Despite his chilling mention of war, reminding her that even now the newly formed Continental Army had the British redcoats under siege in Boston, Anna flung herself at Papa with a glad cry. "Oh, Papa. At long last, and sooner than I could have hoped!"

"'Tis become a matter of urgency," Papa said when she released him with a kiss upon his scarred cheek. "Should William not take ship soon, it may be impossible for him to do so. I only hope he'll not come kicking and screaming."

Anna laughed at the notion. "Why should he?"

Papa looked at her with eyes that flashed so quickly from feeling to feeling she only half grasped his lack of certainty. "This is William's home," she said. "We're his family. I know you'll wish to write and tell him, but . . . may I mention it in my letter?"

Papa said of course she might, then with a smile rooted more in sorrow than happiness, left her to continue her letter with hands that shook again, but with excitement. William was coming home!

Only one thing might have made the news more perfect. If Papa had decided it a day sooner, she could have told Two Hawks.

1776
THE MOHAWK RIVER VALLEY—
NEW YORK

*D*ifficult to credit it may be, but I tell you there are times I forget my great sin, forget that a scholar at Oxford who bears my name wasn't the son I saw pulled from between the thighs of my wife as the mortars screamed above our heads. Ashamed as I am to own to it, it has been easier with an ocean between us.

But look you, I ought never to have let him go. I took him. Claimed him. I should have had the making of him, whatever the burden to my soul. But I have been a selfish man, grasping for an illusion of freedom from that burden. Illusion? Just so. For though I forget for a time, always something brings me hard up against my self-wrought chains. A comment in a letter, a reference to an ancestry he presumes his own. Or it is the dream, the one in which I am hunted. Or the shade of that dream visiting me waking—an Indian plying his canoe on the river, a copper face to launch the question like an arrow at my soul: Is he the one, the father of the lad I call my son? Has he come for me at last?

For nigh on twenty years I have lived this lie. I caused my wife to live it to her death, never knowing. I cause the lad to live it still. Yet in this craven heart there is longing for him, the only son I shall ever know. Have I a right to a second chance with him, when I had no right to the first?

If I deny myself all else, can there be atonement?

I was a man of the People, a hunter, a warrior, and strong. But not always a good man. Sometimes a foolish man, and cruel, when I had the trader's rum in me. Now I am a man of the People forgiven by Creator. Born-again, the preacher calls it. This thing I tell you is true. But still I feel in me the presence of that first man. That man I was before. I have not forgotten how to hunt.

He took my firstborn son. That is what that redcoat did. Not a day passes that I do not feel the wound of it. Am I now to turn the cheek and offer that same redcoat the other son, whose heart I see leading him far from us?

In the heart of my people beats a drum-call for vengeance. And whatever else I am, I am still a man of the People.

25

2 January 1776
Queens College, Oxford

Dear Anna,

*Received your letter of November last along with another from
Father, besides a kind note from Lydia on paper that has made
my rooms to smell of Rosemary and reminds me of her old Shop.*

*More than I can express in words was my appreciation of your
Condolence at the loss of Mama. For all she had her shortcomings,
she was my Mother and I honored her as such. You and I will, I
trust, never comprehend the horrors she and Father endured at the
fall of Fort William Henry, nor the Damage inflicted upon her
delicate Mind—not to mention the death of all my poor little
brothers—but it is clear from your letter that you have reached a
like Conclusion and have, I dare to believe, forgiven her rejection
of your Tender Affection, which you would have lavished upon her
as a Daughter had she permitted it. There is nothing but Grace in
your words of her, no matter how I look between the lines for the
old hurt and wistful regret. Moreover, there is a Compassion I do
not believe feigned, for when did you ever feign Affection?*

*Which begs a Question I have meant to ask. I have reread
some of your Missives from years past (Yes, I save them; forebear
to Tease!) and I detect an Alteration—a general Elevation of
Mood—which I fix at a Twelvemonth past. Something changed
you. Will you tell me what—or should I say <u>who</u>—it was?*

*Of course ere long I shall judge it for myself, and while
I confess to Excitement at thought of seeing you again, despite
what you have written on the Matter I cannot come to terms
with Father's thinking and confess myself as consternated over
the Whole Affair as I was during Michaelmas Term when he
wrote of his Grand Plan. I know the pair of you are "thick as
thieves" as Mrs. Doyle has put it in her letters, that you hold him
in the highest Regard and Fatherly Affection, but I wonder if
this has clouded your view of the Situation? I beg leave to note
that it does not seem to me, judging from your letter, as if Father
has shed sufficient light upon his Reasoning for your benefit
either, yet where you are accepting of his Plans and Purposes, my
heart and mind teem with questions. Why sell the Estate? Why
summon me home before my studies are concluded, if I can still
call home a land where so many of its Citizenry stand in open
Rebellion to their King? Be glad you needn't endure the talk I
hear daily in the halls of Queens and in every public house
beyond its walls—that a ragtag band of farmers and shopkeep-
ers styling themselves an Army would take on the might of
Britain's forces is cause for the rudest scoffing and Indignation.
I blush for the ribbing I endure from those who know me not
Welsh-born, but a Colonial. Mayhap it shall be short-lived, this
Rebellion, and swiftly crushed. The only battles I wish to wage
are fought among dusty tomes and even dustier Tutors. And in
these battles I am being tempered, proven a worthy Warrior.
I have a Life here! How if I were to refuse to abandon it? Stage
my own Rebellion, plant my feet in Oxford and vow to remain?*

*Of course my musket lacks powder, and my bayonet is
waxen. Father's Factor is already neck-deep in the process of
divesting the family of our Ancestral Estate, and I am soon to be
landless and penniless, and Degrees are not granted for Charity's*

sake. Back across the Ocean I am bound come Spring and am
meant to be thankful for the Allowance Father grants me to
finish out the present Term.

But enough. I shall style myself the Dutiful Son and return
to New York. I do long to see you again—never doubt it despite
my ill-tempered Foot-stamping in these pages. Perhaps then I can
make Father see reason. In the meantime I have every Intention
of discovering what lies behind the aforementioned change in
your letters. Spare me the Suspense. Write soon and give answer
to your most obedient and curious Brother,

William Llewellyn Aubrey

28 February 1776
Schenectady, New York

Dearest William,

Your letter of January last comforts and troubles me, which
ought come as no Astonishment since that is what you are to me,
Consolation and Vexation, oft times concurrently! I say that with
all due Affection and with Assurance that you could say the same
of me, though do refrain, at least for the hour of our reunion.

William, I long for you and Papa to be of one mind about
your Homecoming. It aches my heart that the two of you have
grown apart in your thinking on so many Issues. Papa has
endured such Loneliness these past years, and I have not been
equal to the task of assuaging it. As strained as things were before
you left, given the state of her unhappiness here, still I believe
Papa missed your Mother as much as he has missed you. As for
the state of Matters beyond the confines of our Farm, I confess
myself too uninformed to attempt to persuade you to think on

*things Political in any manner other than you do. But speaking
to your Comment that what is happening here is not your
Quarrel, you may see that it is mine, and it is Papa's, and it is
Lydia's, and that of everyone you name Family, Friend, and
Neighbor in New York. Perhaps Papa did not mention in his
last letter the News of Sir William Johnson's son, Sir John, how
he sent a letter to Governor Tryon in which he expressed his
intention to raise a Loyalist Battalion for the British cause,
including some five hundred Indians—right across the river at
Johnstown!—to retake the forts in the west being held by our
militia. General Schuyler, along with the Tryon militia,
managed to bring that to naught, disarming the men he'd
assembled, although Sir John was paroled and set at Liberty.*

*Perhaps once you are home for a time your heart will follow
your feet? Papa and I, and the Doyles, desire above all else to
have you with us again as we face these Uncertainties, and
toward that end I bend all my Hope and Prayers to Heaven for
you daily, lifting you before the Throne of Grace for safety in
Travel, health of Body, and contentment of Soul, resting assured
that our Heavenly Father has you in His hands, which is a cause
of utmost Comfort as you are dear (dearest!) to us all, most
especially to the Heart of your sister,*

Anna Doyle

*7 April 1776
Crickhowell, Breconshire*

Dear Anna,

*Do not think I failed to note the Lack of Response to my
Query. Far from brushing the Matter aside, your silence only*

*whets my Curiosity and compels me to ask again. What is it
that causes this depth of Joy I sense in you these past months,
that even as you talk of heartache at my hands, you bless me
with your Affection and Prayers? Of course, what I have
greatly feared has come upon me! I must endure a sea voyage
ere I have my Answer, as I shall myself be hot on the heels of
this letter and perhaps outrace its Journey, if the Winds be fair.
There is nothing for it but to possess my Soul in patience,
which seems to be the lesson Providence has Designed for this
Hour. Term is ended. I, with my trunks and my folded up
Dreams, am home at Crickhowell. I'm to retrieve several
Artifacts of our family that Father has asked I convey to him,
and a few which I fancy for myself—including Grandfather's
bow. Then what is left but to wander these rooms and passages
a final time and visit Mother's grave. How sad to think of her
resting here alone in years to come.*

*I send ahead my Gratitude for your faithful Prayers. I do
not know how I deserve them, but confess myself glad of them,
and you. I shall refrain from addressing the subject of our
illustrious Neighbors across the River. Let us discuss them and
their doings upon my arrival. Better yet, let us instead take a
run through the Beeches and sit by your Waterfall and see if for
that Hour at least we may wink at the Wide World and pretend
what concerns us is of such small Matter as when last you sat
there beside your most dutiful Brother,*

William Ll. Aubrey

26

April 1776

"*I* have it in mind to supply General Schuyler with a few of our bateaux—more than a few, actually," Reginald told Ephraim Lang, who'd accompanied him from the Binne Kill into town on an errand to the cooperage, where Sam Reagan was employed when not piloting bateaux on the Mohawk. He'd held his tongue and saved the announcement until they'd passed several townsmen and women, so as to not be overheard.

Lang raised his brows. "In addition to the grain shipments for Boston's relief?"

"Aye. What say you of the prospect?" Reginald lifted his hat to an elderly woman who passed them near where the McClaren apothecary had stood. Now a haberdashery, he couldn't see it without experiencing a pang of sadness for Lydia.

They strode on, the captain scratching at his whiskers, blue eyes bright in his sun-leathered face. "Well now, Major, reckon I'd say *huzzah* and *hallelujah*. Only I'd be inclined to say it quiet-like . . . unless you mean to use the occasion to hoist a Liberty pole over our corner of the Binne Kill?"

"To which you'd say *huzzah* as well?" Reginald inquired, brushing absently at wood shavings clinging to his coat sleeve. Before Lang could reply, Reagan's voice called to them.

"Mr. Aubrey, I've those buckets you ordered here." They'd reached the cooperage. In the yard, Sam Reagan was holding a trussing ring steady round a circle of staves, while the master cooper cranked the windlass to tighten them into proper barrel shape. Reagan jerked his chin toward the interior of the shop. "Be just a moment."

"Take your time," Reginald said, then noticed Reagan's left eye, bruised, the skin around it swollen. He quirked a brow at it.

"What? Oh," Reagan said and shot them a cheeky grin. "Serves me right, talking politics in taverns."

The cooper, a burly man with a scar through his lower lip, glanced up from their work. "If ye'd pick a side and stick to it, ye'd maybe not arouse the ire of your neighbors quite so much."

A look of . . . *something* too brief to read sharpened Reagan's features, before his hazel eyes danced with a careless light. "So I like playing devil's advocate. I'll take the punishment that comes with it."

The cooper grabbed a metal hoop and a pair of mallets. He tossed one at Reagan, whose hand shot up to catch it. "Punishment's what I'll be dealing out presently," he growled, "do ye no' keep your mind on what ye're doing."

Reginald shook his head, amused . . . and perplexed. Devil's advocate? Whatever that meant, Reagan seemed to have a knack for creating drama wherever he turned up. While the rhythmic thuds of hammering went on behind him, he turned back to Lang. "It's no poles I'll be hoisting. No need to announce our doings, but none to hide them, either."

General sentiment in the Mohawk Valley was leaning sharply away from England, to the point that Colonel Guy Johnson, who'd stepped into William Johnson's role as superintendent of Indian affairs, had decamped from the valley, leading more than two hundred loyalists and Mohawk supporters to refuge in Montreal.

Though he'd signed every declaration of association and loyalty oath circulated by the Continentals' Committee of Safety, and abided by every trade boycott, Reginald had left it to louder mouths—like Reagan's—to spout their opinions in Schenectady's streets and taverns. Nominally a member of the Albany militia, there was no denying the crippling wound taken in the Old French War would make campaigning in rough country difficult, if not impossible. But there were other ways of serving. Having evacuated Boston in March, the British had left behind a stunned and starving populace. As had other Mohawk Valley farmers, Reginald had sent grain east.

How long, and how widespread, the present conflict would prove was anyone's guess, but with Guy Johnson in Canada, it didn't take a prophet to foresee the need to garrison the colony's western forts along the Mohawk River and the Oneida Carry. General Washington's army would stand in need of bateaux for the supplying of those garrisons.

"We won't have to send the bateaux anywhere," Lang confirmed, his voice carrying in the sudden hammerless quiet. "Just have 'em ready for Schuyler when the need arises."

Glancing aside, Reginald noticed Sam Reagan staring at them. He opened his mouth to inquire about the buckets, when a decidedly feminine voice spoke his name.

"Reginald?"

Putting his back to the cooperage yard, he found Lydia standing behind him, looking trim and lovely in a blue gown and matching sweep of hat. "Lydia. Well met, and good day to you. Were you merely passing or . . . ?"

The dazzling smile she gave him set his pulse to quickening. "I'm in need of a piggin, but I meant to come down to the Binne Kill after. Is it a bad time?"

"Not at all," Captain Lang cut in, making her a brief bow. "I'll just have a talk with Sam here about his trip upriver tomorrow. Your servant, ma'am." Grin barely concealed, Lang left them in the yard and hauled Sam away through the open shop doors.

Reginald waited while Lydia and the master cooper haggled over the price of a piggin, then Lydia came out into the gray of the overcast afternoon, carrying the small bucket by its elongated handle.

"Had you something to discuss with me?" Reginald asked. Above them thunder rumbled. They both glanced skyward. The clouds sagged, heavy with the threat of moisture.

Lydia glanced about the yard, the wide brim of her hat casting her features in shadow. "I . . . Yes, I do, as a matter of fact."

Clearly she didn't wish to discuss it there. Distracted, warmed, and inordinately pleased by her presence, Reginald offered his arm. "Come you back to the quay with me then. We'll talk—and maybe beat the rain."

Perhaps she'd something concerning Anna to discuss. They did so, from time to time. Though Anna was always eager to tell him—oft times in too great detail—about the babies she'd helped birth, or something new she'd learned, he valued Lydia's perspective on his daughter's burgeoning skills and calling and was gratified she took the time to keep him appraised.

They'd nearly exited the yard before Ephraim Lang's drawling voice called, "Don't worry about the buckets, Major. I'll see they make it down to the Binne Kill."

He'd forgotten Lang, the buckets, and his head, apparently. He and Lydia pivoted as one to see his boat captain *and* his crewman both attempting—a halfhearted effort at best—to stifle their grins.

Blushing—at his age. He couldn't deny it. Nor could he deny his awareness of the woman whose small hand lay warm in the crook of his arm as they walked, moving quickly with a renewed clap of thunder on their heels. Thirty years of age she must be now—or was it thirty-one?—and still she was as shapely and inky-haired as she'd been at twenty.

At four-and-forty he was by no means ready to admit himself an old man, but Lydia's youthfulness made him aware of his irrevocable middle age—complete with inexplicable aches that plagued him of a morn and the all-too-explicable pain of his hip, which rarely gave him respite now. Even so he'd kept active, on horseback or the river most days, and could boast of an otherwise reasonably preserved physique below the neckcloth, which felt of a sudden constricting, though he'd tied it loosely for the day's labor.

He did his best to suppress his limp and keep to their brisk pace, wanting her to think . . . Well, maybe he was an old fool after all, but he wanted her to find him appealing as a man, not one to be pitied. Thankfully it was a short walk to the quay. They were already in sight of the river.

Lydia was unusually silent.

"Is it Anna you wished to speak of?" he asked her. "'Tis been some time since we have." Anna was at the farm at present but due to come into town with him on the morrow. "How fares our girl these days?"

He liked the way it felt to say. *Our girl.*

"Oh," Lydia said vaguely, as if he'd jarred her from another train of thought. He glanced down but could see only half her face for that sweeping hat. "Anna does well," she said, warmth infusing her voice. "In some ways better than I do. She has a tender way with patients I admit I lack at times. She's very patient."

"Patient with the patients, is she?"

Lydia laughed, a bit too lavishly for so lame a jest. He'd the impression something was making her unwontedly nervous.

They'd reached the boatyard before the first drops of rain hit them. In seconds the drops became a deluge, but they were already scurrying for his office door. He wrenched it open and stood aside for her. She swept in with her piggin, and he followed.

The air inside was stuffy. Despite the rain now gushing down in sheets beyond it, he left the door wide and proceeded to remove his dampened coat, then to turn up the sleeves of his shirt in preparation for the afternoon's work. "So then, do you think she'll follow this calling for a good many years?"

"I . . . Actually, Reginald, I don't know."

Lydia's words were rushed, slightly breathless. He looked up from his sleeve-turning to find her watching him, gaze riveted on his bared forearms, and he realized belatedly what he was doing in front of her. Too late now to rectify it.

Lydia set the piggin on a bench inside the door and, taking his cue, pulled the pins from her rain-soaked hat and set it on the bench beside her new purchase. Her cap, worn toward the back of her head, left the hair swept back from her brow a framing shadow, with a few loose strands left to curl about her ears. When she spoke, her voice just carried above the drumming rain, and she kept her face turned toward the window, where smudged light fought to penetrate the rain-streaked glass.

"Anna has a bright mind and is good at midwifery—at every aspect of the healing art I've taught her. And as I said, she has a very nice way with people."

He wished she'd look at him. "Am I hearing a *but* in there somewhere?"

Lydia sighed. "I don't sense in her the same . . . *need,* I suppose, that I feel when it comes to healing—have felt for as long as I can recall. I do think, if she chose it, she'd make an excellent midwife for the rest of her days. One thing I've noticed about Anna, when she sets her mind to something, she does it well."

Reginald warmed at the praise. "Aye, that she does. And another thing about Anna, she loves you. I'm sure half the pleasure she derives from this arrangement comes from your company."

Lydia appeared startled but deeply pleased. She glanced at him, then away again, turning toward the window. "I remember the day I came to the farm to tell her I was marrying Jacob." A smile came into her voice. "She thought it the end of our friendship, and it had barely begun . . . But I don't see Anna devoting herself to midwifery lifelong. I fully expect she'll marry, have children of her own, but until then . . ."

She turned to him, blue gaze searching, as if she expected him to say something. A frown appeared between her brows.

"Lydia? You've plainly something on your mind besides Anna. Is there ought amiss?"

"Not amiss, no. I want to ask a question of you and am having difficulty finding the words to begin."

He smiled at her. Even in professing hesitation, she came at it straight as an arrow. Though not always a comfortable trait, it was one he admired in her. He'd gone behind the counter, but now he rounded it—trying not to limp—and took her hand in his, turning her so that what light the curtaining rain permitted fell upon her face. "You mentioned friendship before. How long is it you and I have been friends?"

Surprise flared in her eyes, at his touch or his question he didn't know. "For my part, since I was twelve years old."

Reginald had in mind another period of their lives to mark the start of what might properly be called their friendship—around the time of her marriage to Jacob, actually. But her response added weight to his reassurance. He squeezed her hand between his and released it. "So you know you can tell me whatever it is. Mind you, if there's aught I can do for you, you've but to ask it."

She smiled softly, perhaps hearing the Welsh lilt strengthen in his voice, as it often did at times of deep emotion. Did she know that?

"Very well." Though seeming reassured, the smile disappeared. "Of necessity I've refrained from saying this for months—years, if I'm honest—but now that things are altered and what once stood between us as insurmountable does so no longer . . ." A tide of pink surged into her cheeks. "You see, I've often thought . . . that is I've felt that I—that you—"

Fumbling to a halt, Lydia breathed out audibly through her nose. He watched her, fascinated by this uncharacteristic ineloquence.

"I wish to know . . . I *need* to know, Reginald, where your heart and head are concerning Heledd."

He stared, lost in the blue of her eyes as her words tumbled round him, graspable as the rain still pouring in runnels from the lintel of the office doorway. His heart and head? His heart was in his chest, whipped to a rib-bruising gallop. But the mind of which she inquired was gone utterly blank. "You wish to know . . . about Heledd?"

"Yes." She waited, staring at him.

He waited, staring back. The rain had slacked off to a steady patter.

"This is more difficult than I feared." Lydia seemed to gather her small person, drawing herself up straight and looking him in the eye. "Reginald, I am attempting to say that, should you be so inclined to bestow them, I would welcome your attentions in such a manner as might, in due course, lead to our mutual and *united* happiness."

In the face of his stunned silence, she colored up again and added with less articulation than haste, "Should it not be too forward of me to invite them. Should it not be too soon after . . ."

"Heledd," he finished for her. He thought his knees might buckle and drop him to the floor at her feet. It was a near thing, but he stayed standing. "Lydia, I—you—my *romantic* attentions?" he asked round a tongue as clumsy as a block of wood.

"Exactly." She gazed up at him, obviously relieved he'd understood.

Something like a Roman candle burst inside Reginald's chest, shooting giddy sparks out from his center. He could only stand there and let it sweep through him, mute and lightheaded with the wonder of it, when he wanted to shout, to take her in his arms and twirl her around.

Perhaps those desires had made themselves known on his face. A tentative smile curved her lips. "So it's not too precipitous to be speaking of such things?"

Precipitous? He'd been waiting a decade, he realized, to have this conversation, the want of it—of her—darting at the edges of his soul through the years, never invited, never entertained, never allowed to bleed into the realm of the possible. Yet always it had been there, *she* had been there, in the shadows of his heart and mind.

Heart and mind. She'd asked about those. And Heledd. At last he found the words. "I lost Heledd years ago, when she took William to Wales. Long before that, truth be told. What I feel at her passing now is a grief I've carried long. Nothing prevents . . ."

Prevents what you ask of me, and what I want with all my heart to ask of you in return. Your heart and mind.

They were the words he'd meant to say. The words he remembered, almost too late, that he could never say. The speaking of William's name checked his flight and sent him plummeting back to earth, Icarus with melted wings.

Instead of the words, a strangled sound escaped his throat. He turned from her, half staggered to the counter, reaching for a ledger, opening it blindly. Putting his back to the bewildered pillar of silence that was Lydia.

"You've a fair point," he said, the words bitten off like a wince. His gut twisted with the need to face her, to explain himself and what he was doing to her. To them. Instead he took up a quill, removed the cork from an inkwell, and began writing—he barely knew what. "About Heledd . . . and with William coming home . . .'tis best I keep a narrow focus. He's unhappy about this turn, see, but I think given time he'll settle into life here with content."

He wasn't sure he believed his words, but they were the only ones that came to him to say. He couldn't say he feared to take her to his heart and cherish her. Feared if he did so, she would be taken from him.

A punishment long deferred.

Behind him, like a presence in the room, was Lydia's hurt at being brushed aside. Her humiliation. When she spoke, her voice was slow and thick, as though merely forming words now was a challenge.

"So you're saying . . . it *is* too soon?"

The quill stilled in his hand. "Aye. Too soon."

Too late. What had he been thinking, to have assumed for even an instant there could be a future for them? She didn't know him. She only knew the man everyone knew. The man they believed him to be. Not the man who stole a babe, abandoned his own dead child . . . Lydia would despise that man, reject him utterly. And that he couldn't bear. Let them go on in friendship, if that was possible after this. Let her go on seeing him as the wounded soldier, the broken hero, the man who brought Anna into her life. *Let that be enough.*

Behind him Lydia said, "Reginald, are you certain? Because I don't think that's what you began to say to me."

He tried to swallow so he could give her answer. It was like trying to force down a gourd. "You took me off guard. I never expected . . ."

"That I love you?"

"Lydia." Her name came out a groan. "Don't . . ."

He could never recall exactly what she said to cut short the interview, but he would never forget the raw wound in her voice as she asked, with all politeness, whether she should expect Anna on the morrow as usual. He'd said "Yes, of course," and the tap of her heeled shoes had retreated out onto the quay, into the rain still falling, though gently now.

The quill dropped from fingers shaking too badly to hold it. He pictured himself turning, running after her, catching her before she was away into the town, telling her he hadn't meant it, that he'd admired her since she was the girl who named his Anna, that her coming to him today was both honor and joy, that he loved her as he'd never loved any woman. And he would kiss her, and kiss her, until memory of the pain he'd caused her was drowned between them.

He dared not grasp at such unbridled happiness. Dared think no further ahead than William's homecoming. William, to whom he owed a debt the lad must never comprehend. Sin compounding sin.

But there was time to make it right, to strengthen the fraying ties that bound them, to be a father to the lad. Toward that end he must bend all his mind, and for that he would need blinders to keep his heart from straying after other needs, other hopes.

Lydia. Had the Almighty prompted her to make her feelings known, knowing full well the guilt he bore would prevent him pursuing the joy of a union with her?

Reginald folded onto the bench by the door and put his head into his hands. The ache in his chest rivaled the pain of his hip, yet the stone lay firm across his soul. The burden hadn't lifted. Lydia wasn't punishment enough. What more must he deny himself? He dared not bring another cherished face to mind. It was only a matter of time ere God required payment in full.

27

Thunder Moon 1776

*T*wo Hawks found his mother kneeling at the fire, packing a carry-ing basket, when he came breathless into her lodge with news that had him torn two ways in his soul. "Where is my father?"

Good Voice's long braid whipped like a panther's tail as she turned, in her hand a sewing awl. Surprise at his abrupt appearance changed to plea-sure. "He is gone to the fish camp. He left yesterday with his uncle to put the camp in order. The rest of us will follow in the morning. It is good you are back in time. Are you hungry? There is corn soup." She waved toward a gourd bowl set near the fire. "Not so warm now."

"I am not hungry." He was too full of news, and worry, and regret, to think of food.

"You eat too little, so I do not know how your bones have grown so long. Maybe that girl you go to see is feeding you? Maybe you prefer her food to mine?"

His mother smiled as Two Hawks crossed the lodge and hung his rifle and bow above his sleeping bench, hiding the ache her teasing caused. He sat on the bench and leaned forward to meet her gaze. "I cannot go to the fish camp. When I tell you why, I think you also will not wish to go."

His mother's smile faltered. She seemed to gather herself, though she didn't rise. The gathering was all in the planes of her face, splashed golden by the fire's light, in the blue eyes, creased now at the corners. *She knows what I am going to tell her. After all these times of going to Anna Cathe-rine, she knows this time it has happened.*

Then memory jolted him, making him less certain what was in his mother's mind. Two things of importance had happened in the spring-leafed wood where Anna Catherine found him waiting for her, but only one had to do with him. The other was about—

"He-Is-Taken." The name passed his mother's lips like a prayer.

"Yes," he said, knowing now which of those two happenings had flown swifter than his running feet and embedded itself in his mother's heart. Two Hawks wished it might have been the other. "My brother is coming home. Already he is on the great water in the ship that is bringing him."

Saying the words didn't make the news feel more tangible to Two Hawks than when Anna Catherine had all but shouted it.

"William is coming home!" she'd called before she reached him, breathless from running across the clearing. "I've been waiting all winter to tell you. He's already on his way. He'll be here in a fortnight—maybe sooner. Around the middle of May."

Anna Catherine's eyes danced with joy. She was looking at him expectantly, but his throat was a knot of dread. As his heart thundered beat after beat and the silence stretched and only a bird in the trees nearby sang, the light in her face dimmed. "Two Hawks, did you hear me?"

"I heard," he said and wanted in a rush of frustration and longing to tell her everything. Who he was. Who William was. What the man she called Papa had done to his family. And mixed with all that, he yearned to take her by the arm, lead her up the hill to the cave where he'd waited, and make her his in the oldest, surest way he knew—now, before his brother returned and everything changed.

These were not the thoughts of a Christian, but they were strong in him. Two Hawks didn't know what to say, or even to feel.

Anna Catherine was frowning. "Aren't you happy William is coming home?"

"I did not know it would be so soon."

It was not an answer, but the words must have seemed fitting, for she smiled again, so happy about William that she was quickly put at ease. "I've had months to grow accustomed to the news. Papa told me right after I last saw you—the very day after. I wanted so much to tell you then. Had I known the path to Kanowalohale, I'd have come running after you."

Her words made it hard for him to breathe. "Bear's Heart . . . come up the hill with me."

Though he wanted to go to the cave, he knew he mustn't take her there. He turned aside to the little waterfall, and they sat on the rock they'd shared many times, touching all down their sides because the stone now barely fit them both. On her other side the water fell with its small plashing.

The air was cool. Somewhere in the woods, a fox barked.

She clasped her hands between her knees as though she felt a chill. He wanted to take them between his own but didn't trust himself to do even that much.

It was wise that he didn't. She glanced up, and he knew she was also thinking of the cave, and what he asked her to do for him when they were inside it. Thinking of how she'd taken her hair down for him, letting it spill around her, letting him touch it.

He felt the pull of her to his core. "There is something I must tell you."

She leaned away from him, searching his face. "What is it?"

He wrenched his gaze to the greening forest spreading out from the slope on which they sat.

"I am not the firstborn to my mother. I had a brother born before me. We were two-born-together. Twins. Not long before this, my mother was captured by redcoat soldiers, and it was among them she birthed us, in an English soldier fort. Afterward she escaped those soldiers, taking me to my father, but before she could get away, one of the redcoats, an officer, took my brother from beside her while she slept and in his place put a dead baby—his own, we think—and that is how my brother was lost to us."

The words had poured from him like a spring bursting from the rocks, so fast Anna Catherine couldn't have squeezed one of her own in had she tried. He looked at her. She was staring at him, open-mouthed.

"A British officer stole your brother?"

"Yes."

"And your mother couldn't get him back?"

"No. The fort had surrendered. The English left. She never saw his face."

"Two Hawks . . ." She went on staring, a dozen more questions crossing her eyes before she said, "Why are you telling me this?"

"Because it happened."

She shook her head. "I mean, why now? Why haven't you told me before?"

"I could not." His father wouldn't be happy about the little he'd already said, and yet . . . he didn't wish the words unsaid. They'd beat inside him to be spoken for so many years. He only wished he could tell her more, and in wishing it his feelings for her came surging up and he didn't want to think about William anymore.

He lifted a hand to her face. She wore a cap today. Her hair was pinned up beneath it, but in his mind she was in the cave with it down around her shoulders. That was the moment he would go back to and live in, if he could choose a moment. But time was moving forward, out of his control. Would there ever be a moment like that again?

"Anna Catherine, I would keep things as they are now, if I could." No brothers. No fathers. No peoples. No wars. Just the two of them alone, like first man and first woman Heavenly Father put in His garden. He ran his thumb along her jaw to her chin, then brushed it across her lip. "Will you keep a place in your heart for me?"

He felt her shiver, but her breath flowed warm across his hand as she said, "Of course I will."

Telling himself to be content with that, he drew back his hand, even as hers lifted. Her fingers brushed his cheek. He sucked in a breath.

Like a child caught stealing another's food, she snatched her hand away and dropped her eyes. Her touch on his skin lingered as though all his nerves had awakened singing. "Bear's Heart. Look at me."

Her dark lashes swept up. She glanced over his face, then away.

"No. Look at me as you did when we were children. Without fear." He wanted her to drink in his face as she once had—with the innocent fascination of a child for the strange and new. He wanted her to look at him and never stop looking so he could drown in her eyes.

She was trembling. "I cannot."

"Why can you not?"

"I . . ."

Which of them moved first, Two Hawks didn't know. Did he tilt her face up to him? Did she find the courage to lift it? The meeting of their mouths was gentle, a brushing of lips. When she didn't pull away, he fitted his mouth closer to hers. A groan came up from her throat, a feeling sharp and sweet lanced through him, then his arms were around her, pulling her across his thighs, the earth spinning away beneath him, and it was *joy*.

She swayed in his arms and put out a hand as though to catch herself. He tried to hold her tighter, but her reaching hand found stone and she used it to push herself away, scrambling off him in a tangle of skirts.

She found her feet and stood, breathing hard.

He sprang off the rock and reached her in a stride. She didn't back away nor resist his arms enfolding her, his mouth seeking hers again, until with a small cry she thrust free.

"Two Hawks . . . I cannot think when you do that. I need to think!"

He couldn't think either and didn't want to. Her mouth was full and red from his kissing it.

"I only need you," he said, all his love and wanting in the words, in his eyes. He held nothing back, and maybe that was his mistake. Maybe it was too much, even for a woman with a bear's heart.

She whirled from him, and before he could move she was halfway down the hill.

He stood as he had that first time she—a scared little white girl— took fright and ran from him, leaving him watching helplessly as she disappeared into the beeches across the clearing.

My brother is coming home. Already he is on the great water in the ship that is bringing him. Her son's words wrapped themselves around Good Voice's chest and throat like vines. She couldn't swallow past them, couldn't breathe. At last she forced out words. "Coming here?"

Two Hawks's brows soared. "No. Where he lived with Anna Catherine."

Of course her son wouldn't come there. He knew nothing of them, his true family. *But he might soon learn.* The thought sank into her, down through flesh into bone, and started her trembling like a frail grandmother. She put her hands over her face.

She was unaware of Two Hawks stirring until his arms encircled her. They were a man's arms.

As it did from time to time when she stopped and looked at Two Hawks, really looked, and her thoughts would fly to that shadowy newborn who lived in her mind and she'd know *he* was also a weanling, unsteady on fat legs, or a skinny little boy, or a tall, gangly youth, it struck her now that, like his brother, He-Is-Taken would soon be nineteen summers. A man. But a white man in his heart.

Will he want to know me, even so? She clung to Two Hawks, her hands moving in a mother's instinctive caress, under them the long, lean back she'd often stroked, the shoulders nearly as wide now as his father's.

Then she gathered up her pieces and gently pushed her son away.

She'd tried to absorb what she could of this person called William Aubrey from the scraps Two Hawks brought her over the years, stories the girl told him, things he read in his brother's letters. Her whole being yearned toward that young man on his way across the water, stretching toward him like the flames his brother was staring at now with a troubled gaze.

So troubled the muscles of his jaw clenched and his nostrils flared as he drew breath to speak.

"I am sorry," he said.

"Why are you sorry?"

The sound that came from his throat was too strangled to be called a sob. "Sorry you have carried this pain so long. Sorry I have not known my brother. Sorry I have probably ruined things with Anna Catherine."

Brown eyes reflected firelight, and a pain that made an answering ache twist in her belly even before what he said took on substance in her mind. Good Voice felt a dryness in her mouth. "What do you mean, ruined? Have you . . . done a thing to hurt her?"

Ai-ee, she thought as regret rippled over her son's face. She waited in choked silence for him to tell her what he'd done.

He looked away, miserable with guilt. "I kissed her."

Good Voice waited, breath suspended, but Two Hawks clenched his jaw tight and said no more. "You kissed her? That is what you did?"

He didn't seem to hear the relief in her tone. "Yes! And now I do not know if she wants to see me ever again. She ran away, back across the fields to her home. I waited for her to come back, until what food I had was gone. She did not come."

"Then you *must* be hungry." It was a reflex, a mother's response, certain her child needed to be fed, just as certain he hadn't the sense to know it. But he wasn't a child, and that he wasn't hungry after so long a fast told her more than anything how deeply he felt for this girl he called Bear's Heart.

Good Voice steadied herself, afraid there was more he wasn't telling her. "Did anyone see you do this?"

That would be bad, if any of the girl's people had seen it. She should never have let Two Hawks go so many times alone to her. Why had she let him get so close to the man who stole his brother, and close in another way to this girl who had turned his heart inside out?

Because of that cherished, tenuous link to her firstborn, forged through Two Hawks's friendship with Anna Catherine. She'd allowed him to endanger himself, body and soul, because she couldn't bear to give it up. What sort of mother was she to have done this?

"No," Two Hawks was saying, looking as though he carried the weight of all their choices on his shoulders. "I do not think anyone knows about me. Or my father. Or you. At least . . . Anna Catherine did not tell them about us before. Maybe she has now. I do not know. Even if she does not tell, it will be harder now for me—for us—to get to William. It will be harder without Anna Catherine to speak for us. That is why I am sorry."

Knowing that wasn't the only reason for his pain, Good Voice reached for him, putting her hand on his dark head. "We will see your brother. God will make a way." She stroked his hair, silently thankful that it wasn't plucked away like a warrior's. Not yet.

"Do you love that girl?"

"I want her for my wife."

As he drew away, Good Voice felt the blood leave her face. She had known this girl was special to him but . . . her son wanted a white woman for a wife? Not one adopted and raised one of the People. One with no mother for her to speak to, to carry gifts to, to persuade her of Two Hawks's worthiness to marry her daughter, to join her clan. There would be no clan for him to join. His children would have no clan. Had he thought about that?

"I am afraid of what my father will do when he hears William is returning," Two Hawks said into the silence. "If he hurts Anna Catherine's father, she will hate us. Hate me."

"Stone Thrower will not hurt her father." She said the words, but the instant they were out of her mouth she doubted them.

So did Two Hawks. "Do not try to tell me so. I have heard him say with his own mouth that he still has vengeance in his heart. That the dreams still come. They have a power over him, a part of him that he has not given over to Creator."

Good Voice clenched her fists as rage boiled up in her heart, not against Stone Thrower but against the man she still thought of as Redcoat Aubrey. It dismayed her to know there was part of her she had held back as well, held back from being made new and clean. She forced her hands to relax, hoping her son was too distracted to have seen.

"I cannot let him hurt Anna Catherine's father," Two Hawks said. "Or I will have lost her. And it may be we will lose William. Or do you not know that after all this time that man is his father, too?"

That was true enough.

Good Voice was thinking now, hard and fast. Should they keep this knowledge from Stone Thrower? Two Hawks was right. His father had admitted he'd never truly laid aside the need for retribution. And William . . . He was no longer a baby who could be taken back by force, molded to a way of thinking, of being, but a man who could only be persuaded. Spilling blood that might be precious to him now would persuade him of nothing but hate, as Two Hawks had said.

Then she thought of something else. She was the one who lost their firstborn. It was from her side he was taken. Perhaps it had happened this way, this news coming while she was here and Stone Thrower wasn't, so that she might have a chance to do what she failed to do years ago.

Guide me, Father in Heaven.

"We must tell your father your brother is returning," she said. "But we do not have to tell him right away."

That brought a flaring to Two Hawks's eyes, hope leaping, stretching up tall in a steady flame. "When you go to the fish camp, do not tell him.

I will go back and see if Anna Catherine comes to look for me. If she does not, I will go and put my fist to the door of their house to see her and give her father warning."

Give the redcoat warning. That thought had never entered Good Voice's mind. Looking into her son's pleading eyes, she had a revelation: he had determined to forgive Aubrey, forgive completely, for the sake of his love for the man's daughter. And in the heart of his gaze, she saw his hope that she would also forgive the man.

Hadn't she forgiven the redcoat, long ago as she knelt outside the window of Kirkland's house? What was this rage still doing in her heart? It wasn't a killing rage, as Stone Thrower struggled with, but it wasn't forgiveness.

Only one thing was certain in her mind. If there was any chance of William being part of their lives, then they must go to the man who raised him not bearing a war club but with the white beads of peace.

Stone Thrower had buried those beads and refused to dig them up again.

It felt like a dagger in her heart, excluding him from what she meant to do, but she couldn't risk the old rage getting the best of him and ruining what might be their last chance to bridge the chasm that divided their son from his blood, his family, his people. "I will go to the fish camp. And I will keep this knowledge from Stone Thrower."

"What will you say of me?" Two Hawks asked.

"I will think of something. I do not know how long we will have before your father questions your absence at the camp. Go back to that place quickly, my son. Even tonight. And Heavenly Father go with you."

28

May 1776

*P*apa had left her at Lydia's and driven a wagon to Albany to meet the sloop coming up the Hudson, bearing William home. Since they couldn't be sure of the exact day of his arrival, Papa meant to hire a room while he waited. That had been four days ago, and it was all Anna could do not to prowl Lydia's house like an agitated cat. She ran a rag over the dining room's sideboard, breathing fumy linseed oil, her thoughts batted like a shuttlecock between William and Two Hawks.

The notion of Two Hawks's twin, stolen at birth, haunted her. To never know where he was, whether he lived . . . It was almost too horrible to dwell upon. Perhaps it was so for Two Hawks. He'd no sooner told her about his brother before he dropped the subject as if it were a snake, turned to her and asked her to keep a place for him in her heart, then swept away all thought of missing brothers as the world narrowed to his mouth on hers—

"Anna?"

Startled, she snatched up the polishing rag she'd let fall to the floor. Lydia had entered through the kitchen passage, arms around a stack of pewter dishes. "I didn't hear you come in."

"Obviously." Lydia grinned as she set the dishes on the sideboard.

Anna clenched the oily rag and returned to polishing, nearly as mortified to be caught reliving that kiss as she'd have been had anyone come upon her and Two Hawks in the midst of it.

I only need you.

Because she hadn't known what *she* needed, she'd run like the frightened child she'd once been. Every moment since, when she wasn't thinking about William, she'd wondered what would have happened if she hadn't run but let Two Hawks go on kissing her.

"I think we can use it for a mirror now." Anna's hand jerked to a stop as Lydia set a candle atop the sideboard and peered at the flame's reflection in the gleaming wood. She gave Anna's face careful scrutiny. "Shall we break for tea?"

In the kitchen, Lydia brewed a pot of what she called her garden blend, which changed from day to day. This time it was strawberry leaf and lemon balm. Anna had scrubbed her hands and removed her soiled apron. Both she and Lydia were overdressed for housecleaning; they wanted to be ready whenever William and Papa arrived. *As ready as may be.*

Anna's heart gave a thud. She curled her fingers round the steaming teacup and stared at a smudge on the blue cuff at her elbow. Lydia, in plum linen, sat across the table from her and sighed. "Waiting is most wearisome." When Anna didn't respond, she added, "But what news we'll have to tell when they arrive—though like as not they'll have heard about Sir John already, fast as news flies to Albany."

Anna's thoughts flew not eastward but westward. Did Two Hawks know the late Sir William's son, John Johnson, had followed Guy Johnson's lead and fled to Canada?

"And all those families loyal to the Johnsons gone with him." Lydia paused to sip her tea. "To think of women and children forced across those mountains. Poor things must be half-starved by now."

Anna scoured her mind for something to say. She'd heard that General Washington looked to draw the Six Nations in as allies, woo them away from the British, if possible. Surely not the Mohawks, so loyal to the Johnsons and the Crown. Probably not the Senecas, closest to the British in their lake forts. The Oneidas alone among the Six Nations seemed inclined to support the colonists, but what of the Onondagas, Tuscaroras, and Cayugas? Would the Great Peace between the nations be broken, as Two Hawks feared it might be?

She longed to speak of these things to Lydia, but conscience stopped her. Lydia would want to know why she cared, why she knew so much about it. It was Papa she must tell first about Two Hawks. And soon.

I'm being courted. By an Oneida brave.

Feeling warmth steal into her face, she took a gulp of tea and nearly scalded her mouth. She didn't know how Indians went about such things as courting, but surely Two Hawks wouldn't have kissed her as he had if he didn't want . . . more. Was it marriage he wanted?

Anna's belly turned over at the thought. Would Papa countenance such a thing? She was nineteen, old enough to be contemplating matrimony. With a tradesman. Or a farmer.

But Two Hawks was a Christian. *More of a Christian than anyone I know, barring Lydia.*

How sweet was her memory of that Day of the Bear, as she thought of it now, when he prayed with her and she opened her heart to a faith she'd somehow known she lacked. Bear's Heart, he'd called her that day. A woman baptized in courage.

Why then had she run from him? She ought to have been braver, taken him home and made everything open. She ought to have done so long ago when all there had been between them was friendship. It was more than that now. Anna closed her eyes, shutting out Lydia, the tea, William's imminent homecoming, remembering the naked longing in Two Hawks's eyes . . .

"I suppose we shan't recognize William." Anna opened her eyes to find Lydia watching her with a curious, almost speculative look. "Too bad we've not had even a sketch of him all these years."

Anna's belly turned over again. Now she hadn't only Papa to tell about Two Hawks but William as well. Unless William was the one she should tell first. *Perhaps we can tell Papa together if—*

From the street came the rattling approach of wheels. Anna held her breath. Across the table Lydia's teacup paused midway to her lips. When the rattling faded, they exchanged a grin, acknowledging their nerves.

Lydia sipped her tea, then fingered the rim of her cup, a frown knitting her brows. "William hasn't mentioned anything of the sort in his letters to you? What he looks like now."

Anna shrugged. "I suppose he looks as he always has, only . . . grown up. Like me."

Lydia swept her with a wry look, but the question made Anna think of the William she remembered from nine years ago. A blue-eyed boy in breeches, racing through muggy cornfields, fetching her treats behind his mother's back.

Lydia had fallen silent. Anna looked up to find her expression, momentarily unguarded, drawn with unhappiness. Was it to do with Papa? With a prick of memory, Anna recalled the poorly concealed strain between them when Papa saw her into Lydia's keeping before he left for Albany. Lydia had made no mention of a quarrel. In fact, she'd barely mentioned Papa the past four days.

"Lydia," she began. "Is there something the matter between . . . ?"

Out in the street came the grind of wheels again. This time it halted without passing on.

Abandoning their tea, they hurried into the sitting room, which opened to the narrow front entry. Voices outside. One of them was Papa's.

Lydia gave her hand a squeeze and went to open the door. Anna's insides writhed as late spring sunlight spilled into the entryway, illuminating Lydia's sweep of plum skirt and the winter cloaks hanging in a row, pattens lined below them, not yet put away.

"William!" Lydia exclaimed, stepping out of view.

Anna wanted to rush forward, but her feet had taken root.

"Lydia," said a young man's voice. "Look at you—so small you are!"

Papa came first into the sitting room, limping from long hours in the wagon, looking tired, strained. Behind him another figure, lithe and tall, dressed in a tailored brown suit with a high white stock and buckled shoes, stepped into the light from the sitting room windows, removing his hat as he did so, uncovering thick hair tailed back—not the blond-brown Anna remembered but a darker shade.

The young man caught sight of her and halted.

Anna felt the ponderous thudding of her heart, an eternity of bewilderment stretching between each beat as she sought for a scrap of resemblance to Papa, or Heledd Aubrey, or her hazy memory of the boy she'd known, in the person standing before her now.

All her mind could scream at her, impossibly, was *Two Hawks.*

The likeness wasn't perfect. William's hair had darkened, but not to black. The startled eyes fixed on her were blue, not brown. His complexion was swarthy for a white man's, but only a little. Yet in every other way he might have been Two Hawks: the wide, bladed jut of cheekbones, the smooth sweep of brows, the molding of his slightly parted lips, curved at the corners as though hiding a smile.

"William?" she said, certain her eyes deceived her.

"Anna—" He took a step toward her, clutching his hat, then shot Papa a look of stunned accusation. "Father . . . you ought to have warned me she'd grown into such a beauty." He uttered a shaky laugh, and it was Two Hawks's laugh. Two Hawks's voice. The same timbre, the same tones, but with a lilt as thick as Papa's.

Lydia and Papa were hanging back on opposite sides of the room. Papa said something in response to William, but the words didn't penetrate because William had gained possession of himself and come closer . . . was standing in front of her . . . was reaching for her hand even as she lifted it for him to take. His lips brushed her knuckles, as over her hand his eyes grinned down into hers. "Well, Anna. Did I not tell you I'd one day be bigger?"

She heard Lydia give a small laugh. Without intending to do so, Anna snatched back her hand and flung her arms around her brother. With her cheek pressed to the breast of his coat, she held him and burst into tears. "You're here. Oh, William—you sound like a Welshman!"

He rocked back, then steadied himself, arms coming around her. She heard the beat of his heart, pounding like hers, as in a voice half-choked he said, "It's what I am then, aye?"

No, she thought. *It isn't.* Because except for the clothing, holding him was exactly like holding Two Hawks.

Anna jerked her head back to stare up at his face, understanding flaring like a musket flash, leaving behind a choking billow of denial. It couldn't be. William was Heledd's son, Papa's son—William Llewellyn Aubrey, born during the siege of Fort William Henry, saved out of the massacre in which her parents had perished, from which Papa had rescued *her.* Fort William Henry . . . where there had been plenty of soldiers in red coats. British officers. Like Papa.

And captive Indian women?

No. He never said it was Fort William Henry. Besides, William was *white.*

"Anna?" William's brows tightened in a look of concern so dizzyingly familiar that she stepped back from him, trembling. "You look as though you've seen a ghost. Look you, I promise you I'm truly here."

She was making a scene, one she couldn't explain. She glanced at Lydia, standing awkwardly in the dining room doorway. "I'm sorry. I didn't expect to be so . . ."

"Overwhelmed?" William suggested. "I would have to concur. In fact . . . I believe I'd best sit down just now."

It broke the tension. Papa came forward, giving her a lopsided grin as he propelled William to the settee. Anna's gaze raked across Papa's smiling mouth, his scarred cheek. Her hands would not stop shaking.

William folded himself onto the settee and stared round at them all, his gaze returning to Anna, rooted in the center of the room.

"Sit, Anna." Lydia was moving into action now, asking about tea . . . supper. Anna somehow made it to a chair. Somehow she spoke without stammering about things a sister speaks of with a brother she hasn't seen in nine years, while she tried not to stare, while suspicion fermented in her belly and disbelief roared in her head.

But she couldn't look at Papa, with that beloved scar across his cheek. Not and keep the smile fixed on her face.

Anna had moved her few belongings into Lydia's room, leaving to William the room at the top of the back stairs. The plan had been to return straight-away to the farm once William arrived. Anna wasn't sure whose notion it had been for them to stay a few nights in town, but that evening over sup-per Papa brought up the Binne Kill and talked at length of its expansion over the years, his trade upriver, Captain Lang and his crew. Papa's eager-ness for William to see it for himself was plain.

William had pushed the food around his plate and said little, though he hadn't objected to the change of plans.

Supper past, Anna brushed out her hair in Lydia's room, recalling the unhappy tone of William's letters in the weeks before he sailed. Glad as he was to see them again, Anna feared William felt he no longer belonged in Schenectady. She was all but certain he was right, though not for the rea-sons he imagined. Dare she admit of her suspicions?

And if she was wrong? She would have needlessly complicated the rebuilding of a relationship between William and Papa that was already showing its cracks. And what would it do to Papa to know she'd imagined him capable of stealing another woman's child?

Anna set down the brush on Lydia's dressing table. The uncanny re-semblance William bore to Two Hawks *could* be coincidental. People un-related by blood could bear a likeness to each other. *But Two Hawks admitted he has a twin . . . somewhere.*

Here, under Lydia's roof?

Papa wouldn't have. Couldn't have. *Could he?*

Over the course of supper she'd managed to shove thoughts of twins and stolen babies to the back of her mind, and found the self-possession to converse of things that would have been of absorbing interest only yester-day—the farm, her experiences as Lydia's apprentice, Sir John Johnson's flight to Canada, the war with king and parliament yet to be declared a war but which everyone knew was war. The likelihood of more soldiers in red coats coming to their shores.

On that last subject William had guarded his words, but she knew what he was thinking. Or how he was thinking. He was thinking like an Englishman. Not like Papa. Yet there was still a bond there. She'd bid them good night in the sitting room, turning back to see Papa clasp Wil-liam's arm and draw him into an embrace. A stiff embrace, but still an embrace.

Let me be wrong. She finished plaiting her hair, not bothering to tie it off, and was reaching for her nightcap when she realized she'd left it hang-ing on its peg behind the door. Upstairs.

She slipped on a wrapper, took a candle, and crossed the shadowed passage toward the narrow back stairs, pausing at their foot. Talk wafted from the other end of the house. Lydia and Papa, their words indistin-guishable. She started to climb the steep treads when Papa's voice rose.

"Lydia . . . let it bide now."

Lydia's softer reply held a note of pleading. It struck Anna that though they'd freely spoken to her and William, Lydia and Papa had exchanged no more than polite words all evening. What was the matter between those two? And where was William? Not in his room abed, she hoped.

She reached the top of the stairs to find the door open, the room within dark. She slipped inside and held the candle high. William's coat draped the straight-backed chair where she'd sat to compose many a letter to him, but aside from its furnishings and William's trunks, the room was empty.

She pushed the door aside, snatched the linen cap off the peg behind it—then turned and caught her breath.

William leaned against the doorframe, undressed to shirt and breeches, neckcloth hanging loose. It might have been Two Hawks standing there looking at her . . . if Two Hawks had been born white.

"I forgot my nightcap," she got out, holding it up as if he couldn't see it clutched in her hand. His blue eyes swept from the braid hanging over her shoulder, half-unraveled now, to her bare feet. She made for the door, meaning to edge past him. "I'll go—let you rest. You must be tired—"

"Anna." His hand on her arm froze her, though his touch was warm.

She looked down, and the hairs on her forearm rose. Even their hands were alike. The candle shook in hers.

William released her with a smile that bespoke a shyness they'd never known as children. "Do you remember what we discussed in our last letters?"

Her mind was a blank.

"About going to the waterfall together. Not the first hour of my arrival, plainly. But . . . the first hour home at the farm? You still wish to, don't you?"

Of course, Anna started to say, then knew she couldn't. What if Two Hawks were there waiting for her? She wanted him to be, needed him to be. But not with William, whose eyes in the candlelight were a darker blue, his cheekbones thrown into sharper relief. One second doubting her eyes, the next believing them, she bit back half a dozen things she wanted to say.

"Are you truly glad to see me, Anna?" Uncertainty shadowed William's gaze, and suddenly it didn't matter about Two Hawks, or Papa, or who or what William was. He was *William*. Here, with her.

"Very glad. Oh, I've missed you so. But . . . are you glad to be home? Are you still quite angry with Papa over it?"

William's mouth stiffened. "There is a subject to spoil a moment. Can we let it bide?"

Papa's words to Lydia, or nearly so. "But—"

"For now?" William's expression softened. "I'm more than glad to be with you again."

Eyes flooding with warmth, he raised his hand to grasp the braid that fell across her shoulder and gave it a tug.

"Anna, I—" Whatever he'd begun to say, he changed his mind, and with a glance toward the stairs said, "Best go on down. Good night to you."

"Good night, William." She bit her lip, added, "See you in the morning," and smiled, for in spite of everything it was wonderful to say.

29

*T*hree days in the lad's company, and Reginald found himself still unable to quell the impulse to stare.

They'd spent the better part of yesterday in the workshop, Reginald giving William a taste of the boat-building craft. He meant to give it another go today. On the way he'd paused in the office and opened the ledgers, explaining his decision to step up production to aid the Continental Army. William listened with glazing eyes and pinched brow, clearly preoccupied, or bored. Thus far he'd shown no more than polite interest in any aspect of the boatyard. Absent was the passion Reginald hoped to kindle.

But one didn't always get a catching spark on the first strike of steel to flint.

At the dinner table, plied with questions by Lydia and Anna, William spoke animatedly—about English law, his tutors, pranks he and his fellows had played, lectures of particular interest. Even if he'd resigned himself to being in New York, William's heart remained in Oxford. And who had Reginald to blame for it but himself?

Shame washed its sick tide through him at the jarring reminder. Whatever blood flowed through his veins, William was—had been since Reginald carried him out of that hospital casemate—an Aubrey. As Welsh now, by raising if not birth, as Reginald. His son, whom twice he'd plucked up and replanted in soil not of the lad's choosing.

Hoping resignation wasn't the best he could expect, Reginald glanced toward the office window and saw, out on the quay, Ephraim Lang arriving with a loaded bateau, back from Fort Dayton at German Flatts. He left

William frowning at the books and went to the bubbled glass to watch the crew make their nimble landing on the quay.

"That's him, is it? Your partner?"

Reginald turned from the window. William was looking up from the ledgers with markedly more interest in the activity on the quay. "It is, aye. Captain Lang."

William's brows puckered as he strained to see through the distorting glass. "He's older than I expected. You've known him since Fort William Henry?"

"Aye. Just after." Reginald's chest burned with the same amalgamation of relief and dread that had churned inside him upon seeing the lad off the sloop in Albany, gaze raking for signs he'd feared to see. Those he found—the darkened hair, the almost nonexistent hint of beard, the faintly tawny complexion—might evidence a truth none but he knew. Or not.

Reginald had known Frenchmen more swarthy than this lad, and not for the first time found himself grasping at doubt. Had he taken up two orphans, not one? William had looked nothing like the other child, so clearly a half-breed . . .

"That's not Reagan's crew, is it?"

William was looking past him now, through the window. Sam Reagan, not due to leave upriver until the morrow, had come down to the Binne Kill to meet the returning crew.

William's annoyance was poorly concealed. "Does he always hang about so?"

Reagan had engaged Lang in conversation, most likely about the river, with an eye toward his own imminent departure. In four years Reagan had proved himself dependable and was routinely put in charge of trading trips whenever Lang wasn't along. The men liked him, deferred to him, sometimes without knowing quite how they'd been talked into it, which was fine as long as Reagan kept a sober head on his shoulders—and his mouth shut. More than once of late he'd fallen to fighting in the street over politics, but such lapses never resulted in harm beyond scored knuckles and blackened eyes. If there was a reckless edge to Sam Reagan—and behind the affable hazel eyes and ready charm, Reginald suspected there was—the young man minded himself on the Binne Kill.

William, however, had taken an almost instant dislike to him. Little wonder, seeing as Anna had been present yesterday when the two met. Reagan lost no time in engaging in his usual flirtation with her, barely tempered by the presence of a glowering brother fresh off the boat from England.

"He works with a cooper in town when he's not piloting for me," Reginald said. "But he's free to come and go as he pleases."

William gazed darkly through the window a moment longer, then muttered something that sounded like, "Glad I am *someone* is."

Reginald hoped he'd misheard.

Ephraim Lang entered the office, introductions were made, then the captain and Reginald fell to talking of the trip upriver, until behind them William said, "Father, here is Anna come down from—and there *he* goes pestering her again."

Reginald broke off conversation to peer through the window. Anna had arrived on the quay with Lydia nowhere in sight, though Reginald looked for her trim, dark figure with an eagerness he tried to quell. He'd turned in time to see his daughter waylaid by Reagan. The window glass distorted their expressions, but their body language had a predictable aspect. Anna, nearly as tall as the boat pilot, had no need to raise her chin to smile at him before making to move past with a half-playful, dismissive wave of hand.

All might have been well had Reagan let her go. Instead he caught her waving hand, forcing her to check and turn back. In so doing she looked directly at the office glass. Her expression might have reflected impatience, amusement, or an appeal for assistance. Though the latter was unlikely, William was out from behind the counter and bursting onto the quay before Reginald could react.

"William!"

Almost lazily Lang said, "Let him go, Major. Reagan's got brains enough not to damage his employer's son."

It had taken only heartbeats for Reginald to reach the same conclusion—and for William to cross the quay to where Anna and the pilot stood, still bound by clasped hands. Surely they would break apart, Anna would diffuse the situation, William would—

William struck, landing his fist on the point of Reagan's chin.

Reagan's head snapped back as Anna cringed away. The river pilot kept his feet, and his cool, while William cradled his fist, no doubt regretting his aim.

"He'll know to pick a soft spot next time," Lang said. "I like this boy of yours, Major. Many's the time I've wanted to do that to Reagan."

Reginald was heading for the door before Lang finished speaking. Not on account of the brawl in the making but its unwitting cause— Anna. The office door stuck fast. Uttering an oath, he wrenched it free and limped onto the quay.

He'd missed vital seconds of the confrontation. William's posture had changed. Ignoring Reagan now and the crew who'd stopped work to watch the drama, he was looking after Anna, who was fast retreating, shaking the dust of the boatyard from her buckled shoes.

Grabbing William by the coat sleeve, Reginald yanked him around. "Explain yourself, sir!"

"Father, she—he . . ." William faltered, as though uncertain himself what had just transpired. Reagan, self-possessed as always, watched Anna disappear around a corner, then slid a look at William, cool and assessing.

Anger flared in Reginald's chest. "She'll be away to Lydia. Do you go after her—the pair of you—and make your apologies."

William shot him a rebellious look. "No sir. I mean, yes sir, but—not *him*."

"You'll both go," Reginald said. "And sort yourselves out between you on the way, see. If word gets back to me you've laid so much as a finger on the other, you," he said to Reagan, "will no longer have a place with me. As for *you* . . ." He met the blue blaze of William's eyes. "For Anna's sake you will make amends. And when you've done so, we're going home."

He shoved William in Anna's wake, leveled a gaze at Reagan as good as a shove, and the pair trudged off along the quay, refusing to look at each other.

Lydia was minding a syrup on the hearth when she heard Anna come in off the street. She gave the kettle's contents a stir. Sweet, medicinal steam rose up to curl the hair escaped at her temples as, behind her, Anna's footfalls came through to the kitchen.

"Did you find someone to home—to explain the dosage for Mr. Jansen?" Spoon in hand, Lydia turned as Anna plunked herself down onto a worktable bench, breathing hard, face clenched in fury.

"What is it? Mr. Jansen?" The old man could be difficult, but she doubted Anna would be in such a state over his querulousness. "Has he worsened?"

"No," Anna said shortly. "I went to see William and Papa after."

Lydia stiffened at mention of Reginald and the hurt that inevitably came fast on its heels. She moved the syrup away from the heat, then sat at the table across from Anna.

"Did something happen at the Binne Kill?"

With a spate of angry tears, Anna told her about William hitting Sam

Reagan in her defense. "As though I'd ever need defending from *Sam*. Then Papa came onto the quay—yelling at William—but by then I'd run away. I'm *always* running away!"

She reached for a square of linen from a pile on the table, leaving Lydia groping for understanding. Always running away?

"What was William thinking?" the girl demanded.

"Oh, Anna. You've grown into a lovely young woman." She doubted William felt anything of a romantic nature toward Anna, but certainly it had seemed the two of them were stunned by the other's altered appearance. That alone would take time to sort itself out. "He was just being protective of you. Figuring out how to be your brother again."

Lydia couldn't fathom the look Anna gave her at that. Was it startled? Dismayed? What was going on? Everyone she loved was behaving themselves as if she'd never known them at all. Was it only to do with William's reluctant homecoming, or something more?

"Whatever his feelings," she went on, "they're surely running high right now. Think of all he's had to adjust to in the past few weeks."

"I suppose so . . ." Anna sighed. "You're right. I shouldn't have been so angry."

So why did the girl appear unassuaged? Lydia hesitated, then ventured, "Is something else the matter, besides what happened on the quay? Something to do with William?"

"What do you mean?" Alarm—and comprehension—registered plainly on Anna's unguarded features.

Lydia was stunned. She'd given no hint, hadn't mentioned Reginald at all, yet . . . there it was, staring from Anna's eyes. She knew.

But she couldn't . . . not *that*.

For an instant Lydia was back at the farmhouse, in the room where Reginald lay fevered . . . the heat of the fire . . . the grip of his hand. His broken confession.

"Lydia? What is it?" Now Anna was staring at her, looking every bit as stunned as Lydia felt. "Is there something about William *you* know? Something to do with . . . Papa?"

The question jarred so, Lydia thought she was going to be sick. She'd kept Reginald's secret for years, thought never to let it pass her lips, yet it seemed . . . she was almost certain now . . . that Anna knew it too. Or did she only suspect?

Why should she? How?

Did it matter how? William was home, and unhappy, and if Anna knew . . .

"Yes," she said. "I know about William. I've known for a very long time."

30

*F*or the third time in as many days, Anna felt the world slide out from under her like a rug yanked from beneath her feet. Her mind swirled around Lydia's tale of Papa's confession—one he'd no memory of making all those years ago, as far as Lydia knew.

"It's true then. William is . . ." She clapped her hand over her mouth in time to prevent Two Hawks's name slipping out.

Two Hawks *knew.* He'd always known. That was why he came to the wood's edge. Not for her. He'd come because of William. *His brother.*

A pressure like a fist squeezed her heart.

Lydia had paused, looking as thoroughly wrung from the telling as Anna felt at hearing it. "But, Anna," she said now. "How is it you know? Reginald never *told* you?"

Anna pressed her fingers more firmly to her trembling lips. No one had told her anything. No one. And what was *she* to tell?

Secrets. She was choking sick of them.

Removing her hand, she gulped a breath and told Lydia everything, starting with the day she was eleven and missing William like her heart would tear out of her chest and go flying to Wales—the day she and Lydia walked to the creek and she'd ended up racing off in tears, running for the waterfall where she'd longed to find William and instead found Two Hawks.

She spoke faster, grinding out how Two Hawks came to see her over the years. How she shared William's letters. How Two Hawks learned to read them for himself. How they played together and picked berries and shot arrows and grew up. How a bear almost attacked them. How Two Hawks prayed with her and her heart opened to God. And to him.

That was the hardest part to tell, because now she wasn't certain if anything she'd believed about him was true. "Two Hawks told me, just days ago, that he had a twin brother taken at their birth. Taken from his mother's side by a British officer who put a dead baby in his place. But he never said it was *William*. It wasn't until I saw William—saw how much he looks like Two Hawks—that I ever imagined *Papa* was that officer."

She had to stop, breathe, steady herself. Only there seemed nothing solid left to cling to. "Why? Lydia, why did Papa do it?"

"Grief can work a twisted logic on the mind." Lydia's answer came so readily that Anna knew she'd thought about it dozens, if not hundreds of times. "We cannot imagine the horrors he and Heledd endured inside that fort. Then to have his newborn son die—"

"I'm sure it was terrible. I understand that. But, Lydia, he took a woman's *baby*. Her name is Good Voice. William is *her* son. Surely he is."

"Good Voice," Lydia whispered, her gaze on Anna pained. "Please don't misunderstand me, Anna. I'm not excusing Reginald. But I've had time to reason through why he may have done what he did."

"Then why are *you* upset with him?" Wariness came into Lydia's eyes. "Oh, Lydia, don't deny it. You've hardly spoken to each other in days, and . . ." Anna bit her lip. Perhaps because her heart was already so raw, clutching at anything that hinted of wholeness, of truth, she asked, "Do you love Papa?"

Lydia hesitated only a moment. "I do. I love him very much."

A week ago those words would have filled Anna with happiness. Now . . .

"Knowing all this time what he did?" Feelings of anger and grief, pity, compassion, encompassed a sense of loss so devastating she could hardly begin to comprehend it. Good Voice's and Stone Thrower's. Papa's. Two

Hawks's. William's. Her own. "He's made Two Hawks's family suffer and grieve—shouldn't he be held accountable for that?"

Lydia's mouth trembled. "Anna, I can't know all the workings of your father's heart and mind—how I wish I did—but I've watched him over the years, and it seems to me he has punished *himself* ever since he took William from that fort. He's kept those around him, even the Almighty, I think, at arm's length. It would explain so much—the strain between him and Heledd, and why he never attends meeting, and why he won't let himself return my affections when I know he—" She faltered, then amended, "At least I *think* he feels . . ."

"He does. I've seen how he looks at you when you aren't looking at him." She watched joy, regret, frustration play over Lydia's face, and was saddened at the thought of Lydia loving Papa and Papa loving Lydia but refusing them both happiness because . . .

She frowned. "Lydia, how do you know that's why Papa won't return your affections?"

Lydia's face flamed a deeper red than Anna had ever seen her blush. "Because I went to him and all but asked him to marry me."

Anna gaped. "You did? When?"

"Before he left for Albany, for William. We met in town, then walked together down to the Binne Kill, and for a moment I thought . . ." Lydia's face clouded with memory. "I saw it in his face, Anna, clear as though he spoke the words. He wanted what I was offering—my heart, my life, everything."

Anna thought her heart would wrench in two. *Papa.* She bit her lip, willing back a fresh surge of tears as Lydia went on.

"I'd never seen such a look of joy on his face. And then it was gone." Lydia snapped her fingers. "Like a candle snuffed. He'd remembered."

"Fort William Henry?"

Lydia nodded. "In his heart, I believe Reginald never left that wretched fort. I can only conclude he fears that one craven act will forever define him, that if it was known, he would lose what he has—your love and William's, the respect of the Doyles and Captain Lang. And the friendship he and I have enjoyed."

Anna reached across the table to grasp Lydia's hand. "But he's lost that—your friendship."

"For my part, he hasn't. I went to him that day hoping he would trust me. That we could break open that festering wound and find healing at last. Together. But he wouldn't even show it to me." Lydia gripped her hand, eyes shimmering. "I don't believe he feels himself deserving of happiness, and so he goes on denying himself—crucifying himself for his own sins. Maybe he thinks he's atoning."

Anna drew back from Lydia and put her hands to her face, rubbing her fingertips hard across her eyelids. Did Papa deserve happiness? What about Good Voice and Stone Thrower? What about Two Hawks?

It was too much.

"There's one thing I haven't told you yet, Anna," Lydia said. "You've already asked the question. I know why Reginald did it. It was for Heledd."

Anna lowered her hands. "How do you know that?"

"He told me, when he was fevered. I should have stopped him, I know. I was young—younger than you are now." Lydia rubbed her temples as though they hurt her. "I've had long to think about this, and what I think is that Reginald feared to tell Heledd their son was dead, feared her mind couldn't bear it. Knowing her as I did, he was probably right. He must have seen the Indian woman—"

"Good Voice," Anna cut in.

"He must have seen she had *two* babies. It was wrong," she hurried to add. "Of course it was wrong. But in that moment, telling Heledd the truth must have seemed unbearable."

Anna shook her head. "But it didn't work."

Lydia frowned. "What do you mean?"

"Giving her William. It didn't save Mrs. Aubrey's mind. Not after what happened when they left the fort. The massacre."

"I don't know," Lydia said. "I never knew Heledd before Reginald brought you to live with us. I do know he loved her. And I can understand how love could drive a person to do something they might later regret. Like keeping secrets."

"Keeping secrets isn't the same as doing what Papa did!"

"Anna—" Lydia's voice broke. "Don't judge your father too hastily. Please don't. He once called you the one pure thing in his life. Whatever else he's done, he's loved you from the moment he rescued you on that road to Fort Edward."

Anna winced, the image of Papa's scarred cheek flashing across her mind. The one pure thing? *Oh, Papa.* She didn't know what she felt, or whom she felt it toward. Her life was crumbling before her disbelieving gaze, reshaping into something unrecognizable.

"Do you think Mrs. Aubrey knew?"

"No," Lydia said. "I doubt her mind would have allowed her even to suspect it. William was her only consolation. Until she returned to Wales."

And there was yet another appalling thought. William . . . thinking all this time he was an Aubrey, a Welshman, when he was really the brother of Two Hawks. The son of Oneida parents.

He had to be told the truth. Hadn't he?

What if someone told *her* that Papa hadn't saved her, orphaned on that wilderness road, but stolen her from living parents? Parents who still grieved her loss. Would she want to know that? What would she do with such knowledge? Thought of telling William what amounted to the same was enough to make Anna quail. What if he hated Papa? What if he wanted nothing more to do with him? With any of them? What if she lost him in telling him the truth? But he had parents, a brother . . .

Two Hawks. She needed to find him, make sure beyond all doubt what they had pieced together was the truth. But it *had* to be.

Or ought she to warn Papa first? Tell him about Stone Thrower. Her earliest memories of the tall Oneida warrior came vividly to mind, the rage, the anguish, the dark intent she'd sensed from him—perfectly understandable in light of this terrible revelation.

But Stone Thrower was Caleb now. A Christian. Papa couldn't still be in danger, could he?

"Doesn't the Bible say the truth will set us free?" she implored.

"There is only one Truth with the power to set souls free," Lydia said. "Jesus Christ and Him crucified. The truth of another's sins? Only God knows what will come of—"

"Anna!" a deeper voice called through the house.

She and Lydia shared one half-panicked glance before William's tall frame filled the kitchen doorway. His tailed hair was disheveled. The knuckles of his right hand were scored and swollen. Anna saw no further evidence of his fight with Sam, save the remorse in his gaze.

"Anna . . . I'm sorry. I didn't mean to upset you."

Anna lifted a hand to her face as though she might hide behind it. Did William think she'd been crying over his scuffle with Sam? It was hard to remember back to that scene on the quay. A quarter of an hour since? It seemed days.

"I know, William." His name trembled on her lips.

"You do?" William's brows shot up. "Mind you, I thought I was defending your honor. You're not angry with me?"

"No. I'm not angry."

"Oh. Well then." Her answer had disconcerted him, but her tongue felt stuck to the roof her mouth, preventing her saying more. "I wanted to be sure you were all right, see . . . before Sam and I head to the tavern for a pint."

She gaped at him. "You and Sam?"

"Aye." His face colored as he gave her a rueful smile. "Father gave us a dressing down, then we fell to talking for a bit, Sam and I—he sends his apologies too, by the way. He's waiting for me on the street." William shrugged, as if unable to better explain. "But look you, Anna. I'll not go if you'd rather I didn't."

How jarring it was now, hearing Papa's manner of speaking coming out of William's mouth. She looked into his earnest blue eyes, thought of marching him up to his room and telling him everything . . . and to her chagrin made the choice Lydia must have made a hundred times.

"There was no good reason for you to hit Sam. He doesn't mean anything by his flirting. He was just being . . . Sam."

"I tell you, I know now." William held her gaze, tender, conciliatory. "So you don't mind if he and I . . . ?"

"Not if you don't. Is—is your hand all right?"

"What? Oh." He glanced down at the appendage, made a fist, and grinned. "Better than his jaw."

Half in a daze, Anna rose and followed him to the front door, where he turned and said, almost as an afterthought, "You'll want to be packing your things, Anna. Father says we're going home to the farm directly. Now I best hurry if I mean to have that pint." He opened the door, and there was Sam with his bruised jaw, waiting in the street. He waved to her. She raised a hand, weakly, and watched them head off together, looking for all the world like becoming friends.

"I don't understand men," she murmured. "I just don't."

Lydia had followed her from the kitchen. "If ever you manage it, my girl," she said, a welling of sympathy in her gaze as she shut the door, "be so kind as to enlighten me as well."

31

*I*t took less effort than Anna had expected to delay a visit to the waterfall. Mrs. Doyle, in her eagerness to shower William with nine years' accumulated attention, did most of the delaying for her. Mr. Doyle, while less transparent about it, was keen to reacquaint William with Papa's land and livestock, including the new saddle horse Papa had acquired, a homecoming gift.

"Ah, she is a beauty," William said as he stroked the mare's dappled neck, his face aglow with appreciation, making Papa look happier than Anna had seen him since the day of William's arrival.

The sight wrung her heart in a dozen directions, even as William turned to her, smiling. Her mouth mirrored his, but she mustn't have been wholly convincing. Papa gave her a curious glance.

William, distracted by his new horse, noticed nothing amiss.

The moment passed but not Anna's dismay. It churned within her as she trailed William from house to field to barn, unable to prevent her gaze straying to the undulation of trees beyond the sprouting corn.

If Two Hawks waited, there was no telling.

On his second morning home, William rode into town with Papa. Anna tidied the kitchen hearth, wiping the pewter dishes and putting them in the hutch. Mr. Doyle went to the barn. Mrs. Doyle drifted off to other chores. When the kitchen door closed behind her, Anna put the last plate in its place and went to fetch her gathering basket.

He wasn't among the beeches. Or in the clearing. Afraid her voice would carry too far, Anna refrained from calling his name as she started up the hill. But as she neared the shelf of rock over which the spring flowed, the hedge of rhododendron screening the cave higher up rustled. Two Hawks emerged, his face lighting up at sight of her.

"*Shekoli,* Anna Catherine. At last you—"

"Was it Fort William Henry?"

She'd cut him off before he could extricate himself from the cave's low entrance. He did so as she reached him. He wore only breechclout and moccasins. His eyes were grave as they sought hers. "I have waited long for you. I did not know what to think when the days passed and you did not come."

"Two Hawks—was it Fort William Henry where you were born?"

A moment more he looked at her, his gaze unreadable. "It was."

"Why did you never tell me?"

His long legs seemed to fold beneath him. He sat at the cave's mouth and held out a hand to her. When she didn't take it, he let it fall. "I told you some of it when last we met."

"You should have told me everything!" She laced her arms across her chest, fighting back the urge to cry. "There I was in the room with William, unable to believe my eyes, trying to behave as if I hadn't just had my world overturned."

"He is home then." A spark of joy lit Two Hawks's eyes, then he bowed his head, lacing his hands behind his neck, and groaned. Abruptly he pushed himself to his feet. "I am sorry it was hard for you, these last days. It has been much hard for me, for my parents. For a long time."

His words cut through her anger, breaking it in pieces along with her certainty that she ought to be feeling it at all, at least toward him. But what about *them*? Did he feel anything for her—for her own sake, not because she was his link to William?

"Have you told my brother?" he asked, jerking her thoughts sideways with his query. "Told him who he is?"

"No. I had to be sure. I just . . . I couldn't . . . I don't . . ." She was lost for words. Her hands were shaking.

"Did you tell Aubrey that you know?" Two Hawks asked her, and she realized now he was calm. Perfectly calm.

"Of course not. If I couldn't tell William until I was sure, I couldn't bring such a charge against Papa."

During a final hurried conversation in Lydia's room, they'd agreed to wait until that last scrap of doubt was obliterated before confronting either William or Papa. It was gone now. She stared at Two Hawks's bare chest, stricken by the distance she felt between them. Yet even when Two Hawks drew near and put his arms around her, it wasn't bridged.

"I am sorry. I did not want you to bear this burden of my family, all those years when there was nothing to be done about it."

Slowly her fists unclenched and spread against his chest. Then she was holding him, breathing in the clean smell of him, saying through her tears, "I wish you had let me bear it. William is *my* family too. Isn't he?"

Through the linen of her cap, she felt him kiss the top of her head, felt the press of his jaw as he laid it there. "That is going to be for William to decide." He stroked her back, his voice rumbling beneath her ear. "I am sorry to cause you this pain, when what I want is to bring you joy."

"But you do bring me joy," she protested, in a voice so thick with misery they pulled apart and, despite everything, shared a watery smile.

Amusement was swift to pass. She stepped away from him. "I only wish I'd been the one you were coming here hoping to see all these years, instead of William."

She hadn't meant to admit to such a selfish thought. Hearing it, Two Hawks's brows nearly met over his nose. He took her hand in his. "Listen to me. Long ago, when we were small, you told us William was gone across the great water, that he would not come back for many years. Still I came here, yes?"

"You did," she admitted.

"Why do you think I did so?"

She bit her lip, knowing what she wanted the answer to be. "To hear of William."

"It is true I came because I wished to know of my brother, but it is also true that I wanted to see my friend, Anna Catherine, who has become Bear's Heart, the woman I love."

The woman I love. It was all she could do to keep from melting at his words. She marveled that he could love her, the daughter of the man who tore his family asunder, who caused them such pain.

And yet . . . had Papa never taken William, I would never have known either of them. Never loved either of them. That was the last thought in her head before Two Hawks took her face between his hands and kissed her. It was gentle at first, almost a question, but when she didn't pull away it deepened with a stirring need. *But is my love strong enough to prevent my losing either of them?*

At that thought she stiffened in his embrace. He released her, looking stricken. "Do you not want me, now that you know the truth? Or is it that you no longer trust me?"

She wanted him. Loved him. Ached to say the words. But there was too much between them that needed to be settled. He'd had years to reconcile his feelings for her with what Papa had done, with the suffering of his family, their loss.

"I don't know what to trust anymore," she said.

Pain flickered in his gaze, but he said, "Trust Heavenly Father. He has seen all that has happened and is bringing it to light now. It is His time. Hold tight to Him, Bear's Heart. As I am doing." He looked beyond her toward the farm, visible through the trees. Longing to see his brother was plain on his face.

"How can you comfort me? You should hate me. And Papa. Lydia believes he did it because he couldn't bring himself to tell his wife their son had died. He feared she couldn't bear it, so when he saw Good Voice, saw she had two babies . . ." The words were spilling from her like water. "I don't know why I'm telling you this. Nothing I can say will make any of this right."

He put a hand to her chin, lifting her face. "You are saying these things because he is your father. You love him and fear for him. But I would never hate you for something Aubrey did before you were even his daughter."

His daughter. She didn't understand how Two Hawks could be so perceptive, but he was right. No matter what Papa had done nineteen years ago, she hadn't stopped loving him. Or William.

"He looks like you," she said impulsively. "Yet he's different from you, too. I can see his Oneida blood—I know to look for it now—but I think to most he looks . . . white. How can that be?"

Two Hawks was nodding, as if this all made sense to him. "My mother has told me many times of when we were born. It seemed to her that one of us took all of her blood and one of us took all of my father's blood. That is me, the one who took my father's blood."

Anna's frown tightened. "William took your mother's blood? What do you . . . ?" All at once she realized what he meant and only wondered why she hadn't deduced it. William showed so little evidence of being Oneida, and for that to make any sense at all . . . "Your mother's white? Why did you never say? Or is that another secret?"

"No secret," he said. "It is not a thing I think much about. In her heart my mother is Oneida, though she was not born to the People—but how is William like me?"

The eager question distracted her from the revelation about Good Voice, jarring her with a memory of William in his room, unearthing from a trunk the bow he'd brought from Crickhowell. He'd taken a stance and drawn the weapon, making his shirt pull snug across long, lean muscles . . . making her see Two Hawks in the forest with his bow.

"He's as tall as you," she said. "And he's knit like you. His features are much like yours. His skin is lighter—you know that already—and his hair, and his eyes are blue."

"My mother thought his eyes would be like hers." Two Hawks's smile was swift but faded quickly, as if quelled by the magnitude of what was coming for the families they loved. For William, the unknowing cynosure of it all.

"I should go back," she said, though saying it felt like tearing out her heart.

"And I." Two Hawks's gaze held such intensity she felt herself melting toward him again, despite the words of imminent parting. "I want peace between our fathers. I do not know how that can be, but I believe Creator sees a way. I will do all in my power to make it happen, as He shows me how."

Two Hawks took her hand in his but held her away so he could go on looking into her eyes. "Tell Aubrey about me and that I do not wish him evil for what he did. Nor, I think, does my mother. I will bring her to see him and to see William. But I do not know what my father will do."

He made no mention of it, but it was in his eyes; he hoped for peace between their fathers, not just so he could know his brother, his parents their firstborn, but so he and she might have a chance at a future together.

"I'll warn him," she said, her grip on his hand tightening. "Jonathan . . . pray for me. As I will for you."

"With every breath," he said, drawing her close for a last embrace.

32

June 1776

*L*ydia thought long about what to take to the Binne Kill. She thought long about whether to take *herself* to the Binne Kill but couldn't bear another day of not knowing what, if anything, had transpired at the farm. Days had passed without word from Anna or Reginald, though William had visited twice, giving no indication he suspected—much less knew of—his true parentage. Which didn't mean Anna hadn't revealed her knowledge of it to Reginald. Had Anna decided not to bring her into it, despite Lydia's assurance she needn't go through this alone?

She would have to go and face Reginald, look him in the eye, to know whether Anna had yet spoken. She didn't mean to go empty-handed, but if Reginald looked like spurning the plum cake she'd made, still warm from the oven, she'd pretend it was for William.

"How can this have a good ending?" Anna had asked before their parting. "If we give William back his birth family, it will wrench him from—from all those ancestors who looked down at him from the walls in Crickhowell. From *us*. What will that do to him?"

It would devastate him. But beyond that devastation, might there be healing . . . for everyone? Even Reginald?

There was no sign of William when she reached the quay, nor was he in the office when she opened the door. Reginald stood behind the counter, head bent over his books. He looked up, the beginnings of a smile on his lips. Surprise froze it there, half-formed. Emotions passed in swift succession across his eyes, ending with a guarded unease.

"Good day, Reginald. I brought plum cake." The words hung between them, bereft of context. The mantle clock in the sitting room ticked. She set the basket on a bench by the door. "Is William about?"

"Ah . . . no." Reginald's gaze shifted to the front window. "He's away into town. With Reagan, I think."

Despite their rocky beginning, the unlikely pair were often in each other's company now. The few times William had visited her, he'd spoken of going out on the river with Sam.

"I see. I'll leave this then." She gestured at the basket, adding, "It's for you as well, of course."

Reginald nodded briefly. "As you wish."

A pain took Lydia in the center of her chest, a pit of disappointment opening beneath it. Reginald's hands gripped the counter. His posture was like an arm outthrust, keeping her at bay. "Actually, I came to see you as well, about Anna. She hasn't sent word since William's homecoming. Is everything all right?"

At mention of Anna, Reginald seemed to let down his guard. As though struck by the belated impulse to greet her properly, he rounded the counter, in his stride the hitch that told her his hip was paining him more than was usual. Why hadn't she brought a white willow tea, or a lavender and comfrey rub, instead of useless plum cake?

Reginald halted well out of reach. "Anna's fine. It may be Mrs. Doyle needs her help more than we've become accustomed, now William's home. She hasn't mentioned coming into town." He glanced at the basket on the bench. "Kind of you to be thinking of us here. I've missed your plum cake."

Never mind he hadn't said he missed *her*. Here at last was a crack in the wall he'd flung up between them. If only she could melt and pour herself through it. "You're sure Anna's all right?"

His expression held no hint of the wrenching grief and guilt she'd witnessed that day she removed the cloth fragment from his suppurating wound, the day she'd heard his feverish confession.

Why hadn't Anna said anything? Had she spoken to William's twin? Were they all at sea with their conclusions?

"Anna's fine," Reginald repeated. "Shall I tell her you asked after her? I'm sure she'll send you word—or come to you soon herself."

Again Lydia felt dismissed but couldn't bring herself to leave. "Did I interrupt you in the midst of something important?"

He followed her glance toward the counter. "You'll have heard General Schuyler has decided to reoccupy Fort Stanwix, between the Mohawk and Wood Creek?"

Lydia nodded. A woman with a boil to be lanced had brought her the news, as well as a good deal of chatter about the Continental Army's fear of invasion from the west, now the British had retaken their territory in Canada and opened the St. Lawrence River.

"I was going over a list of supplies we'll be shipping upriver for Stanwix's garrison. Colonel Dayton will be bringing his New Jersey troops through. They'll need provisions, as will whatever militia is attached to the garrison."

"Sounds as if war has been good for business." She regretted the frivolous comment the instant it was out of her mouth.

Reginald looked at a loss for a response.

William, bless him, chose that moment to come into the office from the quay. He greeted Lydia warmly and was more forthcoming when she asked after Anna. Reginald, she noted from the corner of her eye, used William's presence as an excuse to retreat behind the counter.

"Anna's all right," William said. "I think. She's been quiet the past days and I wondered . . . But there now, I've been gone so long it may be I'm not reading her rightly." He smiled and shrugged, more perceptive than he knew.

"William," Reginald cut in. "It would be good if you could look over the accounts here. What we expect by way of supplies you should know, so that when they arrive you can attend to them if I'm otherwise occupied."

William tensed. "I was coming to ask would it be all right did I go with Sam. He's taking a canoe down to the falls to do some fishing—"

"I tell you we've supplies to receive." Reginald jerked his head toward the workshop. "And a bateau needing to be finished."

William ran his lip through his teeth. "'Tis for a few hours only. Besides," he added, stepping toward the counter. "Do you really think supplying the rebels the prudent course?"

Lydia slipped out onto the quay, shutting the door on the conversation. Neither Aubrey seemed to notice her leaving. She was no nearer understanding what was going on at the farm than when she'd taken the plum cake out of the oven. Quite apart from the pressure building inside her over Anna, Reginald, and William, she was bothered by what she'd left behind in the office. Another pressure on the build.

As she strode back through the streets of Schenectady, minded of the angry boil she'd recently lanced—a painful, messy business, but needful for healing—Lydia made a decision. There was a babe due to be birthed any day now, perhaps any hour. Once she'd seen it safe into the world, if she'd heard nothing from Anna by then, she would ride out to the farm herself and see about another sort of lancing.

As though she thought he could overlook her going, Lydia chose the moment William's question demanded his attention to take her leave. When Reginald glanced past his son again she was gone, out onto the quay. His spine jerked, sending a lancet of pain down his thigh as instinctively he made to go after her. He'd been rude—unforgivably so—when all she'd done was show concern for Anna. But William went on speaking.

"Do you not think it shortsighted to be so blatant about it? Where will that leave you once the Crown's troops arrive and this rebellion is put firmly down?"

With Lydia disappearing down the quay and his son challenging his politics and business acumen, Reginald felt like a weaver watching the threads of his work unraveling under his fingers. He hadn't hands enough to hold them all in place. It was the vibrant blue strand called *Lydia* he let go, with a pain in his chest he feared bespoke a permanent snapping of the weft.

"William—" Hearing the agitation in his voice, he said again, "William, I am doing what my conscience bids me do and nothing less."

"Conscience, sir? You're defying an army and a king you once served. You cannot have forgotten. Captain Lang still calls you *Major*."

"And there is the scar on my face and the pain that bedevils me daily to remind me as well." Reginald forced a laugh, trying to diffuse the tension. "An old, tired soldier I am, true enough."

Frustration clouded his son's gaze. "That wasn't what I meant to imply. If you will not—or cannot—fight again for the king, can you at least refrain from aiding his enemies?"

The words lashed Reginald's heart. "Look you, William. Who among the men of this valley do you see fence-sitting? Was that where I wanted to be, someone would come along directly and knock me off it. To do nothing, say nothing, refuse to sign the petitions and oaths, that is now tantamount to proclaiming oneself for the king. And a Tory I am not, see."

"Sign them then, but stop this." William gestured to the quay, to the bateaux being prepared for the morrow's trip upriver. "Mrs. Doyle sits to home knitting hose and hemming kerchiefs for the militia. All Mr. Doyle talks of is the acres of grain he's sowing to feed Washington's ragtag troops. Do you tell me *this* is why you sold your birthright in Crickhowell? A pot of porridge for a band of rebels?"

"The Doyles act according to—"

"Conscience, aye. But now you've brought me back here against my will, shall you not suffer me to do likewise?"

Fear washed cold over Reginald. "What mean you?"

"I'm not saying I'm ready to call myself a Tory." William's throat convulsed over a swallow. "But only yesterday Sam was saying—"

"Reagan? What's he to do with any of this?"

"He's minded the colonials cannot hope to hold out long."

"Is he then?" Reginald said. "Since when?"

William frowned. "Since first I met him. Why? Has he said otherwise to you?"

He'd thought the young man a Patriot, but Reginald waved a dismissive hand. "Never mind Reagan. It is you we were speaking of."

"No sir. Begging your pardon, it was *you*." William's jaw was set, but he made a visible effort to relax it. "Look you, Father, I'm only trying to be objective, to view all sides of this present conflict, to look ahead."

"As am I. Looking ahead to your future." Reginald could barely meet his son's challenging gaze.

"He means to leave your employ, sir."

"Who?"

William firmed his mouth. "I shouldn't have said that."

"Who?" Reginald pressed. But he knew.

"Word has come that Sir John Johnson is raising a regiment in Montreal. Sam talks of following him there and enlisting. Perhaps he has the right idea."

The breath *whooshed* out of Reginald's lungs as though he'd been gut-punched. Thought of his son fleeing to Canada, donning a red coat, drained the blood from his face.

"Father—" William grasped his arm as if he thought him set to topple over. "I don't know how we've come to be quarreling so. Might we just . . . let it bide?"

That sounded good to Reginald, who didn't think he could bear the unhappiness in his son's eyes another moment. He pulled away, standing straight. "Aye, let's do. There's work to be done, by my hands, leastwise. Go downriver with Reagan if you're so minded."

William took a half step back, as if Reginald had told him to go to Canada. Or the devil.

There was movement on the quay—Sam Reagan talking with the crew, the summer sun shining off his pale hair, laughing easily, face turning toward the office, looking expectantly for William.

That young man wouldn't pilot another bateau for him. Not so he could take word of what he saw upriver at the forts straight to the ears of Sir John and his loyalist followers. By his blood, Reginald thought, he would not. Nor would *he* stoop to begging his son to take an interest in his work.

"Get you then to fishing," he said. "If that is what you wish."

33

June–July 1776

onfronting Papa about William proved a thing easier to resolve to do than to actually do. He was away to town more than was usual, what with the Continental troops and militia under Colonel Dayton bound upriver for Fort Stanwix. The pressing needs of soldiers on the move and merchants and farmers eager to provision them kept Papa moored to the Binne Kill. Only twice had she come upon him alone in the sitting room when she knew William to be safely out of hearing. Each time, courage deserting her, she'd crept away to soak her pillow in prayers, listening to the crickets below her window or the distant hoots of owls along the river. Wondering what had happened to the courage Two Hawks believed she possessed.

At last an evening came when Papa returned from town before supper without William—and little explanation of William's absence other than he'd last seen him in Sam's company.

She and Papa supped alone. Mrs. Doyle had taken supper to Mr. Doyle, down at the barn with a cow fixing to calve. Anna barely tasted the few bites of food she managed to force down. Papa's furrowed brow when he'd spoken of William's absence further unsettled her nerves. They were none too pleased with each other, those two. And she was about to make matters between them infinitely worse.

Once she'd tidied the kitchen for the night, Anna went into the sitting room and found Papa settled with his pipe. She tried to sit with a book, but the lines of text swam in the candlelight. She looked up. Papa was staring into the empty grate as though a fire blazed there, pipe to his lips. William could return at any moment. If she was going to do this . . .

Sensing her gaze, Papa glanced at her. "I suppose I should take myself down to the barn, see how Rowan fairs with the calving."

Anna's belly turned over in a sickening mingle of relief and dismay. She was about to say she'd go along when he yawned hugely, and abruptly changed his mind.

"No . . . Was anything amiss he'd send to fetch me. May it all come well for the beast, for I'm done in. I've spent the day since dawn helping load supplies for Stanwix—and provision to accompany Schuyler to German Flatts."

"German Flatts? What is General Schuyler doing there?" She'd sounded breathless, nervous. Papa didn't seem to notice.

"Meeting with the Six Nations, trying to talk them round to staying clear of Fort Niagara and the British. Nothing for you to worry over." Sighing, Papa settled deeper into his chair, his face lined with fatigue. "Never have I sent so many boats upriver at once. Aside from Schuyler's council, a fair number of Oneidas have been attached to the garrison at Stanwix and must be fed."

Silence stretched. Smoke from the pipe wafted toward the ceiling. Anna's gaze fixed on the thin scar across the curve of Papa's cheekbone, as old as her adoption. She swallowed, knowing it had to be now. "Oneidas are scouting for the army. Spying on the British and their Indians at the lake forts."

Papa lowered the pipe from his lips, studying her quizzically. "How come you to know that? Been talking to William of it, have you?"

Anna's face and fingers chilled. *Talking to William about Oneidas?*

She was on her feet with her next breath, dizzied by what she was about to do. "No, but I mean to. I—I know about him, Papa. I know the Oneidas are scouting for the army because William's brother told me."

Papa's face blanched. "What did you say?"

"I'm trying to say that I know who William is. Or was."

Papa's blank expression lasted but a heartbeat before understanding seized his features, freezing them in a look of startled horror. "*What* do you know of William?"

"I know he has a twin. An Oneida twin. He's called Two Hawks." The pipe slid from Papa's hand and fell to the rug, but Anna kept talking. "I've known him for years, only he never told me who he really was, and because I hadn't seen William in so long I didn't realize—"

Papa wrenched out of his chair, crossed to her, and took her by the shoulders. "Hush you. Hush!"

He'd never before touched her with anything but kindness. Not even to smack her bottom when she was small. His roughness now shocked her. Then a smell hit her, pungent and sharp. Where the pipe had fallen, the rug was sending up wisps of smoke. "Papa—the rug!"

He let her go to stamp the rug, the heel of his shoe coming down on the pipe's stem. It cracked with a pop like breaking bone.

Papa bent, wincing, picked up the pieces from off the scorched rug, then he stood, looking at her from a face she barely recognized. "How is it you can know of a brother—an Indian—what was it you called him?"

The acrid stench of burnt fibers caught in her throat, cracking her voice like the pipe's stem. "His name is Two Hawks—but his Christian name is Jonathan. I met him after William left for Wales, in the clearing where we used to play. They were just . . . there one day. They'd found you. Only it was too late for finding William."

Papa clenched the broken pipe. Clenched his face too, as if to keep that from breaking. "They?"

"William's brother. And their father."

"Not . . . the mother?"

Anna shook her head. "I've never met Good Voice, but . . . she isn't Oneida by birth. She's white. That's why William looks as he does."

"I know." Untold remorse lay behind those whispered words. A lifetime of lies and deception. William's lifetime. Lydia was right.

Anna's throat closed over a terrible ache. "Papa . . . why?"

It was the wrong question to ask. Papa's face hardened until it appeared chiseled in stone. "How many times is it you have gone across that creek to see these Indians?"

"I haven't seen their father since I was a girl."

"But this other. The son?"

Anna hoped the candlelight was too dim for Papa to see the heat that rushed into her face. She was afraid now to say how often. "I don't know. I'd find him there waiting sometimes when I went to gather herbs or pick berries. I used to read William's letters to him."

"And you are telling me you never knew who he was? All this time, you never suspected?"

"Why would I have? Truly, Papa. I didn't know. Not until I saw William again, at Lydia's."

"And since? Have you seen the Indian since? Does he know William is come home?" Papa's mask of control was cracking.

She hated to tell this part, the part that was going to change everything. "I had to tell him. I had to be sure it was true. And he told me to tell—"

"Enough, Anna. Enough! Just . . . go to your room."

She stood her ground, too stunned to obey. "But I haven't told you yet—they don't know what Stone Thrower will do when he learns William is here."

"Stone Thrower?" Papa's face lost what little color remained, as if he had no need to be told of whom they spoke. "Anna, go to your room. You will say nothing of this to William. Not a word, see? I forbid it!"

She'd never had such sharp words from Papa, such a stinging look. "Papa—"

"Have you thought this through? Thought what this will do to him? I've tried to make it right for the lad, to give him a good life. A purpose. A place. Now you come wanting me to tear it all down—tear William to shreds. Is that what you want me to do, Anna?"

How could Papa think he could keep the truth from William now? It was out of their hands. Two Hawks had gone to bring their mother . . .

"Of course I don't want to hurt William. I love him." Her mouth quivered over the words, and she couldn't hold back the tears a moment longer. "And I love *you*, Papa. But I love Two Hawks too, and he and his parents have been—"

"What?" Papa had put his face in his hands when she said she loved him. He jerked it up again, in his eyes shock and dismay, and she was left to wonder how things might have turned out had she not said that part about loving Two Hawks.

The news reached Kanowalohale that the Americans' council at German Flatts was going badly. Warriors early to arrive were misbehaving. Some Mohawks, foolish with rum, shot at a bateau full of flour sent upriver to feed them and sank it.

Two Hawks stood with his father and Clear Day as they talked about the situation. He waited to see what his father would do, relieved when the two decided to journey to the council that was getting off to such a bad start, to see if they could help bring order. Or whether the rumors were even true.

"If things are going so badly, I do not know how long I will be gone," Stone Thrower told Two Hawks and Good Voice by the fire that night, as he prepared to leave. "Will you be all right without me?"

The fishing and the hide-hunting were done for the summer, such as they had been. There was still hunting for meat to do—always that—but to have his father occupied for days up on the river at German Flatts . . . They couldn't ask for better circumstances to help keep William's return secret.

"We will be all right," his mother said, quick as he to come to this conclusion. "I pray you bring a wiser head to help those others. Both of you," she added, turning to include Clear Day sitting nearby, listening and watching. Watching very closely.

"I will hunt if need be," Two Hawks said, wanting to hold his father's attention, keep him from noticing what wasn't being said between the rest of them except with eyes. "We will be well."

Stone Thrower paused in filling his pack to smile at his son. Two Hawks found it hard to hold his gaze.

In the morning Stone Thrower and Clear Day left for German Flatts, with other warriors and sachems curious what the white general would say to them. Watching them go, Two Hawks's blood stirred to be doing something as well, maybe to be out watching the borders of their land for any who might make war across it. Some of the young men he'd grown up with were volunteering to do such things for the soldiers at Fort Stanwix.

He stilled those thoughts. It wasn't for him to do those things. Not yet. Anna Catherine had promised to speak to Aubrey. And to William.

"I will go back to her." He said this to his mother after Stone Thrower and Clear Day walked out of the village, headed east, though not as far east as Two Hawks meant to go. They stood beneath the arbor outside her lodge. He felt his mother's hand grip his and looked down into her face that in the morning light showed its sorrows and its hope. "Will you come with me this time?"

Never had his mother hinted she might want to see the place or the people who had had the raising of his brother. He felt the shudder that rocked her now as she looked in the direction his father had taken. Two Hawks knew she was looking far beyond the river valley to the lake called George. She stood in memory at the edge of a forest, a dead white baby in her arms, looking at the fort where he and his brother were born.

"I will come with you," she said. "I will see my son again at last."

34

July 1776

*A*t the knock on her door, Anna abandoned the window and dove beneath the rumpled bed covers. She was safely tucked between stale linens before the door opened and Mrs. Doyle peered into the room.

"Anna, dearie, how—" One look at her face, peeking over the summer coverlet, and Mrs. Doyle didn't finish the question. She shouldered into the room with a tray of tea and toast, the only nourishment for the past two days she'd persuaded Anna to accept.

"Thank you," Anna mumbled, sounding as if her nose was swollen shut. It was, but not from the summer ague she'd been claiming to suffer.

Mrs. Doyle set the tray on the foot of the bed. "Can I bring you aught else before I'm out to the garden?"

Anna sank down the pillow until her face was buried in the coverlet. "No . . . thank you."

The feather tick sagged under Mrs. Doyle's weight. "Anna . . . you're sure 'tis nothin' else the matter? The Major bid me let you rest, but William's worried. He said you wouldn't see him again this morn."

She'd heard the concern in William's voice through the bedroom door, when he'd all but begged her to open it and let him see her. She longed to do so, but how could she and not blurt everything Papa had forbidden her to say? One look at her and he'd *know* something was terribly wrong.

"Is it to do with William?" Mrs. Doyle persisted. "Has he done aught to upset you?"

"No." Fresh tears came hot into her eyes. She pressed a wad of linen to her face to staunch them. "I'm not upset with William."

Papa hadn't told Mrs. Doyle about their quarrel, or she wouldn't be fishing for an explanation of Anna's misery—beyond the state of her health. As tears were most definitely not a symptom of a cold, she kept her face hidden in the covers. "Papa's right. I want to rest."

What she wanted, desperately, was to get across the fields to look for Two Hawks. But she couldn't.

"You will go across that creek no more," Papa had told her, during that distressing encounter in the sitting room. "You will confine yourself to this house and yard, else you will pack your belongings and go to Lydia."

As she'd stared, barely recognizing him with his hard-set jaw and unflinching gaze, a wave of rebellion had swept over Anna. His threat was empty. He would go into town again. When he did, she would slip across the creek and find Two Hawks—or at the very least leave him a note, explaining what had happened. She'd kept her lips shut over *those* words, but she might as well have shouted them in Papa's face.

She hadn't come down to breakfast next day, pleading tiredness when both Mrs. Doyle and William tapped at her door and inquired. When William and Papa were gone to the Binne Kill, she'd dressed and crept from the house. She'd barely started down the lane between the fields before Mr. Doyle stepped across her path.

Whatever else Papa had kept secret, he'd told Mr. Doyle she'd been meeting an Indian in the wood. Mr. Doyle informed her flatly that she wasn't to go across the creek, that he knew what she'd been doing there, that she had lied to Mrs. Doyle about it, and it was never to happen again.

She might as well have placed the lock on her cage. Knowing he'd every right to see what she'd done as lying, she'd fled back to her room and hadn't come out again, and by now she felt sick in truth, with apprehension, grief, confusion.

"All right then, dearie. I've brought you fresh tea. And there's toast. I'll be down to the garden if you need me." The bed shifted as Mrs. Doyle rose and went out of the room.

The stairs creaked under her descent.

Anna flung back the covers and padded barefoot to the window. The sill was cool to her touch, there on the west side of the house. A breeze came in thick with the scent of corn and cows and the river. She looked to the line of trees that marked the creek. Was Two Hawks there, expecting her to bring William? What would he do when she didn't come?

Movement below her window made her start. Rowan Doyle stood at the edge of the cornfield, looking up at her. She stepped back, heart beating like a netted bird's.

"Come down from her room yet, has she?" Reginald kept his eyes on the brush in his hand, and the horse he groomed between himself and Rowan Doyle, who leaned in the open box stall.

"Not to my knowin'. You'll be after askin' Maura to be sure."

Reginald's gut twisted at thought of his daughter, confined to her room, pretending to illness. Sick at heart she was.

"I'll talk to Maura directly I'm done here." He was home from the Binne Kill, just ahead of the dark—and alone. William had stayed in town, saying he'd be late. Not saying it was Sam Reagan he was going to meet with. No need of saying it.

The widening gulf between them was a worry and a grief, but it was not a new grief. This estrangement with Anna . . . There was a crippling to his soul. It had taken him unawares, and there was no fixing it, no expunging from her mind the things she knew. No more pretending he was the man she'd thought him to be.

Beneath his hands the horse quivered, pleased to be relieved of its saddle and the sweat of the day. Light from a hanging lantern fell warm across his hands. Dust smells and manure smells and warm horse smells filled his nostrils, but the only sound in the barn was that of industrious chewing and the occasional stamp. Until Rowan cleared his throat.

"She hasn't left the house in body, but her heart is well away. She's at her window starin' across the fields for hours at a stretch. Maura would know—how soon shall we be expecting Indians on the doorstep?"

Reginald fumbled the brush, chasing it with clumsy fingers along the horse's spine. The animal shifted its weight and stamped a hoof in agitation a hair's breadth from his shoe.

"You've told Maura?"

"Maura can tell a weepin' binge from a summer ague. When she asked me straight did I know what was wrong, I had no wish to lie."

Rowan waited.

"It is over now, with that Indian. She will get past it." Reginald circled the brush over the horse's side, loosening dirt thrown up from the road, his left hand smoothing behind. Anna would have to get past it. Perhaps he should insist she stay with Lydia now regardless, to keep her away. To keep her safe . . .

But no. She might defy him and have that conversation with William, there in the town, where he had less control of the pair of them.

Control? Did he still have such a thing?

Rowan looked unhappy with his answer, but he let it stand. "William did not come home with you?"

"He'll be along. He's for socializing, is all." Reginald took up a softer brush to sweep away the hairs and dust he'd loosened.

At last Rowan bade him good night. When his footsteps faded,

Reginald raised his gaze to the open barn doors. Beyond them twilight was darkening. Gazing into the wall of corn across the lane, he saw nothing but leaf blades and shadows shifting with a papery rustle and the last of the evening's fireflies winking like feral eyes among the stalks.

Perfect cover for creeping feet.

The dread of a hunted thing stirred in his blood. Thinking he heard a sound—a step—he whirled to look behind him, deeper into the barn, startling the horse again.

"There is nothing," he said, soothing the creature, if not himself.

He winced from memory of the hurt in his daughter's eyes as he told her she wasn't to speak to William of what she knew or see the Indian again. *William's twin.* After so many years he'd almost persuaded himself that tiny brown infant could bear no relation to the one he'd taken. Perhaps the woman had no connection to William either, for she'd been with Indians and couldn't be expected to birth a child so white it might have been his own.

She had, though.

Good Voice. He longed to carve the name from his mind. He was as terrified now as that night in the encampment outside Fort William Henry, when he'd stood between Heledd and their changeling, and the Indians prowling the firelight. Again he stood between, though he couldn't see the Indian staring back at him now. That terror from his dreams had known where to find him. Could have long since taken his revenge.

That he hadn't meant one thing. He meant to have his son back first.

"Papa?"

Anna's voice gave his chest a wrench so sharp he dropped the brush to the straw-littered earth. Abandoning it and the horse, he moved into the aisle to see her standing at the edge of the lantern's glow, arms crossed at her waist. The night was a sheet of black behind her.

One look at her sorrowing, swollen eyes and he was overcome with the need to gather her safe into his arms. He spread them wide and she flew to him, face crumpling in relief.

"Papa, I'm sorry—"

"Dear girl—"

She cried into his shoulder, and he pressed her to him, crooning to her, every other thought consumed by the love bursting like a mortar in his chest.

At length her crying quieted and he fished a kerchief from his coat and she blew her nose, the undignified noise making them both laugh. He'd missed the sweet sound of her laughter.

She wiped her nose and said, "Oh, Papa. I don't want to quarrel."

He touched her cheek, brushing away a tear. "Nor do I, my girl. And I'm sorry for it. More than you can know."

She stilled beneath his hand. Hope bloomed in the eyes more brown than green in the lantern light. "But I do know, Papa."

Relief bled away. He dropped his hand to his side. "No, Anna. You cannot possibly know. There are things beyond your scope of understanding, and for that I am glad."

Her face was stubbornly earnest. "Lydia explained it to me."

"Lydia." Her name came rough to his lips. "What does Lydia know of this? Has she been here to the farm? Did you tell her?"

"She already knew, Papa. She's known about William for years."

The admission hit him with a doubling force. "How could she know?"

"You told her. That last time you were fevered from your wound, and she came here and tended you."

He told Lydia? All those years ago? An instant's scouring told him well enough he had no memory of doing such a thing. "Do you tell me the truth, Anna? This isn't some ploy to get round me and across that creek to—"

"I'm not lying!" She was tearing his heart out again with her wounded

eyes. "Lydia kept your secret all these years and would have gone on keeping it forever if she hadn't realized I'd guessed it too. I had to tell her, Papa.
It was too much for me."

And he it was who'd laid that burden on her. Reginald grasped hold
of a slat in the nearest stall. *Lydia . . .*

"She was sure you didn't remember. You were out of your head with
fever when you told her about Fort William Henry, about Good Voice and
William."

Reginald winced as an image of the woman with her golden braid
rushed in, a face frozen young in his mind, no older than his Anna was
now. He gripped the stall so hard his nails dug into the wood. "I'll have no
more talk on this, Anna. Go now and pack your trunk. In the morning I
will take you to Lydia and—"

He broke off at the scuff of a boot at the barn doorway, the blow of a
tired horse. He hadn't heard William's coming.

Anna whirled round to see what Reginald had already taken in, the
bruise spreading dark across William's left eye. The scored knuckles of the
hand that gripped his mare's reins. The burn of his bewildered gaze, taking in the two of them.

"Let her speak, Father. What is it about the fort where I was born that
has Anna in tears and you banishing her to Lydia's? And who is this other
she named—this Good Voice? What has she to do with me?"

35

*W*illiam—" Anna's thoughts spun faster than she could grasp them: William was here; he'd heard what she'd said; he was injured. "You're hurt!" She took a step toward him. He stopped her with a look.

"The price of being Sam's friend," William said, his voice tight, impatient. "I managed to extricate him from the brawl with limbs intact."

"Brawl? How badly are you hurt? Come up to the house and—"

"Never mind it, Anna. You claimed to be ill, now here you stand looking hale but miserable, and I'm thinking Father is the cause of it." William's gaze flashed back to Papa. "What is this upset between the two of you? I'll have the truth of it now."

Behind her Papa made no answer. He'd been silent this whole time. She thought to turn and seek his guidance, permission, *something* . . . but couldn't take her eyes off William standing there looking so much like his brother that longing pierced her—longing for Two Hawks to step out of the cornfield, to come and stand beside her. Help her find the right words.

At last she tore her gaze away. In the lantern light Papa's face appeared that of an old and broken man, hollow-eyed, haggard. He moved a step nearer and the shadows shifted, leaving only the brokenness.

"Let us do as Anna wishes," Papa said, a hint of desperation in his voice. "Go to the house. We'll speak of it there."

William was immovable. "We'll stay as we are. Tell me what Anna meant by what she said. What about that fort where I was born can have her so upset? What is all this to do with me?"

Papa came forward to stand even with her, as though her nearness could lend him strength. She had no strength to lend, only a fraying hope that the brother she cherished wasn't about to be obliterated before her eyes.

"William, do not make me say this," Papa said. "For your own sake, I am begging you."

"My sake?" William challenged. "I'm thinking it is for *your* sake that you would have me pretend I didn't hear what I did. We do not move from this spot until you tell me."

Anna looked to Papa and saw that everything Lydia had told her, there in her kitchen when they'd confessed their secrets, was true. Regret and guilt, fear and dread, half a lifetime of it, ravaged his eyes, his face. Her mind flashed back to that night of her birthday, years ago, when she'd found him sitting with William's letter in his grasp, looking as if the weight of the world was upon him. She'd thought it had to do with the things William had written about his mother and her. No doubt it had, but it was more. So much more. The memory of other moments like it came rushing back to her, of the heaviness that clung to him, weighing him down, noticed in passing but never understood.

Let William see. Let him be merciful. It was the only prayer she had time to fling heavenward before Papa resigned himself in the face of William's implacable demand.

"William . . . you are my son," he said, the words rough as gravel on his lips. "But you were not born to me."

There was silence in the barn, a breathless, hair-raising stillness like the pause between lightning and thunderclap.

William's head reared back. The eye that wasn't bruised flared wider. "You . . . are not . . . my father?"

He spoke the words with frightful care, as though in a language barely comprehended. Whatever he'd thought was the matter between them, he hadn't been prepared for this. Anna had prayed for mercy, but who could be prepared for this? She ought to have waited at the house, not come down to the barn to persuade Papa of his danger, that it was too late to bury the truth.

It was buried no longer. God help them.

"Not by blood," Papa said, the words dredged out of him as if by great force. "I am not."

The color bled from William's face. His throat worked, forcing down a swallow before he said, "Mother?"

Pain wracked Papa's face. "Heledd wasn't the mother who birthed you, no."

William closed his eyes, grimaced, then opened them. They were blue as glass even in the dimness where the lantern's glow met the crowding dark of night. Blue and shattered. "Who then? Who is my mother?"

No sound left Papa's lips now. His jaw was set like a man enduring a slow and terrible wounding.

"I'll tell it," Anna whispered, pain for them both a strangle in her throat. "If you want me to—"

William had turned his gaze sharp on her, but Papa's hand on her arm held her silenced.

"No, Anna. This is for me to do." He released her and to William said, "You were born to another woman at Fort William Henry. A white woman taken from a band of Indians before the siege. She was held in the fort until it fell to the French. You were born to her the same hour my son—mine and Heledd's—came into this world."

Anna realized she was clenching her ribs, squeezing them as if to keep the tension stretching inside her from snapping her in two, her gaze fixed in silent pleading on William, who was shaking his head like an ox stunned by a blow.

"There is no sense in what you are saying. You had a son, but he isn't me? Where is he then? *Who* is he, and why am I in his place?"

She reached for Papa, but he didn't notice her clutching hand. He stood remote, accepting no comfort, no support. Anna let her hand fall.

"But an hour after his birth," Papa said, "he died, that son of mine. I took you from your mother's side, she asleep and unknowing, and put him in the place where you had lain."

Anna had no memory of crossing the space between them, only of looking up into William's stunned face—the bruise dark against his pallid skin—at his eyes staring at Papa as if from some great distance. Her fingers touched his coat sleeve, but William didn't break the stare that locked his gaze with Papa's.

They stood alone, separated from her by a veil transparent but impenetrable.

"It was moments before the British evacuated the fort," Papa was saying. "And the French took possession. In that confusion no one knew what I had done—"

"How?" William cut in. "How could she not have known?"

Anna knew who he meant. So did Papa.

"Heledd was half out of her mind with the fright of the siege and overcome by the birthing. She barely saw . . . *him* before she slept, never knew he died beside her. I took his body into my arms still warm and walked out into the casemate. I was looking for the courage to tell her of it when I saw you. And her. Your mother."

William's silence was terrible. The sounds of the stock in their stalls and the trill of insects outside the barn could make no dent in it. It was the ringing stillness after cannon-fire, reverberating in Anna's soul.

"*She* knew. My real mother." William at last looked down at Anna. "Is that who you spoke of before? What did you call her?"

"Her name . . ." Anna's mouth was almost too dry now to speak. "Her name is Good Voice."

William scowled. "What sort of name is that?"

"*Onyota'a:ka*—Oneida. Good Voice is white, but she's been Oneida as long as she can remember. She—"

The horror dawning on William's face stopped her cold. "He said . . .

she'd been with Indians? But how is it *you* know this?" He drew back a pace, crowding his mare, who tossed her head and danced. He dropped the reins and stamped a boot on them, holding her fast. "How is it you know, Anna, and I do not?"

The words thrust at her like blades, pushing her away even as they demanded answer. Pushing her away as he was pushing Papa. "Because I know them. Your family. At least I know your brother."

"Brother?"

"Your twin. His name is Two Hawks. He's also called Jonathan . . ."

She trailed off as William, looking sick with the shock of it, gazed down at his lifted hand, fingers spread in the lantern light. Softly he said, "So that is what I am? An Indian. A half-breed."

"You are my son!" Papa started for William, who snatched his horse's reins from the ground and backed the mare onto the track.

"I am not, though, am I? You've said as much." Before Papa could reach him, he vaulted into the saddle. "There is none of it true. Wales, Oxford, this place—my *name*. None of it is mine."

Anna pursued him. "William, no. Please, just listen—"

"How long have *you* known of this, Anna?" William swung the horse away as she grabbed for his foot. She staggered back, hardly aware of Papa rushing past her, trying to catch William as she'd failed to do.

Eluding him as well, William heeled the mare into a gallop back along the lane. They vanished in the dark, reappeared briefly in the glow of a candle burning in the cottage window, then the night swallowed them, save for the drumming of hooves headed for the Schenectady road.

Mr. Doyle came down from the cottage, having heard William's horse thunder past. Anna's head was banging, her throat thick with grief. The lifting of a hand to brush at tears felt like pushing through deep water. It had all gone wrong. So terribly wrong. Was it her fault? She'd chosen the time and place to confront Papa. It must be her fault.

"Get you up to the house, Anna."

She jerked her head up to find Papa astride his horse, Mr. Doyle swinging onto the back of another. She'd heard them talking but hadn't really noticed they were saddling the horses. "Papa, I'm sorry . . ."

"Go you now," he said, closed to her, unreachable still. "I will watch to see that you do. Maura will come to stay with you."

She didn't think to add *to be my guard* until later. For now all she saw was Papa's face looking years older than it had before William's flight. She didn't think a shift of light would be enough to change it back now.

Mrs. Doyle had asked a dozen questions. Anna, too stunned and upset to be coherent, tried to answer them but ended up dissolving in tears. At last Mrs. Doyle took pity and, despite her own fretting, sent Anna off to bed.

Anna went gratefully to her room but with no intention of sleeping. She couldn't know how wide a margin of time lay between Mrs. Doyle finally nodding off to sleep in the sitting room and Papa and Mr. Doyle's return. Hours? Minutes?

It was nearing midnight before she extricated herself from the house. Through rustling cornstalks, across the chattering creek, into the inky whisper of the beeches, she never allowed herself to think that Two Hawks mightn't be there. She needed him to be there.

The beeches opened to the clearing. By starlight she saw her way to the hill rising dark where the spring flowed down. She made a racket of falling stones as she climbed, heedless of stealth. When she was not quite to the height of the waterfall, a voice called to her from above. She scrabbled to a halt, the better to hear it.

"Bear's Heart?"

Relief brought her near to tears. "Two Hawks!"

They met at the level by the fall. Wordless, she reached for him and felt his arms enfold her, pressing her close.

"I have waited days for you and am glad you are come. But you have never come in darkness. What is wrong?"

"Everything!" All but drowning in her sense of failure, she told him how William had learned the truth and then ridden off into the night, devastated, angry. "Papa and Mr. Doyle went after him. If they return and find me gone, it might make matters worse. I don't know. I've already made a ruin of it!"

Two Hawks held her again and stroked his hand down her braid.

"Though I am sorry for this pain, Creator saw what would happen this night. He has a plan for us."

She felt the wild beating of his heart, knew he was far from calm, despite his words. As if he sensed her thoughts, he held her from him.

"I have long thought about how it would be if I was the one taken, only to learn the truth all these years later. What would I think? What would I say? I may have done worse than what William has done."

Anna wished it wasn't dark. She wanted to see his eyes, which barely caught the starlight as he looked down at her. As if her fingers could make up for what the darkness denied, she touched his face. "I'm glad you're here. I didn't know what to do. I've missed you."

"And I you." He bent his head and she lifted hers, inviting him to kiss her. Before their lips could touch, the scuff of movement above them startled her. She clung to Two Hawks, fear racing up her spine. Was it Stone Thrower?

A figure was climbing down the rocks, a slender person moving with grace and care, a long braid swinging in the starlight like a panther's silvery tail.

Two Hawks's hand squeezed her shoulder, reassuring. "*Né: ka'í:kʌ aknulhá.* Here is my mother come to meet you." His voice had taken on a formal note that mingled respect, pride, affection, and a sudden shyness. "Here is *Ha'tiyo,* Good Voice of the Turtle Clan, also called Elizabeth."

Though it was dark, Two Hawks stood back to give Anna Catherine and his mother a chance to fix upon each other without him as distraction. His nerves were strung bow-taut.

"Good Voice." In Anna Catherine's whisper, he heard the same shyness afflicting him. Also much feeling rushing from her through her words. "I've wanted long to meet you."

He wished this moment was happening under the sun so he could see the small signals of their eyes and lips, to know how they were looking at each other, what they were thinking.

Anna Catherine wore a cap. The white of it glowed in the starlight. It seemed to draw his mother like a moth to a flame.

"You are the woman my son loves? You are Aubrey's daughter?"

"Yes," Two Hawks said, eagerness betraying his nerves. "This is Anna Catherine."

His mother's face turned his way, the angle of it hinting at amusement. Then Good Voice reached out her hands. Anna Catherine lifted hers. As they clasped, his mother said, "The woman both my sons love."

Anna Catherine froze, held in greeting. "Yes," she said, her voice breaking as she added, "But he—William—is angry with me now."

"Two Hawks has told me much of you. You have been true in your heart to the son born first to me, as a sister is true. He will remember that." His mother held Anna Catherine's hands and looked at her as if the darkness was no barrier. "We have each nurtured one of my sons, in our different ways. I think it is true we each have loved them both."

"Good Voice . . . I'm so sorry, for all of this."

He could tell Anna Catherine was crying. He could also see their hands, joined where the starlight fell between them. A bridge formed of slender fingers entwined.

"As am I," his mother said. "I heard what you told my son, that his brother has fled. Will Aubrey bring him back to that house across the fields?"

"He means to. He's looking for him. But William can be stubborn."

Two Hawks grunted. Good Voice looked at him. "As can be his brother," she said. "Has he been a good father to my son, that man you call Papa?"

"He wanted to be. I know he tried to be. But now I know what has stood between them all these years." Anna Catherine hesitated, then said, "Papa wouldn't listen to my pleas for his safety. Where is Stone Thrower?"

Two Hawks stepped to Anna Catherine's side as Good Voice let go her hands. "My father does not yet know William has returned. He has gone to German Flatts, to the council there with Schuyler. There is time for us to decide what is best to do."

She nodded, acknowledging his words. "Good Voice, what is it you want to do? Tell me. If there is any way I can help, I will."

Two Hawks felt his chest warm with pride. This was his Bear's Heart talking now. He put his arm around her, claiming her wordlessly in the presence of his mother. Sides pressed together as if they were already one, they waited for her reply.

36

*A*nna returned from the woods to nary a sign of Papa or William. Mrs. Doyle still slept. There was nothing for it but to retreat to her room to pace—pausing at the window to gaze into the night—and wait.

"I have come to see my son," Good Voice had told her. Could Anna contrive to bring him across the creek to them?

"I'll try my best, if Papa brings him home." It was all she could promise, standing by the little fall, loathe to leave them, yet eager to return before her absence was discovered.

"I hope we yet have some days," Two Hawks told her. "Before my father returns from German Flatts and learns we are gone. He will come here—bearing the hatchet is what I fear. But if William is here and will stand between our fathers . . ."

Though the night was warm, a chill had raced up her spine at the words. William stand between Papa and Stone Thrower? If asked to do so now, he was more likely to stand back and let them fight it out.

Good Voice had taken them each by the hand. "My son may know that in my heart I forgive the man who stole his brother. It is not easy to do, but I tell you, Aubrey's daughter, I wish him no harm. What my husband wishes I do not know. But there is One who does."

Good Voice had raised her face to the night sky and prayed. She'd prayed in Oneida, but Two Hawks whispered the English words into Anna's ear. Good Voice had asked for guidance and protection, for truth and grace, with an eloquence and trust that caused the words to rebound through Anna's soul. *I forgive the man who stole his brother.* If Good Voice could forgive Papa, dare she hope William might . . . in time?

Two Hawks had led her back as far as the beech grove. There he'd pulled her into his arms and held her with a fierceness that made her think he feared never do so again. She'd taken his face between her hands and drew him down to kiss her . . .

Now at her window she lit a candle, a tiny flame she hoped was visible to him, out there in the darkness with his mother.

She paced, and waited, and prayed. Between prayers she tried to piece together her impressions of Good Voice. It had been too dark to glean more than a suggestion of features, of deep-set eyes and high-arched brows, strong hands larger than hers, a braid that caught the starlight and would be blond under the sun. A low, pleasant voice offering courage and trust.

"*Ha'tiyo* . . . a good voice," she murmured and wept a little in this one relief.

Curled at the foot of her bed, she dozed, until the creak of footsteps in the hall had her bolting upright. She was off the bed and at the door before fully awake. "Papa—"

She'd run smack into a broad chest, but it wasn't Papa's. "Anna . . . *hush.*" Taking her by the arm, William steered her back into the room. "You'll wake Mrs. Doyle."

"Where have you been?" She stepped back to search his face in the candlelight. His blackened eye had darkened. He reeked of smoke-filled taverns. "Papa and Mr. Doyle are searching for you."

"Aye. There's the devil of a time I had getting round them to the road." William turned to heft a knapsack, to which was tied a bedroll and shot bag, onto her bed. Slung at his back were a rifle and the bow he'd brought from Crickhowell, with its quiver.

Anna stood in the center of her tiny room, gutted by their implication. "Where are you going? To Lydia's?"

William slid the weapons to the bed, then perched beside them and removed his hat. He raked a hand over his tailed hair. It was as rumpled as her bed, as if he'd performed the gesture repeatedly the past hours. "I came to tell you where. First there is this I must say—how I spoke to you earlier, at the barn . . . Look you, Anna, I'm sorry. You deserve better of me. Whatever lies *he* fed me my life long, you and I have been true. Haven't we?"

How well Good Voice knows her son, though she's yet even to meet him. The thought flashed through Anna's mind as she took in the disillusionment and hope at war in William's eyes. Eyes that grasped for her amidst the spun-away pieces of his world.

"William . . . yes." She moved to the bedside to stand before him, taking his hand in hers. "And I'm sorry too. Sorry you found out like that. I wish now I'd come to you at once. But it's only been days since I—"

"No, Anna." William raised his fingertips to her lips. "Please . . ." He dropped his hand from her mouth but with the other gripped hers tighter, almost bruising. "Did you know they've announced a formal separation from England?"

"Who?" she asked, bewildered by the shift.

William's lip pulled back. "The Continental Congress. They've dissolved all connection between themselves and the Crown. 'Twas read in Philadelphia. A Declaration of Independence, they're calling it. Sam told me."

Anna pulled her hand away. "I don't care about that. I care about you and Papa. You didn't give us a chance to explain."

"Save your breath, Anna." William stood, his hand closing hard on her shoulder. "What excuse is there for stealing a stranger's child and leaving a dead one in its place? For naming that child, raising him to think he was something he isn't? There are no words you can say that will justify any of it in my eyes."

"I didn't say *justify.*"

William let her go. "Save your breath, I said. I came only to fetch my things and to tell you where I'm bound."

"You cannot go. Think about—"

"I don't want to think!" William snapped off the words, then lowered his voice. "Do you not see? I am sick in my soul for thinking."

"But your mother and brother want to see you. Aren't you even the least bit—"

"Curious? To meet strangers—Indians—who think they have some claim on me?" Emotions passed across William's eyes too quickly for her to read by candlelight, but last to emerge, and linger, was bitterness. "Who is my mother and my brethren?"

"William! Do not use the words of Christ to—"

William clapped a hand across her mouth, cutting off the exclamation. She glared at him over it, until he took it away. "Only listen, Anna. This declaration of war has decided Sam. He's headed north, to Quebec. Sir John is there, raising a loyalist regiment. Sam means to join, and he's asked me to come with him. So I suppose this is me declaring *my* independence."

Anna's heart dropped down and down, as if into a bottomless well. "You're leaving us?"

William took her shoulders between his hands, dizzying her with the resemblance to his brother he bore, even to the way he was touching her. "*We* don't have to be parted. Come with me. Here is no less a web of lies for you than for me. You needn't stay caught in it."

Anna shook her head. "It's not all lies."

"Fair enough," William allowed. "He came by you honestly—the great war hero. But you cannot want to stay here now, with *him.*"

He couldn't even call Papa by name. "William, please. There's so much you still need to hear. Once you do, you'll think differently."

"Not about him. He had no right to me, yet he took me. Then soon as Mother—Mrs. Aubrey, I should say—was in her grave, again he yanks me from my life with no more thought than was I one of his blasted boats."

Anna pressed her hands to her temples, trying to think. "Then don't stay for Papa. Stay for Good Voice, for Two Hawks. They're right there." She pointed past him to the window. "Waiting to meet you."

William stepped back from her, pivoting on his heel as if he expected his mother and brother to materialize from the shadows of her room. "Where?"

"At our place. The waterfall."

"We never did go there," he said, but the wistfulness in his voice didn't touch his eyes, which were filling with suspicion as he faced her again. "'Tis your place with *them* now, is it? Tell me something—why is it you are in such sympathy with these Oneidas?"

Anna's heart leapt with hope. "They found me there. Your father and brother."

"Stop calling them so!"

"William . . . all right." Though her mouth was dry as dust now, Anna told him how she and Two Hawks met, only weeks after his leaving for Wales, that she hadn't known who he was to William, until William came through the door of Lydia's house. "I realized then that he'd been coming here all these years because he and your parents never forgot you. How could they? William, they want so badly to see you. I had to sneak out of the house after Papa left, but I found them waiting and—"

"He forbade you to see them again, didn't he? That's why you've been shut up in your room for days, playing sick."

Nothing she had said had softened William in the least.

"Papa needs time," she began, but he had no wish to hear it.

"I don't care what he needs. I've made *my* decision, Anna. Now I'm asking you to make yours. Do you love him more than you love me?"

Anna felt her face blanch. Was he speaking of Papa, or could he have somehow guessed her feelings for Two Hawks? She shut her eyes, trying to sift through it all to what mattered most now. "I do love you. You know I do."

"Then come with me, Anna. Leave this place, leave all of it. We can have a new life. One not based on lies."

Not based on lies. Based on what then? Denial of the truth?

"I want you to come with me, Anna." The candle was behind William, his face in shadow, but the hope in his voice broke her heart.

"Please . . . don't ask it. I cannot leave him."

"Who? Who can you not leave?"

She mustn't say *Two Hawks.* She mustn't. "Papa!" she said on a sob, knowing that answer was no better to him.

William's features twisted, a grimace of pain. "So it's him you choose. I suppose I oughtn't be surprised. He always loved you more."

"No, William. That's not . . ." But she couldn't say it. What if it *was* true? *The one pure thing,* Papa had called her.

Turning his back, William took up rifle and bow, slung them over his shoulder, then the knapsack. Anna watched him from beside the door. She couldn't look away, couldn't stop time and keep him with her though everything in her screamed for it to stop. On the threshold of her room he paused, looking down at her as if he meant to memorize her features like a landscape he expected never again to see. In his eyes was desolation.

"Give my love to my family."

He was gone through the door before he was done speaking the bitter words.

Anna came downstairs in the gray of dawn. William had made it out of the house without waking Mrs. Doyle, who was beginning to rouse as

Anna drifted past the sitting room, through the kitchen, and out the door
to find William's mare in the yard, reins trailing in the grass it was busy
cropping. He'd left on foot rather than take the horse Papa gave him. Or
had he left by river? Which way should she go to try to catch him?

In a daze of fatigue and heartache, she picked up the reins, gathered
her petticoats, and raised a foot to a stirrup. Mr. Doyle came around the
house on his horse. William's mare stepped forward in greeting and Anna
fell in a sprawl on the grass, bare feet wet from dew. She'd forgotten to put
her shoes on.

"Anna." Mr. Doyle dismounted, caught her by the arm, hauled her up
off the ground. "Where is William?"

She blinked into his face as the first crest of sunlight fell upon the yard
and knew by the way he was looking at her that there were no more secrets.
"I couldn't make him stay."

It was all she had time to say before the kitchen door opened. Mrs.
Doyle stood in the doorway. "Rowan? Where is Reginald?"

Mr. Doyle let go Anna's arm. "Go to the cottage, Maura. I shall come
and tell you everything once I've seen to the beasts. A long night of it
they've had."

Mrs. Doyle seemed only then to register the gray mare. "That's William's. Where . . . ?" She broke off that question to fix Anna in her gaze.
"What about—"

"She's to wait in the house for her father."

Anna roused from her daze. "But William will be gone!"

"That he will be." The look Mr. Doyle shot her held no warmth. Had
he set his heart against Papa? Against them all? Whatever it meant, another piece of her world had crumbled away. "Maura. Come you now."

Mrs. Doyle opened her mouth, then shut it and stepped into the yard,
clutching her shawl to her bosom.

*L*ydia's eyes felt gritted with sand as she came within sight of her doorstep. After a night and a day sleeping in snatches by an unfamiliar hearth, she was weary enough to drop her midwifery case in the rutted lane and crawl the last steps home—though less weary than the woman who'd spent most of that time laboring to deliver her firstborn through hips almost too narrow for the task. To Lydia's profound relief, the grueling effort had paid off at last in a loud and lusty baby boy, if an utterly exhausted mother and midwife.

Her bleary thoughts returned to a concern as consuming as the one just shed, giving her the push needed to reach the house. No further word had come from Reginald, which she hadn't expected. But neither had there been word from Anna. It was hard to think past the buzzing in her head. She wanted to fall across her bed and sleep the rest of the day through, but as she let herself into the house decided instead to don a fresh gown, eat something, and if any strength remained, saddle the horse and . . .

The horse. A neighbor lad cared for the beast when she was called away overnight, but she ought to make sure all was well. Shutting the door, she hefted her case and summoned strength to reach the kitchen. *Just one more push.*

On the kitchen's threshold she halted. Reginald sat at her table, shoulders bowed, unshaven face etched with devastation. He said nothing, only stared at her through eyes that looked as hers felt, desperate to close and shut out the world but denied the mercy.

Lydia forced herself into the kitchen, set her case on the table, and gripped it for support. "What has happened?"

"Well enough you know, having played your part in it."

The words came from his lips—she saw them move—but the graveled voice might have issued from a stranger's throat.

Lydia lowered herself onto the bench across from him, mustering words she'd waited half her life to say, finding them now with great effort. "Whatever has happened, bear this in mind. I've known the truth about William since I was barely seventeen and—for my part—have counted you my dearest friend for much of that time."

His eyes flashed to hers. "The truth about William, is it? Here is truth—he's gone. To Canada. All night we've searched for him, Rowan and Ephraim and myself, with naught to show but that scrap of news. He's gone with Sam Reagan to join the regiment Johnson is raising. So I'm here at last to see you, for I am desperate. Do you know which road my son has taken? Did you aid him in his going?"

"Aid him? This is the first I'm hearing of Canada." Lydia wanted to reach across and cover the man's hand with hers. His haggard eyes forbade it. "Reginald . . . had I kept quiet and not 'played my part,' it would have left Anna caught between you all with no one to stand beside her. Would you have had me abandon her?"

Reginald ran a hand over his face, wiping hard at his eyes. Lydia hesitated, then asked, "When last did you sleep?"

He stiffened, jerking his hand from his face. "When did you?" Even he cringed at his harshness. "Lydia . . . there has always been with you a love for my Anna. And you say you've held me in regard—though I cannot fathom it, knowing how long since I must have come crashing off the pedestal you set me on as a girl. I'm come crashing down in the eyes of my children now as well. I've lost them both."

Lydia wanted to weep. Held him in regard? Loved him beyond all reason was what she'd done. Dull pain throbbed behind her eyes, but they were dry of tears. "I don't believe that's true—especially of Anna—but even if it is, there is only one loss that matters now."

Wariness sprang to his eyes. "What is that?"

This moment had caught her at the end of her strength, and she feared she would find only wrong words to say. *God help me.* She flung the prayer heavenward and started in.

"Shout at me, rage, whatever you like, if I'm wrong in this, but I believe that on the day you took William, you lost the man you thought yourself to be. Because of it, you suffered an even greater loss and *this* is the loss of which I speak. You put the Almighty at arm's length that day, I think, and have held Him there since. You separated yourself from His mercy, out of mistrust, anger, grief—I don't know—but it's left you striving to atone for that one great sin before you dare approach Him again. You have crucified yourself, but that work will never be finished, Reginald. It cannot be. You are not Christ."

Reginald didn't shout at her, only stared at her with the look of a prisoner hearing himself condemned. She hurried on, too exhausted for anything but honesty.

"Leaving aside for the moment what you did nineteen years ago—you, Reginald Aubrey, are a man of more merit than any other of my acquaintance. You loved Heledd and were faithful to her, when she was difficult to love, even when she took herself across an ocean from you. I know you love Anna and William. You have spent yourself daily, often through pain, to give them good lives. And I know, had the truth of William's parentage never come to light, you'd have gone on devoting yourself to their well-being until your last breath."

Across the table Reginald's lips quivered. He pressed them tight.

"But in the end," Lydia continued, "it wouldn't have brought you nearer to what it is you need. No amount of sacrifice can atone for a single sin, not the smallest sin, or earn a right to God's forgiveness. You never lost that right, Reginald. He's always been as near to you as your next breath."

Come at last to the end of her words, Lydia wanted nothing more than to put her head on the table and cry. It was all she had to say, but it wasn't enough. Else she'd said it with too little tact. With a sinking in her soul, she watched Reginald's face harden.

"Where was God when I called to Him inside that fallen fort? Where was God when I held my son dead in my arms and cried to Him?" He held up a hand when she would have spoken. "No. Answer me only this—if you will have her, I will send Anna to you, not for a few days but to live. There is her safety now I must consider."

"Her safety?" He must fear William's Oneida family meant him harm. Had Anna not told him everything? Had she not said that she and Two Hawks were in love? Or was that the threat to Anna he most feared? "Of course I'll have her, but—"

Reginald stood, screeching the bench across the flagstones, wincing in pain at the movement. "I'll bring her myself. Before nightfall. I'm bound for the Binne Kill to speak with Ephraim. I'll be leaving my affairs in his hands for a time. I must overtake William before he enlists."

"Overtake him? How?" He was in pain just standing there.

"I'll take a bateau up the Hudson River."

"In the middle of a war?" Lydia pushed to her feet, wishing she'd the strength to tackle the man, restrain him until he came to his senses. "Reginald, you have to let William go. Trust him to the Almighty . . ."

He'd turned away as if she wasn't speaking, limping for the door. There he stopped, not turning to look at her as he spoke a final time. "There is sin that is past forgiving, Lydia. I have always feared it was so."

Why couldn't he see how wrong he was? The question had long since translated into prayer, an endlessly repeating refrain as Lydia saddled the horse and rode for the Aubrey farm. Anxiety had staved off her exhaustion. The need to reach Anna drove her as she turned her horse down the lane between the cornfields. Under a westering sun she dismounted. There was no sign of Maura in the yard, no indication Rowan was about. She looped the reins to a length of rail fencing and crossed to the house, but hadn't raised her fist to the door before it flung wide and Anna was pulling her inside.

"Oh, Lydia. I prayed you'd come. Two Hawks and Good Voice are waiting, but I couldn't keep William from leaving, and now Papa is angry and the Doyles are shut up in their cottage, and it's all my fault— everything!"

Lydia shut the door and led Anna into the kitchen, where they sat at the worktable, gripping hands. "Don't take such blame onto yourself. You could no more control how William and your father are contending with this than you could have prevented it happening in the first place."

Anna wiped at her tears—the poor girl looked to have been crying for days—and stared at her through pools of misery.

"Would it have been better for Reginald to have found an angry warrior on the doorstep demanding his son back, with no warning at all?"

Anna shuddered. "No."

"Can you conceive of a good way for William to have learned the truth?"

Again, the answer was *no*. "But have you seen Papa?"

Hope rose in Anna's eyes when Lydia confirmed she had, only to dim as Lydia recounted their conversation. "He knows of William's plans and means to follow him. He's gone to the Binne Kill to talk to Captain Lang."

Anna closed her eyes, shoulders sagging. "When William left, he was angry with me. He asked me to come with him to Canada."

"Did you tell him about his brother and you?"

Anna's face bloomed pink, but she gave her head a shake. "No. He thinks I stayed because I chose Papa over him. Lydia, what do I do? I cannot leave Two Hawks and Good Voice wondering what's happening. William was so close, and now they've lost him again. It's too cruel."

Fatigue was catching up with Lydia, buzzing at the back of her head again like a swarm of agitated bees. "Two Hawks is there now, across the creek? And his mother with him?" That fact was late in registering. It did so now with startling impact. "William's mother is here?"

Anna took her hand, the light coming back into her face. "Yes. She prayed with us. And Lydia, the most amazing thing . . . She's forgiven Papa."

Lydia felt hope flare, fragile as a new-struck spark. "She told you so?"

"Yes. And there's something else you should know. Maybe you already do. While she's Oneida in every other way, Good Voice is white."

Of course she was, Lydia realized. She'd have to be for William to look as he did. "What about their father? Is he there? Has *he* forgiven Reginald?"

Anna's face dimmed, shadowed by fear. "Stone Thrower went to General Schuyler's council in German Flatts. They're worried he'll discover where they went and come after them. And Papa."

"And Reginald has it in his head that he must go after William." Lydia paused, trying to think her way through. Surely the Almighty had a plan for them through this tangle. *Please.*

"Go across the creek, Anna," she said at last, seeing but a step of the way forward. "Go as quickly as you can. Bring William's family here. I'll stay in case Reginald arrives first."

"I was hoping you'd think that best." Anna was already rising to go. She wavered long enough to ask, "But . . . the Doyles?"

"Are they here? Then I'll speak to them while you're gone fetching Two Hawks and . . . or is it to be Jonathan? What am I to call him— them?"

Something near a smile brightened Anna's face. "I guess you can ask them when you meet them."

"I will," Lydia said, with a nervous twisting in her belly. What would Reginald have to say to her when he returned to find the woman whose child he stole—and that child's brother—sitting at his kitchen table? "You do trust this woman, Good Voice? You trust her, about Reginald?"

"As much as I trust Two Hawks," Anna said. "And you."

Lydia stood in the doorway and watched Anna head for the track toward the creek, hope speeding her like wings. "May I prove worthy of it," she whispered, then turned her gaze to the cottage across the yard, in time to see a face behind the window glass hastily withdrawn.

*A*nna raced across the stretch of ground between the farthest cornfield and the creek. The terrible consequences of confronting Papa with the truth had paralyzed her with doubt, but no more. Lydia's arrival had been the shove to set her moving again. Though the day was cooling, sweat trickled from her temples, stinging her eyes. She couldn't run like this the whole way, ribs aching beneath suffocating stays, but she'd run as far as she could.

She reached the footlog, which she'd crossed countless times. Only once before had she done so running—the day she met Two Hawks. Then she'd been light and small. She was taller now, and not thinking about where she put her feet. She didn't feel the old log give until it crumbled under her. She staggered into flowing water, shallow but bedded with stones that caught her foot while the rest of her sprawled onto the bank.

Pain twisted through her ankle as she fell.

Though she knew the Doyles were within, Lydia's knocking had fallen on deaf ears. Neither opened the door to her. There was nothing for it but to stable her horse and retreat to the house to await Anna's return with William's Oneida kin. The minutes ticked by, marked by the mantel clock in the sitting room, the moving slant of sun on the floorboards, and her pacing from window to window.

It was Reginald who arrived first. The sun was beginning to set when she heard his horse coming down the lane, a tired, lagging pace. She stepped into the yard to meet him, thoughts a swirl of dread and hope and half-formed explanations. He straightened in the saddle upon seeing her, and despite everything that should have quelled it, her heart sang out with longing that this should be a thing between them each day, for all their days, her standing in the yard to welcome him home. Then he rode near enough for her to see his haggard features, burnished by the sun's westering light. He showed no surprise at finding her there. Nor did he look pleased.

"Where is Anna?" His voice, roughened when last she heard it, grated now like sand scrubbed over floorboards.

"She's gone across the creek, to fetch William's mother and brother."

For a second he stared at her, mouth open, hooded eyes blank. Then he wrenched a leg over the horse and, with an audible pop of his bad hip, dismounted. In seconds he had her by the arm. "How long since?" When she hesitated, he gave her a shake. "Lydia—how long?"

"A bit too long actually." Seeing the alarm her words kindled, she hurried to douse it. "She's likely having to convince them to come. She trusts them, but—"

"I trusted you—foolish woman! What if *he* is there?"

Stung by the words, Lydia fought to make sense of that last. "You mean their father? But he isn't. Not yet."

She doubted whether Reginald even heard her. "They'll take her. When they learn William is gone, they'll take my Anna instead—or worse!"

Shoving her away, he tore off down the track between the fields, heading for the creek. Without the horse. Without rifle or pistol. The limp in his gait was enough to break her heart.

"Anna means to bring them here!" Lydia shouted, but he didn't so much as slow his hitching stride. Sending up a wordless prayer, she ran after him.

Anna felt a fool—so careless—wasting precious time hobbling through the beeches, then across the clearing, pain shooting through her ankle with each step. She was spared the hill. Only seconds passed after she called his name before Two Hawks appeared among the rocks above. He and his mother descended the steep path, Good Voice looking beyond her and then back with expectant eyes. In the slanting light of evening, they were the exact shape and hue of William's.

She stood with her twisted ankle favored. Two Hawks took her by the arm. "You are hurt?"

She slipped her arm around his waist. "I fell crossing the creek. It's only—" She'd meant to say *a bit sore,* but a test of her weight on the foot made her gasp.

Good Voice was standing a little apart, watching them, braced and still. Anna saw she was a handsome woman, with a face both strong of bone and delicate of feature, blown by strands of blond hair caught in a breeze coming off the river. "My son has not come with you," she said, hiding admirably what must be crushing disappointment.

"He returned home, just before dawn. I tried to stop him leaving again."

She felt Two Hawks stiffen. "He has gone? Where?"

"To Canada, probably to join the British army." Into their stunned silence, she added, "Papa means to go after him. Lydia told me so. She's at the house."

"That is the woman who teaches her healing," Two Hawks told his mother.

"We think it best you come to the house with me, meet Papa when he returns, talk to him." She appealed to them both. "Will you come?"

It didn't take long for them to agree—though it seemed an eternity while their gazes held, searching, speaking. "What else is there to do," Two Hawks said, "but return to Kanowalohale?"

Good Voice nodded, sorrow and wariness in her eyes. Anna ached for words to reassure her, knowing that even with Lydia on their side, Papa might turn William's kin away, refuse to see them. Or worse, treat them with hostility. She prayed his heart would soften as they started across the clearing, Two Hawks supporting her as she limped.

It soon grew clear they had a more immediate problem. At the rate she was moving, it would be nightfall before they reached the house. Two Hawks swept her into his arms, grunting with the effort, and carried her forward into the rays of sun streaming threads through the tops of the trees. Good Voice came behind, looking at them as if unsure what to make of her, cradled in her son's arms. The warmth of him radiated through his shirt. Though Anna's impulse was to turn her face into his neck, draw from him the strength she'd need to face Papa, shyness in front of Good Voice prevented her.

"It's too far to carry me," she began in protest, when across the clearing a figure emerged from the beech wood and staggered into the open.

Papa.

Good Voice made a noise like an indrawn hiss. Two Hawks stopped, arms tightening around Anna until she felt his heart beating hard and fast.

Papa saw them and halted. "Anna!" Panic strained his voice as he lunged forward again. "Let her go!"

"No . . . Papa!" Anna cried in a burst of understanding. "He thinks you're taking me away. Put me down!" Two Hawks set her gingerly on her feet. She clutched his arm, watching Papa approach, his limp pronounced. He carried no weapon that she could see.

"Let me talk to him." She took an awkward step forward, wincing.

Good Voice stopped her with a touch and a flash of resolute eyes. "I will go and meet him. As it should be."

Two Hawks took Anna's arm and pulled her to his side. In that instant, Good Voice was striding forward to meet Papa. "Pray, Bear's Heart. Pray to God with me."

She heard him praying, but her own mind was frozen, wordless in its appeal.

Papa had halted in the center of the clearing, seeing Good Voice marching toward him. She moved with the stride of a younger woman, her long braid shining in the light that arced a golden path from her feet to his. Papa's gaze jerked past Good Voice, flying to her and Two Hawks, then back it snapped to the woman bearing down on him. When she was but a few yards off, his face constricted. He sank to his knees as though felled by an arrow, launched from an unseen bow.

Good Voice halted briefly, then proceeded on. So focused were they on each other, Papa and Good Voice, that neither looked away when Lydia emerged from the beeches.

She wasn't the only arrival. Across the clearing to the west a shout arose. A man's shout, speaking words in a language Anna knew for Oneida. A tall, broad-chested figure strode from the wood's edge, moving with purpose. Though it was years since she'd seen him, Anna knew him at once. Stone Thrower, bronzed face shining in the fading sunlight, black hair grown long and full, tied with feathers, flowing behind him. He strode across the clearing, war hatchet gripped, shouting at Good Voice and Papa.

Beside her Two Hawks groaned out a word she knew meant *Father.* "He is fulfilling his dream. He must not."

The words, inexplicable to Anna, were uttered in a moan of distress. What dream did he mean? She clamped his arm in desperation. "Go. Help. Please, go!"

The support of his arm slid away, leaving her to find her own balance. Two Hawks was loping, stride quickening until he ran full out. But he wouldn't make it in time.

Papa saw Stone Thrower bearing down on him and lurched to his feet, twisting to favor his lame hip. The pain must have been great, for he staggered back to a knee, hands to the ground to keep from sprawling.

Good Voice lunged to get between Stone Thrower and Papa. Stone Thrower didn't look at her but must have uttered some command for she hesitated, then let her husband pass. Fear pulled at Anna's stomach, cleaving it to her spine, as Stone Thrower loomed over Papa. Helpless on the ground, Papa looked up into his face. If either man spoke, Anna was too far away to hear their words.

Good Voice must have heard her son's pounding footsteps. She turned and raised her hands, palms flat in a command to halt. As if he'd run into a wall, Two Hawks stopped short.

An icy cold shot through Anna's veins. Were they going to let Papa die? Had she misunderstood all this time? Had this been what they truly wanted? *Revenge.*

Papa bowed his head, hands going slack on his knees in submission. He was going to let it happen. He was going to let himself be killed.

"Papa, no. God, no." She started forward, though it was too far—impossibly far. As she hobbled toward them, Stone Thrower raised the gleaming hatchet. Bending, he placed a hand on Papa's head.

Swift movement at the corner of her eye drew Anna's glance aside. Over toward the beeches, Lydia was running, not toward the center of the clearing but along its edge. Anna saw the blur of her petticoat but forced her gaze back to Papa—as a rifle roared to life. The crack of it fell like thunder from the clear sky. Anna jarred to a halt and watched, uncomprehending, as Stone Thrower dropped to his knees.

Good Voice and Two Hawks broke apart, both crying out. Good Voice rushed forward. Two Hawks sprinted toward the cloud of powder smoke drifting at the edge of the clearing near where she'd last seen Lydia. Still, it took a moment for Anna to comprehend that it was Stone Thrower who'd been shot. Rowan Doyle had shot him. He and Lydia were at the edge of the wood, grappling over a rifle. Two Hawks reached them, plucked the gun from both their hands, then ran with it back toward his father, who was on his knees with Good Voice leaning over him, gripping his shoulder. A dark patch was spreading down one deerskin legging.

Stone Thrower put out a hand, clutched at Good Voice, then firmly pushed her away. She stood erect, looking down into her husband's face, then stepped back.

Hardly aware of her own pain now, Anna limped forward, trying to reach them. Why was Good Voice not moving? Why did she raise her arm to hold off Two Hawks, who staggered to a halt with the rifle that had wounded his father? They stood there looking down at Stone Thrower and Papa, both men on their knees, facing each other. Stone Thrower's mouth clenched tight as he looked into Papa's face. His fingers still gripped the hatchet's long handle, though when he raised it again, it shook in his grip.

"Papa!" Anna cried as the blade came down—into the seeded grasses beside Papa, driven deep into the earth. Two Hawks hurried back to her, but she was already near enough to hear what followed

"*Atahuhsiyost*. Listen to my words, Redcoat." Stone Thrower spoke in the deep voice she remembered, grated now with pain. "This hatchet you see . . . I bury it in the ground between us. I cover it with dirt. With it I cover every bad thing that has long been between us. I bury it out of sight, out of my heart, that it might cause no more grief to me . . . and to my family."

He paused for breath, his gaze never leaving Papa's face that was so wretched with fear and grief. Guilt, remorse, and pride. It seemed to Anna that he hadn't the strength to hide a single thought or feeling. Not from this man. Not from Stone Thrower. She gripped Two Hawks's hand, straining to catch every word as his father continued.

"Since before the time of the grandfathers, it has been the way of my people to take a captive from an enemy to replace our dead . . . to ease the grief of our women who have lost brothers and sons. This is a thing I have thought long on as the years have gone around . . . as I have thought of you . . . and of my son you took and called your son."

The last of the sunlight was fading now, pulling westward as dusk crept in. Anna heard footsteps coming with the shadows and the winking of fireflies. Lydia joined them, her face pinched with fear, but a fear fast giving way to puzzlement. There was no sign now of Mr. Doyle. Two Hawks held the man's rifle. He met Lydia's gaze as she came to stand beside them, in his eyes a question. She shook her head, as if to say the Irishman would be no further threat.

"Your father?" she asked, taking a step toward Stone Thrower. "He's hurt."

Good Voice stopped her. "Let him be. Let this happen. He will not want you to interfere."

Anna looked back at the big Oneida on his knees in front of Papa, bleeding into the grass, ignoring his wound. From the sash at his waist he drew something long and white. Three strings of beads. *Wampum.* To Anna they seemed to glow with a light of their own in the settling dusk.

"What is this? What is he doing?"

Good Voice uttered a small cry at the sight—one of gladness, Anna thought. She stood straight and still, fists clenched at her sides, and Anna knew despite her words that it was taking all her self-possession not to rush to her husband's side. On her face was a look of profound joy.

The same look was coming over Two Hawks. "It is the condolence ceremony," he said, barely above a whisper. "Or something near to it. My father is offering your father condolence."

"For his son," Good Voice said. "His son that I took away dead from the fort."

Stunned, Anna turned to Lydia. She was crying, tears falling unashamedly, and though her face was white with strain, there was the beginnings of hope in her eyes, as Stone Thrower held up the three strings of beads.

"The woman who gave birth to the male child you took . . . and that child's father speaking now . . . they have mourned his loss. For many long seasons they were not consoled, knowing he lived far from their eyes that wished to see him, their hands that longed to touch him, their hearts that loved him." Stone Thrower's mouth trembled. He firmed his lips, bloodless now and thinned. "But Creator was watching. In His time He gathered their broken hearts to Himself. He has been their consolation, though the path has often been a difficult one to see and follow. But you also lost a son, and no one mourned with you, for the thing you did was done in secret. So I give you these strings . . ."

Papa gaped at the beads held out to him. Then, like a man in a dream, raised his hands to accept them.

"With them," Stone Thrower said, laying the beads across Papa's upturned palms, "I wipe the tears from your eyes so you may see clear. With them . . . I open your ears so you may hear what we say to you. With them . . . I clear your throat so you may speak to us what is in your heart." He raised his empty hand to Papa's shoulder. "Now it must be that He-Is-Taken, called by you *William,* is returned from over the water, or why would his mother come here as she has never done all these long years of our waiting? So I ask you, Aubrey—" Stone Thrower's voice faltered. He was leaning close to Papa, struggling not to fall over. Still Anna heard his final words, replete with a lifetime of anguish and hope. William's lifetime.

"Where is . . . my son?"

Then like a great tree toppling, Stone Thrower slid sideways. Papa caught him and laid him in the grass beside the buried hatchet.

39

For all her imaginings of how a meeting between Papa and William's Oneida kin might unfold, for good or ill, Anna hadn't expected this.

She stood back from Papa's bed, holding a candle, though Lydia no longer needed light beyond the hearth and the candles on the clothespress, to see to her work. She'd cleaned and dressed Stone Thrower's wound. The rifle ball had passed through the muscle of his thigh. Probably it had cracked the bone on its way. Miraculously, it had severed no major arteries. Stone Thrower was weak from blood loss, but if wound and bone healed cleanly . . . The next few days would tell.

Hovering over him now, Lydia checked the linen strips holding the dressing in place across his thigh. Good Voice sat in a chair by his head, while he gazed at her with eyes brimming alternately with wonder, relief, anguish. They'd been speaking to each other in Oneida, about William, and something about a dream coming true. Anna caught only the gist of that. The part about William was all too plain, as was the grief they shared. They'd lost their firstborn again.

Lydia poured a cup of water, handing it to Good Voice. "He needs to drink as much as possible. I'll see about a broth as soon as I can."

"I'll see to that, Lydia." With a sudden longing for Two Hawks, Anna set the candle on a trunk beside the door and went out of the room.

She found him alone in the kitchen, standing with arms crossed, looking rather lost. He turned sharply when she entered, dark eyes questioning in the light of the hearth fire he must have tended while she helped tend his father.

"He's going to be all right, I think." She crossed to him and touched his arm. "Where is Papa?" He'd left after seeing Stone Thrower into Lydia's care, pausing long enough to pull Anna fiercely into his embrace, before bolting from the room.

"He went out that way." Two Hawks nodded at the door to the yard between the house and cottage. "He barely looked at me."

She gave his arm a squeeze. "Go and see your father. I'm sure he'll want to see you."

"Has my mother told him William is gone?"

"Yes. Just before I came out."

He hesitated, then put his hand behind her head, pulling her to him gently. "I did wrong by my father, thinking he would give way to vengeance. I did wrong by Creator, not trusting Him with the power to change my father. Among my people it is thought that dreams—night dreams—have power. If a man has a dream he cannot get out of his mind, then it is good for him to make it come to pass."

She leaned back, looking up at him. "Any dream? Even strange ones?"

Two Hawks breathed a laugh. "Sometimes strange things are done. But my father . . . He dreamed of hunting your father and taking his revenge." His smile wavered even as she felt her own vanish. She let her arms fall from him, but he took up her hand. "This dream troubled him often over the years. He was driven to see it come to pass—even after he came to know Heavenly Father's path. It is what we thought was happening back in the clearing, my mother and I. At first."

Anna caught her breath, then frowned. "I thought I heard Stone Thrower say, 'The dream was a true one.' I must have misheard."

Two Hawks's eyes were radiant. "You did not mishear. In the dream he never killed your father. It always ended with him standing over Aubrey with a hatchet raised, or a club. All this time he thought it meant he was to take his vengeance and kill. Instead he buried the hatchet."

"He forgave Papa. *That's* what he's been dreaming all these years?" Anna felt her chest expand with the wonder of it.

"In giving the white beads, my father was trying to set *your* father free, but it was his own heart that was freed." Tears had welled in Two Hawks's eyes. They coursed over the blades of his cheekbones as he added in a voice that swelled with the same wonder she was feeling, "And we were there, all of us, to see it."

"I'm so glad." Anna reached to wipe away his tears.

Two Hawks studied her with a look of such tenderness that she felt the force of it course through her.

"You are my candle flame," he said. "Shine for me now—pray for me to have good words for my father, healing words, for I have never been so proud to be his son as I am this night."

He'd made it out of the house before the retching overtook him. Down again on his knees, Reginald vomited at the edge of the cornfield. He missed the approach of quiet footsteps and jerked in violent surprise at the touch of a hand on his shoulder. A woman's touch.

"Lydia," he croaked, throat raw from the ravages of the past hours. "For pity's sake, leave me—"

"It is me. Good Voice of the Turtle Clan. I have words to say to you, if you will hear them."

Her voice was a shredding to his soul. More words? He'd had words enough. Forgiveness? A buried hatchet? It was his nightmare, turned on its head.

No. The true nightmare stood before him, wearing William's face.

Too dark to see it now. He didn't need to. Sight of her walking toward him with the day's last light upon on her, shining with the aspect of an avenging angel, was blazoned upon his mind as though she stood now under the noonday sun. What could she want from him? He hadn't even her son to return to her. Reginald wiped his face and pushed through agony to his feet, swaying in the dark.

"I have words to say," she repeated when he stood. "Words of the son you left with me, the day you took mine."

Reginald's chest seized with a pain so sharp he feared it was the end of him—wished it *was* the end. But still his legs stood him up, there at the edge of the cornfield, his constricted heart went on beating. And the words of William's mother kept coming.

"He has a grave, that son. I dug it for him, good and deep. I put him in it with my tears. With my hands I covered him."

He had no right to tears, not before this woman, but was helpless to stop them. He put his hands over his face. "Why do you this?"

"Good Voice? Papa? Are you all right?"

Another quiet shadow had joined them. Anna, his dear girl, still holding out to him her heart, in spite of everything.

They would kill him with their mercy.

He staggered as he started for the cottage, recalling he must speak to Rowan before he fell over unconscious. But he didn't move fast enough to keep from hearing his precious Anna speaking wistfully the name of William's twin.

"It is soon to speak of it," Good Voice told her. "Too soon for him."

Anna replied, but Reginald closed his ears to it. *Two Hawks.* It was agony even to look at that young man, so like William, so unlike. His mind flashed back to the two of them supporting the big wounded Indian between them, their straining arms touching in the falling twilight, those features hovering near, disconcertingly familiar, unnervingly strange. No wonder Anna looked as she had at William's homecoming. As if she'd seen a ghost.

Reginald shook off the vision and fixed his gaze on the candlelight falling through the cottage window. He refused to think beyond the fact that he must explain to Rowan and Maura that these Indians were there to stay. For now.

Good Voice had rejoined her son at her husband's bedside. Though she wanted to give the family their privacy, Lydia didn't leave the room until she was certain Stone Thrower's dressing would hold and the bleeding had nearly ceased. The threesome hardly seemed to notice her, so absorbed were they in each other. Clearly a healing of another sort was happening between them. Filling the room was a weighty, peaceful presence Lydia recognized from long acquaintance.

Finally satisfied her patient wouldn't bleed out onto the bed, Lydia left them, slipping from the room with a basin to empty. In the shadowed passage outside, a solitary figure stood. Faint light from the other end of the house barely reached him.

Lydia clutched the basin, startled but not surprised. "Reginald?"

His voice came up from a place deep within, dry as an empty well. "I spoke to Rowan. He meant only to protect me, even knowing . . . what I've done."

Lydia had been furious with the Irishman, but no longer. She understood Rowan Doyle had acted out of loyalty and ignorance. "I tried to let them know what was happening. They wouldn't open the door to me. I'm so very—"

Reginald held up a hand. "There is no need for you to apologize, Lydia, but there is for me. For the terrible words I said to you. I called you foolish, knowing full well that one thing you have never been is a foolish woman."

A host of words staggered across her tired brain. Just as many emotions pressed against her breastbone. The man must feel his list of sins growing by the hour.

"You were terrified for Anna. I've already forgotten it." She hadn't. Not quite. But she would. And still it took everything she had by way of self-control not to touch him now. Compassion rushed in, overwhelming any thought for her own heartache and hope. "It will be weeks before Stone Thrower can be moved. Rowan and Maura . . . Can they accept that?"

"I told them as much. Whether they stay or go is for them to decide." Reginald's glance strayed to the door of his room. "Who is with him?"

"His family. But he asked for you. Will you go in to him?"

Even in the half dark she could sense him stiffen, but he said, "I've taken William's lifetime from the man. He may claim of me whatever he wishes."

Resolve weakening, she freed a hand from the basin and touched his arm. "Don't wait too long. He would take no laudanum to help him sleep, not until he says whatever more he means to say to you. But once he's said it . . . please, Reginald, make him take it and then you get some sleep as well. Somewhere. Anna and I will look after everyone."

In danger now of either bursting into tears or flinging herself into his arms, she turned and hurried down the passage toward the kitchen.

Her name on his lips stopped her.

"Lydia," he said, and there was longing in it, as she'd never heard before. "Lydia . . . you could do so much better than me."

There was a chair. She put the basin on it, then went back down the passage to him. She took his drawn, unshaven face between her hands and kissed him full on the mouth. It made him groan.

His arms came around her and he kissed her back, crushing her to him, as though she were all that was keeping him from drowning. The taste of him was salty with tears. Her own and his mingled. When at last he let her go, breathless with half a lifetime of wanting, she said, "I honestly cannot imagine how."

He made a sound that might have been a sob or a laugh, and he kissed her brow.

She touched his shadowed face. "Sleep, Reginald. Soon."

Remembering the needs of her patient, she found the strength to pull away and leave him, forgetting the basin, so dazed was she with the joy of such tenuous promise.

40

*A*nna set bread on the kitchen table with a sliced round of cheese, then limped to the hearth where a broth simmered and returned with the kettle steaming for tea. Her movements seemed a blur. How long Lydia stood watching her, drenched in glorious, bruise-tender hope, she didn't know, before Good Voice and Two Hawks sidled past, casting her curious glances. She shook herself into action.

"Anna, sit down and rest that ankle. Good Voice, Two Hawks, please sit and eat, and . . . be welcome."

Two Hawks ate what was set before him, his gaze rarely straying from Anna, but Good Voice didn't touch the food. She stroked the table, tracing its scars with a fingertip—perhaps imagining William touching them, making them with his own small fingers? Lydia was reaching to clasp her hand when the door latch's lifting caused every head to turn.

Maura Doyle pushed open the door to the yard and came within. She surveyed them all, brows raised, then moved aside. Lydia glimpsed a figure behind her. An older man, but not Rowan.

Sounding more than a little dazed, Maura said, "I found him in the yard on my way over. He's claimin' to know these others here."

Lydia's gaze fixed on the man who came forward into the hearth light, an Indian with a blunt-featured face, wrinkled and faintly pitted. His gaze took them in, as if he searched for a particular face among them. In English he said, "Where is Stone Thrower?"

His voice even more than his face snapped Lydia's memory back across the years, to a day in her father's apothecary when the Mohawk healer, Hanging Kettle, had visited with an Oneida warrior. "Clear Day?"

The man looked at her, eyes narrowed. "Black-Hair-Girl?"

"This is she?" Good Voice asked, standing from her place at the table. "This is McClaren's daughter, who spoke to you of Aubrey?"

"I—he—McClaren was my father's name," Lydia stammered. "I met Clear Day in his shop."

"Daniel Clear Day he is called now," Two Hawks said in a voice that, despite its dissimilar cadence, rang with a tone like William's. "Uncle, my father is in this house. Come. Sit at this table. We will tell you about it."

Anna turned to look at Two Hawks, standing in the doorway of William's room. It was the only spare bed in the house. She'd changed the bedding and opened the windows to a cooling breeze. "Will it be hard for Good Voice, being so close to William's things?"

Not that many were on display. William had been back in the room so brief a time. What possessions he hadn't taken with him were still put away in trunks. Yet standing in his room, all Anna could think about was their last exchange, their bitter parting. She made for the door. "I sleep right across the passage there. Not far."

Two Hawks made way for her but said, "Anywhere not beside me is far."

The words stole her breath and sent the blood surging warm into her face. His eyes were dark in the glow of the candle she'd brought upstairs. These moments alone were fleeting. She wanted to hurl caution and conscience aside and spend them in his arms. But William had squeezed between them. Was he still in Schenectady? On his way north with Sam? Did he regret not staying to see his family? Did he regret anything?

"May I see where you sleep?" Two Hawks asked.

Though she feared the specter of William would linger even stronger there, she took up the candle and they crossed the passage to her room. Two Hawks halted in the doorway. Anna strode to the window. All was darkness beyond the reflecting glass. She set the candle on her desk and turned.

Two Hawks took in the tiny space, desk, bed, press, trunk, and little else. In his long linen shirt, leggings, and moccasins, with his quilled sheath knife hanging at his chest and his black hair falling past his shoulders, he seemed to her a beautiful, exotic bird that had strayed into her familiar surroundings. Until she looked at his face, then it seemed the most natural thing in the world he should be standing in the doorway of her room.

"William asked me to go with him to Canada." The words were out before she knew she meant to speak them. Two Hawks didn't move from the doorway or take his gaze from her. The silence gnawed at her composure before he spoke.

"Did you want to go?"

She let out the breath she'd been holding. "No."

"Iyo," he said, and there was no mistaking his relief as he smiled in invitation. "I will not cross this threshold, but will you come here to me?"

She went to him, trying not to limp. He raised a hand and stroked his fingers down the back of her head. She wore no cap, had lost it somewhere between the woods and home. His fingers brushed her neck, making her shiver with pleasure.

"I love you, my Bear's Heart."

She was drowning in his eyes. They pulled her to him, making her forget how to speak. Or breathe. At last she managed both. "And I love you."

His hand found hers, raised it to his lips. She closed her eyes as he kissed her fingers, then her open palm. His lips were gentle but far from tentative. A promise that made her heart beat with desire.

"Then I am going to ask your father for you, to let me have you as wife. If that is what you also want?"

"I do." Anna knew an instant of utter happiness, before a thousand tiny arrows tipped in alarm pierced it through. "But Two Hawks, I don't think now is—"

"Hush." Deep in his throat he was laughing softly. "It is much soon. My eyes are not so blind with wanting you that I cannot see that." He pressed her hand, still tingling from his kiss, to his chest. "But I am going to court you, however it is done. Will you tell me how an Oneida man courts a white woman?"

She had no idea. "We may have to devise it as we go."

"We will so. In a good way, with honor and respect."

Anna thought of Papa walking away into the darkness. "He'll need time, Papa."

Two Hawks gave her hand a squeeze. "You have beaten a straight path to my heart. I will clear such a path to the heart of your father. With Creator's help."

"And with mine," Anna said, wrapping her arms around him. "I'm done with running away."

Two Hawks kissed the top of her head, then took her gently by the arms and put a space between them. "My Bear's Heart, we must not touch like this again under Aubrey's roof. Not without his blessing."

A sound like a whimper formed in her throat. She bit her lip, embarrassed to have been so transparent in her disappointment. But he was smiling. "It will not be easy. But it is right."

As if to put himself at a safe distance from her, he stepped backward into the passage. "You have made a good place for us. Shall we bring my mother up so she can rest?"

The night was warm. Though the fire in the hearth had died, Reginald added no wood. He'd barely glanced at the silent Indian lying still in the bed when he entered the shadowed room. Now he kept his gaze on the taper he dipped to an ember in the ashes, quelling the tremble of his hands. Not even the aftermath of Fort William Henry's fall could touch the ravaging the past hours had wrought upon him, body and soul.

He set the taper in the remains of the one that had guttered before it, carried it to the press, then eased his aching frame into the bedside chair. From his waistband where he'd tucked them, he removed the three strands of wampum and laid them across the rumpled tick. Then he looked at the man in his bed.

Stone Thrower had been watching him the while, dark eyes glittering with pain. On the press by the candle awaited the laudanum Lydia meant him to consume. But first—according to Lydia—he wanted to talk.

Reginald waited for him to do so.

"That one who shot me . . ." came the voice from his pillow. "What is he called?"

"Rowan Doyle. He'll be offering you no further harm."

"That is good to know." The man kept an astonishing control over his face. It was hard to tell in the candlelight whether the glint in his eyes had anything of humor in it, but Reginald thought so. The Indian was intent on shattering the perception of him that had sustained two decades of nightmares. Perversely, Reginald was finding it hard to keep from scrambling after the pieces. It was easier to hate. To fear.

He watched warily as Stone Thrower's hand moved from his side, but it was only to touch the white beads. "These you put between us . . . I do not need to see them to remember the words that went with them. They were from my heart."

With them I wipe the tears from your eyes so you may see clear.

Reginald's tongue lay in his mouth, useless as a shattered hull.

"If I could turn back the years," he finally rasped out. "I'd walk past what was yours and never touch them. I'd leave them whole to find their way back to you."

Stone Thrower's head moved on the pillow, nodding. "There was a time I also wished to turn back the seasons, to go back before I had done the wrongs I was ashamed of and choose instead not to do them. But that is not a thing we get to do."

"What *would* you have me do?" The question tore from him, spewing from his lips like bile, bitter, burning. He waited, longing for the Indian to pronounce some sort of sentence, penance, something.

Stone Thrower said, "Years ago . . . my people took a child from the whites and made her *Onyota'a:ka*. That child grew . . . became my wife. From us a child was taken and made white. It is a thing to make one think."

Reginald put his head into his hands. He didn't want to think. "I would give him back to you if I had him to give."

He heard the beads click, looked to see Stone Thrower's fingers wrapped around their ends. "My sons are men now. They must choose to give or take themselves."

Reginald saw at last the grief and disappointment—long years of it—the man restrained. The broken pieces inside Reginald shifted toward it, slicing pain through him in all directions. "'Tis not from you that William is running, but from me."

It was hard to bear that gaze searching his, knowing it read more than he wanted the man to see.

"Maybe it is from us both. You will go after him?"

Reginald blinked, eyelids weighted with fatigue. "I'll not face my son in a red coat, across the barrel of a musket."

The words thrust between them like a sword. *My son.* Had the Indian lunged up from the bed and set his hands to Reginald's throat, it would have been the least he deserved, and no surprise. What did surprise was the look that rose into the dark eyes. *Relief.* As though the acknowledgment of his paternal bond with William was a thing the Indian had long wondered about.

"Is that what you ask of me? To go after him? I tell you I will do it. I will find him—or die trying." Maybe, if he managed it, God would look on him with as much mercy as this man confessed to look.

"No. You will not."

In the wake of those words, emotions rose, ugly things surfacing through the morass of exhaustion. Affront. Jealousy. Anger. Humiliation. One by one they clotted in Reginald's throat. One by one he swallowed them down.

Stone Thrower watched it all with patient eyes. "You do not understand. You will not find him on your own, but *together* we may do it."

The hand Reginald long believed would end his life lifted from the beads and stretched toward him, brown and battle-hardened. He stared at it, prepared to refuse it. This calamity was of his making. He'd torn William from the life he should have lived, uprooted him so many times, little wonder the winds of war had blown him north to the British like a drifted branch. He alone should bear the burden of setting right his wrongs.

And yet . . . there went his hand rising from his knee, as if another will lifted it. And there went his voice—what little remained—uttering words he'd never imagined he would speak, as across the white beads he clasped Stone Thrower's hand.

"Together then," he said.

AUTHOR'S NOTES AND ACKNOWLEDGMENTS

Some years ago, while deep in research for a novel called *Burning Sky,* I read numerous accounts of the Haudenosaunee (the Six Nations of the Iroquois Confederacy) and their experiences during the Revolutionary War. Those six nations are, east to west as they dwelled across what is now New York State, the Mohawks, Oneidas, Tuscaroras, Onondagas, Cayugas, and Senecas. My focus during that early research was on the Mohawks. But another nation, the Oneidas, kept snagging my attention as I read book after book and followed countless research trails online.

Of all those nations long united under their Great Law of Peace, the Oneidas went against the majority of the Haudenosaunee and sided with the Americans during the Revolutionary War. Though some individuals managed to remain neutral, the rest, by and large, sided with the British. This brought about a breaking of a confederacy that had existed for centuries, amounting to a tragic mirroring of what was happening among the European colonies—a civil war. As I came to understand the tremendous pressure the Oneidas found themselves under during this time, the heavy price they paid for following their convictions, and the contributions they made to the founding of an American nation, I couldn't resist attempting to tell their story, at least in part. That story outgrew the bounds of a single book, and has become the Pathfinders series, of which *The Wood's Edge* is the first.

During the 1760s–70s, more than one Presbyterian missionary was living, teaching, and preaching among the various Oneida towns and settlements. For narrative simplicity I chose to focus on Reverend Samuel Kirkland. His adventures among the Senecas before he settled with the

Oneidas fit well with the story I wished to tell, as did his influence among the Oneida people, not only in sharing the gospel, but for his friendship with key warriors and sachems who in turn influenced their people's choices during the Revolutionary War. Kirkland's wife, Jerusha, and his assistant teacher, David Fowler, are both historical figures; the details of their lives presented in this novel are based on research, though Jerusha's appearance is drawn from my imagination.

Speaking of research, for the many threads of history that form the weft of *The Wood's Edge*, I'm indebted to the following historians for their scholarship and writing, and offer this short list of titles to readers desiring to learn more about the Oneidas and other historical aspects of this novel:

Forgotten Allies: The Oneida Indians and the American Revolution by Joseph T. Glatthaar and James Kirby Martin
The Oneida Indian Experience: Two Perspectives by Jack Campisi, Laurence M. Hauptman, editors
The People of the Standing Stone: The Oneida Nation from the Revolution through the Era of Removal by Karim M. Tiro
The Iroquois in the American Revolution by Barbara Graymont
Life of Samuel Kirkland, Missionary to the Indians by Samuel Kirkland Lothrop
Bloody Mohawk: The French and Indian War & American Revolution on New York's Frontier by Richard Berleth
The Siege of Fort William Henry: A Year on the Northeastern Frontier by Ben Hughes
Fort William Henry 1755–57 by Ian Castle

The Haudenosaunee have a culture rich in tradition and ceremony. Among these traditions is The Wood's Edge, a ceremony used for greeting strangers who approached a town or village. Pausing at the edge of the surrounding forest, the visitors would wait until a delegation came forth to meet them. If found friendly, the strangers would be invited into the village as honored guests. As I've come to see it, the wood's edge was a world between, a realm that existed as much in the minds and hearts of human beings as a clearing bounded by the spreading boughs of mighty oaks and chestnuts. At the wood's edge strangers found welcome, minds were expanded, hearts deepened by the extension of friendship and hospitality.

The process of a novel's creation has its parallels to the wood's edge. As always, many minds and hearts contributed to its creation and refining. My thanks to my editors, Shannon Marchese, Nicci Jordan Hubert, and Laura Wright, for their invaluable input. I'm so glad we're a team. It's an honor to work with you. And to Kristopher Orr, much joy and appreciation for the beautiful cover art that speaks deeply to one of this story's central themes.

I hope readers of my debut novel *Burning Sky* enjoyed getting a peek into the back story of Joseph Tames-His-Horse, one of the main characters from that book, as well as a larger look at a minor *Burning Sky* character, Daniel Clear Day. You'll see more of these characters and other familiar faces in *A Flight of Arrows,* the second book in the Pathfinders series, releasing from WaterBrook Press in 2016.

Until then, dear readers, you'll find me online at loribenton.blogspot .com or on Facebook at www.facebook.com/AuthorLoriBenton. I look forward to hearing from you!

Blessings and happy reading,

Lori

READERS GUIDE

1. Reginald Aubrey made a choice that would carry lifelong repercussions for everyone closely connected to him. Could you sympathize with him in this choice? Have you ever made a choice in the heat of the moment, big or small, only to look back later and realize it altered the course of your life?

2. What was your perception of Reginald in the early chapters of the story? Did that perception change throughout the novel? For better or worse? Why?

3. Lydia van Bergen is a woman of purpose. Although initially thwarted in many of her deepest desires (love, motherhood, vocation), how did she find fulfillment in these areas? Have you ever had a dream fulfilled in unexpected ways?

4. Good Voice experiences one of the greatest heartbreaks a mother can know, the abduction and loss of her child. Yet she comes to know peace as she seeks healing and wholeness for her broken family. How was this possible? What do you think was her greatest test?

5. Stone Thrower is a man plagued by dreams, to which he gives power—a power that long torments and imprisons him—according to the traditions of his culture. Have you ever allowed a harmful force or influence to have power over you? Was it something of which society or culture approved? What enabled you to break free?

6. Lydia chooses to keep secret Reginald's confession and her deductions about William. Would you have made the same choice? Why or why not?

7. Two Hawks states, "If knowing God in my heart means losing a little of what it means to be Oneida—I do not think it means losing

THE WOOD'S EDGE 385

everything, as the sachems fear—I think it is only what must be remade in every man who comes to Creator through His Son, Jesus. White, black, red, and any other sort of man. If I have lost anything, what I have gained is a trade in my favor." He is in agreement with Paul who states in Philippians 3:8, "I count all things but loss for the excellency of the knowledge of Christ Jesus my Lord." Have you given up something of significance, or something that defined who you were, because you sensed a higher calling? How did that affect your relationship with friends and family?

8. Anna is a woman caught between the people she loves, her sympathies and heart torn two ways. How might this story have unfolded had she told Reginald, or Lydia, much sooner about the friend she was meeting at the wood's edge?

9. Heledd Aubrey is a tragic figure, traumatized by violence and loss, but was she sympathetic? Why or why not? Lydia believes Heledd never suspected William wasn't her natural son. If you were in Heledd's place, would you have wanted to know the truth?

10. Of all the characters, William has had the least amount of time to come to terms with the truth of his identity and Reginald's deceit. Was his choice to run away from such devastating revelations one you might have made? Why or why not?

11. The theme of finding God's path through life is explored from many points of view in this story. Which character's path did you find the most compelling or relatable? What caused you to connect? Which characters are still seeking that path, and what might be hindering them?

12. Forgiveness isn't always a feeling, but it is always a choice. Good Voice, Stone Thrower, and Two Hawks have chosen to forgive Reginald for stealing their son and brother. What were some of the challenges they overcame to do so? Do you think this choice will need to be made again? And perhaps again?

13. Did Stone Thrower's ultimate decision concerning Reginald, during the confrontation in the clearing, come as a surprise? Why do you think his last request of Reginald was not to go after William on his own?

14. Two Hawks learned to speak and read English not only in hopes of communicating with his lost brother but also to serve his friendship with Anna. Do you think he is prepared for the task he has chosen— clearing a path to the heart of Reginald Aubrey and winning his blessing? What challenges might he and Anna face as the story unfolds in the next book?

GLOSSARY

ONEIDA/IROQUOIS WORDS

a'sluni—white person

Onyota'a:ka—People of the Standing Stone, the Oneidas

hanyo—hurry

tekawiláke'—two babies

Haudenosaunee—the Longhouse People, the Six Nations of the
Iroquois

kutiyanéshu—clan mothers

ukwehu-wé—an Indian person

Tewaarathon—the little-brother-of-war game, played with stick and
deer-hide ball, played traditionally to entertain the Creator; lacrosse

Atahuhsiyost—Listen carefully

sekoh—a greeting (Mohawk)

shekoli—a greeting

ola:ná—corn soup

iyo—good

o-kee-wa'h—farewell

Náhte' asilu—How do you say . . . ?

yotahyú:ni—lots of berries

a'ʌ:ná—bow

kayu:kwíle'—arrow

ashale'—knife

A'no:wál—Turtle Clan

ohkwa:lí—bear

Né: ka'í:kʌ aknulhá—This is my mother

ha'tiyo—a good voice

Kanien'kehá:ka—People of the Flint, the Mohawk

ONEIDA 13 MOON CALENDAR

Moon	Month
	approximate correspondence
Snow Moon	January
Midwinter Moon	February
Half-Day Moon	March
Thundering Moon	April
Planting Moon	May
Strawberry Moon	June
Green Bean Moon	July
Green (or New) Corn Moon	August
Harvest Moon	September
Storing Moon	October
Giving Thanks Moon	November
Hunting Moon	December
Long Night Moon	

ABOUT THE AUTHOR

LORI BENTON was raised east of the Appalachian Mountains, surrounded by early American history going back three hundred years. Her novels transport readers to the eighteenth century, where she brings to life the colonial and early federal periods of American history. These include *Burning Sky*, recipient of three Christy Awards, and *The Pursuit of Tamsen Littlejohn*. When Lori isn't writing, reading, or researching, she enjoys exploring the Oregon wilderness with her husband.

MORE CAPTIVATING TITLES FROM
Lori Benton

One woman torn between two worlds. Can love cross the boundary of her heart?

It took courage to leave home, and the cost of freedom may be less than the price of true love.